GIFTS

FOR THE

DEAD

GIFTS

FOR THE

DEAD

JOAN SCHWEIGHARDT

RIVERS ❖ BOOK 2

A FIVE DIRECTIONS PRESS BOOK

ISBN-13 978-1947044234

Published in the United States of America.

Cover image: Bird-of-paradise flowers vector art © berry2046/Shutterstock.

FIVE DIRECTIONS PRESS

Dedicated to Michael Dooley

MORE BY JOAN SCHWEIGHARDT

Novels
Before We Died
The Last Wife of Attila the Hun
The Accidental Art Thief
Virtual Silence
Homebodies
Island

Children's Titles
No Time for Zebras
Zoe and Zebra Play Hide-and-Seek

Contents

Part 1: 1911–1919 iii

  1. Nora 1

  2. Nora 11

  3. Jack 22

  4. Nora 23

  5. Jack 33

  6. Nora 44

  7. Jack 56

  8. Nora 61

  9. Jack 63

10. Nora 71

11. Jack 79

12. Nora 83

13. Nora 86

14. Nora 90

15. Jack 96

16. Nora 98

17. Nora 104

18. Nora 116

19. Nora 120

20. Jack 131

21. Nora 134

22. Jack 141

PART 2: 1927 149
23. NORA 151
24. JACK 157
25. NORA 174

PART 3: 1928 185
26. NORA 187
27. JACK 202
28. NORA 210
29. JACK 219
30. NORA 226
31. JACK 237
32. NORA 250
33. JACK 260
34. NORA 267
35. NORA 279
36. JACK 284
37. JACK 296
38. JACK 302
39. NORA 310

ACKNOWLEDGMENTS 318
THE AUTHOR 320

Part 1

1911 – 1919

1. Nora

WE WERE TO EXPECT a knock on the door, Clementine said, any day now. In her vision she saw Maggie, who would be the one to answer it, squinting into the faces of the visitors—two of them, big boys from down on the docks. The squinting detail suggested it would be early morning, with the sun just coming up over the Hudson. The boys would explain they'd come to confirm they'd had good word from their shipping cohorts that both Maggie's sons, Jack and Baxter Hopper, had perished in the South American rainforest, where they'd gone two years earlier to make their fortune tapping rubber trees.

This was not a shock to us; Clementine had been warning us for some time that things had gone *obliquo* for Baxter and Jack. The fact that we'd had no word from them in ages did not encourage us either. Furthermore, the newspapers were full of horror stories of men who'd gone to tap for rubber only to lose their lives in unimaginable ways. Nevertheless, we *prayed*; even though not one of us was a churchgoer, we all believed in a higher power and we all prayed all the time that just once Clementine was wrong.

I told my boss, Mr. Fitzgerald, about Clementine's prophecy, and knowing of her reputation firsthand—she'd foretold his daughter's pregnancy, which everyone else, including the doctor, had given up on—he suggested I take time off from the bookstore so that I could mourn my loss—Baxter and I were to have married—though he hoped in this one instance Clementine would be dead wrong too. I would have asked to take off anyway, because I wanted to be with Maggie if and when the fateful knock came. Clementine wanted to be there too. There was a time when Clementine had charged Maggie a full three dollars just to walk through the front door; that was long ago, and the intimacy they'd shared since, sitting at the kitchen table attempting to communicate with Baxter Sr. and other dead, had led to a friendship that was akin to sisterhood. Now Clementine only wanted to protect Maggie, as did I. Maggie's life had been nothing but heartache, and we didn't know how much more she could endure before she perished under the weight of it.

And so it was that each day for the next two weeks we gathered together early and waited. Sometimes we sat in the parlor, but mostly we sat at the pine table in the kitchen, to be closer to the tea kettle. Maggie, who had embroidered colorful flowers on thousands of handkerchiefs over the years, kept a supply of hankies there. She wailed into them when the pain got bad, and she dabbed at her eyes and nose when it eased off. And all the while Clementine, who liked to hear herself talk, mumbled clichés as they occurred to her, her gnarled hands continuously lifting from the table edge like birds that couldn't quite attain flight but would never stop trying. "One day you gonna join them," she said regularly, her Italian accent thick. "One day, yeah, *si, si,* but not now. So what you gonna do now? I tell you what. Now you gonna learn to live with *il tormento.*" Sometimes when she said that she'd rap her fist on her heart. "What women do," she'd mumble. As for me, I sat dumb as a rock most of the time, thinking of everything and nothing. Sometimes I felt Clementine staring at me. When I gave her my attention she'd pat my hand if it were available and say, "Don't worry, *la mia bambina*, you gonna meet another nice *amante*," but it was more a wish than a genuine prediction. Anyway, I didn't want another nice *amante*. If I couldn't marry Baxter Hopper, I didn't want to marry at all.

Twice before the real knock, the one Clementine had prophesized, other people came to Maggie's door. The first time I answered, fearlessly because it was already past noon. And who did I find out on the stoop but the frizzy-haired neighbor from down the road, Biddy O'Brien, whose red cat, Lucky, had gone missing again. *Biddy Oh No*, as Bax and Jack and I called her behind her back when we were kids, was Maggie's age and a widow too, a tall, thin, nervous woman who loved gossip and talked continuously—to everyone, including the children she found in her path. We called her *Oh No* because that's what we said to one another when we saw her coming our way.

Ordinarily I would have told her politely that we hadn't seen the cat and shut the door before she could get in a single word more, but it occurred to me she might be just the one to distract Maggie, who'd been crying all that morning. And so I invited her in for a cuppa, as Maggie called it. As she followed me down the narrow hall into the small kitchen Biddy revealed that Felix Martin, who lived across from her, had left his wife for another woman. With barely a nod to Clementine and Maggie, she plopped herself down between them and went right on with her story, saying she'd seen Felix and his *loosebit* out walking down near the docks where the kids went to smooch.

She would have had more to say on the matter, but she made the mistake of coming up for air, and Maggie, who believed in "good Irish manners" above all else, interrupted to introduce Clementine, whom she referred to as her fortuneteller. Biddy, whose mouth was open and ready to fire, blinked a few times. "Fortuneteller, you say?" she said, and before Clementine could deny it, Biddy remembered why she'd come to the door and begged Clementine to try to "see" the whereabouts of her cat. Then she spent five minutes describing him so that Clementine wouldn't confuse him with the other red cat on the street.

Clementine waited her out and then told her to go home and look in the privy behind her house, because she'd accidentally locked him in there when she'd been for her morning visit. A look of pure wonderment passed over Biddy's face, and she got to her feet at once, her tea, which I'd seen about, untouched on the table. She wasn't gone a minute when Clementine declared bitterly that the cat was not in the privy, that she'd only said that to get the horrid woman out the door. She had no idea where Lucky was and cared less. She shook her head at me, exasperated that I'd let such a person in in the first place. Nevertheless, the distraction—Biddy's grand entrance, Clementine's hijinks—did us all a world of good, and we actually laughed, the three of us, just as we were wont to do in the old days.

The second knock came not an hour later, and Clementine sighed and got up herself and Maggie and I, bored by then, got up and followed. The caller was a salesman—I couldn't place his accent—who announced he was peddling Persian rugs. Still huffy from her encounter with Biddy, Clementine struck a pose and demanded to know how a Persian rug could fit into a sample case as small as the one the fellow carried. The salesman winked and strode right past her, past all of us, through the parlor and down the hall into the kitchen—as if he already knew the layout of the house (which he probably did as all the workers' houses, built initially for Irish brick masons, were the same: narrow structures with tiny bedrooms on the second and a storage attic above)—and opened his little case on the table. We gathered around to see.

Inside the case was not one Persian rug but twelve, all tiny rectangles not much longer than my finger, tacked to a thin board covered over in black wool. Each rug was perfectly formed, with silky fringe at the short ends, and each with a different design. They were wonderful—beautiful, perfect replicas of the real thing.

Maggie asked if he wanted tea and he said yes and sat himself down where Biddy had been and began to teach us the names for the various rug designs. Most of them were called after the faraway places where their patterns had first been conceived. When I asked if he was from one of those places, he laughed. Then his long thin face got longer and his gray eyes went dark and he looked at Clementine and me in turn (Maggie was at the stove with her back to him) before saying, "I'm Russian, a Russian Jew."

"A Jew!" Clementine exclaimed. She sounded delighted.

The salesman lifted one hairy brown-gray brow. "We fled our homeland, Missus, all my family and me, and four of us died along the way. Two uncles, one cousin, and my own baby sister." His eyes implored us to consider the weight of the burden he carried.

Maggie turned toward the table with the teapot. "I crossed from Ireland me miserable self," she said.

"Ah, then you know! Different but the same."

Maggie clicked her tongue. "And to arrive knowing you'll be treated like a mucker just 'cause where you're from!" she bemoaned.

The salesman nodded eagerly. "Yes, exactly how it was!"

Maggie poured his tea and refilled her own cup and sat down, and as if the two were dear old friends who hadn't seen each other in far too long, they began at once to share persecution stories. Maggie told him how Baxter Sr. had been robbed in Liverpool by a young lad of twelve or thirteen, but as she had most of their money in a secret pouch she'd sewn into her undergarments, the thief didn't get away with enough to make their passage to America impossible. The salesman talked about the bugs in the mattresses in the steerage compartment, how he didn't sleep the first two nights, then on the third night he fell into a dreamless stupor, and when he awoke he learned his baby sister had died. He never got to say goodbye to her—an injustice I understood all too well myself.

On and on they went, for two hours or more. Never once did Maggie mention that she was at that very moment waiting for even more suffering to befall her (though he must have seen how red her eyes were), and never once did he—his name was Isak Rabinovich—remind her that he'd come to try to sell her a Persian rug. When he finally left, Maggie excused herself and went directly to her room, and Clementine, who had fallen asleep at the table, her chin rising and falling on her ample chest and her eyelids fluttering the way they did when she prodded herself into a trance, roused herself and left soon after.

And so it was that I found myself sitting there in the darkening kitchen alone, imagining having all of those little rugs for myself. Though I was a grown woman now of nineteen years, I allowed myself to envision a dollhouse with rugs in every room, and the dolls—a mother, a father, and a daughter—moving back and forth on them hundreds of times each day, all in the course of being a proper happy family.

❖

The real knock came the following week. Maggie had lost several pounds by then, and her throat had gone raw from so much wailing. Clementine, who was showing signs of fatigue, had taken to stretching out on the sofa and falling asleep almost as soon as she arrived. We were in the parlor like that—Clementine on her back on the sofa, her hands folded over her girth, and Maggie in her rocker, and me in the wing chair—when the knock came, and when I saw how quickly Clementine went from snoring contentedly to sitting bolt upright, I knew this was the one we'd been anticipating. Clementine looked at Maggie, and Maggie looked back at her, and a communication passed between them. Then Maggie nodded and rose from her chair—with the dignity of a woman facing the gallows, innocent but reconciled to her destiny—and went slowly to the door and opened it just enough to peek out... And there she stood, staring.

Clementine and I sat forward, waiting for the messengers to be asked in. But Maggie only continued to look out at them, saying not a word, and if they said anything on their end, we didn't hear that either. A full minute passed that way, and then Maggie simply closed the door as gingerly as she'd opened it and stood with her back to it, staring at Clementine with eyes that seemed to fossilize in their sockets.

Clementine leapt from the sofa at once, and motioning Maggie aside, she opened the door herself—and she too took a moment to stare. Then she regained her faculties, and next I knew she had thrown the door wide and was yelling orders at the dock boys, and in they came, two burly macs I knew by sight, hauling between them an old man—his body was skeletal, and his skin tinted blue-grey—so sickly, so feeble, that he could not even stand on his own two feet. His chin bobbed on his chest as if he were no more than a wooden puppet.

My first thought was they had the wrong house, these boys, that after all the grief we'd suffered, Clementine had had a vision meant for a neighbor. I regained my wits when she hollered for me to run and fetch a tea towel to wipe the dried blood from under the old man's nose. It was the right house all right, of course it was, and while the half dead man had not been part of Clementine's prediction, he was ours as well, though I could not say whether he was Bax or Jack, and there was no room in my head at that moment for holding a preference.

The macs placed him on the sofa Clementine had just abandoned, an ugly French antique thing with a hand-carved frame that took the form of a hill sloping gently down from left to right into a valley. The fabric was ruby red. Maggie had bought it at a public auction, held after the death of a resident in town. How Baxter Sr. used to tease her about it, saying that it had lived in a brothel long before it ever found its way to Hoboken, New Jersey, that it had stories to tell that he for one would like to hear. "Oh, you cheeky stook," Maggie would say, and she'd slap his arm and chuckle at his nonsense.

But the sofa was not long enough to accommodate a man of any stature, and while this one had no meat on his bones at all, he did have length. Clementine and the macs placed his head near the hill end and stuffed a cushion in the valley and lifted his feet so his ankles could rest over the arm on that end. It was only when the macs backed away, their job finished, that I got a good look at his face: Jack, half dead, but Jack all right, with a note pinned to his jacket on which was written in childish block letters, "Hoboken, in America." My heart sank to a deeper place than it had ever been before.

"Bill Thorn, and he's Michael Weber," the larger of the dock boys was saying, using his thumb to indicate the other fellow and addressing himself to Clementine. (Maggie was still near the door, which had been left open. She could almost be said to be hiding behind it, her hands crossed over her throat as if she were suffocating.)

"He's not contagious," Clementine stated, but it was meant to be a question.

Bill Thorn responded with a bark that was almost a laugh. "Our boss spoke to the boss on the ship he come off, Missus, and he said no one had been on the ship caught anything and he never worried they would. But one of our crew, German fellow, pipes up and says he wouldn't be surprised—"

Michael Weber elbowed Thorn in the ribs and Thorn shut his mouth. "We'll go now," he said when it opened again.

"There wasn't another?" Clementine asked as the boys backed to the door. "The other brother?"

"No, Ma'am," Bill Thorn answered. "Only this one here. We known 'em both a'course, from when they worked—"

Weber elbowed him again.

"What now?" Thorn asked.

"It's *know*, not *known*, in this one's case anyways," Weber shot.

Bill Thorn glanced at Jack, stock-still on the blood-red sofa. He removed his cap and bowed. "My apologies. *Know*, not *knew*, as my friend here says, and rightly so, regarding this one. He's alive all right. He breathed in my ear all the way over here. But his brother is gone for a fact, passed in the jungle, they says on the ship, and buried there in observation of nautical sanitation rules and no way to haul him out anyway. That's what we learnt and what we was told to relay to you."

There was a noise from the corner and we all turned to see Maggie stepping forward, her hands still crisscrossed over her neck, her face a mask of horror.

Thorn turned back to Clementine. "I'm sorry for your troubles, Ma'am," he said.

Clementine glanced at Maggie. "Go, go," she said, flicking her hand at the young men. "You've let all the heat out of the house."

The macs turned and ran off, and Clementine closed the door behind them. "Well," she said, "*questo è quanto*." *That's that.*

2. Nora

I WAS EXTRACTED FROM our flat as soon as my parents began to cough.

I stayed at first with a family in the building next door, the O'Sullivans, who had three children of their own, all boys and all of them bullies. The first night I slept on a pallet on the floor in their room. Half the night they took turns jumping down from their bed to pull my blanket off me and try to grab my feet before I could get in a kick. But I got my share of kicks in anyway, and when I told Mrs. O the next morning that I would not sleep in that room again, her eyes slid off to the side and she shook her head, whether at my whining or her sons' antics, I will never know. I was only four years old at the time.

I identified a closet in the parlor that was not overly full, and Mrs. O helped me to move the boots and shoes out of the way and fit my pallet into the floor space that remained. It was better after that, though it didn't keep me from missing my parents every minute of every night and day.

Sleeping in the closet with the door ajar, however, afforded me an opportunity to eavesdrop on Mr. and Mrs. O late at night when they conversed over tea in their kitchen, and I learned things I didn't know before: for one, I learned the Irish were despised there where we were in Manhattan, in a section called Five Points—something my parents had never mentioned. I also learned I was not wanted in the O'Sullivans' flat, that I was "a bricky little thing," and "one more hungry mouth" when Mr. and Mrs. O were alone, and "poor wee Nora Sweeny" when Mrs. O's sister dropped by for a late night cuppa. But none of what they said was truly useful to me until the night they mentioned the rooftop, a subject which came up because one of Mrs. O's sister's children had gone up there with another boy on a day he was to have been in school. "It doesn't help the door being just there in the hall," Mrs. O's sister lamented.

I thought about nothing else after that, though it would be awhile until I found myself up on the roof. The problem was I had to keep myself awake until everyone else in the flat was asleep, and that was a trial for me at that age. Then one night I managed it; I stayed awake until I could hear both Mr. and Mrs. O snoring, and then I crept out of the flat and went along the dark hallway with my hand swiping the wall—until I found a door that didn't have the same feel as the others. It was wider and there was cold pressing up against it. I was certain I would find the stairway behind it that led to the roof.

And then there it was, the stairway before me as I had envisioned it, with just enough moonlight coming in through the upper door's small window to guide my way. But when I got there I encountered another problem. The door at the top of the stairs was too heavy for me. I could not get it to open more than a crack before it fell back into its frame. I was in tears struggling with it—until I noticed a block of wood with a plane on one side in the corner of the landing. And remembering how my father always jammed a woodcut under my door at night to keep it partly open so I wouldn't be afraid, I figured out how to use it as a wedge, pushing the door and kicking the wood until I'd made a space I could just squeeze through.

I had no sense of orientation at that age, and at first I could not get my bearings to identify the apartment building that had been my own. I was surrounded by buildings, and they all looked the same from my viewpoint. I had to stand on my tippy toes and lean over the perimeter wall to see down to the street, where I hoped to find a door or stoop that was familiar. And it was cold up there on the rooftop, very cold, and I hadn't thought to bring a coat. I wasn't even wearing shoes, and as I navigated the endless space, I stepped on things that felt like shards of glass. But finally I found the building, and by counting up from the bottom I found our floor and then our one and only window. And then it happened, the miracle.

There was a lamp lit in the parlor, and I could see into the room. And what I saw was my parents, dancing, close and slow, staring into each other's eyes. They didn't look sick at all to me! They looked like two beautiful people who loved each other heart and soul.

My own heart was beating wildly by then, and though I was shivering with cold, I was prepared to stand there through the night if only I could continue to feast my eyes on them. As long as I could see them, the world was right! I imagined I could hear my father humming. He loved to hum when they danced. Sometimes the sound of his humming would reach me in my child's bed and I would get up and go into the parlor. They never saw me at first, but when they did their mouths would drop open with surprise and delight, and I would run to them and my father would lift me high into the air and then the three of us would dance together.

I don't know how much time passed, but at some point they stopped dancing and merely stood there, looking at each other, searching each other's faces as if they expected to find all the answers to all the questions in the world there. My mother had to tilt her head back, because my father was so tall. It made her silky red-gold hair fall low on her back, almost to her waist. I thought she looked like an angel with her hair loose like that. My father must have thought so too, because he lifted a strand from the shoulder of her nightdress and bent his head to press his mouth and nose into it. When he released it, she moved into his arms and they embraced. Then she turned from him and came nearer to the window to put the lantern out for the night. And just before the room went dark, she looked my way, and while I knew even at my tender age that she couldn't possibly see me—my head was no more than a bump at the top of the brick parapet—I saw her clearly enough; I saw her beautiful sad smile and I knew she was thinking of me.

I didn't plan to tell anyone about my adventure, but as soon as I heard voices in the kitchen the next morning, I dashed out of the closet and ran in and spilled everything. I could hardly catch my breath, the details of my story came back to me so quickly. The boys laughed and called me a liar and a trickster while Mr. O scolded them for being uncharitable, his eyes never leaving the magazine he was reading. When I turned to Mrs. O, I saw her face was as rigid as the cast iron stove she stood beside.

Later that day, after Mr. O had gone to work and the boys were out in the alley playing whip-tops, Mrs. O chastened me. "You couldn't have found your way up there in the dark," she began. "Look at the size of you! And you wouldn't have survived in this weather anyway. The wind would have picked you up and carried you away. And besides, the super keeps the door locked at night, to prevent children like you from getting themselves into trouble." Her voice grew louder, and there was a bluish vein jumping under the skin of her pearly white forehead. "And for the record, little miss, your parents have a nurse with them day and night now, and they aren't allowed even to leave their beds; that's how sick they are. Dancing! What a foolish child you are! Dancing is the last thing they're thinking of at this point. You dreamed the whole thing." She raised her hand, which was trembling with her anger, though something kept her from striking me. "You made it up," she snapped. "The boys are right; you're a liar. And now you can stay in the closet until you're ready to admit it."

I admitted nothing, but I spent the rest of the day in the dark wondering if it was possible that I was little more than a wretched girl who could not tell the difference between the things that were real and the things that came and went in dreams, which often seemed just as real to me. And that night, though I was still awake when the flat went quiet, I did not go down the hall and climb the stairs—not because I was afraid of Mrs. O but because I was afraid Mrs. O might be right and I would find the windows to our flat dark. Then the next day, I got a surprise. My Aunt Becky, my father's sister, a woman I hardly knew, showed up at the flat, and Mrs. O said, "There she is; I can't handle her no more myself."

I hadn't known I was leaving! I was sitting on the closet floor, still in my nightdress, my blanket around my shoulders like a shawl. Aunt Becky sighed. "Let's get on with it then," she said, and while Mrs. O and her boys—who were lined up beside her, sniggering behind their filthy hands—looked on, she pulled me and the sack containing my few possessions out of the closet and began to dress me.

She was fast and rough, nothing like my mother. Although there were two pairs of clean knickers in my sack, she left me in the same ones I'd been wearing since my arrival and chose a dress I didn't care for and buttoned it all the way up to the top, pinching my neck in the process. When it came time for my stockings, she had me sit on a stool and lift my feet. "What's this?" she cried, holding one heel in her palm. "Your feet are dirty and cut to shreds." She pulled something out from between two toes. "And look here! A pebble? Is that what this is?" She turned around to show the thing between her fingers to Mrs. O, who stared back at it and said nothing. When Mrs. O's gaze shifted to me, I grinned.

In no time I was fully dressed and Aunt Becky took my hand and said to Mrs. O, "I'm sorry for your trouble with her."

Mrs. O walked behind us to the door. "She's a liar or a hellion," she said. "One or the other. God knows which is worse."

I turned back and flashed her one more smile before she closed the door behind us. I seemed to sense that was the thing to do. Perhaps I'd seen my mother do it once or twice when she was right and her adversary was wrong. As we walked down the hall, Aunt Becky asked me if it was true I'd gone up on the roof in the middle of the night all on my own without anyone's permission and watched my parents dance. I looked up at her. My father had been born in New York, but Aunt Becky, who was older than him, had stayed behind with a relative when their parents crossed over. She didn't come to America until she was nearly fourteen. Yet she had not a trace of an Irish accent. But she didn't speak quite right either. She spoke slowly, each of her words a solitary thing until the next one came on board beside it. I said it was true; I'd been on the roof and I'd watched my parents dance. She nodded once and said, to my surprise, "Good girl."

She didn't say anything more until we were outside the building. "We can't go up there to say goodbye," she said then, talking into an icy wind that seemed to want to push us back indoors, "but before we take the ferry across the river, we can stand here and wave goodbye to them." And that was just what we did.

After the macs left, Maggie sat in her rocker, bent over and crying into her palms, for an hour or more. Every now and then she'd look over at Jack and say, "Oh, me boy, me sweet, sweet boy." Jack showed not a shred of evidence he even knew she was there. Eventually Maggie got up and hesitantly put her quivering hand alongside his slack face, but his lack of response only set her entire body quaking, and fearing her heart might shred from so much grief, I turned her away from him and took her upstairs and got her into bed. The last thing she said before I left her room was, "You'll stay with him, won't you? You'll make sure he doesn't die in the night? Promise me that, lass."

I came back into the parlor just in time to catch Clementine bending over Jack and asking him outright, in a razor-sharp voice, if Baxter was truly dead. I guess she had to hear it for herself, though she must have realized Jack was beyond responding; poor fellow couldn't even keep his eyes open, and when they did fly open, they seemed to focus on nothing, and then they closed again. But I will admit he did appear to nod, just once, in the seconds following her question. Clementine nodded too, as if to agree she had her answer, though I thought it more likely Jack had had some kind of spasm, something involuntary happening in his body just at that moment. I could have told her myself that Bax was dead—because I had known Jack and Bax Hopper nearly all my life, and they were both as upright as they came. Sick or not, Jack would no more have left his brother behind in the jungle than Bax would have left him.

My grief was suddenly physical. It pushed me down so fast and hard in the wing chair that the cushion whooshed beneath my rump, and for a moment I wondered would I ever get to my feet again. The memory I had of my parents dancing as a child was never more than a wish away, and I beckoned to it now, to come to me and help me make sense of a senseless world. Softly, I began to hum the tune I'd decided my father had been humming that night.

I was not so silly as to think my beautiful memory was a pure one; surely I'd embellished it over the years. But what mattered was that I *had* seen them; my dirty cut feet were proof. Except to tell the O'Sullivans (who, thankfully, I never saw again) and Aunt Becky (who never spoke of it again after the night she came for me), I'd never told anyone until Bax and I became sweethearts. Telling him was a test. If he laughed—which he well might have done, because he laughed at everything—I would have ended it between us. But he didn't laugh. He said the way I told it made him see them dancing for himself. I loved him all the more after that.

Later, after Clementine had gone, Dr. Burns came to the house. He visited with Maggie first, up in her room, and then he came down and examined Jack. He was very clear with me that Jack was in his final days and would die soon enough. I let him babble on about how all Jack's systems were shutting down and why it would be only cruel to try to feed him anything because having to digest even a liquid would only cause him unnecessary pain.

When he finished his lecture, I saw him to the door, and then I turned and went into the kitchen and warmed up the chicken soup I'd made for Maggie the day before. I was supposed to go to a meeting that evening—women's rights, which was all important to me—but I could neither bring myself to awaken Maggie (Dr. Burns had given her a sedative, even though I'd told him not to) nor leave Jack on his own. I'd have to sleep in the wing chair; I'd have to stay the night.

I pulled Jack up gently and stuffed a pillow behind his head, and then I brought in the bowl of soup and a tea towel to tuck into his collar. He didn't so much as open his eyes. But he did open his mouth, just slightly, when I touched the warm spoon to his bottom lip, and some of the liquid went in and I saw him swallow, or try to. I threw my head back and emitted a sigh of relief. My subsequent efforts were not so successful. While I might have gotten a drop or two more into him, most of it dribbled down his chin. Later I fed him water with the same spoon, and again some went down, and I saw him swallow.

The last thing I wanted to feel for Jack Hopper was resentment, but he was there and Bax was not, and I was wretched. And while anyone looking in on us might have mistaken me for Florence Nightingale, I could not help but think about the meeting I was missing, how reassuring it would have been to get with the girls and tell them what happened and be comforted by them—or even to be able to go back to work and be comforted by Mr. Fitzgerald and our regular customers, all of whom knew I'd been waiting for word of Bax. I'd have preferred even to be home in my tiny dark flat—the one I'd shared with Aunt Becky from the time I was four right up until she'd left me on my own not yet a year ago—because my things were there, scant though my possessions were, and I thought the sight of them might bring me at least a pittance of the comfort I desired.

I put the spoon aside and removed the tea towel. "Jack Hopper," I said, perhaps more harshly than I aught have, "we are all depending on you. You are all that's left now that your father's dead these years and your brother has gone and joined him. Think about your mother, Jack. How cruel would it be for you to pass on and leave her alone?"

I looked around the room, deliberating. "Think of me," I barked at last.

Bax used to make a joke of the fact that Jack had always been sweet on me. He would imitate his brother staring at me, his eyes all moony with longing and his lips in a sulk. The truth was, Jack never looked at me like that, though I will admit I caught him staring often enough. Bax was simply unkind, a terrible person, and I would tell him so. But he would keep it up, keep making what he called his "sullen Jack face" until he got me to laugh, which never took all that long. As we got older, he let up a bit. But every now and then when the three of us were together, which was almost all the time, and Jack was talking to me earnestly the way he did sometimes, going on about some book he'd read or some idea he'd had, Bax would move off where Jack couldn't quite see him and make the face again, the sullen Jack face, so that while poor Jack was trying his best to impress me, I was quivering with suppressed laughter.

I was bad, and Bax was worse. I turned my head aside in case Jack should open his eyes in that instant and catch me chuckling behind my fist. And chuckle I did, remembering all that, until the tears came.

I knew about grief; I'd learned its lessons at a very early age. When it came for you, you had to surrender to it, because it was a monster that fed on combat; it only got larger when you tried to fend it off.

I stayed awake all night, slouched in the wing chair with grief curled up on my chest like some enormous snarling cat. It moved off when the light came, and by the time Maggie came down the stairs, I had had a few hours' sleep and was more or less functional again.

3. Jack

SHE WAS GOING TO be in a parade, she said one evening. It would be across the river, and it would be a grand event with banners and drums and thousands of marchers and even more spectators. She and some other women from Hoboken had made leaflets, which they planned to distribute to the crowd. "How I wish you could come and watch us," she whispered as she bent over him, and he nearly laughed.

Nevertheless, he had no idea what she was talking about at first. He let her words bounce in his head until he could find an image in his memory to correspond with them: Parade, yes! Big noisy events. A sea of people. So much humanity!

Even though she made no sense half the time, he liked it when she bent over him and touched his cheek and whispered his name. "You seem so peaceful, Jack," she said once. "I don't think I've ever seen anyone so at peace. You're quite beautiful, you know, despite the fact you're nothing but a bag of bones. I almost envy you. It seems cruel to disturb you, to insist like this. But your mum and I are not at peace. We can't go where you are. We must have you back in our world." But another time she slapped him, across the face, hard enough that it stung, and he felt her weight lift from his side, and he knew she'd stalked off in a huff.

4. Nora

I HAD THE *New York Sun* with me, and I held it up in front of his face. His eyes were open at that moment and he seemed to be focusing but I could never be certain. "Can you read the headline?" I asked. I slid my finger along the words. "It says, *Women Demand the Vote.* Do you know what that means, Jack? We want what you have, and I don't mean your stones and the rest of it."

Maggie, who was sitting in her rocker embroidering yet another handkerchief, chuckled. I'd said it purposely, to keep her engaged. Besides trying to bring Jack back to life, it had fallen to me (and Clementine when I was working or off with the girls) to keep Maggie from spending the day in bed. Sometimes it was exhausting.

I flicked the news page with my finger. "Jack, are you paying attention to me? Look at the picture. See us all marching? Don't we look lovely in our whites? And see the banners? They say, *Votes for Women.* And look at all the people leaning in towards us from both sides of the street. You can almost hear them, can't you, Jacko? Some of them booing, and others—though not many, I will admit—cheering us on? But mostly they just watched, dumbfounded, as if they'd never seen anything like it before, and most likely they hadn't. Think about this, Jack: If you'd been there, would you have been booing or cheering? Which one?" I gave him a moment to digest the question. "If you can believe it, it was the women spectators who were the nastiest, calling us names and screaming at us as we went by," I added.

I glanced over at Maggie. She'd stopped her work, her needles at rest in her hands and her eyes unfocused, an ominous sign. She wasn't paying attention to my commentary either. I would lose her soon.

"Look, Jack," I cried loudly enough to be heard at the house next door. "That's me! Can you see me there in the crowd? Look right here, just above my fingertip. And see who's next to me? That's Susie Gilpin! Do you remember her? Little Susie Gilpin, we used to call her. She used to be sweet on you back in the day. Still is for all I know. She's lovely now all grown up, isn't she?"

I pulled the paper away and swept it in front of Maggie's face. She shook her head once, fast, as if to bring herself back from wherever she'd drifted. "You remember Susie, don't you, Maggie?" I cried.

All my life I'd called her Mrs. H, but one day *Maggie* slipped out, and when I saw that it was pleasure that followed her quick gasp of surprise, I decided I'd call her Maggie from then on out, right up until Bax and I married, at which time I'd call her Mum, as the boys did. Now that would never happen. It was mostly at night I allowed myself to think such thoughts. But every now and then they snuck in when I was otherwise occupied. I took a deep breath to keep myself focused. Maggie leaned towards the newspaper. "Look at you," she said at last. "How thin you are. You need to put some pounds on, me sweet lassie."

I sighed and turned back to Jack—and found he'd closed his eyes. I could almost convince myself that his lips were slightly upturned at the corners, as if he understood my ordeal on some level and was amused. "And think of it," I exclaimed loudly, determined to get him to open his eyes again, "some of those women saying we could never bear the burden of politics. As if it's something you carry on your back and not in your head and your heart! They said we were making a public spectacle of ourselves, marching like we were, that we were unladylike. They didn't see the irony at all, them all grouped together shouting at passersby in a most vulgar way. Nothing ladylike about that, wouldn't you agree? Jack Hopper, would you agree with me there or would you not?"

I put the paper aside and dropped my head into my hands, and in spite of myself, I began to cry.

Over the next few weeks Jack's appetite increased to where I could get four or five or six spoonsful of soup down him in a single sitting. He drank water too. And he kept his eyes open more and focused them on me when I sat at his side and leaned right over where he could see me without having to turn his head. But he remained expressionless throughout it all, and there were times I thought to myself, *This is my life now. I've committed myself to keeping a dead man alive when he would much prefer to be dead.*

When Maggie was not in the room I took to throwing his blankets off him—suddenly, to shock his system (and sometimes his eyes flew wide open and I felt certain I had succeeded and then I laughed like the witch I was). I stretched his arms and rotated his legs, and not always so gently. I pulled on his fingers and rubbed his palms. I bent and unbent his toes. I turned his head from side to side to stretch his neck. I massaged the muscles of his face. I snapped at him. "You can't just lie here and expect us to wait on you forever. You're trying my patience, Jack Hopper!" And still nothing! As soon as I pulled his blankets up to his chin, he closed his eyes and sank back into full impassivity, suspended between two worlds like a footbridge nobody bothered to use.

After Baxter Sr. died, Maggie and Clementine met almost every week. The communications Clementine picked up from Baxter Sr. in the beginning were clear—especially when he suggested that Jack and Baxter, who were inconsolable, do something to change their lives. But they became vague over time, and eventually Maggie and Clementine's meetings became less about Baxter Sr. and more about practical matters, such as the whereabouts of a bracelet Baxter Sr. had given Maggie (it took two full sessions, but Clementine did finally pinpoint its location, on a shelf in the cellar with the hammers and nails, of all the strangest things!) and how much coal it was likely to take to heat the house for the winter.

It was only after Jack and Baxter left for the jungle that I began to sit with Clementine and Maggie during some of their sessions, more for the pleasure of their company than for any other reason. I liked the idea that the dead were there on the other side eager to answer our questions and offer us guidance when we asked for it, but in my heart of hearts, I was not so sure calling out to them wasn't in some way impeding their progress. I'd never had the sense that my parents were trying to communicate with me, and I never asked Clementine to try to reach out to them on my behalf. Nor did she suggest it, which only deepened my conviction that they were too far gone from earthly matters. But I kept an open mind, reading books about the hereafter during stretches between customers at the bookshop, and most of the authors I read agreed it was only healthy for spirits to move on over time into a deeper stratum of the abyss where they might find opportunities to communicate with others of their kind, and even to decide whether or not they had good cause to come back again, in another form.

Once, when Baxter Sr. had been gone a long while and was no longer relaying messages for Clementine to relay to Maggie, Clementine suggested that she try to get some messages going in the other direction, from Maggie to him. She told Maggie to make a list of whatever she most wanted him to know, and, since Clementine was all but illiterate, to read the list, one item at a time, and she would send it out there, for Baxter Sr. to find or not. Mostly Maggie's list was regarding things she was sorry for. She was sorry she'd called Baxter Sr.'s sister a lazy mucker on a few occasions when they were all still children in County Wicklow, back in Ireland. She was sorry she'd insisted Jack be named Jack when Baxter Sr. wanted him named Abban, after his father. "You think he's listening?" I asked Clementine when Maggie paused to chew her fingernail and think up her next message.

"*Chissà?*" she replied, her hands flying up from the table. *Who knows?* "Maybe yes and maybe no. Not for me to say."

I liked the idea of leaving messages for the dead, to be deciphered or not, rather than imposing on them to stop what they were doing and respond to questions that no longer concerned them. And I liked the idea of writing them down. We had some lovely cloth-covered notebooks in the bookstore, and I bought a green one and asked Mr. Fitzgerald to order more. I addressed all my early entries to my parents after that. Yes, in essence it was really only a diary like any other, but as I began to fill up the pages of the first slim volume, with my mother and father front of mind, I did truly begin to imagine that some of what I wrote found its way to them, that they were interested in some vague way, that they smiled sometimes thinking of me here on Earth sharing my mundane existence.

As soon as Maggie felt strong enough, she asked Clementine for a session to try to reach Baxter, but Clementine said Bax was hovering, gone from this world but not yet at home in the next. Sometimes when they were like that, she said, they didn't even know they were dead yet. It wouldn't help him *mescolare* (I think she meant "assimilate") if we broke the news before he was ready to hear it; nor would it help us to know we'd been the messengers of such tidings. And besides, Jack was only in the next room, and while he didn't seem to be alert to anything, you never knew what was going on in his head.

We didn't argue with her, but it seemed odd to me that she'd begun communications with Baxter Sr. almost before his body was cold. I wondered if she knew something she wasn't telling us. I switched journal colors not long after that, from green to blue, and I began to address my entries to Baxter. I never mentioned his death, in case Clementine was right in saying he was between destinations. I never mentioned his status at all. I simply wrote news about myself, what little there was to tell, and of course I told him how Jack and Maggie were faring.

Once I went back to work, Clementine and I didn't see each other all that often. When I came to the house, in the early mornings and late afternoons, my job was to feed both Jack and the furnace in the cellar. Clementine's job, when she came in the middle of the day, was to wash him down head to toe and change his nappies. Maggie, who was no longer taking the medication Dr. Burns had prescribed, had the graveyard shift; every night when her grief awoke her (like me, it was the nights that were worst), she would come down the stairs and sit with him, grieving for Bax and willing Jack back to full life.

One day in late March we had a blizzard, and Mr. Fitzgerald closed the store early in the afternoon. The snow was falling so hard and fast by then that I was afraid of finding myself unable to get out again once I went home, so instead I went directly to Maggie's. Clementine had only just arrived herself. I made us tea, and as Maggie was upstairs napping, we took our cups into the parlor and dragged our chairs to the window and watched the snow pile up outside.

I hadn't liked Clementine at first. She was the kind of woman who said whatever came to mind, even if it wasn't always kind. I'd been accused of that myself a time or two, but I knew for a fact I was seldom as crass as she was on a regular basis. But over time she grew on me. I began to understand that many of her meanest comments were meant to be humorous. At heart, she wanted to make people laugh. She liked to tease, and before we lost Bax, Maggie had kept right up with her. Clementine's Italian accent was heavy, and of course Maggie had an accent herself, and the two of them enjoyed poking fun at how the other spoke. And they both made fun of me when I used a word they'd never heard or phrased something in a way they thought of as uppity, saying, if it were Maggie speaking, "But ain't she Miss Prim?" and *"Una saccente"* (a pedantic) "this one is," if it were Clementine. And then they would have their laugh, and go on smiling awhile after.

Clementine almost always dressed in black, and her hat, which was twenty years old if it was a day, featured a dead crow, his wings and tail feathers spread out to suggest he was just about to take flight. I was opposed to people wearing dead birds on their heads, but the crow—unusual in itself as most women who still wore taxidermy preferred terns or pigeons—was so much a part of Clementine's unique personality that I never mentioned my opposition in her presence. She wore it all the time outdoors, and sometimes she kept it on inside as well. It was an extension of her person, and I believed that she believed that it was responsible, at least partially, for her psychic abilities. She always wore it when she was preparing to go into a trance. As for her appearance, her eyes were as dark and direct as gun pistols, and they could be as frightening when she turned them on you. And her nose, well, it was witchlike. Jack and Bax had called her "the hag." They had joked that her look alone could curse a person, and if they happened to come into the house when she was visiting, they'd greet her with their heads tucked—Maggie, with her insistence on proper manners, would have had something to say if they didn't at least say hello—and run for the shelter of their room.

Today Clementine was subdued. I was too; the snow, and the half-dead body of Jack Hopper on the blood-red sofa behind us, had rendered me so. The only words that passed between us in our first hour together occurred when a red cardinal happened to land on a branch of the maple tree in the yard. All the world was white except for that red bird. "Look at him," I muttered.

Clementine didn't comment at first, but a moment later, after the cardinal had flown away, she reached up and touched her hat and said to me, rather sharply, "When I fly, you put this good fellow in the ground with me. You. No one else will do it." I looked at her, thinking at first she was trying to be humorous, but she turned her gaze back to the window at once, and the site of her shrewish profile—with the added indignation in the set of her lips—kept me from asking her what on earth she was talking about.

A half hour later a noise broke through our dream spell, a kind of croak, and we both turned our heads at once toward the staircase. Maggie was waking, I thought, and I placed my long-empty teacup on the floor, thinking to jump up and put the kettle on for her. But before I could move, the noise came once more, and I realized it was coming not from upstairs but from the sofa.

It was an awful noise, harsh and grating. Clementine and I looked at each other, both of us with our brows raised and our mouths dropped open. "He's dying," I cried. "That's the death rattle!"

I got up at once and dashed to Jack's side. My tears were flying already. I had worked so hard, against all odds, to bring him back into the world—for Maggie's sake, and because the hard work of keeping him alive day after day gave me purpose; it had become the counterpoint to my grief.

The noise came again, and it was even more horrible at such close range. It sounded like something was stuck inside him and he was trying to bring it up and spit it out. His chest heaved. His eyes were squeezed tight.

I took his hand. "Jack," I cried. "What can I do to help you?"

"Hush," Clementine ordered. She had gotten up too now and was standing just behind me. "How I gonna hear with you?"

I forced my sobs inward, but strange squeaks and squawks escaped me anyway. My Jack. He made the rasping sound again. It was so deep inside him it might have been coming from his gut. All at once his eyes popped open and he looked right at me, beseechingly, his chest rising and falling with his wheezes.

I gasped. I was horrified. I didn't know what he wanted from me. "Move, move," Clementine cried loudly, pushing me away. She took my place and put her ear right up close to Jack's mouth. *Let him die in peace, please*, I thought, but there was no sense saying so because peaceful he was not.

I thought he must be crying for help, because he couldn't breathe, wanting someone to end his suffering. I half expected Clementine to open his mouth and stick her gnarled hand in deep and fish out the thing that was killing him. I glanced at the staircase, weighing whether or not to run up and awaken Maggie. So many things in my head at one time… His pillow was right there, under his head. I tried to picture myself pushing Clementine aside, pulling the pillow out from under him, holding it over his face until he went limp. Could I do such a thing? Probably not. I couldn't even move at the moment. But then the noise came once more and a few seconds later, Clementine turned her wicked witchy face toward me, and I saw that there was a glimmer of light in her dark pistol eyes, her brows thick and arched high above them. And all at once she began to laugh. "Privy!" she cried.

"What?" I screeched.

"He's saying privy!"

That wasn't what I heard. That wasn't it at all. The man was dying.

But then he said it again.

"*Meno male!*" Clementine cried. "Run up and get her," she demanded. "Then run down the cellar and get boots, for all of us. It'll take us three to get him there in this snow."

"You can't be serious. He's—"

"*Vai, vai,*" she cried. "Who knows best? I do. That's who." She hit her fist on her chest. "*Sono io*, Clementine!" she cried.

And off I ran.

5. Jack

Jack went down to the docks, to the shipyard where he'd worked previously—before the jungle—before he'd died, as he liked to think of it, because he *had* died, as far as he was concerned, and he'd come back a new man, a stranger to everyone including himself. As soon as he got close enough that they could recognize him, all the workers within view stopped what they were doing to stare, their mouths agape. No one had thought he'd make it. Jack's mouth was open too. He felt so much like an intruder in the world that the actual sight of these once-familiar men—lifting freight, calling out to one another, cussing—was jolting.

He took a breath and approached Frank Bäcker, his old boss, and asked him outright for a job. Bäcker looked him up and down. He was skin and bones; he knew that. Bäcker shook his head sympathetically. "Ahearn," he yelled, his eyes on Jack, and a moment later Daniel Ahearn appeared at his side.

"What, boss?" Ahearn asked, his eyes on Jack too.

Bäcker jerked his head toward a wooden crate the size and shape of a coffin. It was marked "Steel fittings, Canada." He said to Jack, "You take one end and Ahearn here will take the other. I can't use you if you can't work."

Jack understood that. He looked around. Even the men who had gone back to work were keeping an eye on him. He sensed they were rooting for him. He and Bax had always been well-liked, as much by the Germans as they were among the other Irish, just as their father before them. He squatted down and grabbed one end of the crate and Ahearn took the other. They lifted on Jack's nod and up it went. But Jack could feel right away that he wasn't going to be able to keep it up, to walk with it. Ahearn was watching him for a signal. Jack could feel his face turning red as he strained. Finally he shook his head; it wasn't going to happen. It took every last bit of strength he had to put the crate back down on the ground without dropping it. He barely had the energy to straighten his back and walk away.

He could hear his mother moving about in the kitchen when he got home. He didn't want to go in, but if he went directly to his room, she would guess anyway, and then she'd want to comfort him there, at the side of his bed, and that would be worse. He forced himself to enter, and when she turned from the stove with a wooden spoon in her hand and the question on her face, he shook his head. She turned back to the stove. "Well, I could have told you," she began, but some sudden insight kept her from finishing. What she would have said, if not for the burst of reason, is that it was too soon for him to be out looking for work, that even the doctor had said so. What she said instead was, "Sit yourself down, Jack Hopper. I'm going to fix you a cuppa."

Jack sat. His mother kept the kettle full and half on the wood-burning part of the stove almost continuously. The water was hot in just a few minutes. She poured a small amount into the fine blue china teapot his father had bought her only weeks before he died. Then she added the tea strainer and followed it with more water. Everything had to be just so when it came to her tea and her teapot. Sometimes Nora prepared the tea, and Jack had noticed that his mum followed the teapot attentively whenever Nora handled it. Once, when Nora was carrying it to the sink—jabbering, as always—she accidentally hit it on the edge of the porcelain basin, and his mum squeezed her eyes shut and cringed.

Jack was touched. She'd lost everything, his mum—her homeland, her husband, and the better of her two sons. All she had now was him, and he wasn't worth a hill of beans, was he? Yet she could still take pleasure from something as simple as a cup of tea. A cuppa. To her it was a magical substance. He'd heard her say to Nora several times that she couldn't have gotten through her troubles without her tea—or the hag, Clementine, or Nora, for that matter.

Jack stretched his legs beneath the table and let himself relax. They drank in silence, and when he finished he put his cup in the sink and came behind her and wrapped his arms around her shoulders and pecked her on the cheek. "Oh, now stop that," she cried, but he could see she was pleased as Punch.

The tea got him thinking, and the following day he got up early and took the ferry across the Hudson—the underground had opened by then, but while he'd never had any qualms about traveling on the river, he couldn't cotton to the idea of traveling beneath it—and walked several blocks to the Lipton Tea building. He'd read in the *Tribune* they were looking for help, and while he knew for certain now that no one in their right mind would hire him to load or unload freight, the Lipton building at least dealt with freight. And he greatly admired Sir Thomas Lipton. Who didn't? Well, Nora perhaps. If he got a job in the Lipton building, she would surely bring up the fact that Lipton owned slaughter houses too. He hoped she would. He would defend him, reminding her how Sir Tea gave money to the poor all over the United Kingdom. And anyway, the great man had come to purchase his slaughter houses after the creation of the Pure Food and Drug Act. Surely he didn't run them the way his predecessors had. "You like your beef now, don't you?" he would say if she started with him.

He had come to resent Nora of late, though he couldn't say why. He mulled it over as he approached the Lipton offices and warehouse, looming large on the corners of Franklin and Hudson a few blocks ahead. His contemplation generated only questions, no answers. Was it because she'd seen him at his worst, weak and helpless and dumb as a dote? Or was it somehow tied to his hodgepodge of feelings regarding his brother? Or was it simply because she was always so contrary—as stubborn as a Missouri mule, his father would have said, not that he'd ever been to Missouri or interacted with a mule—always fighting against the grain? He had to laugh at himself. What she was always fighting for was justice. Why should *that* bother him? Before he'd died, he'd always admired her for being who she was.

The streets held so many more automobiles than he remembered. And there were more people walking along the sidewalks too. The fashion had changed, he couldn't help noticing. He was wearing a plug hat, pushed back on his head, and a brown pinstripe sack suit that had belonged to father. The men he saw all around him were wearing fedoras and smart three-piece suits with pleats at the back of their jackets. One part of his new temper regarding Nora, he realized, was guilt. Here he'd been in love with his brother's sweetheart most of his life. But he *had* kept it to himself. He had to keep reminding himself of that. That had to count for something.

He was so tied up in his thoughts as he entered the front door to the Lipton offices that he bumped right into a man making his exit. "Sorry," he mumbled, but when he looked to see who he was addressing, he sucked in his breath so quick he almost gagged on it. It was the man himself, Sir Thomas Lipton, wearing the very same yachting cap he wore in most of the newspaper photos Jack had ever seen of him, and sporting his great white mustache too! "I'm very sorry," he said again. He was sure he didn't look sorry. He was smiling ear to ear.

Thomas Lipton grinned back at him. "That's quite all right, young fellow. Quite all right. I wasn't looking where I was going either." He cocked his head. "May I ask your business and direct you?"

Jack couldn't wait to tell his mum he had literally bumped into Sir Tea, almost knocked him down. He imagined how her face would brighten, the way it had so often in the old days. "I've come to apply for a job," he said.

Lipton regarded him, his blue eyes twinkling with amusement and curiosity. His pipe wasn't lit, but he put its stem into his mouth and drew on it anyway. "I've got some time," he said, finally. "Let's sit down and have a cup of tea, shall we?"

He turned and led Jack down a wide hallway. He opened the door to a small office off to the right that was empty except for a rectangular pine table and four chairs, and in Jack went, as giddy as a shill. A large chalkboard took up all of one wall, and a window looking out onto Hudson Street another. Lipton stayed at the door, looking out into the hall until he caught someone's attention. He made a hand signal that Jack couldn't quite see, then nodded, and leaving the door ajar, he came in and sat down himself.

"So, you're looking for work," Mr. Lipton said. "What kind of background do you have? What kind of work have you done?"

It had been too long since he'd made conversation with anyone, and here he was sitting across the table from one of the people he admired most in the world. Still, he wouldn't have traded the moment for anything. "I was in the jungle," he said. He hadn't said a word about the jungle to anyone since before he'd boarded the launch that helped him escape it.

A plump youngish woman in a bright red dress came in with a silver tea tray and Lipton thanked her. As Lipton was pouring, Jack tried to picture what Nora's face would look like when he told her he'd met Sir Tea. Would she try to minimize his experience? "In South America, in Brazil," he went on. "I went to tap for rubber. Before that I was a longshoreman, just across the river."

He wanted to say that he'd gone to Brazil with his brother, but he feared the mention of Bax might bring on some unanticipated emotion and ruin the moment. "The fellows I was with, in the jungle, they all died," he said instead. "One bit by a spider; another lost his mind and went running off, and we never did learn exactly…" He stopped talking. In his mind's eye he saw Teddy's head, or what he had taken to be his head, dangling from a crossbeam in one of the huts of the Indians he and Bax had come to know. The Gha-ru. They had liked him and Bax but they hadn't liked Teddy apparently; no one had.

Lipton put his cup down. "And now it's all come to a bad end, hasn't it?"

"Sir?"

"I've got tea plantations in Ceylon. I visited some of the rubber plantations in the area last time I was there. I saw for myself how the production works. Interesting. Very interesting indeed. Unfortunate we didn't meet earlier. I could have told you rubber production was shifting to Asia."

"Not to offend, Sir, but no one would have believed you back at the time I was there. No one thought rubber trees could grow anywhere but in the jungles of the region where I was. It was difficult, though, Sir, getting to the trees in the thick of all the vegetation."

"So I've heard. And they couldn't be grown on a plantation there because of some sickness?"

"Yes, Sir, blight. If the trees are too close, the blight, it jumps from one tree to another and kills them all. At least that was what we were told by our *mateiro*, our guide..." He drifted again, seeing C's ugly mug the way he'd seen it last, blood dripping from his mouth and rain dripping from his person as he bent over Jack, his foot coming forward for one last kick, the one that would break one of Jack's ribs. Jack cringed. He could feel the burn of that last kick all over again, as if someone had just executed it now. "But I guess there's no blight in Ceylon if you say the trees are doing well."

Thomas Lipton laughed. "They're doing more than well. Tapping in the jungles of South America is all but come to an end."

Jack stared at him. Except for the help-wanted ads, he wasn't reading these days. It was a strain and it put him to sleep—and frankly he wasn't all that interested in the world anymore. "You're certain about that, Sir? The whole industry?"

He laughed again. "Don't you read the papers?"

"Sir, I come back sick." He pulled his father's jacket away from his scraggy chest. "That's why I look like this. But you say it's really over, huh? For good then?"

"From what I understand there are pockets of tappers still working, but for the most part..."

Lipton went on talking but Jack's mind wandered off again. If the tapping had stopped, that meant the killing had too. It was too late for the Gha-ru, but other tribes might still flourish.

He was elated, though he had two other thoughts: If the *patrãos*, the barons at the top of the industry hierarchy, left Manáos because there was no longer money to be made there, Manual Abalo, his *patrão*, might well be here in New York. And if he remembered Jack was from the area, right across the river, it was possible he'd seek him out and kill him. The thought amused him. He was already dead, so what would it matter? The second thought exhilarated him, though it was fleeting: If his brother had managed to keep himself alive this long... But no. How likely was that? If he was alive, he'd be home by now.

Lipton was talking about his lust for adventure now, and how he'd traveled penniless to America when he was Jack's age or maybe younger, to seek his fortune, and how he came to love ocean travel ever since.

"I saw your boat race once, Sir!" Jack cried, remembering. "It must have been in '99, because I couldn't have been more than a lad of nine or ten. My father, he worked at the shipyard too, and the Germans, the bosses, allowed all the workers and their families to board one of their smaller ships for the first heat. We traveled to Sandy Hook, and from there we watched..."

He remembered it well now. His mother had not come on board. It was just him and Bax and his father and two of his cousins. His mum had wanted to go, badly, but her sister Emily had come all the way down from upstate New York by train to be part of the festivities surrounding the American Cup races, and then one of Emily's girls, Caroline, refused to board the ship. She was so scared that she began to scream when the others tried to coax her, and finally Emily said she'd stay behind with her, and then Maggie, ever well-mannered, said she'd stay behind too. Nora wouldn't have volunteered to stay behind for all the tea in China—as they used to say before Lipton came to fame—but she made the mistake of telling the man taking tickets that she was not family, not exactly, and she was refused passage. So as the ship pulled away, there was Jack's mum, wearing the new green taffeta dress she'd bought especially to show off on the ship, standing with thousands of others at the docks, burning mad, knowing no part of the race would be visible to her. And there was Nora, with her hands on her narrow hips, seething, sticking her tongue out at Jack and Bax and their two cousins as they laughed and pointed at her from the rails.

"We cheered for you, for your *Shamrock*, my da and me."

He'd left out Bax again, but this time he forgave himself. It was his mother's fault, and Nora's. They almost never spoke of him. It was as if they were conspiring to get Jack to believe he'd never existed. Only once had Nora said to him, "Jack, did he die of the same thing you had when you came back?" When Jack nodded, she asked, "And did you or someone else bury him there in the jungle?"

"Someone," Jack had mumbled. "I was too sick myself." And that was that, the end of the story.

Lipton laughed. "You mean to say you didn't cheer for the *Columbia*, the American sloop?"

"Nah. Where your people are from, in Shannock Mills, Sir? Well, it's not far from where our people come from, in Wicklow. You'd just go due east a wee bit and then drop south..." He laughed at himself. He'd seen Shannock Mills on his mum's map. It wasn't really close at all. "And because you went there first, to Ireland, when you needed someone to build your ship? My da was pleased as Punch to hear that, he was. He would read us out loud at the supper table night after night, how Scotland was your second choice when it turned out that no one in Ireland was equipped for the job. Even so, you called her *Shamrock*, and we was all so proud, Sir." He laughed. "My mum even bought a green dress special for the occasion." He shook his head. "We heard the whistles blowing the night the *Erin* come into the harbor." He and Bax couldn't sleep that night, they'd been so excited. They'd wanted to run to the docks, but their father managed to convince them that the *Erin*, Lipton's steamship, would be anchored too far south for them to see anything.

Lipton was laughing heartily. "Such flattery. Now if only I'd won."

Jack looked the great man in the eye. "But you did, Sir. You won the hearts of all the country, Irish or no." He shook his head and smiled at his teacup, which he hadn't yet touched. "The fireworks. The celebrations all through the city. We had magicians on our street corner, across the river in Hoboken—"

"Is that where you're from, Son, Hoboken?"

"Yes, Sir. The kites that were released here flew across the river, right over us in Hoboken. I found one. It needed fixing but then it was swell."

"Is that so?"

He could see it! It was brown, a light canvas fabric, with colorful ribbons tied to the tail, homemade. The spine cracked when it fell to earth, and he and Bax planned to replace the frame. That night they lay in their cots looking at it up on the chest of drawers they shared, whispering across the narrow space between them about the lad who'd made it and what he might be like, and how they owed it to him to fix it up and take care of it. How could he have forgotten all that until now?

"We had family come in for the race, Sir. We had people sleeping everywhere in our small house. But we ourselves were there for the parade in the days before the race too. My father was a great admirer of Admiral Dewey. We saw the governor, Roosevelt, that day too." He hesitated. "No, truth was we were too far to actually see him, but people shouted back that he was going by, on his horse. But we did catch a glimpse of you."

Lipton laughed. "There were a great many soldiers and sailors that day. And marching bands."

"They were good times, Sir," Jack agreed, and he dropped his head and reached for his teacup.

6. Nora

"YOU CAN SEE IT's still weighing on him, whatever happened," Maggie said.

We were in her kitchen, Maggie at the stove and me carrying plates and glasses to the table. Jack had found a job and moved out of the house—much to Maggie's dismay—a few weeks earlier. But he came dutifully to supper at least twice weekly. And when he was coming and I didn't have a meeting, Maggie begged me to come too. She never came out and said so, but it was clear she was afraid if it were just the two of them, Jack would eventually stop coming around.

I understood her concern. Jack had been living inside himself ever since he'd come back from the jungle. Yes, it was true he was out and about now, no longer sick like he was, but he seemed always to be looking through things—and people—without actually seeing them. He wasn't interested in things he used to care about. Talking to him was like talking to a withdrawn child about his school day. I had to drag it out of him about how he'd come to get the job with Lipton. "You met Sir Tea himself?" Maggie exclaimed when he'd finally come clean with that little detail. And then, as if her exclamation didn't require a response, Jack shut down. He looked at his mother and he looked at me, and he picked up a wedge of bread and dipped it into the bowl of stew I'd set before him and proceeded to eat. "Well, did you talk to him or not?" I cried. Jack nodded, chewing. "And what'd he say? What was he like?" I interrogated him for Maggie's sake, because she was looking back and forth between Jack and me like she was sinking and one of us had better throw her a life preserver before she drowned. But Jack only mumbled, "Nice enough fellow. Didn't say much," and I simply gave up after that.

Maggie and I stopped what we were doing to share a quick look when we heard the front door open. "We're in here," I shouted, as if he wouldn't have guessed. I took a deep breath to prepare for his gloomy presence and promised myself that I would get him to talk tonight, for Maggie's sake, if it killed me.

He appeared in the kitchen and stood just under the arch that divided it from the hallway and smiled—if you could call the twitch of his lips that much. His mother went right to him and he took her gently into his arms and kissed the side of her graying head. I nodded at him and he nodded back at me over her shoulder. "Jack," I said.

"Nora," he responded.

It was sort of funny how formal we'd become with each other. You'd never know we'd known each other for years. You'd never know *I* was the one to bring him back from the dead.

He released his mother and pretended (or so it seemed to me) to take in a good long whiff of the aroma. "Smells good in here," he managed.

Maggie twittered. "Shepherd's pie!" she cried. She'd been waiting all day to say those words to him.

"So I thought," Jack said flatly.

I wanted to break a dish over his head just then, but instead I said, "Let me get that," and Maggie sat herself down and I opened the oven and removed the steaming pie and set it on the trivet at the center of the table. Maggie was looking at Jack affectionately, her lips pressed together and her eyes dewy with mother love. She'd shopped for the ingredients for her pie in the morning and then spent the entire afternoon preparing it. "Maggie love, you've outdone yourself!" I cried. That's what Baxter Sr. used to call her, Maggie love. We all called her that now and then. The two words seemed to fit together like a hand in a glove, and she was a love; no one could deny that. "This is the most beautiful shepherd's pie I've seen in all my long life!"

"Indeed," Jack put in.

I sat myself down. "So," I began, "what did you dine on at the boarding house last night, Jack?" I filled Maggie's plate and reached for his. "Schweinenbraten?"

He looked up, surprised.

"You did say the landlady's name is Herta, right? You put two and two together you get German. And she does cook for the tenants, yes?"

"Yes, but…"

"But I take it by your expression she doesn't make schweinenbraten."

He shrugged. "She made some dumplings…"

"Dumplings? Dumplings and sauerkraut? I had that once at my friend Gerta's house. Gerta, Herta. And I know a Berta too, come to think… But dumplings and kraut. Tasty once you get past the smell, eh?"

I was having fun now. Except for a glance his way now and then, I was talking into my plate, moving food around with my fork. My strategy was to question him relentlessly, but in the most chit-chatty kind of way, so we would not have the same dark cloud of silence hovering over the table on this night as we had during his last visit. I glanced at Maggie. She was chewing but smiling too. She was amused—and happy, no doubt, to have me carry the weight of the moment.

It took just about the entire evening, but by stringing together all of Jack's one- and two-word answers I managed to glean a great deal. He'd rented at Herta's because it was close to Maggie's and also close enough to the ferry station that he could bolt from his bed and make it down to the 6:15 in less than twenty minutes. There was a new gas stove in the kitchen common area and some tenants used it to prepare their own suppers, but Herta always had a pot of something going too, and the tenants were welcome to that as well. It was included in their weekly rent.

Which is not to say Herta was broadly accommodating, at least not with Jack in the beginning. In fact, she called him a *worthless Irish mick* first time he appeared at her door asking for a room! Luckily, he didn't realize right away, because, as he put it, in his most descriptive phrase of the evening, her accent was "thick as her waistline." It came out sounding like *lost Irish army* to him, and as he couldn't make sense of her words, he didn't respond to them.

I asked him how he'd heard about her and he said one of his old dock buddies, a fellow he'd run into at one of the saloons, had told him. He made a point of saying he'd only gone to the saloon to ask about rooms; God forbid we thought he'd taken to socializing! Herta was a widow, the fellow said, whose husband had died on the docks.

Over the course of their introductory conversation, which took place just outside her door as Herta was reluctant to invite him in, Jack said that he would be pleased to help her with any heavy work—feeding the furnace, painting the rooms, beating the rugs—not in lieu of his weekly payments but in addition to, his thinking being that his strength would return faster if he used whatever brawn he still had left. She liked that. He won her over. She let go of the fact that he was a worthless mick (he'd figured it out by then), and not only did she give him the biggest room she had available, but she offered him supper that same evening, and yes, it was dumplings and kraut.

All *that* we learned, thanks to my badgering. And he must have been all right with it because he stayed later than usual.

I'd be lying if I didn't say I was pleased with myself. He was my responsibility, after all. I'd brought him back into the world almost single-handedly. But it wasn't enough for him to be physically in the world but otherwise unengaged. We needed him to engage, with the world, with us.

I visited Jack at work the following month. I hadn't planned to, and of course I hadn't been invited, but I was in the city for another event, and I will admit that I was curious to see for myself if the Jack who worked in the Lipton Tea factory was the same one who came to Maggie's for supper and had to be coaxed to participate in the most elementary conversations.

It was the second anniversary of the Triangle Shirt Factory fire that day, and we, our little group (there were only five of us now that everyone seemed to be getting married and putting aside their political will) of Hoboken activists, had been notified by letter that speakers would be gathering once again, in front of the opera house, to rally for workers' rights. The forecast was for the weather to be bitter cold and windy, and as my fellow protestors declined to accompany me at the last minute, I went by myself. During the first anniversary of the fire, at an event that took place not outside the opera house but within it, a committee had been formed, and it eventually got the state to commit itself to a thorough investigation of the causes of the fire. I had not been part of that committee; there were plenty of good people in attendance, all of them representing large organizations, and my voice was not needed. But I did my part on the street, marching with others and drawing attention to what was going on inside, carrying a sign I'd made myself with the words "never again" printed in large black letters above orange and yellow flames reaching up— but failing—to devour them.

This day's event was over almost before it began, because of the weather. There were a few speakers, but the wind raced away with their words, and in the case of one woman, her hat as well. I stood there anyway, to the bitter end, missing my Aunt Becky, who had begun taking me to rallies right after she took me in. She had no choice. She knew just enough about childrearing to resist the temptation to leave a four-year-old on her own, but she didn't have money to spend on a sitter either. And she was not about to give up her political ambitions in order to raise a little girl who was not her own to begin with.

At first she apologized for my presence on those occasions when she was forced to introduce me to her cohorts. But I was a good little girl and I never bothered anyone, and eventually I was able to understand what the people up at the podium were talking about and comment appropriately (if somewhat simplistically) when my aunt's friends asked me what I thought of the issues. And eventually there came a time when my aunt would take my shoulders and steer me to stand in front of her, so that I would be well positioned should anyone want to speak to me. She was proud of me, I think. In the hope of remaining worthy of her pride, I made my first speech out in my school's play yard, on the subject of women's equality, when I was ten. My teacher that year, Mr. O'Malley, told me I was never to make a speech again on school property, that I was a rabble-rouser who would only upset the other children if allowed to continue.

He needn't have worried. The truth was, there were plenty of people who believed the way I did and could get their point across with more clarity and charisma than I had. I didn't know where to pause when I spoke; I failed to recognize an applause line until I'd already barreled over it. Often I forgot to smile when the moment called for it.

And there was another thing, if I'm to be completely honest: just after the quake in San Francisco, my school friends and I organized a clothing drive and found a church that was still standing out there willing to accept our shipment and distribute the goods. To this purpose, we each made speeches in different parts of town about the importance of participating and the whereabouts of the drop locations. Baxter attended my speech, which was outdoors in front of the train station, and when I asked him later for an evaluation—hoping for unmitigated praise from my sweetheart—he said what excited him most was that my freckles lit up when I became animated. He realized right away he'd said the wrong thing and swore it was only a bad joke, and I in turn swore it didn't bother me in the least, but there was never a time thereafter that I stood up on a soapbox and it didn't cross my mind that my freckles were likely twinkling like little red fire stars across the sphere of my chalky white face.

I would do in a pinch, but I wasn't a great speaker, and I didn't aspire to be one. What I *was* was a presence. I went where I could when I could and stood up for justice and change solely by virtue of being there, another face in the crowd. Aunt Becky always said that was the most important role a citizen could play. *Show up. Be counted.*

While Aunt Becky expected me to behave in a certain way when we traveled together, she allowed me vast freedoms when we were back on our side of the river. The only rule was that I did well in school. She never asked where I went or what I did in my free time, even when I was still very young. All my friends thought that was grand, especially Jack and Bax. Maggie didn't trust her boys at all; she laid down rules and demanded explanations when they weren't followed, which was most of the time. But Jack and Bax were otherwise well compensated by Maggie's enormous love for them. She kissed them most every time she saw them, knowing full well they were rolling their eyes and snickering; she wiped their hair back from their dirty faces and looked into their laughing eyes with longing and said they were blessings from God.

We argued about it; they said I had the better hand. I said they did, though I wouldn't have given up mine for theirs even believing that. I liked my freedom. I always thought I'd make the model parent, combining Maggie's unbridled devotion with Aunt Becky's emotional detachment, dispositions I did not regard as opposites. There was time in a day for both. Of course it was a moot point now.

I asked for Jack Hopper at the front desk and the receptionist told me I would find him up on the fourth floor, three doors to the right if I took the elevator. I could have walked up the stairs; it would have helped to warm me up after walking bent forward, directly into the frigid wind, from the opera house. But I seldom had the chance to use an elevator, and so I rode.

The operator was a friendly older man, and when I explained that I only wanted to have a peek into the room where Mr. Hopper worked but not necessarily to disturb him, he informed me, as I hoped he would, that each of the rooms on the floor had a glass window built into its door, and if I stood at just the right angle, I could observe as long as I liked and no one would be the wiser.

As he brought the elevator to a stop and pulled open the gate and then the steel doors, he winked at me and said, "You don't have to worry though, Mrs. Hopper. The girls are sweet on him all right; I hear them whispering. But he's no cake-eater, that man; he don't pay the least attention." He threw his arm out, a gesture meant to confirm his words were true.

My jaw dropped. Mrs. Hopper indeed!

Now I knew what I'd come to learn; Jack was as buttoned-up at work as he was at home. I could have left right then, but I did not; I blushed easily (the horrid freckles again), and I could feel my face was red and didn't want to have to show it to the operator, a sight that might compel him to react in a way that might compel me to explain that I was *not* Mrs. Hopper, that I was to have been Mrs. Hopper but then everything had gone—as my Baxter would have said—arsewise, and now here I was a single woman who would never get to drag her children to rallies and then hug them senseless when they got home, because she would never have any. I exited the elevator quickly and started down the hall.

I took a moment to compose myself. I could hear the elevator doors closing behind me and I wondered if the operator had stood there and watched me tromp off, perhaps wondering what he could have said to upset me so. It had been two years now since I learned that Bax was dead, and while grief no longer kept me company entire nights, it still visited, often when I least expected it. But whereas in the beginning my bouts with grief left me profoundly sad, now they only made me angry.

I found one of Maggie's handkerchiefs in my purse and wiped my eyes and blew my nose. I took one more deep breath and turned to the window, and there he was, Jack Hopper in the flesh, walking slowly up and down the aisle, his hands behind his back and a noncommittal smile barely perceptible on his face, overseeing the tea packing being done on the assembly lines on either side of him.

As he went along his way, many of the women, especially the younger ones, looked up and smiled, and his own quiet smile stretched just a bit then to adjust to theirs. I could see why they were attracted to him. He had gained back some weight, and while he was still slimmer than he'd once been, he looked good in his white dress shirt and tweed vest. He was handsome; there was no doubt about that. He'd still had a baby face when he left for the jungle; you could tell he was the younger brother. Now his face was thinner, his cheekbones more prominent and his jaw squarer. And of course the blue eyes and the dark hair. If Bax were alive and looked the way I remembered him, they'd pass for twins now.

Once he'd finished his inspection, he climbed an iron staircase that led to an elevated platform that was enclosed with a half-wall gate and overlooked the assembly line. His desk was up there. He sat back in his chair and crossed his ankle over his knee and looked out the small window to his right. His pleasant smile was gone now. He looked heartsick. He sighed once, and then he lowered his leg and turned to his desk and began to sort through some papers, but I could see the sadness remained with him.

I walked back down the hall and buzzed for the elevator. The operator nodded politely when he saw me and I nodded back and we said not a word to each other as we descended.

But when we reached the lobby, he said, "Have a lovely evening, Mrs. Hopper."

I gave him my biggest Irish smile. "And you too, Sir. And by the way, please don't mention to Mr. Hopper that I stopped by."

He ran his fingers across his lips. "My lips are sealed," he said.

I walked away thinking it had been a strange and unproductive day, and it got stranger yet. I had been preoccupied with the elevator operator until I saw Jack. Then I was preoccupied with Jack, until I got on the ferry and Clementine took up space in my head. All this time and she'd still not made contact with Bax. At first it was that Bax wasn't quite settled and ready for company. Then it was that Jack was in the next room and might overhear. Once, when Jack was well enough to climb the stairs and rest in his bedroom, Clementine did try to reach Bax, but she broke off mid-trance and hit her knuckles on her bent forehead and complained it was all Jack's fault, that he was upstairs thinking about his brother at that very moment and his thoughts were so *intenso* they were interfering with her abilities.

Clementine was no longer a young woman. She claimed not to know her age, but whenever the subject came up, she insisted she was somewhere in her mid-fifties, like Maggie, though I would have put her in her seventies myself. It was possible she was losing her abilities and didn't want to admit it. Her nephew, who lived in the same building as her, had an automobile, and the only times we'd seen her over the winter months were when "Louis, the nephew," as she referred to him, had an errand on our side of town and could drive her, and still we had no séances because she had to be ready to leave the minute she heard him toot his horn. The last time she'd come by—she'd talked to Maggie; I was at work—she promised the next time the nephew drove her she would walk home, now that Spring was around the corner. *If she doesn't come up with another excuse,* I thought to myself.

I brooded about her absence from our lives all the way home, on the ferry and then on foot in the biting cold and dark. By the time I finally reached my building and climbed the stairs to my two little rooms, I had already decided I would skip supper and crawl directly into bed—with my grief, which had been waiting impatiently most of the day, and my concern about Clementine—and pull the blankets over my head. But I was delayed by a note I found taped to my door.

I brought it into the bedroom, and having no desire to switch on the overhead, I lit the candle I kept on the table near the bed. The note, written in a hand that was unfamiliar, read, "Aunt Clem suffered failure of the heart today and perished. I went to the house of Margaret Hopper to inform her, and she asked I inform you too. I am leaving this note in the care of your landlady and trusting she will deliver it as she would not permit me up the stairs to speak to you in person. Sincerely, Louis, the nephew."

I blew out the candle and rushed over to Maggie's.

7. Jack

THE SERVICE FOR CLEMENTINE was on a Saturday, and as Jack didn't have to work, he went to his mother's house in the morning with the intention of accompanying her. He didn't know the time of the event and he wanted to ensure she and Nora wouldn't try to sneak off without him. When Maggie had told him of Clementine's passing the evening before, she'd insisted that he didn't have to be there, that he'd hardly known the woman. He saw what she was up to; she was protecting him, trying, as she always did, to shield him from anything that might remind him that Bax was dead and gone. She and Nora had become adept at such artifices. They seemed to think he would crumble if he came face to face with his memories. If only they knew what played out in his head; Bax was always in there anyway. He was going to Clementine's service whether they liked it or not.

Nora was already at the house when he arrived. He could hear them in the kitchen. His mother was crying loudly, saying over and over that she couldn't bear her losses anymore, and Nora was mumbling words of consolation. They were so absorbed in their conference that they didn't hear him. They froze when he stepped into the kitchen.

He looked aside, to give them time to recover. He noticed the table was laid out for baking. A glob of dough sat on the part of the table surface that had been floured, and beside it was the rolling pin and a large bowl of sliced apples. Nora's coat and handbag were on one of the chairs. "We're making pie to bring to the family," Nora said by way of greeting. "But the service isn't for hours, if you were thinking…"

"I'll be fine waiting," Jack answered. He held up the book he'd brought along—Zane Grey's *The Heritage of the Desert*, which he'd found among the stacks Herta kept for her boarders—and turned toward the parlor.

He made himself comfortable on the sofa. This was the very sofa where he'd made his transition, from death to life. He wanted to hate it, ugly thing that it was, but he found he had no feeling for it one way or the other. He lifted his book, but then their voices began again in the kitchen.

He found himself listening, not with intention but out of a vague curiosity regarding what they made of him and why they treated him the way they did—and how he should feel about it. "Maggie, love, I know she wanted me to know!" Nora was saying excitedly. "It was almost like she was there on the ferry, talking in my ear. It was her time; that's what she seemed to be saying. And of course she was reminding me of my promise too."

"Hmmph," Jack uttered. Apparently Nora had a visitation from Clementine. He looked down at the book in his hand and realized he had it opened upside down. He turned it right side up just as Nora walked into the room. He hoped she hadn't seen him righting it. She had her handbag and coat; she was going out. She flashed a quick grin in his direction as she passed. He wanted to ask her where she was headed, but she was gone before he could think how to phrase such a question.

Jack was in the kitchen when he heard Nora come in through the front door an hour or so later. He'd fallen asleep on the sofa and Maggie had awakened him to say she'd baked two pies, one for the service and a second one just for him. He got up and followed her to the table. She made him tea and cut a slice of steaming hot pie for each of them.

"*Mo chroí!*" she exclaimed all at once, *my heart*, and Jack looked up to see Nora standing in the archway wearing the hag's hat. The sight was so shocking that his fingers trembled, and his fork fell back onto his plate with a clanging noise.

Nora laughed. She was as flushed and delighted-looking as he'd ever seen her. "Well, I kept my promise," she said to Maggie. "And it wasn't easy, believe me."

"What happened?" Maggie asked, her eyes on the bird on Nora's head, her hand still protecting her heart.

"I went to St. Ann's and got their address and found their house and told them who I was and that I'd promised their aunt I would see to it that she was buried with her bird. And what a fuss they made!"

"Stooks!" Maggie exclaimed.

"The nephew was all right really, but his wife… On and on she went about how being buried with your possessions is what they did in the old country, some superstition from back in San Giacomo, where Clementine was from. Did you know she was born there?"

"Never said. Italy's all I knew."

Nora turned to the cupboard and got herself a plate and a fork and sat down and cut a large slice of pie for herself. She took a bite. "Good, Maggie, love. Perfect, I'd say. Anyway, I could see she wasn't going to give in, and as I had to have the hat, even if I had to steal it, I changed the subject to talk about how dear Clementine was to you and me, about all the hours we spent together, and when I saw the wife softening, I asked her could I at least have the hat for myself then, as a keepsake to remember her by. And the wife, she smiled and went in another room and returned with it and said to me, *Take the damn thing. It's dirty and it smells. You'll save me the trouble of having to burn it.*"

Maggie laughed loudly, and Jack marveled at how his dear mum could go from tears to laughter and back again all in the same day. "And you wore it home?"

"I put it on the moment she handed it to me, in the parlor, and I adjusted in their own mirror. You should have seen their faces. You'd think I was putting a live snake on my head."

Maggie was laughing so hard that tears were gathering in her eyes.

Jack slipped another piece of pie onto his plate and studied Nora. The old crow had looked just right on Clementine, who had been something of an old crow herself, but on Nora, with her white skin and freckles and carrot-colored hair, it looked ridiculous.

Nora caught him staring. "Do you like it on me, Jack?" she asked.

He didn't know how to answer without being rude. He smiled instead.

"You know, he talked to me all the way home."

Maggie hooted with delight.

"Who?" Jack asked, "the bird?"

"Yes, the bird, Jacko. Who else?"

That evening, things were not quite as funny. His mother could not stop wailing, and she was louder than anyone else there. Jack felt certain she was crying for Baxter as much as she was for Clementine. Nora, meanwhile, sat like a granite statue, listening to every word the priest said.

As Clementine had never married and had no children of her own, most of the people there were nieces and nephews. But there were a few old-timers too. When the service was over, Nora stood up and addressed the congregation, explaining that Clementine had instructed her to ensure the bird was buried with her. She returned to her seat and opened the cloth bag she'd brought along and produced the hat and held it up. There was a brief uproar, with one woman, surely the nephew's wife, shooting to her feet and crying, "You lied to me!" before the man beside her, the nephew, no doubt, pulled her back down and whispered something that seemed to quiet if not calm her. By then other young people were arguing about foolish superstitions from the old country while the older folk maintained that of course Clementine would want to keep her bird. She loved her bird, and everyone knew it.

Nora stood in silence, bird hat in hand, and let the drama play out. When it was over, she cleared her throat and said, once again and with all the authority she could muster, "This is what Clementine wanted. It will bring all of us as much closure as it will her." She stared out at her audience, defying anyone to say another word. No one did, and after a moment she approached the wooden box, and finding no way to fit the hat on Clementine's head without shifting the body, she placed it on its side, next to Clementine's head. Then the priest who had overseen the service closed the box and that was that. Jack and Nora and Maggie were invited to go back to Clementine's apartment for a gathering, but they declined, and after handing over the wrapped pie, they walked home in silence.

8. Nora

MAGGIE WANTED ME TO come in for more pie after the service, but I'd had enough. I'd lost my appetite for it, and I'd lost my appetite for conversation as well. I couldn't stop thinking about the idea of closure. Of course I didn't believe that closing a coffin lid on a dead woman and her favorite possession was true closure, but it was something akin to it. It was a way of marking the end of one moment and the beginning of the next, the moment of reckoning with the parting. I'd been cheated, twice now. I'd never had a chance to say a proper goodbye to my parents; I hadn't even known when they died until well after the fact. And I'd been deprived of the chance to say farewell to Bax too. And yet Clementine, who knew as well as anyone about my losses, had put me in charge of seeing to her last wishes, closure from her end.

It was a puzzle, and it hurt my head to think about it. Even Jack, who was usually too preoccupied with his own misgivings to be aware of anyone else, said to me as we drew near the house, "Why not come back in, Nora? I'll fix you a stiff drink if you don't want pie or tea."

I laughed. Even Maggie snickered. "No, thank you. I'll just walk home."

"Would you like me to accompany you?" he continued.

"No, no. Go in with your mum. I'll be fine."

I kissed Maggie's cheek, and then, without giving it a second thought, I grabbed Jack's arm to get him close and pecked his cheek as well. I could feel the heat rushing up into his face even as I was pulling away.

9. Jack

A WEEK OR SO later, Maggie received a letter from her sister in the Catskills, inviting her to come up and spend some time with her. She didn't want to go, because she was still mourning Clementine, she said. Jack overheard her say to Nora that she would be terrible company, that Emily would be bored and sorry she'd asked her.

But Nora told her gently that it would be good for her to get out of the house and breathe fresh country air, that Clementine would have said the same thing. "In fact she whispered that to me, in my ear," Nora said, tapping her fingers on the side of her head. It was a running joke now; anytime Nora wanted to get around Maggie's objections to anything, she said she'd heard from Clementine directly on the matter. You could tell by the way Maggie looked at Nora on those occasions that she half believed her too. So Maggie packed a valise and boarded a train there at the station in Hoboken. And Nora and Jack, both of whom accompanied her, stood waving until her car was out of sight. As they walked away, Nora asked Jack if he would be all right by himself with Maggie gone for the next few weeks. He stopped walking and stared at her, speechless. "I'll be swell," he said at last, and he turned abruptly and stomped off.

Jack didn't see Nora again until the night before Maggie's return. That evening he had eaten bread, cheese and the bowl of stew offered by Herta, and afterwards he'd brought all her first-floor carpets outdoors and beat them with a broom and replaced them again. Then he sat on one of the rockers on the open porch at the front of the house with the pipe he'd begun to smoke since starting work at Lipton, watching the first bats emerge from the eaves of the house across the way and thinking hard about who he was now that he was not Jack Hopper anymore.

In more ways than one, the old Jack had been no more than a bad imitation of his brother. He had always been the less lively, the less talkative, the less adventurous, the less likely... And he hadn't really minded, or at least he hadn't thought too much about it. It was the way things were. As Bax liked to say, he'd come into the world ahead of Jack, and if he'd stopped to consider it, he'd have found Jack up his arse, because Jack followed that close behind.

Now Jack pretended Bax was sitting beside him, looking out at the darkening sky. He imagined saying to Bax that he'd felt like a poor imitation of him back in the days before they'd died. Bax would have hooted with glee; he'd say, *I'll drink to that, beggar*, and then he'd produce a bottle from thin air, because he'd always been something of a wizard, and the two would have a good hard laugh together. And maybe, when they settled down, Jack would tell his brother about a book he was reading (he'd begun a copy of *A Study in Scarlet*, but to date he hadn't been able to concentrate on more than a few pages at a time), just like in the old days. Or maybe he'd tell him something interesting someone had said at work. And then he might once again hear his brother's even breathing just below the surface of his words.

What he wouldn't give for that.

Although Nora seemed intent on wresting every single detail of Jack's colorless life out of him, she had failed to ask the location of the room he occupied at Herta's. Yet just after he'd gone to bed that night, the door, which he never bothered to lock, opened, and there she was. There was just enough moonlight coming in through the window for him to see her.

She closed the door behind her and stood leaning against it, her hands behind her back, and they stared at each other. She looked indignant, he thought. She seemed to be daring him to have an adverse reaction to her presence in his room. He didn't know how he looked, but he imagined "utterly dumbfounded" might fit the bill well enough. He couldn't think of a single thing to say to her. He glanced across the room, where his trousers were, folded neatly over the edge of the bureau. "Am I welcome here?" she asked at last.

Jack leaned over the edge of his bed and struck a match and lit the candle he kept on the side table. Nora must have been to one of her meetings because she was dressed up, wearing a long light-colored tunic over a narrow skirt, neither of which he'd seen before. On her head she wore a straw hat with a dark-colored bow and a spume of some airy fabric.

There were only two entrances to the boarding house: the one that led to Herta's private residence and the common area on the first floor, and the one that led to the second floor. The latter entrance, the one that Nora had to have come through, was used only after dark, after Herta locked the front door and went to bed. It was gained via a flight of rusty metal stairs on the outside of the building leading to a metal door behind which was a dark hall and the second-floor guest rooms. As Jack's room was on the third floor, Nora had to have gone down the entire hallway, stopping at each of the second-floor boarders' doors long enough to read the tiny name tags Herta had taped to them, and having ascertained that Jack's name was not among them, found the stairway at the far end of the hall. What was wrong with her? Didn't she realize that people already talked about her living alone the way she did?

"I'm sorry to disturb you," she continued when he didn't answer. "I'd have gone to your mum's but she's not there, is she? I needed someone to talk to."

He shrugged. "You can always talk to me," he said, but it sounded bland and insincere even to his own ears.

She went on as if she hadn't noticed. "You're like a brother to me," she said. "Since my aunt left, you and your mum are the closest to family I have."

Why hadn't she said, *Since my aunt left and Bax died*? He found it ironic that she went out of her way after all this time not to mention Baxter. Yet where he mostly forgave himself for his own neglect, it made him even more resentful of her. They were more alike than not, he and Nora.

She propelled herself away from the door and marched across the room with her chin in the air and placed her hat and her little carrying purse on the chair near the bureau. Then she turned back to look at him. She stood erect, her arms at her sides. "Do you remember Florence?" she asked. "We knew her back in our school days, but then when we were twelve or thirteen she moved across the river, and later she married into money."

He nodded. He remembered her vaguely, a tall thin girl with light brown hair and darting eyes, as if she were always anticipating danger.

"She was there tonight, at the parlor meeting. I was speaking. I was saying it's interesting to me that the anti-suffragists are engaged in lobbying legislators to support their views, which is in my mind a political act, so that they can condemn us for fighting for the vote so that we can have political lives. And Florence stood up and said the problem with most suffragists—she made a point to say *present company excluded*, of course—was that they're uneducated and wouldn't know how to make good use of the vote if they had it. They wouldn't comprehend what they were voting for. They could be swayed to make mistakes that would hurt us ever after. Her friends had a good laugh over that. Their elitism will be what kills their cause in the end. These are women of means who don't care about the working poor and don't trust us with the vote."

"That sounds like the kind of lively banter you like," Jack said.

She stamped her foot in frustration. "My point was lost, Jack. They're becoming political beings just like we are, only their sense of superiority is keeping them from realizing it."

"Then you should be glad," he said. "Your war with them is driving them into your camp. Grand how things work out sometimes."

"You're being smug. You're making fun of me."

Her eyes glistened in the candlelight. But it couldn't be that there were tears in them; Nora almost never cried. He thought about when they were kids, how his father always called her the girl who didn't cry. Maybe she wasn't that girl anymore. Maybe she'd changed too. "I'm not, Nora. Go on, I'm listening. I was nearly asleep. I don't even know what I'm saying, but I do want to hear what happened."

Nora looked at him awhile, considering. Then she went on. "I was ruffled. It wasn't just what she said, it was the way she said it. It was mean, Jack. So I said to her, which probably I shouldn't have, that from what I could see, most of her crowd tended their gardens and their homes rather than their minds." Nora took a step closer. "And she laughed. She said I was only jealous because I'd never had a garden. Of course she knew I grew up with my aunt, that my parents are long dead." She lowered her head. Then she lifted it again and spoke in a whisper. "She made the argument personal, Jack. All her friends were laughing. She turned around and smiled, to encourage the ones seated behind her. I'd wanted to say other things while I had the floor. But all I could think in that moment was that my aunt is gone, and... Wretched self-pity. I hate self-pity, in anyone, but especially in myself. But tonight... To have someone like Florence..."

"You were off target, that's all," Jack offered. "Next meeting you'll be yourself again, and you'll say—"

"I need to be held," Nora interrupted.

Jack's mouth fell open. He closed it, and suddenly aware that his eyebrows had shot up, reined them in too. He pushed himself back toward the wall, to give her room to get onto the bed beside him.

He thought she'd come just as she was, wearing her silky tunic, and that did seem to be her intention. She stepped out of her shoes and moved toward the bed and swept her hand down her backside to smooth her skirt. She was about to lower her bum onto the bed when she straightened again. She stared at Jack for a long moment—and he stared back at her, trying his best to read her mind, and all the while hoping she couldn't read his. Then she slipped her tunic over her head and pushed her skirt down over her narrow hips and walked across the room and placed her clothing carefully over the back of the chair where she'd put her hat. He still wasn't certain what was happening. Hadn't she just said he was like a brother?

He thought about Bax almost constantly, but not so much about whether he was dead or alive. He assumed he was dead, but as he couldn't know for certain, there was no place for his mind to go with the question except in circles. It was easier to think about the small things, the cracks Bax would have made if he had seen him do this or that.

Jack found himself wondering what Bax would have to say about his job, about the nearly silent room where he spent his days overseeing the work the women did. How he longed to be back in the midst of the rough and tumble of his fellow longshoremen, sharing a bottle and maybe a vulgar joke or two after a long day's work. Strangely enough, back when he was with them daily, he'd always imagined himself as something apart, him and his books, and now he wanted only to be one of them again. Bax would have said, "See where your books got you, Jacko?" Bax would have laughed to see Sir Thomas Lipton appear in the work room the other day, asking Jack if he'd care to have lunch with him. Bax would have asked how much kissing of Lipton's arse it took to find himself with that invitation. He would have said, "Jacko, look this way a minute so I can see that nose of yours. Ah yes, there it is, the brown streak, as I suspected." And they'd have laughed until their stomachs hurt.

Nora removed her corset, and then her chemise, and Jack wondered what Bax would have to say now. For once, he found no clues in his imagination.

Wearing only her brassiere and drawers, she pulled back the blanket and climbed into the bed and immediately turned to Jack and put her arms around him. He began kissing her, of course; he couldn't help himself. "I don't know," he whispered as he kissed her neck. And he didn't; he just didn't know.

She pushed back from him. "It's what he would have wanted," she said.

He pushed back from her too. It was the first time she'd mentioned his brother that way, speculating what he would or wouldn't have wanted. *Was* it what Bax would have wanted? Probably, probably so. Otherwise he'd have come home with him, wouldn't he? And then he'd be there now, in this moment that by all rights belonged to him, holding Nora in his arms.

Nora was looking at him, her eyes hard as marbles. "All right, Jack, it's what I want," she said louder, assertively, the way she'd spoken at Clementine's funeral service. She turned away from him, and for a moment he thought it was over, over before it began, and that she had seen her mistake and was leaving his bed. But she only blew out the candle and turned back again. "I want you, Jack Hopper. And I know if you look deep enough, you'll find you want me too. We're still here and we need each other."

10. Nora

I DIDN'T MEET HIM at the train the next day as I said I would. Instead I bought food and went directly to Maggie's and let myself in and started supper. My head was near exploding with questions concerning the night before, but I wanted to put some distance between it and me before I tried to answer them.

I really didn't want to see Jack at all, but as I wanted to be there for Maggie, there was no help for it. My body was tingling all over. Sensations just like the ones I'd experienced the night before washed over me without warning, and I couldn't help envisioning how it had been, how it felt to have his hands on me, his breathing in my ear. Our hunger had surprised us both, I think. We'd been ravenous, two wild animals.

I'd never been that way with Baxter. We were only kids when he left. We'd done our share of touching and tumbling around, but our most intimate moments happened, by necessity, outdoors, back near the shrubs that grew along the river bank, where anyone might have walked by at any time. It kept us on our toes, so to speak.

"Something smells good," I heard Maggie coo as she came in the door.

I untied my apron and went to her. "Look at you!" I cried. "You look like the countryside, all rosy cheeks and glistening eyes."

"You've never been to the countryside, lass. How would you know what it looks like?" she quipped, patting my check.

Jack was standing behind her and I could feel his eyes on me, but I didn't dare look at him for fear I'd blush and give away the fact that I remained in a state of arousal.

"If you'll move aside, I'll bring this upstairs," he mumbled, and Maggie and I moved to let him pass with her valise. Her hat and handbag she handed to me and I hung them on the coat tree. We walked down the narrow hall to the kitchen with our arms around each other's waists, our hips brushing the walls on either side of us and her stories already bubbling out of her mouth. Her nieces were all big girls now, she said, and all three had boyfriends. Two were gentlemen and one was a hooligan, and she only hoped he wasn't leading her niece—the youngest, at that—to do things good girls didn't do.

Jack was just coming into the room. This time our eyes met. He offered me a tenuous smile and I felt myself go red.

Fortunately Maggie had a lot to say and didn't seem to notice that Jack and I were tongue-tied. I left right after dinner, claiming I'd been up late the night before and wanted to get a good night's sleep. It was my way of letting Jack know I would not be back in his room again, and I was glad I'd made it clear, because by the time I got home to my dark dingy rooms, I could think about nothing but how much I wanted to be back there.

The weeks flew by, and Jack and I fell into our pre-intimacy routine. When we saw each other at Maggie's, we exchanged weak smiles. While we ate, I questioned him about this and that, but not as rigorously as I had in the past. As if to make up for my holding back, Jack became more forthcoming. He was showing some interest in the world again, if I was not mistaken. He'd bought a few books, apparently when I was not working, and he spoke about what he liked and didn't like about them just as he used to do in the old days.

I liked to imagine I had something to do with his renewed interests, that I was Mary Shelley and Jack was my Frankenstein. This kind of thinking helped me to balance all the negative feelings I had regarding what we'd done. I'd disgraced myself, I'd concluded—not because I'd been with a man; I didn't hold with that kind of thinking—but because I'd dishonored Bax, and I'd led his brother to dishonor him too. I was ashamed, and I was only grateful that Jack did nothing to suggest that he had any desire to see the incident repeat itself either.

In late May, several of us decided to put on a play to raise money for the New York Foundling Hospital, which was doing its part to rescue orphans from across the river and get them onto mercy trains where they might find families in other parts of the country. We knew our fellow Irish would come in numbers to support our effort, and a girl I knew from the bookstore, an Italian, promised to pass out leaflets west of Willow, where the Italians lived too. But as we hoped to get the Germans as well, them being the majority of our town's population, we marched ourselves over to the German Evangelical Church and asked Father Wilhelm if we could use the church cellar for our rehearsals. There were eight of us along on this mission, all ladies. Three were my fellow activists, and the other four were good-deed doers we knew from our school days. Even though the good-deed doers were not suffragists, they agreed to wear white frocks such as we favored for our parades. We wanted to look like angels; we felt that would be the best way to intimidate a man of the cloth into giving us what we wanted.

We needn't have strategized. Before we were anywhere near done with the little speeches we'd rehearsed about the needs of the orphans, the pastor, who seemed amused, pledged the space to us, for rehearsals and for the play itself. He even agreed to mention our play to his congregation and urge them to attend. We were thrilled.

We marched back to my flat afterwards, to celebrate. We'd already decided to do a play based on *Sleeping Beauty*—fairy tales always brought out larger audiences than adult plays—and while there were enough of us for all the major and minor female roles, we had yet to decide which of the fellows we knew might be induced to play the male parts with a straight face. I got out a pencil and some paper and we began making a list of names, ten for starters, and we had a swell time imitating how some of the fellows we knew were likely to sound saying some of the lines, especially the romantic ones. In the end we had to cut five of the ten from our list, so as to ensure our little play did not become comedic. By then it was quite late, and one by one the women began to file out.

The last to leave was Susie Gilpin. She was halfway to the door when she turned to me and said, "I wonder you didn't put Jack Hopper on the list."

I laughed. "Jack! Why, these days you can barely get him to say how he's feeling let alone down on one knee whispering words of love to the likes of a princess."

She shrugged. "I don't think he'd do so badly. I can ask him if you'd like."

I stared at her, and she at me, and what I read in her dark brown eyes and her shy little smile was what she wanted me to know. "You're seeing him," I muttered. Susie had been sweet on Jack all through our school days, and right up until he went to the jungle. She kept it to herself back then, but everybody knew.

I admit I was astonished, not that Susie was still keen on him after all this time, but that the feeling was, apparently, mutual. Back in school I'd say to Jack what a nice girl she was or how pretty she was, to encourage him in that direction, and he would always agree, but only as much as was polite. He'd never returned her interest that I knew. But he was a different man now. He'd left his youth behind, in the jungle. Susie was sweet but somber. Maybe that was what the man Jack had become needed. "I'll be seeing him again Saturday," Susie said. "I can ask him then if you want."

"Sure," I agreed. The word dropped so lightly from my lips I barely heard it fall.

We had another meeting, two days later, and we cast ballots for who we thought should play each of the three major female parts: the princess, the queen and the evil fairy godmother. I cast my vote for Susie to play the princess. It was my way of asserting that I did not think of her as a rival and that I wished her well in every way and hoped she and Jack would find happiness together, if it was meant to be. But all the others voted for me to play the princess, including Susie. So that was that; we were to have a princess with bright red hair and unsightly freckles.

On Saturday I went to Maggie's first thing in the morning before I had to be at work to ask if she had some old frilly garment I could wear for the performance. I'd forgotten my key so I had to knock. She opened the door, and as soon as I said why I was there, her face contorted and she grabbed both my hands and squeezed them tight. She was struggling to hold back her emotion. You'd think

I'd been asked to perform at the Met. A memory flared: me as a child, always observant of those episodes when parents seemed to be bursting with love and pride for their offspring. And now here I was, no longer the observer but the object of parental devotion, albeit not from my own parent. "You wait right here, lassie," she cried when she was able to speak. "I've just the thing. I *knew* you would be chosen princess; I *knew* it. That's how sure…"

She was rushing up the stairs, still going on about how she had no doubt in her mind. Meanwhile I heard a rumble in the kitchen, and thinking she'd left some poor neighbor sitting at the table with a cuppa, I moved down the hallway to see for myself. But there was no one there. Then I realized the sound was coming from the cellar. Someone was climbing the stairs. Before I had time to wonder who it might be, the door flew open and there was Jack, holding a wooden crate containing a hammer and several other tools. "I didn't know you were here!" I cried. "You frightened me."

He looked as surprised to see me as I was to see him. He tilted his head to indicate the tools in his arms. "Herta," he said by way of explanation. Then Maggie was in the room with us, and when I turned to face her, I saw her arms were full of puffy fabric, yellowed but rich with lace and silk. "Me mammy's wedding dress!" she cried, tears pooling in her lovely green eyes again. "Ain't it lovely? And it was *her* mammy made it, for her own self's wedding!"

I took it from her carefully and fingered the sleeves. "Irish lace!" she boasted.

The lacework, mostly over the silky bodice and at the sleeve cuffs, seemed bulky, not what I'd had in mind. But I'd have sooner slit my throat than tell her it wasn't perfect.

"She's putting on *Sleeping Beauty*," Maggie went on, tilting forward to see Jack on the other side of me. "She's the princess!" She nearly choked on her pride just getting the word out.

Jack looked confused. "Brothers Grimm? German, yeah? Would their Sleeping Beauty wear Irish lace?"

"The performance will be at the German church, four weeks out," Maggie answered for me. "You'll attend with me."

He nodded half-heartedly and shifted his gaze back to me. He seemed to have more to say, but when he didn't I said, "You didn't know about the play, Jack? I thought Susie would have filled you in."

His lips parted; I'd shocked him once again. It was time to close my big mouth and take my dress and go home. But on I went, in spite of my best intentions. "She mentioned you've been seeing each other. In fact, she suggested we ask you to play a part. I think she plans to ask you tonight."

"Jack and Susie Gilpin?" Maggie said on the other side of me.

I turned toward her. "Isn't it wonderful? She's grown up very pretty. Remember I showed you her picture in the newspaper?"

Now Maggie looked confused. Her eyes slid from me to Jack and back again. "I remember her well. She was small for her age. Dark hair. Terrible afraid of dogs, that one was, and when she saw one, she would run off home, her skinny legs flying up so high behind her I'd thought she'd kick her own arse. Didn't matter what game yous was playing either. Or how big or small the dog was. I seen her many a time from the window, running away from pups no higher than my ankle."

"I don't think she's afraid of dogs anymore," I said gently.

"Be lovely if Jack settled down, though, wouldn't it?" Maggie went on, but there was doubt in her voice.

Jack was trapped. Maggie and her dress and I, and the kitchen table behind us, were blocking his path out of the house. He could have used the back door, but then it would have been obvious that he was desperate to take his leave. The crate he carried looked heavy. He might have put it down on the table, or the floor, but he chose to hold it to his chest, like a shield. I dared to take in his face and found him staring back at me, his lips pressed tight and his jaw hard, trying to send me some kind of message—anger because I'd told his secret?—that he didn't want to share with his mum.

I turned toward Maggie. "Maggie love," I cried, "I love the dress. It's perfect. I'll take good care of it and get it back to you right after the performance."

As I spoke, I shimmied past her with my bundle of fabric and backed toward the hallway, and Jack, free at last, exploded from his corner and flew by me, mumbling "excuse me" when his crate of tools brushed the dress fabric.

"I wonder what got him so buggered," Maggie said when the door shut behind him.

11. Jack

THEY BECAME REACQUAINTED ONE day when they ran into each other at the bakery, and they saw each other three times after that. The first two were at the house where Susie had grown up and where she still lived. Mrs. Gilpin made their supper the first evening and the three discussed local events, and it was only when Jack commented that it was fortunate they had each other now that Mr. Gilpin had passed that Mrs. Gilpin broke the monotony by raising her voice to say, "I don't think much of any young woman who lives on her own, no matter what her circumstances," at which Susie rolled her eyes.

Jack was speechless. He didn't know if Mrs. Gilpin was insinuating that he should think about marrying Susie, so that she would never live alone, or if Susie and her mum had just come off a clash regarding living options for young women, or if Mrs. Gilpin had simply seen an opportunity to unleash a pet peeve. If so, perhaps she was denouncing Nora in particular. What other young woman did they all know who lived on her own?

The second time Susie made supper, but Mrs. Gilpin, who claimed not to be hungry, remained in the parlor and could surely hear every word that passed between them.

Susie had a sweet smile, and she could be funny in her quiet way, especially in her descriptions of her friends—one of whom, Nora, she mysteriously never mentioned. Still, Jack could not envision a future for them—until later, when they were outdoors on the stoop saying goodnight and Susie took his hand and suggested she might come visit him in the boarding house one afternoon, leaving Jack to wonder if he'd judged her too quickly.

Since it would have been awkward for them to visit in the common room downstairs, from which the other boarders and Herta herself came and went regularly, Jack brought Susie up to his bedroom a week later. Female guests were allowed in the house during the day, and right up until night fell and the front door was locked. Boarders were told to leave their doors ajar when they had a friend visiting, but as Jack's was the only room on the third floor (there was another but it was vacant), he closed the door anyway. He and Susie sat upright, across from each other at the small square table in the corner, and drank the tea that Jack had poured into cups and carried all the way up from the common room and talked quietly of this and that. During a lull in the conversation, Susie smiled at him in a way that he took to be encouraging, and he smiled back, and then he got up and came around to her side of the table and bent over and kissed her passionately. She kissed him back, and there was just enough fervor there before she gently pushed him away that he came to think that if he had one more supper at her house, perhaps two, she would suggest a visit to his room again and he would be able to move the moment along.

He returned to his chair. It wasn't what he wanted.

Weeks later, while Jack was tossing and turning, trying to fall asleep, he heard his door creak open, and his first thought was that Susie, whom he had been ignoring, had decided to pursue him anyway. But he realized at once that it was not in Susie's character to come to him in the middle of the night, by way of the fire escape.

How brazen she was, he thought, to walk through the dark streets alone at this hour, to come to his room like a whore. She was truly a scamp, just as his mum had always said. A grown woman, but still a child who thought she could have whatever she wanted, who took what she wanted when it wasn't offered. What more could you expect of someone who'd been raised without any rules?

Nevertheless, his heart was racing.

He hadn't turned to look yet. For all he knew a killer had entered his room at this ungodly hour, and they'd find him dead in the morning, lying in a pool of blood. He didn't care. The moment was delicious just as it was. If it wasn't her there standing silently at the door, then he didn't want to know until the last possible second. He'd been thinking about her. He'd been thinking how much he hated her, how she'd taunted him about Susie in front of his mum that day, how, when he went to her damn play, she'd looked into Billy Ramon's eyes—it was Billy from their school days who'd played the prince—with lust when they kissed at the end of the last scene. He could swear he'd seen the tip of her tongue dart into Billy's mouth too. It happened fast, but Jack heard others in the audience gasp, and why would they have otherwise?

There was no moon. He could barely see her as she began to move around the room, removing articles of clothing, tossing them this time, over the back of the chair against the opposite wall or leaving them where they fell on the floor. In a moment she was pulling back the sheet and climbing in beside him. She pulled his hand to her mouth and began to cover it with kisses. "If you want, we can tell your mother," she whispered. He could barely hear her over his own breathing, over his heartbeat. "Or we can find some way to let her know gradually, if you think it will trouble her less. I think she'll be happy."

Though he hadn't meant to embrace her, his arms were encircling her already, pulling her closer with a mind of their own. Her body was warm in the warm room. The window was open but there was no breeze, no relief from the summer heat. "Clementine told me there would be someone else," she whispered against his neck.

He nearly laughed. Did she mean that Clementine told her long ago, back when she was still alive? Or had the hag come by to visit her again, from the other side? It had to be the latter. There'd been nothing between them back before she'd died. But then again, there was nothing between them now, but this, Nora Sweeny, in his arms, in his bed. "She said it was only right," Nora went on, "especially now, with bad things happening in the world, that we'll need each other, you and me. I didn't know what she was talking about at first. But now I think she had to be referring to the Archduke and all that bad business. Now the empire will have its excuse. You don't need to be clairvoyant to realize that. Who knows where it will all go from here. I will never leave you, Jack. I'm yours if you want me. And if you don't want me—"

"Shhhh," he interrupted, and he rolled up over her and parted her legs gently with his knee.

12. Nora

I SLIPPED OUT OF Jack's embrace when I was certain he'd
fallen asleep. I didn't want him to insist on walking me
home as he had the first time; I didn't want to give him the
chance to say we should think it over, take it slow... I had
a future now, and so did he. *We* had a future; I'd created it
for us.

He was already there when I arrived at Maggie's the
next evening. He stepped into my line of sight while I was
embracing her. His features were slightly compressed. He
raised one finger, as if to signal he wanted to talk to me. I
wondered if that was what he did at work, when he needed
to get the attention of one of the women on his assembly
line. I released Maggie but held onto her shoulders to keep
her from turning back to the sink. I took a deep breath—
because the time had come, the moment belonged to me,
and I needed to act before I lost my nerve or let Jack's
reservations about Maggie's reaction, which we'd discussed
briefly the night before, influence me. I'd thought it all out
over the last weeks, and I had already concluded that it was
for the best, for all of us. "You're about to gain your poor old
self a daughter, you are, Maggie love," I declared loudly.

"What are you saying to me, dear?" she asked, confused.

"Jack and me!" I cried, as if it were common knowledge. "We're going to give it a go." I looked at Jack. The man I saw looking back at me seemed more a statue of Jack Hopper than the fellow himself.

Maggie's mouth opened, but she couldn't seem to come to terms with what I'd said. She lifted her hand to her heart, and I saw that she'd been holding on to the potato peeler all this time. "What? Who?" she stammered. "But I thought he was after that other lass…" She looked at Jack, who managed a nod and a tight smile.

I laughed. "Susie? That's over," I said. I'd done it right, by my rule book, too. I'd stopped by Susie's house the week before. It had been weeks by then since I'd seen as much as a smile cross her face, so I knew the answer before I asked but I asked anyway. I waited for Mrs. Gilpin, who had never liked me, to leave the room, and then I said, "This is awkward, but I have to know if you and Jack are still together."

I saw her gulp. "We're not," she said. I got up and she followed me to the door. "Shouldn't you be grieving for Baxter still?" she asked. Her words were soft, but there was a bite to them.

I turned to look at her. "How dare you!" I shot back. "What do you know about grief?" But then I thought about how long we'd been friends, and how sad it must have been for her to learn Jack didn't want her. I didn't imagine for a minute that it had been the other way around. I embraced her briefly. "It's just life," I said, "and it goes on whether you give it permission or not," and out the door I went.

"I'm his lass now," I said to Maggie.

"You say you're going to—"

"Give it a go. Yes, me and Jack."

She pulled a chair out from the table and sat down hard. Her mouth was still open, her lips stretched into what looked like a laugh that had frozen. "I'm joyous!" Maggie cried at last, the tears flooding her eyes. "I'm bloody joyous!"

"Then we have your blessing?"

Her brows rose and her mouth opened again, and she began to wail. She covered her eyes with her potato peeler hand. Her shoulders shook with emotion. I took the peeler out from between her fingers and placed it on the table. In a moment she got to her feet and pulled me into her arms. "My own daughter," she cried. "Me own wee baby girl. You always had me blessing, lass."

Our foreheads touching, we laughed and cried and laughed again. We looked at Jack at the same time and found him smiling wildly but swaying just a bit, as if he were woozy, as if he'd just received a blow to the head. He was closer now, and I was able to grab his arm and pull him into our cuddle. His hand opened at once and spread itself flat across my back, and I could feel the passion in his fingers.

And that was that. The deed was all but done.

13. Nora

"I'D STILL LIKE TO see where it happened," Maggie said. We were upstairs, preparing to move her things into Jack's old bedroom because Maggie wanted us to have her room once we married. It was the larger one, she said, though they looked the same to me. More likely she felt there was something unseemly about me and Jack taking up in the space he'd once shared with his brother. She got no argument from me there. "We couldn't go now anyway," she added. "They're saying it ain't safe to be on the high seas, the war and all."

We had opened the windows in both Maggie's room and the one that had belonged to Bax and Jack across from it. A sudden cross-breeze caused Maggie's door to slam, and I noticed that a horseshoe had been nailed to the back of it, the opening at top to catch blessings. I'd forgotten it was there. Now I remembered Maggie telling me the Irish myth that went along with it years before, when I was just a young girl. A blacksmith received a visit from the devil, who, having hooves, wanted to try wearing horseshoes. But the blacksmith, knowing who he was dealing with, made the shoes extra hot and used very long nails applying them. The devil paid (the blacksmith threw the money away as soon as he could) and left with his new shoes. But after walking a distance, pain began to shoot up from his hooves into his legs. He tore the horseshoes off at once and vowed never to go near a blacksmith's again. Thereafter, people hung horseshoes on their doors, to keep the devil away.

"We won't forget Baxter, ever," I told her. Maggie and I had talked many times about going to the jungle to memorialize Bax, but it was nonsense talk. We wouldn't have gone in the beginning, when Jack first came home, because we were worried he'd relapse at the thought of us traveling together so far away, or worse, that he'd want to come. And now it was too dangerous. "All this, me and Jack, isn't about that."

"I know that, lass." She put down the jewelry box she was holding and walked around the bed to where I was piling some of her clothes. She took my hand and squeezed it and smiled sadly. "I know."

Later that day I returned to my flat and began packing my things into boxes. Jack had ordered a wagon to come around the morning of our wedding and pick them up. I didn't have much, mostly books and clothes and a box of paints and other materials for protest-poster making. I wouldn't miss the place at all. A long and often lonely chapter in my life had come to an end.

The wedding took place in the house, overseen by an officiant from the City Hall and witnessed by Maggie and her sister Emily and Emily's three daughters, who had come in by train and would stay with us a week. I myself would not have minded a larger gathering, but I worried Jack would worry his old friends would think less of him for making a spectacle of his marriage to his brother's one-time sweetheart; when he suggested a small affair on a Tuesday afternoon, I readily agreed. Nevertheless, I wore Maggie's wedding gown, the same one I'd worn as Sleeping Beauty, but carefully laundered since the play and adjusted, by Maggie, to fit me perfectly.

"How many children do we want?" Jack asked me the night of our wedding. He was up on one elbow in bed, watching me brush my hair at the mirror.

"I don't know, Jack, four, five, six, seven," I said to his reflection.

He considered that for a moment and then he burst out laughing. I think it was the first time I'd heard him laugh that hard since before he'd gone off to the jungle. I turned to look at him, which only made him laugh harder. Beyond him I could hear Emily's girls screaming at one another. Emily and Maggie were sharing Maggie's new room down the hall, and the girls were spending the night in the parlor. They'd been arguing for the better part of the last hour, the older one and the youngest, about who would sleep on the red sofa, and the one in the middle shouting at them both to shut up so she could sleep. It had been a long time since the Hopper house had been so noisy at this late hour.

Jack finally caught his breath and his chuckles trickled to a stop. He dropped to his back and placed his hands behind his head and smiled up at the ceiling. I put my brush down on the vanity and moved to the bed and lay myself down right on top of my handsome husband, so I could look directly into his lovely eyes. "Eight, nine, ten, eleven, twelve," I said.

He began laughing again. He turned his head to the side to keep from laughing in my face. If I didn't know better, I'd say he'd gone giddy on me. I'd married a stranger, not the boy I knew as Bax's younger brother, but someone else entirely.

"I can see it," he said finally. "Scamps like you, all of them, hanging from the chandeliers, sliding down the bannisters. A house full of monkeys."

That was my vision too. I tried to kiss him, but he'd started laughing again.

I rolled off him but stayed close, with my ear on his chest so that I could hear his heart beat. The girls were still yelling downstairs, and Maggie and her sister were too busy chatting away in the next room—I could hear them too, the two of them with their lovely musical accents—to bother to get out of bed and scold them. I found myself smiling. This was all I'd ever wanted, I realized: family, engagement, the sound of children's voices. I made a wish, that I would always have these gifts, and I glanced at the door to look at the horseshoe I'd noticed there a few days earlier.

Someone had removed it; it was gone.

14. Nora

AT THE END OF July we learned that one of the many German ships that came and went from our waterfront had postponed a voyage scheduled for the next day, and that the passengers who had arrived early and were staying at Busch's Hotel or at the Delaware to await their departure were up in arms about it. We discussed it at supper. "It can't have anything to do with the problems in Europe, can it?" I asked Jack. Austria-Hungary had declared war on Serbia, yes, but we were still praying they'd get no backing from Germany—after all, Kaiser Wilhelm II prided himself as being a peacekeeper—and they'd come to their senses before there was any real trouble.

"More likely there's a mechanical problem that'll get sorted quickly," Jack replied, but his gaze lingered on me and I suspected he was holding back his real concerns so as not to upset Maggie.

There was another cancellation the next day, from another German ship, and then another the day after that. Within a week, the papers were saying all the German ships along the Hudson had been ordered to suspend operations temporarily, and the ones already in passage, some of which had gone as far as four-hundred miles out to sea, had been wired instructions to return to port immediately. And then we learned that Germany had secretly promised its support to Austria-Hungry even before they declared war, and France, Britain and Russia were leaning in support of Serbia, and the next thing we knew, the papers were saying the German ships would not be permitted to sail again until the war was over.

We were astonished that war could break out so quickly and involve so many countries so fast. We talked about it constantly, though not so much in front of Maggie. We began to walk after supper—an activity Maggie had no interest in—for the express purpose of learning what others were thinking. We discussed these new developments with the grocer, the saloon keeper, the neighbors we met along the way. Mostly people were concerned about how it would affect us, the fact that ships would be sitting at dock. It was an inconvenience, they said, not only for travelers, but also for the crews, who were being kept on board to ensure the ships would be ready to sail when they received orders.

In fact, the changes along the waterfront were even more consequential than we could have ever imagined. As kids we had always gravitated to the piers. It was much more fun to gather with our friends in a place where there was lots of activity than at someone's house with parents looking on. Jack and Baxter learned half the bad language that Maggie was always scolding them for there, just by listening to the macs loading and unloading freight, calling out to one another in gruff voices. The nearby train station and ferry station were constantly delivering fresh faces for us to observe, passengers destined for the big ships, runners looking for newly arrived emigrants they could con for a penny or two, and rowdy sailors making for the bars along River Street. You could not live in Hoboken and not feel the waterfront was a part of you.

And then, all of a sudden, activity ceased—or nearly so.

The vacuum it left in its wake only served to intensify the tragic stories people soon began to share everywhere. With no ships to load or unload, lots of macs lost their jobs. Some of the unattached ones left town to look for work elsewhere. The married ones, the ones who had families in Hoboken, set out to look for other work too, but most could find none. Our businesses simply could not support the number of people who suddenly found themselves on the dole. Many began letting employees go, because while the German crews were right there, living on board ships lined up along the piers and waiting for the war to end, they'd had their wages cut, we'd heard, and could no longer afford to spend their money at the bars and cafes and restaurants in town when they *were* permitted to come ashore.

Jack was fortunate he was no longer a longshoreman. Though things slowed down at Lipton too, they did not come to a standstill and he had his job at the same wage. But when I said that to him one evening when we had walked down to the river to marvel at how different things were, he only turned a blank expression on me. He wet his bottom lip with his tongue and looked through me, so that I knew his thoughts were far away. Everything was happening so fast. Germany had declared war on Russia and then on France by then; Great Britain had declared war on Germany; there was plenty going on in the world to carry one's thoughts away.

I took a good look at our surroundings. Two watchmen had stopped to chat in front of the piers. On River Street a woman pushed a baby buggy while several men smoked pipes outside one of the cafés, and a few shopkeepers sat slouched on barrels outside their empty shops. A line of seagulls sat laughing on the sign pointing to the ferry station. That was it. That was the war-time riverfront. And it wasn't even a war we were involved in, though people had begun to speculate about the possibility.

At the end of August I donned my white suffragist dress and tied a black band around my arm and met with my group—Susie had met a man, an older fellow who worked in dentistry, and was all smiles again, thankfully—and crossed the river to march with other protestors in a parade for peace along Fifth Avenue. Jack had asked me not to go. People were saying German Americans were raising money for the Kaiser, while British Americans were raising money for the Allies. There had been skirmishes in the streets. A few people had been beaten. I explained to my husband exactly why I was marching. We all had to follow our own consciences in such times. He agreed with me there.

Mr. Fitzgerald, my boss at the bookstore, began to hold meetings on Monday evenings in the back of the shop, in the stock room, because so many of our customers wanted to talk about what was happening and felt they needed a safe place to do so. Jack and I went together regularly, and we watched the gathering grow from a handful of people we knew to standing room only in no time. Most of the attendees were Irish or Italian, but a few Germans showed up too. Some had brothers or cousins or friends who had found a way to get back to Germany to enlist. But even those who said their allegiance was to America were torn up because they had loved ones back in the homeland.

In the safety of the storage room, almost all our fellow book buyers admitted they felt conflicted about the war. Mr. Fitzgerald said that was understandable, and in our closed quarters we should all feel free to say exactly what we were thinking, even if we surmised that out on the street the same idea would get us in trouble. After all, we were readers one and all, and therefore thinkers, and it only made sense that we would have a variety of opinions.

Hans, a young fellow who had worked at the docks (Jack and Baxter had worked with his older brother) and was now unemployed and living in a flat with his mother, confessed he feared for his safety. German immigrants who had not yet received citizenship were being asked to go to local police stations to be fingerprinted, "as if they expect the worst from us," he lamented. The Irish among us had mixed feelings too. "Why should we help England?" one old fellow spat one night when someone suggested we were likely to be brought into the war and would wind up on the side of the Allies. "What's she ever done for the Irish but interfere in our lives? If the Germans win, they'll free Ireland in good time. I'll wait for that myself."

Each week our discussions were more distressing than the week before. We always started off with reports of what was going on in Europe. Thanks to modern science, weaponry had been invented that could kill more people at a time than ever, and young men "over there" were dying in numbers too great to contemplate. Both sides were using chlorine gas. And the Brits had tanks, metal giants that broke down constantly and turned into fireballs when fired upon by the enemy. There were countless personal accounts of life in the trenches, all punctuated with dirt and rats and lice and human waste and episodes of starvation, and monotony so great that it was almost a relief when a not-too-distant grenade set time moving forward again. It was heartbreaking to consider it all.

"The back-roomers," as we came to call ourselves, agreed it was only a matter of time until we got dragged into the war too, in spite of the fact that Wilson had pledged our neutrality. The U.S. was loaning great sums of money to the Allies, some of the businessmen in the group pointed out.

Bankers were getting nervous. If the Allies lost the war and couldn't pay back the loans, U.S. banking would buckle. They doubted Wilson and his cronies would allow that to happen, no matter what they said in public.

At one meeting someone pointed out that it might *seem* we were less than patriotic if it were known we were predicting our entrance into the war and viewing the possibility with an unfavorable eye. After that we agreed to keep our discussions secret and keep our numbers where they were. There was no room for anyone else by then anyway.

15. Jack

JACK TOSSED AND TURNED and awoke often in the middle of the night, but when he heard Nora's steady breathing beside him, he was usually able to get back to sleep. Once though, he awoke and failed to hear her breath. Fearing the worst in that hazy instant, he turned her way and stuck his finger beneath her nostrils to feel for airflow. And she awoke just then, and slapped his hand away from her face and cried, "Jack Hopper, what in fuck is wrong with you?"

He knew what was wrong with him, but as he couldn't very well say so, he rolled away in the opposite direction and hoped she'd think he'd acted while in a somnambulant state. He was afraid of losing her; that's what was wrong. He'd lost his brother, and he couldn't forget that. And how did he honor the memory of his brother? By allowing himself to be seduced by the woman his brother had loved. By marrying her. A curse had fallen upon him. Upon them. She wanted children, and so did he, and they certainly spent enough time trying, but it wasn't happening, not yet.

Or maybe it was because of the way he'd come home from the jungle, the diseases he'd contracted there. Either way it was his fault. She must have guessed how befuddled he was over the matter, because she took the trouble to put forth her own theory; it was the war, she said; too much sadness in the world, too much uncertainty and confusion. She had girlfriends who were trying too and weren't having any better luck. When the war ended, they would all get pregnant at once. He hoped she was right.

16. Nora

Mr. Fitzgerald was determined to keep the bookstore open. People needed the escape books offered more than ever, he said, and he lowered his prices as much as he could. But business was off, and it was not long before he cut my hours so that I was only going in on Tuesdays to do the accounts, and on Thursdays to help shelve new deliveries—what there were of them. This left me free on Saturdays, and as Saturday was the day Jack went to check on Herta, I decided one week to accompany him.

Jack opened the door into the parlor without knocking and called her name. She appeared at once, wearing a closed-lipped but earnest smile, but as soon as she saw me standing beside him, her expression became grave. She looked put upon, insulted. She greeted Jack from the far end of the room with a nod and ignored me altogether.

Jack had prepared me for this; Herta was not a pleasant person when it came to strangers. I would have guessed that even if he hadn't told me what she'd said to him the first time he'd met her, regarding her dislike of the Irish. Her aversion was there in her comportment, in the way she stood straight and tall with her chin lifted, almost like a soldier. Her brown-gray hair was pulled back tight into a small bun that looked to be as hard as a chestnut at the top of her head. Her long brown dress featured a stiff tight white collar that made a centerpiece of her jowls. The curtains were drawn, but I could see all the furnishings in the room were brown or gray, and the walls were full of poorly-executed religious drawings and photographs of stern-looking men and women. I saw no joy anywhere.

Jack introduced me, saying, with a sweep of his arm, "My wife, Nora Hopper." That was my cue. Ignoring Jack's look of concern and Herta's sudden expression of dread, I crossed the room quickly—nine steps; I counted them—and placed my hand on the old woman's forearm and exclaimed, "I've heard so many good things about you, Mrs. Eckerd. And now I finally get to meet you!"

Her expression softened not at all. In fact, her brows rose with distaste, as though to suggest I was lying. But I was ready for this too, and before she could pull away I produced from behind my back a package wrapped in yellow paper and tied with an abundance of pink and orange ribbons. "It's tea, from where Jack works!" I cried. "Different blends, so you can see what suits you. Jack had them put it together special for you, and I wrapped it." Herta broke rank then and smiled tenuously and took the package from my hand.

And so it was that while Jack was up on the roof working to determine how water was finding its way into the attic, Herta put on the kettle, and once the tea was poured we sat at the table and began to talk. Or I began to talk, asking simple questions about where she was from and how she liked her life in Hoboken, and she began to answer, conservatively at first, but when she saw I really wanted to know, she became more extravagant.

We pushed aside our cups when they were empty, and I reached across the table and covered her hand with mine while she told me the stories she'd likely been waiting for years for someone to ask about. She and her husband had come to America to find land suitable for farming, hopefully in Pennsylvania. But they found themselves without enough money to make their way there, and somehow they wound up spending their lives in Hoboken. Her daughter died at birth, and her son, who was healthy, left home at the age of fourteen, and she and her husband never heard from him again. That was some years ago, and now her husband was dead and she was alone with her grief—wondering constantly if her son was still alive, and if he was, if she would get to see his face one more time before she passed herself—and in the meantime holding down the awesome job of managing a boarding house she had never wanted as she climbed into her sixty-eighth year with bones that ached continuously and a heart that had been broken beyond repair. "Now I have *das geld*," she said. "But now it's *zu spat*, too late."

No wonder she always seemed to have some odd job for Jack.

I wanted to tell her about my own grief, what it had been like to lose Bax, but it would have been tasteless to mention Jack's brother when we could hear the dull tapping of Jack's hammer up on the roof. Besides, she'd worked herself up; not only were her tears flowing, but while she'd been speaking slowly at first, to compensate for her accent no doubt, now each sentence flowed into the next and her phrases were punctuated with so many v's and z's and compound words in her own language that I had trouble keeping up with her. She quieted only when Jack suddenly appeared in the room, the knees of his trousers black with grime and a streak to match across his forehead. She withdrew her hand from mine at once and lowered her head as he began explaining that he'd located and replaced the offending shingles on the roof. Since she wouldn't look up, he gave his report to me. "There were extra shingles in the attic," he said. "It worked out swell."

"Good," I said. "Glad to hear it." I straightened in my chair, and when Herta peeked up at me, I smiled as warmly as I knew how.

Once I asked Bax how it was that I never heard him speak of any of his mum's stories, and he told me she never talked much about "that stuff" with him or Jack, that he knew the basics of the hardships his parents had endured in Ireland and again making their way to America, but none of the details. Later I asked Maggie why Jack and Bax didn't know about her past, and she said she didn't want to burden them; she wanted them to grow up believing that life was fair in case theirs turned out to be. I said to her, "You mean to say you never told them how your grandfather went off during the famine to seek work in Quebec and then never sent the promised ticket to your grandmother, who was pregnant at the time with your mum?" This was a story she'd told me many times. I knew every detail. Maggie's mother was born into poverty in a filthy workhouse on someone's estate. Maggie grew up listening to her mother lamenting her father's betrayal every minute of every day. She blamed her own "dark side," which she always alluded to but I never saw, on her mother's misery.

"Ah, no, lass," she said. "I don't recall I told any of that to them boys of mine."

"Oh," was all I could say in response. As someone whose parents had died when she was still a small child, I was starved for such stories. It was an ache I could never satisfy, no matter how much I learned about other people.

"Her husband's name was Abel, Abel Eckerd," I said to Jack on the way home. "Do you think your father might have known him from the docks?"

"Never mentioned the name that I recall," he said.

"But you knew before you rented from her that her husband had died on the docks. Did you never think to ask her about him, having been a longshoreman yourself?"

"She didn't talk to me about such matters, Nora. Ours isn't the kind of connection where I would ask such a personal question."

"It was a horrible death, Jack. He was helping to unload a barrel of corn syrup when the rigging broke and the barrel slipped and rolled right over him."

"You don't say? I never heard about it. You'd think someone would have said."

"You weren't there at the time. You were still in the jungle." I saw him flinch, as he always did when I threw the word in where he didn't expect it. "She said there were Irish saw it happen and didn't lift a finger to help. She was never going to rent to Irish again after that. But when you came to the door and said you needed a room and a place where you could be of use, she changed her mind. She said there was a twinkle in your eye, but she could see behind it that you had suffered plenty yourself."

He cocked his head in my direction. "You didn't tell her—"

"Of course not. How could I tell her what I don't know myself?"

He ignored my taunt. "She said all that to you?"

"That and more." I stopped walking and grabbed his arm. "Jack, she's terrified she'll be thrown out of her house, for the simple reason she's German."

He turned to face me more fully, his hands on my arms. "Aw, don't worry, Nora. Half of Hoboken's German. The Germans own the ships in the shipyard. The bosses down at the docks—or I should say the bosses who used to be on the docks—were mostly German. Half the businesses here are German owned. Even if we do get involved in the war, they'd need an army to displace a community as solid as Little Bremen."

"You're naïve," I said. I took one of Maggie's pretty embroidered handkerchiefs from my handbag and used it to wipe the dirt from his forehead. "But that's part of why I love you."

I went to step away but realized he was still rooted in place. And then I knew why; I whispered those words when we were making love, but I'd never said them outside of the bedroom before. I could feel myself blushing. What was wrong with me? "I *do* love you, Jack Hopper."

He pulled me toward him and wrapped me in his arms. "I'm the luckiest man in the world then," he said. "And the happiest."

17. Nora

THE GERMAN EMBASSY POSTED an advertisement in American newspapers saying that ships flying British or Allied flags and sailing European waters were subject to attack. A grand British ship called the *Lusitania* was scheduled to leave New York for Liverpool the day after the advert appeared. People were unnerved by the threat, but no one canceled their passage. After all, we weren't ourselves at war. So all America and Britain were stunned days later when the ship was twice torpedoed and twice exploded and sunk within minutes, with well more than half on board—Americans among them—drowned.

Jack had already told Herta he wouldn't be there that Saturday, because Mr. Lipton had asked Jack to meet with him on some matter. But given the sinking of the *Lusitania*, I thought I had better go by myself. I found her sitting at the table in the kitchen crying into her palms. I bent over her and wrapped my arms around her and rocked her gently and let her cry. She'd had plenty of German boarders who might have looked after her once, she said when she was able to speak, but they'd given up their rooms and left town when their jobs were lost. Of the five boarders she had presently, four were Italian and one was from Spain. They came and

104

went and barely spoke to her. "Who will look after me?" she cried, turning her wet face up to me.

On impulse, I offered to take her home with me, at least until we learned whether this horrible act of aggression would bring us into the war. Roosevelt was calling for war, even before the sinking of the *Lusitania*, and so were the hawks who followed him. Several of the large newspapers were for it too. Wilson was still holding out. Although the *Lusitania* had departed from an American port and was carrying Americans on board, it was not an American ship but a British one, and other than penning a letter to tell Berlin not to do anything like that again, he chose not to act. I was thinking Herta could share the bed with me and Jack could sleep on the sofa. He wouldn't like that, but he would do it; the times called for sacrifice. And as for Maggie, the two of them were likely to get on fine, both immigrants with broken hearts. But Herta turned down my offer almost before it was out of my mouth. She needed to be there to run things, she said, to collect the rents and make sure nothing was stolen from her private quarters.

"Please, Herta," I begged. "We can come together daily to check on things."

She wiped her tears away with her hands and smiled up at me. "You are my daughter, *meine Tochter*," she said. She dropped her head. "Hannah," she mumbled. And she began to cry again, but nothing I could say would convince her to leave her home.

"Not much I can do about the war," Jack said when he came in from his meeting and heard my story, "but I can help with her." He put his hat back on and went out the door with Maggie crying behind him that his supper would get cold—though we all knew very well she wouldn't put as much as a piece of bread out on the table until he was back home.

Forty-five minutes later he walked in and sat down at the table and told us he'd knocked on the door of Alfonso, a fellow he'd gotten to know during the time he'd lived there, a pipe-smoker like himself who'd shared some stories with Jack out on the front porch over an evening or two. "Didn't ask me in," Jack said. He looked at Maggie and then turned to address me. "Seems the masher had a visitor already. I could see a woman's bare foot dangling over the side of his bed from where I stood at the door. But I kept him there and had my say."

Maggie put her hand over her heart and feigned to be aghast.

"And?" I asked.

"And I told him we were worried about Herta, that's all." He shrugged. "I said he should come to the house, day or night, and let me know if he sees any signs of trouble. He said he would. I take the man at his word."

The fact that we were not at war did not calm anyone's nerves. The Germans claimed the *Lusitania* was a legitimate target because she was carrying hundreds of tons of munitions. The Brits insisted this was untrue, that there were no munitions, but there were rumors to the contrary. Wilson sent protests to Germany; Germany responded with pledges to end unrestricted submarine warfare. Some months later more Americans were killed when a German U-boat sank an Italian liner.

We were living in a nightmare. No one knew what to believe. Some people were angry that we had not gone to war over the *Lusitania*; others were holding their breath, believing it was only a matter of time before we got involved. Neighbors, people who had known one another for years, people whose children had grown up together, took sides and became instant enemies and encouraged their offspring to do the same. There was an incident right on our road. Some boys made an effigy of Wilson by filling their fathers' old clothes with straw and placing a pair of eyeglasses on the stuffed sack that was meant to represent the head. They hung it from a low branch of a maple tree and set it on fire. The flames went up at once and ignited the picket fence at the home of a deaf woman in her seventies. Luckily one of the boys had the good sense to cry out for help, and as it was a Sunday, Jack and several other men who lived nearby were able to get to the property and begin dousing the fire with buckets of water from the old woman's house. Another incident involved girls. It happened some blocks away and I never did learn the details. I knew only that it began with someone shouting, "We will beat back the Huns," and ended with one poor child tied to a tree with a sock in her mouth.

There was a time when you could walk down the street and greet everyone you passed and know you'd get a smile and a greeting in return. Now people regarded each other suspiciously, or ignored passersby altogether. People were aloof; they read the newspaper even while walking, wanting to be able to confirm that their convictions—whatever they happened to be—were right.

In the spring of 1916 things got worse for those of us with ties to Ireland. The Irish staged an uprising against British rule. They must have thought no one would notice, with the Brits so busy fighting their war. But of course that was not the case. Before the uprising even began, the Brits intercepted a German ship carrying munitions to the rebels and thereafter licked the Dubliners and other fighting Irish on the streets, imprisoning great numbers and executing the leaders of the movement.

Maggie was not one for reading the papers, and Jack and I tried to tell her as little as possible about what was happening back in the land where she'd left her heart, but we lived in an Irish neighborhood, and Maggie had only to step outside on the stoop with her broom to attract visitors from the houses nearby, and it was not long at all before she knew the awful details anyway. She took to verbalizing what the rest of us were thinking—that the world was coming to an end—and she began to carry her rosary around with her, and this in spite of the fact she had not gone to church since she'd left Ireland.

All this and more I told Baxter in my journal. How cheeky I had been to go to Jack's room, to coerce him into marrying me, I wrote. Even for me it was a brazen act, but now when I looked back on it, in the context of the times we lived in, I felt I'd been right on the money when I'd said to Jack that it was what he, Bax, would have wanted. It even occurred to me that maybe Bax had somehow intervened, from where he was on the other side, to push me in that direction, so I would not have to go it alone in the two tiny rooms where I'd been raised. Jack was my sanctuary; his love made it possible for me to forget the world for hours at a time. Out on the streets, I could see that others were not as fortunate.

One night that summer there was a huge explosion that shook the house and shattered our bedroom window. Jack jumped out of bed at once and ran into the hall, and I was just behind him. Maggie's door flew open, and she appeared in her nightdress, her rosary pressed to her heart.

"I'll go see," Jack said.

"They've come for us!" Maggie said in a flat voice.

Jack, who was wearing only the sheet he'd pulled from the bed the instant before, darted back into our room to dress. I reached for Maggie and wrapped my arms around her tightly. "They've attacked us," she cried over my shoulder, so Jack would hear through the door. "The ships at the dock! Torpedoed!"

Jack reappeared and quickly bent to tie his shoes. "You mustn't go out there," Maggie warned, and she tried to free herself from my embrace, but I wouldn't let go of her.

"Hush, hush," I whispered into her hair.

Jack stood and shared a look with me, which I took to mean, *Take care of my mother if I don't return.* I wanted to tell him I loved him more each day, that he had to return, that I didn't want to live without him, but I only nodded and watched as he turned away and ran down the stairs to the door.

Maggie and I moved into her bedroom and watched from her window, the glass of which had cracked but not blown out. It was after two in the morning and it was terrifying to see the sky orange and full of fiery blasts and heavy smoke. People were running up and down the road beneath us, mostly men but women too, yelling back and forth to each other, trying to make sense of what was going on. We could hear police whistles, and in the distance, fire alarms. It had to be a great fire, somewhere nearby. But there had been fires before in Hoboken, and never before had we heard a blast like the one we heard that night. I felt sick to my stomach and I think I would have vomited if I had not been trying to calm Maggie.

As we stood watching and listening, there was a second great blast, and Maggie grabbed my arms and wailed, "Jack, oh, Jack."

"Jack's fine," I whispered, but all I could think was, *What if he's not? What if he's not?*

We waited—Maggie sobbing and me holding back, though barely—and sometime later the front door opened, and Jack yelled up, "I'm home," and Maggie and I both exhaled. "The two blasts," he said, "but nothing since." He must have taken the stairs two at a time because there he was in the room with us, his arms stretching to embrace us both. Maggie turned immediately and began to sob against his chest. "There's glass everywhere, and we've lost our parlor window," he said, "but no real damage to any of the buildings that anyone has been able to determine so far. There are police everywhere and soldiers out by the piers and all along River Street, but everyone's saying it's something south, whatever happened, somewhere near the statue or Ellis. The smell of gun powder is everywhere."

We went downstairs and sat on the sofa—Maggie in the middle and Jack and I with our arms around her—and waited for the sun to rise. Then Jack went out into the streets again to learn what he could. The explosion, he was told by police officers on River Street, had been on Black Tom Island, a mile-long pier on a landfill that was connected to nearby Jersey City. War materials manufactured throughout the northeast had been sitting in barges and freight cars on Black Tom, waiting to be transported to the Allied powers. "How can Wilson say we're neutral if he's selling ammunition to the Allies?" I demanded.

"It's not him, Nora, not the government making the sales."

"They're allowing it, aren't they?"

"It's manufacturers, and they'd be selling to Germany if Germany could afford to buy," Jack said calmly. "It's greed. No one cares where the money comes from as long as it comes."

Not only had the blasts rocked Jersey City and as far out as Hoboken, we learned in the days to come, but parts of New York and much of northern New Jersey and even as far away as Philadelphia had felt the ground shake. Freight cars, warehouses, barges, tugboats and piers at Black Tom had all gone up in the blaze. People had died, including police officers, and injuries were in the hundreds. The Hudson Tubes had been jolted. Monuments in cemeteries throughout the region had toppled and vault doors had come unhinged, causing even the most worldly among us to speculate that the end of times was upon us and the dead would now walk among the living. The Statue of Liberty herself was damaged, by a spray of shrapnel, and windows had broken in homes and businesses as far as twenty-five miles out.

No one knew for certain what had caused the events at Black Tom. Police made some arrests of bosses who oversaw operations there, but in the end they were released for lack of evidence. Law enforcement officials admitted the blasts were just as likely the result of safety violations as an act of sabotage on the part of the Germans. But that assessment did nothing to deter suspicion against the Germans, and there were yet more instances of innocent German people being harassed and beaten in the area and throughout the country.

Except for work and our visits to Herta, we stayed close to home over that winter and read the papers. It was cold in Hoboken, but in Europe, in the regions where the war was being fought, the weather was merciless. We read horror story after horror story, and the three of us became withdrawn, comfortable only together, particularly in silence. We knew what was coming, and in the meantime we were glad to be suspended in whatever calm we could find before the storm, saving our energy for when it would be needed. In February Wilson broke diplomatic relations with Germany. Almost immediately, a German U-boat sank an American liner. Then four more American merchant ships were sunk. And on April 2, Wilson declared war.

The new changes in Hoboken happened so quickly they took our breath away. Only four days after Wilson's declaration, soldiers from Fort Jay on the upper New York Bay marched into our little town and took over all the German-owned ships (there were sixteen) along the docks. The German owners and the Germans who had worked on the ships were all taken into custody. "How can this be happening?" Jack and I asked each other many times each day.

We ventured out into the streets once again to find answers. We had thought others would feel as we did, but as we talked to people—various merchants, a few neighbors, the shoeshine man, the paperboy—we learned that even in Hoboken there was far less backlash to this aggression than one would expect. Apparently the mood was the same throughout the country. All you had to do was look skeptical to be accused of being a German spy, even if you weren't German. And if a German American were to speak out against the war, or portray himself as having a pacifist leaning, he was accused of treason on the spot, no further evidence required.

German schools across the United States closed in the days that followed. German was no longer allowed to be preached from the pulpit, and German-language newspapers were banned while books were burned by libraries. We were at war, for all intents and purposes, in our own country.

We went daily to Herta's, to check on her. Since she was afraid to go out in the streets, we brought groceries with us, and plenty of tea from Lipton's. More of Herta's tenants had moved out, and we suspected she wasn't making financial ends meet. Fortunately Jack was earning enough money that he could afford to deceive Herta about how much we spent in the markets on her behalf. She must have guessed, though.

Mr. Fitzgerald stood up one Monday night and made a speech about how it was no longer safe for the Germans among us to meet at the bookstore. Too many people knew about our "secret" meetings already. All it would take was for one person to reveal that we had, by that time, some fifteen conflicted Germans in our group, and there would be trouble for all of us. He suggested that the rest of us continue to meet as long as he deemed it safe to do so—and he didn't think that would be very long—and that the braver folk among us meet individually with our German counterparts when possible to let them know what we were hearing.

Our town, which had for so long been devoid of activity, filled up with more and more soldiers. We saw them marching along the riverfront. We saw them at the piers, large numbers of them, guarding ships that didn't belong to them, watching for acts of sabotage or espionage. Baxter Sr. had worked for the Hamburg-American line. He'd been one of their top managers for years before he died. The German bosses had loved him like one of their own. When he passed, not only did they pay for his funeral, but they attended it, each and every German he'd worked for and with. The horse-drawn hearse that took him to the cemetery was a vehicle fit for royalty—all ornately hand-carved mahogany—compliments of the Hamburg-American Steamship Company. They made sure Maggie was taken care of too, even though there were no hard and fast rules dictating they do so.

Jack and I became obsessed, spending hours at the riverfront watching history unfold before our eyes. The abuse of the German population in our own country, in our own little town, had brought us out of our shell. It had also brought out the folks who felt called to celebrate our entrance into the war, and there were far more of them.

They stood on the sides of the streets and cheered loudly as soldiers—many of them doughboys heading off to war—poured into Hoboken.

We happened to be out on the afternoon that the soldiers began tacking up posters along the riverside announcing that any German living within a half mile of the docks was to pack up and leave immediately, or risk imprisonment. "Now she'll have to come with us," Jack said, speaking of Herta. "If she doesn't leave they'll take her by force."

That night at supper we came up with a plan. Since Herta feared her absence at the boarding house would result in the ruin of all she had left in the world, we decided we would change places with her. Jack and I would stay at the house, in Herta's suite of rooms, and collect the rents and see to the needs of the boarders and handle the repairs, which Jack had long tended to anyway, and Herta could stay with Maggie. "No," Maggie said, pouting. "I won't have it. I'm afraid when you're not here." She shuddered just thinking of it. "And all for a stranger, someone you barely know!"

She began to cry, one hand over her eyes, but she let me take the other, and when she squeezed my fingers, I knew she understood it had to be done.

Jack went to work the following day, but only to tell his supervisor that he needed the day off, and I met him later at the ferry station and we went directly to Herta's, walking quickly, hand in hand, arguing about the best way to present our plan so she would realize she had no choice but to agree. Just before we reached her door, I stopped walking and took Jack's arm and turned him to me. "What we're doing, Jack? Are you at all afraid we'll be accused of siding with the Germans?"

He looked confused. "I didn't think of it that way," he said.

Jack had begun knocking lately, three hard raps so Herta would know it was us before we walked in. He opened the door and called her name, and when she didn't appear, we walked through the parlor into the kitchen. She wasn't there either, and I was about to return to the parlor and call up the staircase for her when I noticed there were some red flecks on the white wall facing us. Surely my mind was not working right because I could only ask myself, *Why would Herta let food stains remain on the wall like that? So unlike her.* It wasn't until Jack whispered, "We're too late," that I understood.

We couldn't see her, because of the tablecloth. We hurried around to the other side and found her there, lying in a small pool of blood. She'd shot herself in the head. The hole was small, the size of a dime, directly in the center of her forehead. The weapon was still in her hand.

18. Nora

"I WANT A DRINK," I said hours later as we walked back toward the house. We'd gone to the police station to report the incident (no one there had seemed surprised) and then we'd gone to St. Matthew's, the German Lutheran church, because Jack thought Herta had mentioned it once and we hoped the pastor might have known her and would be able to arrange a service. As the pastor was not in the church or on the grounds, we found his housekeeper and asked her to run up to his room and fetch him, and a moment later she came down screaming that his possessions had been turned inside out and he was nowhere to be found. So we went back to the police station, where we had to wait a good long time because by then other people were there telling stories about German neighbors who had suddenly disappeared, and not all of the missing lived within a half mile of the docks either.

The nearest pub was German-owned and as such, it had been abandoned, a sign on the door saying in English, *See you when this damned war is over.* We didn't want to see anyone we knew, so we walked to the Italian part of town and found a pub there. It was dark by then, and we were tired and downtrodden and unable to even discuss what had happened any longer. As we entered, I took in that I was the only woman in the place, but I didn't mention it because I didn't want to give Jack an excuse to keep me from my drink. There were some soldiers gathered in one corner. They glanced at me and went back to their business.

We went directly to the bar and ordered two whiskeys and sat like strangers, rigid and aloof, staring at the people at tables behind us as they were reflected in the glass mirror behind the bar. It seemed otherworldly to see people laughing and toasting one another on this particular day, when an old German woman—a woman Jack had sometimes found ungrateful but for whom he had taken responsibility anyway; a woman who had shared her life stories with me, who had called me "daughter"—had blown a hole through her head. "Here's to us!" a fat Italian man sang as he got out of his seat and raised his glass. "With the Germans gone," he continued, glancing at the soldiers, "Little Bremen will be Little Italy now!" He swept his eyes towards me and Jack and caught our gaze in the mirror. Then he turned back to his friends, who were clinking glasses and crying, "*Salute!*"

"Let's get out of here," Jack whispered, and we downed what was left of our drinks and slid off our stools. Jack opened the door for me and I stepped outside, but he only stood there behind me, still holding the door. "Alfonso," he whispered.

I looked where he was looking and saw a smallish man walking quickly in our direction. I couldn't see his face in the dark. Alfonso, the Italian boarder, I remembered, the one who was supposed to let us know if there were signs of trouble at Herta's. When Alfonso was close enough, his lips stretching into a smile as he recognized Jack, Jack let the door close behind him and grabbed the Italian around the neck and pushed him up to the brick front of the building. "I told you to tell me if anything went wrong," he shouted.

"Jack, what are you doing? Let the man go," I cried. I glanced at the pub window. A few people sitting at a table on the other side of the glass were straining to see what was going on. "You don't know it's his fault!"

"I was coming to tell you in the morning," Alfonso cried.

Jack laughed in his face. "Tomorrow morning you were going to tell me she shot herself today?"

"Whoa! What the hell? Who shot who?"

A long moment passed, Jack and Alfonso staring into each other's eyes, Jack assessing, Alfonso waiting for his question to be answered. Finally Jack let his hands drop to his side but he stayed in Alfonso's space. Alfonso pulled his shirt collar back into place.

"Your landlady, Alfonso. Herta is dead."

"Dead?" cried Alfonso. He glanced over Jack's shoulder, taking me in with his gaze. "*Dio Mio*. Dead?" He looked down at the sidewalk, then up again. "She tell us to get the hell out. All. This morning, early. She knock on our doors, wake us up. *Sie aussteigen*, she yelling. *Sie aussteigen*. Some of us going to work, but she tell us get out right then, take everything, she closing her doors for good. I tell her give me one hour or two. I have to find somewhere to go first.

"I come here, Mr. Jack, because my uncle, he owns this, with rooms upstairs. But with all the officers in town, he have no room for me. So I go looking, up and down the streets. Then I come back and beg, and my uncle, he says he got two officers so cheap he thinks he can make them share a big room so I can have their small one. So he tell me go, get my stuff and he'll make it good with the soldiers."

He turned his palms up, shrugged, and continued. "The landlady standing there with her hands on her hips when I get back, mad as *un bastardo* in a dogfight 'cause it take me so long. I leave some stuff behind 'cause I can't carry and she says I can't come back either. I take only most important, *capisce*? I flinch when I pass her on the way out, 'cause I think she gonna hit me with the rolling pin she got. Then I come back here. Then I go to work, tell the boss what happened so I don't lose my job. Work to end of the day. Then I come back here. And here you find me!" He turned his palms up again. "I coming to you in the morning, to tell you the landlady, *lei sta impazzendo*, she losing her mind. I coming first thing. You believe me?"

Jack took a step back from the man and hung his head. I stepped forward and took Alfonso's hand. "We found her, Alfonso. It was awful. We're still in shock. Jack didn't mean to accuse you so fast, did you, Jack?" I glanced at him. He was watching me expressionlessly.

Alfonso patted my hand with his free one. Then he gave it back to me and turned to Jack. "I should think to find you first, think of moving later."

"Not your fault," Jack mumbled. "My fault. I owe you an apology."

"No! Apology belong to me. I owe *you*. I give my word, then think of me, Alfonso, first. I owe you drinks. Ten drinks. Words count. I know that back in Italy. Come. I buy now." He moved to the door.

Jack reached out and patted his shoulder. "Not now," he said, and he took my arm.

"Okay, you come and find me, okay?" As we began walking away he called out after us, "I buy for you and the pretty lady too. You come back."

19. Nora

THE FIRST SHIP TO be renovated for carrying doughboys off to war was the *Vaterland* (Fatherland), now renamed the *U.S.S. Leviathan*. Meanwhile, various hawkish groups associated with the government decided that the country was not as pro-war as it needed to be and began a series of domestic propaganda campaigns that included the placement of pro-war advertisements in magazines and newspapers. Men and women were hired, not just in Hoboken but throughout the country, to pass out millions of pamphlets defending America's role in the war. A massive advertising campaign for war bonds was also launched.

The girls and I gathered in Maggie's cellar one Saturday to create peace posters to put up around town and also to make a list of the local places where it might be safe for us to speak to small groups about the peace movement that was already evolving to deflect the efforts of the hawks. The only one who didn't come was Susie, who said she was too busy making plans for her wedding, which, to my knowledge, wouldn't take place for months. Either she didn't want to be in the same house with Jack, or the dentist she planned to marry had convinced her to give up her activist ways. None of us had met the dentist yet, but we'd heard he was the pushy type and that his patients complained about his lack of empathy. We were a dreary group, painting in the cellar. We talked about the news; it was all anyone talked about anymore. It was astonishing to find ourselves living in a country where we were being told what we could and couldn't say. Each of us had a personal story or two to contribute, about some abuse she'd witnessed. As for me, not an hour went by that I did not see Herta, on the far side of the table with a bullet hole in her head.

After everyone left, Jack came down the stairs and had a look at the posters, which the girls had left behind because the paint was still wet. He nodded and went to the workbench and returned with a small tin bucket and began to collect the dirty brushes to take outdoors to clean. "I wish you wouldn't do this, Nora," he mumbled.

"Do what?"

"Speak publicly against the war."

You're no better than Susie's dentist, was my first thought. But before I could express my rage, Jack put the bucket aside and pulled me into his embrace and whispered, "I'm not saying I'd ever stand in your way, just that I never want anything bad to happen to you."

Our intimacy was the one thing I could depend on in a world where everything else was spiraling out of control. The anger that had flared seconds ago drained away. I wondered if couples everywhere were relishing in romance in these troubled times. I pushed him away gently and handed him his pail. "Leave me alone," I said softly. "You knew who I was when you married me."

Later I came to think it was an absurd thing to say. How could he know who I was when I didn't even know myself?

A few days later I received a letter, forwarded from the boarding house where I'd lived, from a socialist I'd met some years ago, when I was still going to meetings with my aunt. Having made the assumption that I, like Aunt Becky, was destined to become a lifelong pacifist, Mary Sheen invited me to travel across the river to speak to a small group of people in her home. I remembered her vaguely, a heavyset woman with white hair, peppering me with questions after we'd listened to someone speak about workers' rights in the lobby of a small hotel. *You're a smart young lady*, she'd said to me that day. *I hope our paths will cross again.*

No one had ever invited me to speak before, and I was flattered. I went into the kitchen, where Jack was reading the newspapers at the table, with the letter pressed to my heart and told him of its contents. I had to have been glowing with pleasure. Poor Jack tried to smile, but he failed miserably. He didn't argue with me though. "I would like to accompany you," was all he said.

I wasn't there to speak in opposition of the war, I told the ten or so people who came to listen to me that night. My instincts told me war was wrong, and I personally was against it; yet I understood there were people who believed an American presence could bring this horrible nightmare to a quicker end. What I opposed was the government's insistence that we all declare ourselves to be pro-war, that we refrain from discussions concerning the morality of the war, that we turn our backs on our German American brothers and sisters and chase them from their homes and schools and houses of worship. And I was opposed to the draft, which had been instituted not long after Wilson's declaration of war.

My little presentation was well received, and a spirited conversation followed. Someone pointed out that Emma Goldman, an anarchist—I'd met her once myself, when I'd gone to hear her speak years before with my aunt—had been arrested for telling people to oppose the draft. Everyone wanted to talk about how dangerous it was these days to speak out for peace now that the Espionage Act was in full swing. People were being imprisoned daily for being disloyal to the war effort. There was even a Protective League made up of private citizens willing to betray their neighbors to the government. The whole country, it seemed, had gone daft. People's worse instincts were on display. Hatreds they had kept to themselves were coming to the surface, and every day brought news of verbal and physical confrontations from every corner of the country.

Jack got up one morning a week or so later and informed me that he was taking the day off from work to go to City Hall and fill out a draft card. "What can you be talking about?" I cried. "You're against the war, Jack! We've discussed it a hundred times." I lowered my voice to a whisper. "And what about your mother? She depends on you. And what about me? And who's to say a stint in the trenches wouldn't reduce you to the same half-dead person you were when you got home from the jungle? Why would you do this, Jack? Why?"

"It's what Bax would do. Bax would sign up and he'd be right. It's got nothing to do with how I feel or don't feel about the war."

I tried to blink back the tears that came rushing to my eyes at the sound of Bax's name. The three of us, Jack and Maggie and I, mentioned Baxter regularly these days, but only in the most superficial way. *You and your brother went there with your father that one year, I believe*, Maggie might say at the supper table. Or, *Where's that fishing rod Bax used to keep in the cellar?* Jack might ask. Baxter's name came up in conversations where it would have been awkward *not* to mention him, where the omission of his name would have been louder than the saying of it. But these were instances that were devoid of emotion; they were safe. We never talked about our grief, and we never speculated on how things might be if Bax were still alive.

Jack shifted the subject before I could think how to respond. "Every man between eighteen and forty-five has to register," he said. "It doesn't mean I'll be called. If I'm caught without a registration card, it would be worse. They'd cart me off to jail and beat me daily."

As it turned out, Jack got beaten anyway, not long after. A friend of Mary Sheen, a woman called Scarlett Hines, sent a letter inviting me to speak at her Manhattan home too, somewhere on East 77th Street. Jack, who almost never got angry with me, raised his voice when I told him. "You can't keep putting yourself at risk like this!" he cried. We were standing in the parlor, and his outburst brought Maggie, who'd been sweeping the front stoop, in from outdoors.

"I might say the same to you," I snapped, "since you insisted on getting a draft card."

"Oh, dear," Maggie mumbled, the knuckles of her free hand raised to her mouth. As if she couldn't decide whether or not to stay and witness our argument, she'd left the door ajar behind her.

Jack glanced at her. He seemed to have more to say on the subject, but I knew he wouldn't say it in her presence. He tiptoed around her these days, trying never to do or say anything that might upset her. I took advantage of my shielded position by adding insult to injury. "And furthermore, Jack Hopper," I continued, "I won't be needing you to escort me this time. I'll be perfectly safe without you. In fact, I don't want you to come, you and your registration card."

He pressed his lips together and looked aside. Then he pulled his arm back and struck the wall with his fist, hard,

though not hard enough to break either the wall or his hand.
I almost laughed. It was something Bax would do. Maggie
jumped and dropped her broom. As Jack flew past her to
attain the stairs, he stooped and picked it up and handed it
to her. When he was gone, Maggie shook her head at me. I'd
disappointed her. My triumph drained away, and once it was
gone I couldn't think what had possessed me to speak like
that to Jack in the first place.

Having never argued with Jack before, I was curious to
see how he would behave afterwards, how we would behave
together. When he was a boy and fought with his brother he
would sulk or fight him back. But he wasn't a boy; he was a
man who barely resembled the boy he'd been.

This new version of Jack didn't sulk or fight. Nor did I.
We went about our business as we always did, which is to say
we conversed with Maggie and with each other at supper,
we walked along the waterfront in the evenings, and we
carried on with our unquenchable appetite for the erotic at
night. We didn't speak of my presentation at all, in fact, but
on the afternoon of the day I was to give it, I came down
the stairs dressed and ready to leave and found Jack sitting
in the parlor on the blood-red sofa in his best shirt and with
his summer jacket folded at his side. I was not surprised. Nor
was I displeased. The soldiers who had militarized our little
town had begun arresting women who were found walking
alone in the dark, and it would be dark by the time I got back.
I went into the kitchen to kiss Maggie goodbye, and when
I returned to the parlor Jack got to his feet and swooped in
front of me to open the door before I reached it.

I spoke for only a few minutes that evening in the Hines'
fancy brownstone, but I led the discussion that followed,
which went on for nearly an hour. Afterwards, the men
among us, maybe seven or eight of them, gathered at one

end of the parlor and someone passed out shot glasses and Mr. Hines opened a bottle of whiskey, which he said was almost as old as he was and wouldn't interfere with the president's proclamation that grain be used for food production only until the war was over. We women stood silently watching them—until Mrs. Hines followed a sigh with the question, "Would anyone care for tea?" and the youngest among us, a woman who had introduced herself as a college student, laughed loudly and strode across the room to join the men. Then we all laughed, and Mrs. Hines went off to find more shot glasses, and before long we were all having a swell time, a welcomed relief after the issues we'd been talking about.

Jack and I stayed on after the other guests had gone, for "one more drink," at the insistence of our hosts. George Hines, we had learned during the course of the evening, was in banking, though he didn't say which bank or what his position was. Scarlett wore a good number of oversized jewels, at her ears and neck and wrists. The parlor was large and full of beautiful furniture and art work. It was clear they were quite well off. Had I met them on the street, I wouldn't have guessed they were the kind of people to be against the war—not because they were rich but because their interests appeared to be mostly material.

We were all a bit tipsy before long, and we wound up talking about baseball, of all things, or the men did. I was pleased to stand and listen, because it wasn't often I got to hear Jack speak with such enthusiasm. Apparently Babe Ruth had threatened to punch an umpire in the nose after the umpire threatened to throw him out of a game. I doubt Scarlett Hines knew any more about baseball than I did, but when the men laughed, we laughed with them. No one laughed anymore. We were all so miserable about the war, about the divisiveness in the country. It was a great relief to laugh at such nonsense.

We said goodnight at the front door and ran down the brownstone's concrete steps still laughing and holding on to each other to keep ourselves upright. But we stopped when we saw two men standing out on the street, facing us. One was carrying a wooden club. Even in my addled state I knew what was about to happen.

"Run back in," Jack whispered, but when I looked behind me, I saw a third man, up on the landing, blocking the door. Jack saw him too. "Run," he said. "Now!"

I ran, but only as far as the next building. Jack said something to the men, along the lines of *What do you want with me?* and I heard one answer that they only wanted to see Jack's draft card. Men were supposed to carry them at all times. If Jack didn't have it, it was my fault, because of what I'd said to him. And I knew Jack well enough to know he didn't have it.

There was a stairwell leading to the building's cellar. I hurried down to the door and knocked once, although I doubted there'd be anyone down there at this hour to hear me. I came halfway up the stairs and peeked out of my hiding place. The two weaponless men were moving towards Jack, one of them calling him a dirty slacker. Jack was talking over him, trying to get him to understand that he did have a card; he'd left it home, was all.

The one with the club was moving in on Jack too now, lifting the club slowly as he neared. Jack was still arguing with the other two and I didn't think he saw what was happening. I was about to yell out when Jack turned from his two accusers and slammed his head into the man with the club. The club fell to the ground and Jack jumped on the man, and when he went down, Jack began to pummel him.

Instantly the other two jumped into the fray, beating on Jack and trying to pull him off their friend.

I ran up out of my hiding place at once and somehow managed to grab the club. My blood was racing, propelling me forward. I might have gone after one of Jack's assailants but the four of them were heaped together, one monster with too many moving parts, and I feared I'd hit Jack by accident. I ran up the stairs to the Hines' residence instead and began to scream and bang the club on their heavy wooden door. When I looked over my shoulder, I saw that Jack was in the middle of the road, lying on his back, and all three thugs were coming at me. Then the door opened just in time and George Hines appeared behind it in his pajamas. He had a gun in his hand, at his side at first, but as he took in the situation, he raised it and shot into the air and the thugs shared a quick look and backed away and then took off running.

"Fuckin pikers," Jack mumbled when I reached him. I laughed through my tears. He was alive.

"We've got to get you to the hospital," I cried.

George Hines was just behind me. Jack reached out his arm toward him and George hauled him to standing. Scarlett Hines appeared in a white silk dressing gown, and when she saw the blood on Jack's shirt, she clapped both hands over her mouth and turned back to the house. George yelled for her to grab two towels, one wet, one dry. Lights had gone on now in some of the buildings nearby. I saw faces at some of the windows.

Jack looked at his knuckles, which were full of blood. He stretched his fingers out. "I don't need the hospital," he mumbled.

"You do," I cried.

"He's not as bad as he looks," George Hines said.

I looked at him. How would he know? I wondered, but I held my tongue. It was clear he'd already decided he would not be inviting Jack back into the house. Scarlett returned with the towels, and Jack took the wet one and wiped his mouth. He ran a finger over his teeth, upper and lower. "All there," he said. He smiled widely. "Let's go, Nora. I want to go home."

We argued about the hospital along the way, but Jack insisted he didn't need to go, and he was able to walk well enough with my help. The blood on his shirt was not his, he promised me, and it did seem to be true. Somehow I got him on the ferry, where, thanks to his appearance, we had the entire bow railing to ourselves. I was afraid we'd be stopped by soldiers on the waterfront in Hoboken and he'd be asked again for his draft card, but I helped him to put his jacket on just before we arrived, to cover his bloody shirt, and then I clung to him as we went by the soldiers, so that we looked like the lovers we were.

Once we were back at the house, I sat him down in the kitchen and cleaned and bandaged all his many bruises, and although he cried out a time or two, we managed not to wake Maggie, who would have been horrified to see him as he was. I helped him up the stairs. Then I ran back down and got a glass and a bottle from the back of the cupboard, one of the whiskey bottles that Baxter Sr. had left behind, and brought them back up to our room. I poured the whiskey and had myself a good slog before I raised the glass to Jack's lips. He drank deeply too. "You saved me miserable life," he said. His brows descended and a look of earnestness appeared in his eyes. "For the second time, Nora. Think of it."

He let his head plop back on the pillow. I could see sleep was coming for him quickly. "If the club hadn't rolled away," he continued, "if you hadn't been bricky enough..."

I laughed. "I *was* bricky, wasn't I?" We'd both seemed to have forgotten the incident had been my fault to begin with.

"Yes." He closed his eyes but then opened them half way. "Bricky and foolish. And now you'll have to nurse me back…"

"You're not so bad this time. A few gashes. Don't milk it, Jack."

He pulled me close with the better arm. "Ah, you've got my number, Nora. And you've always had my hea…" He drifted off.

You have my heart… Baxter Sr. used to say that to Maggie all the time when he was alive, in Gaelic: *tá tú mo chroí.* Baxter Jr. used to say it too, to me.

20. Jack

WITH ALL THAT HE'D had to drink he didn't feel any pain that night, but the next day he realized he had at least one cracked rib, and he couldn't get out of bed. He spent the entire day tossing and turning, cautiously—trying to find a position where he could be comfortable—and praying, after the one time he sneezed, that he would never sneeze again, or at least not until he healed. And thinking this: How had the thugs known he and Nora were still in the house after the others had gone? Had there been a stool pigeon in the group? Could it have been their host, the rich banker? Ah, but that seemed unlikely. And this: How could he prevent Nora from accepting any more speaking invitations without ruffling her feathers?

He didn't go to work that week, but after four days he felt well enough to limp down to the Italian pub. There was no doubt in his mind that he was the one at fault for the hustle he'd had with Alfonso, but he'd seen the man on the street a time or two, and the Italian still insisted he was the one who owed Jack and not the other way around. It didn't matter: Jack was prepared to take advantage of his confusion and collect.

The next night, right after they'd all gone to bed, there was a blast—localized; nothing like Black Tom—and then the sound of shattering glass. Though Jack had been expecting it, Nora managed to get into her robe and slippers and out of the room and down the stairs before him. "It's a rock," she called out, aghast. "Someone threw a rock through our window."

He was halfway down the stairs himself when Maggie emerged from her room, crying, "I can't take it no more; the world is ending!"

"It's not ending, Mum," Jack said calmly. "It'll all be all right."

He stepped quickly to Nora's side and she showed him the rock, which he could see quite well as the room was full of moonlight. It was the size of a baseball. "There was a note tied to it," Nora whispered.

He turned. His mother was just at the foot of the stairs. "Don't let her see it," he whispered back.

Nora nodded and slipped one hand into her robe pocket just as Maggie approached, breathing rapidly, both hands over her heart. Nora showed her the rock. "It's nothing," she said. "A prank. It only means Jack will have to replace the glass again."

Jack went out the front door but returned minutes later. "There's no one out on the street."

"Maybe it was one of those bad boys who started the fire that time," Nora offered.

While Nora and Maggie cleaned up the glass, Jack found some wooden boards in the cellar and tacked them over the broken window. After they'd all gone back to bed, Nora lit a candle and she and Jack read the note together. "You Hoppers are traitors and I will see you all in jail if you don't quit your evil activities," it read.

"How dare they?" Nora exclaimed. "How dare anyone...? This was no kid, Jack; you know that. This was someone who's been spying on us!"

"Blasted pikers!" Jack agreed. He paused a minute, realizing his expression of anger failed to match hers. "*Blasted* pikers!" he said again, louder. "But it concerns me to know this person knows where we live. I'm worried about Mum. She's fragile these days." He watched his wife as she mulled that over.

Nora blew out the candle and curled up on the edge of the bed, as far from him as she could get—or so it seemed to Jack. He hardly slept after that, worrying about what she might be thinking. But the next morning she announced that she had no intention of putting Maggie—who was a mother to her, who would be grandmother to their children when they finally came along—in jeopardy. Her speechmaking days were over.

21. Nora

ARMISTICE WAS DECLARED IN November, though we hardly noticed it because in the weeks leading up to it we got another visitor to our little corner of the world: the Spanish influenza. We'd heard there'd been outbreaks at army camps even before the end of the war, but no one thought it would go further. Then next we heard, instances of pneumonia were popping up in certain regions, including our own. And next thing, old Dr. Burns appeared on our doorstep. "The flu is on its way," he said, "and at the rate it's traveling, it will be all over Hoboken in no time." Schools were passing out circulars for the children to bring home to their parents to educate them about what to look for and how to handle it if someone took sick, he said. Since we had no children, he thought he'd better tell us himself.

Jack's head snapped in my direction when Dr. Burns said that. It was a point of contention between us. He worried about me worrying because I still hadn't become pregnant. I told him it was fine, that it would happen when the time was right, and I wasn't upset. But whenever anyone mentioned children, I caught him looking at me, evaluating my reaction. He drove me mad sometimes.

Maggie was probably safe, Dr. Burns continued—he was sitting on the edge of the wing chair in the parlor with a cup of tea on his knee by then—because she was older, as was he. The strange thing was this pandemic—which he believed was far worse than reports from Europe had let on—seemed to be most dangerous to healthy children and young adults. He was worried, he said, about me, and he wanted me to avoid crowds and wear a mask if I dared to go to work at all, which he hoped I wouldn't.

"Me?" I cried. Besides the time I spent in Jack's arms, my two half days at the bookstore afforded me my only moments of distraction. We had less traffic than ever in the store, it's true, but when someone *did* come looking for a book, there was still the opportunity to have a conversation that wasn't about the horrors of the war or the hell our beloved Hoboken had become now that so many people had been evicted from their homes and made to shut down their businesses, now that we had seen firsthand the capacity for evil that lived in the hearts of seemingly good men. "What about Jack?" I cried. "He's young and healthy. Shouldn't he wear a mask too? And what of *his* job, riding back and forth on that crowded ferry?"

"Jack should take precautions too," Dr. Burns said calmly. He turned to look at Jack. He was seated at one end of the red sofa, and Maggie was at the other. "But I am of the opinion, and it is only my opinion to be certain, that what you had when you came back from the jungle was in the same family as this Spanish influenza. I'm guessing you have an immunity." He laughed. "You deserve an immunity, young man, almost dying on us like that." He looked at Maggie and she offered him a forced smile. This flu news was not sitting well with her at all. Dr. Burns cleared his throat and looked back at Jack. "The symptoms of the influenza are not unlike the symptoms of some of the jungle diseases I've read about, and I'm not the first to say so. The hemorrhaging from the mucous membranes, the bleeding from the ears, the bluish skin. Of course you didn't have the cough, but all the rest…" He turned back to me. "My dear girl, I know you can't stand to be left on the sidelines, but I would like to suggest you sit this one out. Don't go anywhere, don't—"

Jack must have seen the indignation spreading across my face because he interrupted by coughing loudly into his fist. "Mum," he said, turning to Maggie. "You have that quare bump on your ankle that you're always clacking on about. Why not let Dr. Burns have a look now he's here anyway."

Within a week of Dr. Burns' visit, the state of New Jersey issued a mandatory order closing all churches, movie houses, saloons, and other places where people gathered to pray or find relief. Nor were people permitted to assemble to memorialize the dead. The schools closed, and one by one other public buildings followed suit. When Mr. Fitzgerald told me he was closing the bookstore for the time being, I cried, briefly. To my own surprise, I realized I was more relieved than dismayed. The prospect of getting the Spanish influenza appealed to me not at all. Maggie, who'd been worrying herself sick about me being out and about, was overjoyed.

That same night at supper she said to Jack, "You watch. Lipton's will close too now, and I can't say the prospect don't make me happy, lad."

"Lipton's is too big to close," he mumbled, a spoonful of peas waiting to be tunneled into his mouth.

Maggie huffed and Jack stared down into his bowl, and the conversation fizzled, but the next day Jack arrived home not long after he'd left for work. "They've dismissed me," he lamented, coming into the kitchen where Maggie and I were preparing to bake bread. "Temporarily, at least. They're staggering hours for those who live nearby, to eliminate crowds, and they're suspending hours for people like me who have to travel."

When Jack saw Maggie's expression go from surprise to pleasure, he turned and left the room.

Jack had taken Dr. Burns' hypothesis to heart; he was certain he was immune. "I don't want to upset her," he said to me that night in bed, referring to his mum, "but I feel I have a role to play."

I admired his resolve, but I didn't intend to lose him either. And for what? Because old Doc Burns had put a worm in his head? It wasn't all that many years ago that Dr. Burns had told me flat out Jack would die, that there was no chance he would recover from the jungle disease he'd come home with.

How could I stop him now that the tables had turned? I wondered. I never said so, but half the time I agreed with Maggie, that the end was at hand and we would all die soon anyway. Just the day before a neighbor had come to the door, to check on us. Maggie didn't ask her in, for fear she might be sick herself and not know it yet, but they spoke out on the stoop, and the neighbor shared the horror stories that were making their way through town. People were dropping like flies, she said, fine one day and gone the next. It began with fatigue followed by fever and headaches. Then the victims turned blue and started coughing, sometimes with such force they tore their stomach muscles open. Foamy blood bubbled up out of their mouths and from their noses and ears. And then... Not everyone died of course. Some people got sick and then got well, though healing did not happen quickly even for the fortunate. "Jack, I forbid you to take any risks, and I don't care what Dr. Burns said," I whispered, but Jack was already asleep.

Jack got the wheelbarrow out of the cellar the next morning and went out. When he returned, he had enough canned food and potatoes and candles to last until the end of time, if that was in fact what was coming. "The streets are near empty," he reported as he opened the Hoosier doors and began to put things away. "The only people about are those like me, looking to buy food or medicine. And a few soldiers just come off returning ships and don't have arrangements to get home yet. The shopkeeper said once he stops getting deliveries, if it comes to that, he'll close down too, so we'll have to make this last long as we can." He lifted a bag of candy out of his wheelbarrow and held it up. "Where's this go?" he asked. I took it from him. "Oh, and someone tacked posters on some of the buildings," he mumbled, "about a town meeting in the morning at City Hall." He shifted his gaze from me to his mother. "I'll be attending."

"A meeting about what, Jack?" Maggie asked.

He shrugged. "That's what I aim to find out."

I turned to look at Maggie too. Her face had gone white and slack and her shoulders were slumping.

"Don't fret, Mum," he said. "I'll wear a mask and sit apart. You have my word on that."

"But, Jack…"

He put down the bag of flour he'd just removed from his wheelbarrow and took her hand. "I'm not going to die, Mum, and neither is Nora. We're going to live through these hard times, and we're going to give you grandchildren to worry over so you won't have time to worry about us so much. Is that fair enough?"

She nodded and tried to smile, but her tears were already racing down her face.

The house was so clean by then you could eat off the floors. Yet Maggie and I somehow found chores to occupy ourselves for the first few hours after Jack left for his meeting the following day. When there was absolutely nothing more to do, we retired to the parlor, me with a book and Maggie with her embroidery basket. Though she didn't say so, it was evident she was worried he'd get himself involved in something dangerous, and truth be told, so was I.

Jack didn't seem surprised to find us sitting, prim and upright, at either end of the sofa when he walked in. As he was turning from the coat tree, he said, "There were twenty of us, I'd wager." He walked into the parlor proper and studied us a moment. Then he sat himself down in the wing chair. "Everyone had masks, and the mayor himself had two handkerchiefs tied over his face. We were a sight, and it was hard to understand what was being said. You can imagine." He studied us again, longer this time. I made a dogear of my page and put the book aside. "Bottom line, you're wondering, yeah? Well, here it is then: The morgue is full, from so many dying so fast. The hallways there are two deep on either side with corpses in boxes. There's no solution but to dig mass graves and bury the dead quickly as possible. The meeting was so the mayor could ask for volunteers."

Maggie made a neighing sound and covered her eyes with her hand. She let her hand slip away after a few seconds, but her eyes remained closed. "Tell me he didn't volunteer," she said to no one.

"There were several fellows from the fire department packed into a row at back of the room," Jack said. "They looked to each other, and when one raised his hand, the other hands went up too. Then the mayor asked, *Anyone else?* And there I was thinking to myself, *I'm immune, if what Doc Burns said is half true, and that's why I'm here, ain't it?"*

"Jack," Maggie said. It was a plea.

Jack went on. "Then the mayor looks my way, stares at me for a few, and finally says, *You're one of them Hopper boys, ain't you?* As if there were ten of us."

Maggie dropped her head. I moved my book to the floor and scooted over beside her and put my hand on her back. I could feel she wasn't crying yet; more likely she was holding her breath, waiting for the next shoe to drop.

"And he says to me, *Them fellows over there can put you to some good use if you're willing.*"

Maggie began to weep, quietly.

"You're going to be a grave digger? Is that what you're saying?" I asked sharply.

He looked at me, and in his silence swam his answer, as big as a whale in a tidal pool. I wanted to scream at him. I wanted to jump up and slap his face. But I only sat there rubbing Maggie's back. I saw his gaze slide to the table by the rocker, where his pipe was resting in a glass ashtray. In a moment he would leave the room with it.

Maggie's head was pressed against my neck, and I could feel her tears dampening the top of my blouse. Jack and I continued to stare at each other. Then he got up and got his pipe and went through the kitchen and out the back door. Maggie lifted her head. "It's not enough Baxter's gone?" she asked me. "Now I got to watch him die too?"

I pulled her back against me. "He's immune," I whispered. I was snarling mad, but I tried to keep it out of my voice. "He'll be just fine. Dr. Burns said so."

"Yeah, and watch if I don't clock Doc Burns one when I see him again. He don't know what he's saying half the time."

22. Jack

He felt a bit like Sir Percy Blakeney, in *The Scarlet Pimpernel*, one of the last books they'd read his final year of school. While he might appear to be some loogin snag who worked as a floor manager for Lipton, he actually had a secret identity; he was the man who couldn't die. And with that came responsibility. Like Blakeney, he was meant to work in the service of others.

While he waited to be called upon to meet with the firefighters to bury the dead, he came up with an idea of his own. He would go to the hospital and comfort the sick and dying. Nora's face went red when he told her, but the silly girl had made such a stink about answering only to her higher self back in her protesting days that there was no convincing argument she could make now to detain him. "I'll be of use," he said. "I know what it's like to die. I came close enough. You could say I'm an expert on the subject."

"These people want to live though, Jack, that's the difference," she said softly. They were in bed, where they had most of their important conversations, curled up in each other's arms and whispering so Maggie wouldn't hear, candles burning on both bedside tables so they could see each other's faces. "You, on the other hand, all but invited

Death to come in and sit for a cuppa," she went on. "Most of them aren't going to survive, and it doesn't seem right that you should try to inspire them back to life when their death is nearly inevitable."

He chuckled. He was thinking it was what she'd done to him, inspired him back to life; and he was glad, because he lived to love her. But he'd had that choice of life or death; it hadn't felt like a choice at the time but it had to have been, or he wouldn't be here now, would he? He doubted there were many who could choose where this flu—a raving mad animal wiping out everyone in its path—was concerned. "Who said that's what I'm planning, Nora? Unlike some people, I know my place. And it's not in other people's psyches."

Her fingers were resting on his collar bone. She gave his skin a little pinch.

"I was thinking," he went on, "I could read to them. I can picture myself doing that."

"And if you get sick and die on me?" she asked, but he didn't answer, because he was remembering something.

"Jack, just tell me you don't have a death wish. Promise me that much."

Her head was resting on his shoulder now. She would fall asleep soon. He could hear it in her voice. He kissed her crown of unruly red curls. "Of course I don't, Nora love. Now that I have you in my life I want to live forever."

There were piles and piles of books on top of the bureau. Some were his and more were Nora's. Jack took a stack of them and dumped them into the dusty satchel he'd found in the cellar, from his school days, or maybe it had belonged to Baxter. It didn't matter what books he brought any more than it had mattered that it was a book about how to be an immigrant in Pennsylvania that he'd read in the jungle. The subject matter was beside the point.

He left the house at dawn, while Nora and his mum were still sleeping. He walked to St. Mary's, the hospital where his father had died. If his father hadn't been sneaking around with the German woman, he wouldn't have been in her building when the fire started, and he wouldn't have died of smoke inhalation. And if he hadn't died, Jack and Bax wouldn't have had a reason to go to South America; they'd have been happy to keep their jobs on the docks, alongside their old man. And if they hadn't gone to South America, Bax would still be alive, and *he'd* be married to Nora. And where would that leave things? It was a train that ran in circles in Jack's head for hours once it started. He hated it, but sheer will was never enough to make it stop.

The woman at the front desk told him through her mask that there was too much chaos going on in the section of the hospital where the flu patients were being quarantined. She said he should go to the school down the street instead. The Emergency Nurses Council had set up a makeshift hospital annex in the gymnasium there. They could use volunteers.

He went down the street to the school gymnasium and explained to the nurse sitting at a child-sized wooden desk in the hallway that he'd come to read to the sick. He thought she'd make a comment of some sort, but she only asked him to sign his name before going in. She retrieved a pencil from the tray at the top of the desk and reached into the cubby and produced a notebook. He signed quickly and thanked her with a nod, straightened, and pushed open the swinging doors. There were twenty or twenty-five cots spread out in the large room, all of them full. A few people were coughing loudly. Others seemed to be asleep. Five or six were being attended to by nurses.

He wasn't sure if he should speak to one of the nurses, to say why he was there. But since the nurse in the hall hadn't been interested in his motives, he decided an explanation wasn't necessary. He saw a boy, maybe twelve years old, lying quietly on his cot, staring at the ceiling, a gray blanket up to his chin. Jack walked over and stood at his side until the boy realized someone was there beside him and turned his head. His skin was a dull grayish color, but otherwise he seemed all right. Anyway, he was alert. He gave Jack a little smile and Jack turned to look for a chair and found a metal one a few yards off and pulled it over to the bed.

The boy was watching him carefully, and Jack had to fight off an urge to look deeply into the child's eyes. Working at Lipton had made a woman out of him, he thought. His hands were soft now, and his heart was too. Dead father. Dead brother, or probably he was dead. Dead soldiers. And now, this, the flu. Dead children. Dead young people. He put his satchel on the floor and reached in and pulled out a book entitled *The White Peacock*. He chuckled. The sight of the book shifted him out of the darkness he'd felt gathering around him moments ago. The bedroom had been dark when he'd left. He'd grabbed from the wrong pile. *The White Peacock* was Nora's book, something romantic, if he remembered correctly. Just what this poor lad needed. He took a deep breath and opened the book somewhere near the middle—like he used to do with the immigrant book in the jungle—and began to read. He read for two hours—his breath hot in his face mask, the sounds in the background, the whispering of the nurses, the coughing attacks of some patients, footsteps moving back and forth across the room— until the boy feel asleep.

When he returned the next morning, a nurse came right up to him and said, "I'm sorry, Sir, your young friend is gone."

Jack looked at the cot where the boy had been. There was a girl there now, a little older. "That one," the nurse said, following his gaze, "her sweetheart died fighting. And now it looks like she may follow. Poor child." The nurse looked side to side. "Someone's taken your chair. I'll find you another," she said, and Jack, who hadn't gotten over the fact that the boy had died, nodded.

It only took four weeks for the Spanish influenza to pass through the town of Hoboken. And only twice in all that time was Jack called upon to work with other men and teams of horses digging trenches for the dead. On both occasions he and the other diggers were gone before the firefighters arrived with the bodies. He was relieved for that. But almost daily he went to the gymnasium, and without preamble of any kind, found someone to read to. Most of the people he read to were too weak to talk but seemed glad for his company. As for himself, never once did he reveal the sentiments he experienced being there with them. Never did he as much as squeeze a hand or touch a cheek or forehead. But many times, in the space it takes to flip a page, he found himself thinking, *I am here and Bax is not.*

On the last day he went to the gymnasium, there were only four patients and one nurse to watch after them. All the other patients had either died or had gotten better and gone home. In all this time Jack had been reading from the same miserable book, because while he had put the books into the case sideways, they had slipped to the flat bottom of the case, and the same book was always on top—*The White Peacock*. He'd told Nora he'd taken some of her books accidentally, and when she heard he'd been reading *The White Peacock* from somewhere in the middle daily, she laughed and made him promise he'd read it through from beginning to end, so he could judge whether he liked it.

He did; in the last few days he'd read it from beginning to end. And he hadn't liked it any better than he thought he would. And so on this, his last day at the gymnasium, he reached to the bottom of the satchel to see what else was there. He was dumbfounded when he pulled out not another novel but one of Nora's journals.

Once he'd mistakenly pulled open the bottom drawer of the bureau, which was her drawer, and he'd seen several of her journals stacked beside a pile of her undergarments, thin volumes covered with blue fabric. He'd quickly closed the drawer and opened the one above it, which was his. He seldom saw her writing in her journals. But now and then she'd go upstairs before him and he'd catch her replacing the pen in its stand and putting her journal down on the night table. The one he held in his hand, he thought, must be a fairly recent one, and that was why it had been out on top of the bureau with her other books.

The young woman whose bedside he sat at coughed, and he looked up, startled. He had forgotten her. Her name was Beth and he had read to her the day before and she had thanked him profusely for spending time with her. She was on the mend. She would probably be released tomorrow. She had coughed not because she was sick but to get his attention. He smiled at her. Then he put the journal back in his bag and pulled out *The White Peacock* once again.

There were people in the streets, most of them unmasked, when he left the gymnasium for the last time. Some of the soldiers from the docks, officers, were walking in a line, laughing. A group of uniformed boy scouts was handing out cards that read, "You are in violation of the sanitary code." Jack had seen them out and about before, when the influenza had only just begun, handing their cards to anyone caught spitting or coughing. Apparently they had plenty left, and after being shut up in their homes for so long, they were enjoying giving the cards out to passersby, whether they had spat or not. One of them handed Jack a card. He thanked the young fellow and put it in his pocket.

Stores and restaurants and saloons had begun opening again, though the schools remained closed. His favorite Irish pub had reopened, and he ducked in and ordered a beer. He brought it to a small table near the back of the room and sat with the satchel at his feet, thinking. When he got home, he would go right up the stairs and put the journal in the drawer where it belonged, because if she hadn't missed it in all this time it could only mean she believed she'd put it away herself. No need to admit he'd taken it with her other books.

He finished his beer and pulled out the blue journal and opened it randomly and read the one line his eye fell on. It said, "Jack was very brave…" He smiled; he'd been right. It was a recent volume. He thumbed to the back of the book, to make sure it was full to the last page. He saw on another line, "…and Maggie would have said so too but then…"

He felt no guilt. He was only confirming that the journal was full and belonged in the drawer. After all, he hadn't taken it purposely. He was about to close the book for good when he saw his brother's name at the top of the page. "Bax, *mo grá*," it said, Bax, *my love*. Quickly, he turned more pages. They were all the same. Every entry was a letter to his brother. He slapped the journal closed and sat with it on his lap for a long time. Then he slipped it into the satchel and turned his head toward the bar. Several men were shouting and laughing there, but Jack neither saw nor heard them.

Part 2

1927

23. Nora

THREE NIGHTS RUNNING JACK went to bed early, saying he had a headache, and each night I came up some hours later to find him asleep, or pretending to be. He almost never got headaches; if he went up early at all it was to work on his pirate story. He'd sent an outline for it—it was to be a novelette—to *Adventure* magazine the year before, and the editor professed to like it and to be "anxiously awaiting" the finished project. But Jack had grown frustrated trying to come up with the right ending. It had to be at least two months since he'd last worked on it.

On the fourth night he claimed a headache, I tiptoed up the stairs not ten minutes later and opened the door as quietly as possible and stuck my head in. He was sitting at his desk, but the moment he saw me he put his pen aside and covered the letter he'd been writing with his arm, holding it just high enough to keep his sleeve off the ink. How did I know he was writing a letter? I didn't, but as he was using the embossed stationery I'd given him for his last birthday and not the yellow note paper he used for his stories, it seemed a good guess. Like a child caught in the act, he shrugged and offered me a weak smile. I smiled back, faintly, to match him. Then I closed the door quietly and went back downstairs to my book.

But I didn't read, because I was preoccupied with the realization that the little scene I'd just participated in was emblematic of the direction our marriage had taken. We lived in the same house—our own small row house not three blocks away from Maggie—and we worked at our same jobs, Jack at Lipton's—now relocated right in Hoboken, and me still at the bookstore. We walked together most evenings, we talked, we listened to the radio or played records on the phonograph and danced, and we made love, but we were always holding something back, giving each other more space than we needed, even when we were in the same room and sitting side by side.

Space had grown around us and between us. Somehow we had allowed that to happen. Part of it, I think, was that the world was a sadder place than it had been before the war and the epidemic that followed. We had lost our innocence; all the survivors had.

Ordinarily I would not have read Jack's letter, which is to say, I would have given him the space he needed to write what was evidently a private communication. But I made up my mind that night that I would close the gap between us, and if I couldn't, then at least I'd examine it more closely, and when Jack went out the kitchen door the following morning—with his pipe, which meant he'd be gone for a good while—I climbed the stairs to search for the thing.

I found it quickly enough. He had a stack of Edgar Rice Burroughs books at the back of his desk: Tarzan titles. The letters were under the books, five of them, all the same letter in various stages of completion. The one at the top was the longest, and unlike the others, there was nothing scratched out. It appeared to be the final version, lacking only his signature.

Dear Mr. Ford,

You won't have heard of me, but I was one of a small percentage of American men who ventured into the jungle in Amazonas nearly twenty years ago, when the boom was in full swing, and made it back to tell the tale. I thought to make my fortune there—first as a tapper and then as an overseer—but nothing of the sort befell me.

It is not my purpose to bore you now with the details of what actually happened to me. You will have come by plenty of horror stories yourself, all more intriguing than mine, in particular those of your friend the former President Roosevelt—may he rest in peace. But I did want to let you know that along with countless other lessons, I did learn virtually everything there is to know about Hevea brasiliensis, *which of course is the name for the Amazon rubber tree. So naturally when I heard you were planning to establish a rubber plantation in Amazonas, I felt I must write to you.*

Mr. Ford, it is with all sincerity that I warn you against such an undertaking. You may be thinking that because rubber is now growing successfully on plantations in English settlements in the Orient that it can be made to grow on plantations in the Amazonian jungle as easily, but that is not the case. Nature spreads the rubber trees throughout the jungle forests for a reason; there is a fungus in South America that attacks rubber trees as part of the natural order of things, and if the trees are planted too close together, the fungus jumps from one otherwise healthy tree to another. I have seen this with my own eyes, and I know that if you had an entire plantation of trees, before they reached the age at which they could be made to bleed, one of them will have become diseased, and by virtue of its proximity to the others, they would all then fall ill, and all your hard work and good intentions will have been for naught. The rubber tree—in Amazonas at least— can only survive in its natural state, which is to say, separated from its fellows by all manner of thick jungle vegetation.

Besides the problem of the fungus, commonly known as Leaf Blight, there is also the problem of the soil, Mr. Ford. You might think the soil in the jungle is very rich because it supports such a diversity of trees and plants, but the opposite is true. The nutrients lie all in the soil's uppermost layers. When you strip the jungle of the plants and trees that are natural to it, as would be necessary in clear-cutting to make ready for a plantation, you leave the nutrients no choice but to run off into the rivers when the big rains come. Or worse, without the jungle, which is itself a rain-generating machine (the constant heat in humid terrain produces rising air that becomes cloud cover that falls as rain), there might not be the necessary precipitation—at least not if your plantation is as large as people are saying (which I have heard could be the size of the state of Connecticut)— in which case you would wind up with a desert. And Hevea brasiliensis *would no sooner grow in a desert than would your loyal customers give up their automobiles and return to horse and buggy!*

I know that all the country is behind you, Sir, and that everyone believes you will succeed, as you always do, and I know that you are not likely to listen to me, a mere manager for a tea-packing plant (Lipton, I'm proud to say, here in Hoboken, New Jersey), but I feel I must reach out to you on the off-chance that you may take me seriously and reconsider your plans.

Besides what I have said here regarding the Leaf Blight and the soil, there are additional reasons to avoid the jungle, matters of which I could only bring myself to discuss with you in your presence. And I am not talking only about the many diseases that bring sickness or even death to those who try to make a life there. Should you desire me to travel to Dearborn, to speak to you in person and discuss these additional issues, then know that I am your willing servant and will come at once. In fact, I would be pleased to travel with you to the lands where you intend to build, to show you firsthand what I learned all those years ago about blight and soil and other complications.

I could hardly make myself move, even when I heard the screen door slam and then Jack coming through the house and up the stairs. I pushed the letters back beneath the books at the last second and moved to the bed and straightened the quilt and began to punch the pillows into shape. My back was to him when he entered, but he must have seen some rigidity in it, or maybe it was the way I was attacking the pillows, because I heard only silence behind me for several seconds before he finally said, "Nora, are you all right?"

I forced a smile and turned to face him. "Course I am, Jack."

But I wasn't. I left the bed half made and went out of the room.

Certain things Jack and I didn't discuss. One was the fact that we didn't have a water closet. We had running water of course, accessible through pipes in the cellar, but we had never installed an indoor lavatory.

It had to do with the children we didn't have—because the most logical room for a water closet was the one we had designated for the nursery when we bought the house seven years earlier and still believed we would have a family one day. In a moment of reckless enthusiasm we'd even put up Mother Goose wallpaper. It looked ridiculous now, gaggles of geese frolicking in fields of daisies in what had become a storage room for furniture Jack meant to fix and my posters and paints and boxes full of who-knew-what that we seemed to accumulate without ever trying. Soon we would be the only people on the street who still used an outdoor privy, but as neither of us could bring ourselves to admit we had given up all hope of having a family, we left the room the way it was.

The other thing we didn't talk about was the jungle, what had happened there. I'd asked, plenty of times in the beginning, but Jack always treated my questions like an invasion of his privacy. He never actually rebuked me, but he found ways to answer evasively or change the subject. Then, after the war, there were so many stories of men coming home uninjured physically but unable to adjust to the lives they'd led before, men who were gloomy or cross where they had been perfectly swell before, men who seemed to have endured some invisible injury, an imbalance in their thinking. They called it *shell shocked,* because the common thinking was that these soldiers had been too close to exploding artillery. But not everyone was so sure artillery was the culprit.

Once I began to think of Jack as shell shocked, I stopped asking him questions. But now, in his letter to Ford, he had said more about his time in the jungle than he had said to me collectively in all the years we'd been together. And worse, he had offered to go back there, with him. I was furious.

24. Jack

JACK VISITED A FORTUNETELLER named Isabella a few years after the war. He knew he'd made a mistake long before then, but he was able to postpone rectifying it because, by comparison with what was going on in the world, his lapse in judgment seemed inconsequential. What did it matter if he had been right or wrong to keep a secret from his wife? It was enough to get through a day, to know Nora was safe and at his side. And afterwards, when the war was over, there was the residue that followed in its wake, the sense of utter wastefulness, so many lives lost and more destruction than could ever be addressed. It was a burden to know you had lived through such a dark age.

He'd always been opposed to the idea of psychics, but it got to the point where he didn't know where else to turn. He'd tried the local gathering place—a room at the back of the grocer's where a man could have a drink in spite of Prohibition—a few times, hoping a chat with one of the fellows might turn into something more, but it never happened. In the end, there was no one among the men he ran into—mostly fellows he'd known from his school days and now and then someone who'd worked with him and Bax down at the docks—with whom he could imagine sharing his dilemma. They'd think he was mad; half of them thought he was mad to begin with, because of how changed he was when he'd come back from the jungle. He'd even thought to unburden himself to his boss, Thomas Lipton. There'd been a fire at the Lipton building in Manhattan just after the war, and Mr. Lipton had become interested in moving his operation to Hoboken. Jack had been instrumental in helping him make the arrangements, and they'd spent a lot of time together as a result. But Lipton was all business during their meetings—as pleasant as ever, but his mind was on the details of the move—and in the end Jack couldn't bring himself to inject the subject of his personal failures into any of their conversations.

Jack began walking back and forth to work once Lipton relocated to Hoboken, however, and every day he passed an address he recognized from a newspaper advertisement for fortunetelling. He always slowed as he went by it, to allow time in case he should suddenly find himself prepared to act, or in case the fortuneteller should open the door and emerge at just that moment. But neither occurred, until one icy cold late November afternoon when the sky was a drab brownish-gray and he was feeling particularly somber. By then he had imagined turning off from the sidewalk and approaching the establishment so many times that he almost didn't realize he was actually doing it until he was nearly to the portico.

The building was a three-story brick apartment house, and the newspaper text had indicated that the fortuneteller lived in 1B, on the first floor. If there had been signs or posters on the outside advertising her business, he would never have stopped. But the place looked like any other on the block, and as the only people about were three boys playing Stoop Ball at the entrance to the building next door, he took a deep breath and knocked.

She came to the door right away, and his first impression was that she was dowdy. He was used to seeing women at work with bobbed hair and makeup and smart clothes. Isabella's dark hair was longish and unkempt, half of it tied up on her head with a rubber band and the rest hanging down along her neck, as if she had been at some physical task and had wanted to have it out of the way. He could see she was full-figured, even though her faded shapeless house-dress was wrapped loosely around her torso. On her feet she wore slippers, men's slippers if he was not mistaken. He took her to be in her forties.

He mumbled something about having seen her advert in the paper and said he'd stopped to see if he could make an appointment. Of course he didn't really want an appointment; he wanted to be asked in right then, on the spot, before he had time to change his mind. The fortuneteller turned from him when he finished talking and looked behind her, into her flat, as if to ascertain whether she was in fact open for business. When she turned back, she was smiling. "Yes, you can come in now," she said cheerfully, opening the door wider, and Jack was left with the distressing conclusion that she had been listening to his thoughts and not his words. "There's a coat tree just here," she said, pointing to the right as he entered, "and the table's just there, ahead. Make yourself comfortable and I'll be with you in a moment."

It was nearly as cold inside as it was out, and worried that he might want to leave sooner rather than later, Jack decided to keep his coat on. He went directly to the table—a small, square card table, it was—which was pushed up against the far wall, with straight-back wooden chairs on the three open sides. He ignored the chair facing the wall, which would have put him beside the fortuneteller no matter where she sat, and chose one of the opposing ones.

A candle burned in a brass holder at the center of the table and he stared into its flame for a moment while he collected his thoughts. But instead of reviewing what he wanted to say, he found himself wondering if she had lit the candle just before he knocked, knowing he was on his way. Ah, but he was a fool. The woman was saving on electricity; it was that simple. He and Nora did the same.

He looked up. She was across the room, drawing the curtains on the window—which looked out on the street and the vestiges of the vanishing cityscape across the river beyond it. He cleared his throat. "I don't want a séance," he said. "And I don't want any card readings."

When she turned from the window she was beaming with amusement. "You just want to talk then, yes? Is that what you're saying?" She looked much younger than he'd first thought, maybe in her early thirties now, and not so dowdy at all when she smiled like that. But then again, the room was quite dark.

He smiled in response and she sat down across from him and slid the candle off to the side. As he followed her movement he noticed a deck of cards just there near the wall, and he was glad he'd told her ahead that he didn't want a reading. Still, the sight of the cards put him in mind immediately of Bax; he and Bax had won and lost a good deal of money over the years playing cards with various chaps, and they'd had a lot of laughs both ways. Some of their most spirited conversations had been about who was a natural bluffer, who was too poor a player to even know he had a nut hand, who was a piker, and who had the luck of the Irish—theirs by all rights, they'd always joked, unless there was an actual off-the-boat Irishman at the table. But of course the cards on Isabella's table weren't for playing poker. Her deck was longer than a regular playing deck, and the design on the back featured not the standard blue-and-white or red-and-white curlicue pattern he was used to but the head of a woman wearing a gypsy scarf, surrounded by stars and planets, all against a black background.

Clementine had never brought cards into the house as far as Jack knew. She got her messages directly from the dead, his mum had explained when the hag had first started coming around all those years ago. He doubted that, and when they were alone, he and Bax agreed the only dead thing that might bother speaking to her was the bird she wore on her hat, and the only message he was likely to have was *Caw Caw*. They would have laughed about it, but that was just after their father died and they weren't laughing much about anything.

As much as he found the sight of the fortuneteller's cards unnerving, there was a part of him that wanted to pick up the deck and riffle the cards between his thumbs, just for the pleasure of the sensation. They looked warn, soft at the edges; he could imagine what they would feel like, what they would sound like as they fell into place. There was a sense of agency that came with being the button, the one shuffling and dealing—everyone waiting, their attention fixed on your hands, your own attention fixed on the feel of the shuffle, on finding the precise moment when the cards felt just right and ready to pass along to the next chap for the cut.

Isabella picked up the deck and placed it on the seat of the empty chair between them. "We wouldn't want them to distract you," she said, "unless of course you've had a change of heart."

Jack shook his head. "No," he responded quickly. He'd always wondered how anyone with even the most basic understanding of science could imagine that the drawings on a bunch of cards, created not by some divinity but by an ordinary man at the request of some wealthy Italian family that liked to play games some hundreds of years ago—Nora had told him the story—could be thought to have meaning. In his mind, people who professed to be able to "read" cards— or clouds or tea leaves or palms or crystal balls—were con artists. All of them. Now he wondered why he'd stopped. And why she had even let him in without an appointment. She had to be a hustler herself. *I'm about to be hustled*, he said to himself.

But there was something pushing up against his thoughts about her trickery, about trickery generally, and it was this: He'd had an experience himself, back in the jungle, with the Gha-ru, the natives they'd shared the forest with, unwittingly until four of them showed up at their rubber camp and took Jack and Bax prisoner. But instead of harming them, the Gha-ru chief cured the terrible foul-smelling open wound on Bax's leg—which would have killed him otherwise—and, for the next two weeks, the Gha-ru treated the brothers as part of the tribe, teaching them various skills and even allowing them to participate in their ceremonies. It was during one such ceremony, following a long period of chanting and then a share of the golden brown liquid being passed among the men, that Jack had his visions. In one, he saw Nora and his mum and Clementine, engaged in a playful conversation about potato cookies. In the other, his father came back from the dead, smelling of White-Cat, the cigar he favored, just long enough to squeeze Jack's knee and tell him he would be all right. He'd never told anyone about his visions, because who would have believed him? He tried not to believe it himself. He tried to write it off as a hallucination, a result of the drink they'd given him. But deep down he knew he'd seen what he had.

He had no idea he'd drifted again until he looked up and saw Isabella's face, her bemused smile. She lifted her eyebrows, as if to suggest, he thought, she'd been there with him just then, in his memory of the jungle. "You never answered my question," she reminded him. "Did you come here just to talk?"

"Yes," he whispered, smiling apologetically. Talking was exactly what he wanted; he wanted to pay a stranger to listen to him divulge his secrets so he could put them behind him. It was no more complicated than that.

She sat back and folded her hands on the table. While they both waited to see how he might begin, he found himself thinking that her lips were rather beautiful. He hadn't noticed before. They were full, the upper one protruding just a bit beyond the lower. They were slightly parted at the moment, the strip of white behind them aglow in the candlelight. He took a deep breath. "Where my parents are from, back in Ireland," he began, "we have a word—*an-ghá*. It means to desire something—or someone—so badly you can think of almost nothing else." He felt his cheeks burning. It was agonizing to be talking about desire to a stranger. All the times he had rehearsed these words, he had imagined saying them to someone like Clementine, an old hag with a witch nose and a ridiculous bird at rest on her head. Isabella: He'd picked her name out from the others in the paper because it sounded Italian, because he'd imagined Clementine.

Isabella nodded. "This is at the heart of your problem?" She chuckled. "Or, I should say, this is then a problem of the heart?"

He nodded. How could Isabella be helpful to him? he wondered. She seemed too… lighthearted. He guessed she'd never experienced the loss of a loved one, the kind of agony he lived with day after day. "Yes," he said. "I love my wife too much." There, it was out. "I loved her when we were kids. I've loved her my whole life."

Isabella cocked her head. "Lucky woman, I'd say. So, is the problem that she's leaving you?"

He looked down at his hands, which he was surprised to find wrapped around the edge of the table, as if he was expecting it to rock, or lift, as people who attended séances sometimes described. He could no longer remember the rest of what he'd planned to say. "My brother died," he grumbled. It came out sounding harsh, like an accusation. He looked up at her, hoping she could piece the rest of the story together without him having to spell it out.

Her lips remained motionless for a moment. The she asked, "Was she in love with your brother?" She unfolded her hands and stretched them out on the table. Nora's hands were long and slender, a bit boney. Isabella's fingers were shorter and slightly plump. They would be soft, he guessed.

He admonished himself at once. It was not at all like him to scrutinize strange women in this way. He was suddenly certain she'd cast a spell on him. *Something* in this small dark room had caused a shift to occur in his psyche, just the way a shift had occurred the night he drank the brew the Gha-ru offered him. But the drink had heightened his senses; it had dissolved the thin veil of distance and death that separated him from his loved ones. Now he felt only dull-witted, not connected but isolated. Helpless.

She was nodding. She knew everything already; he could see that. She knew it was only under false pretenses that Nora had turned to him. Maybe she would say that it was a trifling matter, his deception, that he should put it behind him and get on with his life.

Isabella leaned forward, and reaching across the table, she took both his hands and slid them toward her and held them there, at the center of the table. "There, that's better," she said. "Now tell me everything."

And he would have, because her hold on him—in senses both tangible and not—was that strong. But just at that moment the door flew open, and along with a burst of frigid air, in ran a boy of ten or so.

Once Jack recovered from the shock of the intrusion, he recognized the child as one of the lads he'd seen outside playing ball. He tested Isabella's grip to see if she might free his hands now, but when she felt his fingers twitch, she only held on more tightly. "The door," she sang, and the boy stopped midway in his gallop through the room and returned to the door and gave it the little push it needed for the latch to fall into place.

"Sorry, Mama," he said. He glanced at Jack.

"Check on Millie, would you, my love? If she's up from her nap, bring her in the kitchen and give her some crackers and milk."

"Yes, Mama."

"And feed Kitty."

"Yes, Mama."

"Good boy," she said, and mother and son exchanged a warm smile before the boy disappeared into another part of the flat.

"Now, where were we?" Isabella asked.

Jack had no idea. Here the house was full of life, children and animals, and he hadn't even known. He heard a door open and close somewhere, and then the boy's voice, sweetly greeting his younger sister, or maybe the kitty.

"You were going to tell me how you came to be married to the woman who was in love with your brother," Isabella said.

Had he said all that? He didn't remember saying that. He was suddenly hot sitting there in his coat. He wanted to unbutton it. He wanted his hands back. He wondered if her husband would walk in next, and what he would think to see them holding hands across the table in the candlelight. It dawned on him that he might know the chap. How awkward would that be?

"It's all right," Isabella said. "My children are well behaved, and no one will bother us now that Felix has come indoors. George, my husband, is a traveling salesman. He won't be home for some hours yet."

She had read his thoughts again! "What does he sell?" he asked nervously, hoping to mask his discomfort with affability.

"Waffle makers."

"Waffle—"

"I just realized," she interrupted. "I never asked your name!"

"Jack," he said. He only hoped she wouldn't insist on a surname. If she did, he decided quickly, he'd make one up. Murphy, he'd say. There were Murphys all over his part of town.

"Jack. Let's start over again, shall we? Tell me why you're here today. How can I help you?"

Jack sighed and began slowly, his gaze moving back and forth between the flicker of candlelight and the steady beam of Isabella's gray eyes. He told her first about the other men he and Bax had traveled with in Amazonas, and then about the two young fellows from Pittsburgh who became their campmates, how well it had all gone at first, and how it fell apart over time. There were holes in his narrative, sure there were. It had all happened so long ago. He knew he was jumping around, leaving out connections that would make his story more lucid. But as Isabella didn't seem bothered, he marched on, through the tensions that arose among the four of them once they were deep in the jungle—especially after their guide left and they found themselves alone, with no means of escape—through what it was like to work night and day, weak, sick with near constant bouts of malaria, through what it was like to know you were starving, dying… Whatever goodness any of them had peeled away over time, and each of them became a repulsive, vile version of his former self. And when the other two fellows were gone—one of them having died and one having simply disappeared—how it was between him and Bax, the last men standing, what it was like to find himself the target of his brother's wrath, to have grave doubts about his brother's intentions, and, to be honest, his own.

The more he talked, the more he found he had to say, though he continued to stumble through his narrative, mixing relevant events with digressions that seemed relevant until he began to recount them. He was vaguely aware of the passage of time. When he stopped to take a breath he heard the children talking in another room. Once he heard what he guessed to be a ball bouncing off a wall—just the one bounce. He imagined the little girl had thrown it and the boy, Felix, had reprimanded her before she could toss it again. But all that might as well have been happening on another planet. It had nothing to do with this room, this dark, this candle, these lodestars that were Isabella's eyes.

Finally he got to the end. He explained the circumstances that had led Bax to put him on a boat half dead in the hopes he might find his way back to New Jersey on his own while Bax himself stayed behind to fight a battle he could not win. It was Bax who suggested—in the last moment, when they could hear the approach of the boat that Bax had secured to get Jack as far as the port in Manáos—that Jack tell Nora and their mum that Bax had perished in the jungle. That way the women wouldn't hold out hope for his return, Bax said—or implied; Jack couldn't remember his exact words anymore, but that was the gist. That was what Bax wanted. And that was what Jack did.

Isabella let go of his hands, finally. His found his palms were clammy and his arms were prickly from being in the same position for so long. "Did you think that would be best for them?" she asked gently, referring to Nora and Maggie.

"Yes, of course." He thought about it a moment. "But if I'm going to be level here, I have to say they arrived at the same conclusion more or less on their own. I was sick, don't forget. I was not myself." He cleared his throat. "Though I did nothing to correct them, you see. Maybe I even nudged them further in that direction, with vague responses to their questions. It's damn hard to remember now exactly how it went down. And then, when I began to get better, it seemed it was the best outcome anyway, because, well, Baxter *did* stay behind. How could I tell them that? How would that make them feel, that he had chosen not to come home? And it's likely he did die shortly after I left. I can't see how it could have gone otherwise under the circumstances."

Isabella regarded him cautiously, her head at an angle and her eyebrows raised.

"And then Nora appeared in my room one night," he continued, "which changed everything, you see. I was square with the decision I'd made until then. It wasn't keeping me up at night, anyway. Have you never deceived someone? And then wanted to set things straight afterward, but each passing day it gets harder?"

She didn't answer. He shifted his gaze from her face back to the candle flame. "Besides, I saw I could have Nora for my own if I kept my mouth shut." He looked up again. "And why not? If my brother had wanted her so much—"

"Likely," Isabella interrupted.

He had to concentrate a full minute to see what she was getting at. Apparently she'd heard nothing he'd said after he admitted it was only *likely* that his brother had died after he'd left. "I had moments of clarity, sure," he went on, defensively. He was leaning forward; he wanted her to see the sincerity in his expression, for he felt that he was losing her and he was suddenly desperate for her to say that any man would have done the same, that what he'd done was forgivable. "I almost told her a hundred times, a thousand times, during those early months."

He sat back and looked down at the table. "There's something else."

"And what is that?"

"My father died of smoke inhalation, in an apartment building fire that happened not too far from here. Back in '07, this was. Maybe you... Anyway, he'd been inside the building when the fire broke out, with a woman who lived there."

He studied her for a reaction but didn't detect one. "Bax and Nora knew something about her, this woman, but I'd been left in the dark... Until the night of the fire. When Mum asked what Da had been doing in the building, I thought to tell her the truth, for the simple reason it was the truth and it seemed to me she had the right to know. But Bax cut me off, saying Da'd been coming home from his work at the docks when he saw the fire and ran in to help. Then the next day Nora got me alone and made the argument that if Mum ever learned about the woman, she would feel she'd lost Da twice—once to death and once to, well, this other woman. She made me promise I would never tell."

"What has that to do with the lie you told your wife?"

"Don't you see it? Essentially, the promise Nora extracted from me when my Da died and the... And my lack of honesty

169

years later regarding Bax are based on the same premise. Hell, it's one I learned from Nora and Bax in the first place. It's about not adding fuel to the fire if you can help—"

"Excuse me," Isabella interrupted. Her expression was suddenly stern. "Nora was trying to protect your mom from unnecessary heartache. As far as I can see, what you did was deprive your wife and mother of the finality they needed, what the behavior scientists call *closure*."

Jack was speechless.

Isabela sighed. "Listen, Jack. I've been telling fortunes since I was a child. But you don't need a fortuneteller to tell you what you need to do. You must tell your wife the truth. You must. Or you will never be at rest."

"It's bloody complicated," he mumbled.

"It's not complicated." She reached across the table, but this time he pulled back before she could touch him. "You're making it complicated. Every day you don't tell her, you make it a little more complicated. You're giving your secret all your energy. Once you tell her, she'll be angry, perhaps very angry, but she'll get over it, and then you can give your energy to your marriage, where it belongs. Otherwise, your secret will destroy you both. That's how much power you've given it."

"It's not like she doesn't have secrets of her own," Jack said sulkily.

"What do you mean?"

He thought about it a moment. He wasn't sure he wanted to tell her. "I found one of her journals once, just after the war," he said finally. "I opened it quickly to be sure what it was before I put it back in its place. All the entries were addressed to my brother." He dropped his head, ashamed.

Her question was a moment in coming. "Did you say anything to her that you knew?"

"Nah. What could I say?"

"Is she still addressing her entries to him?"

"She stopped writing them some years ago. Far as I know. No, she stopped. I would know if she hadn't."

"Maybe that means she found a way to let him go on her own. It's good you didn't say anything. It's no one's business what goes on in our hearts, is it? It's not like lying, which steals something from the person deceived."

He could only stare at her, dumbfounded.

"I'll tell you this, Jack. I was in love once before I met my George. It's no crime. We all have first loves, or many of us do. And sometimes they are the hardest to forget. Would you think her having a first love was so strange if it didn't happen to be your brother?"

"Yeah, but..." He lowered his head again.

"Jack," she said softly, and she waited until he looked at her. "Did you never have a first love?"

"Nah, not really." He thought of Susie, but he hadn't loved her; it had been the other way around. Next he thought of Bruna, the girl he'd met in Manáos when they'd first arrived in Amazonas. Had he loved her? Maybe. He'd come out of the jungle at the end of the tapping season to argue with Abalo about his failure to pay him and Bax what they'd been promised. Before heading back to report the result of his effort to Bax, who'd stayed behind, he spent a night with Bruna, on an empty fishing vessel tied up on the docks. That was a night in which he'd given not a single thought to Nora, maybe the only one in his life since he'd known her.

Isabella slapped the table with her palm and the candle flame jumped in reaction. "Our time is up," she said brusquely, and she got to her feet.

Jack didn't want it to end this way, with so much ambiguity, but he got to his feet too, clumsily after sitting so long. Accidently he bumped the empty chair between them with his foot, causing the card deck to slide to the edge of the seat. His reflexes were quick, and he managed to stop the deck from falling by thrusting his leg up against it just in time. Only one card slipped through the barrier he'd created. He gathered the cards together and handed them to Isabella and then bent to pick up the one on the floor. It had fallen face down, but he turned it over instinctively, half expecting it to be an ace, or a one-eyed Jack, always his favorite in his poker days. The card depicted a man bent over, struggling to carry a bundle of sticks or branches without dropping any of them. "The Ten of Wands!" Isabella exclaimed.

He nodded. He didn't want to know what it supposedly represented. He wanted to go home now that he was on his feet and the spell had been broken. Nora had gone to one of her meetings. He hoped to beat her back to the house so he wouldn't have to lie about where he'd been. But Isabella spoke anyway. "He's struggling with the weight of his burden. Do you see that, Jack? The town he's headed for is just ahead. He'll have the opportunity to lay down his burden there. But the way he's got his head bent and pressed into the wands—as if he needs his head as well as his body to balance all that weight—he's likely to bypass the town altogether and continue carrying his load." She put the card face up on the table beside the rest of the deck and looked at him meaningfully. "He may go on carrying his burden for years to come, until he is an old man. He may take it to his grave."

Jack bit his lip. What did she expect him to say?

"But the ten gives me hope," Isabella exclaimed cheerfully. "Ten represents the end of a cycle. Jack, has it ever occurred to you to travel back there, to the jungle?"

He looked at her sadly. That was a question he could answer without giving it any thought. "Every day."

"It's not a bad thing to act on one's impulses."

"Hmph." The truth was he could not think past the impossibility of telling Nora that, that he planned to return to the jungle without her, for closure, as Isabella had put it, for the thing, he knew now, he'd denied his wife.

Isabella smiled and reached out to embrace him. When she released him, he thanked her profusely and paid her twice what she asked. But just as she opened the door to the wind and the cold, he thought of something else he'd wanted to ask. "Do you think there's any chance he might still be alive?"

Isabella grabbed the fabric of her housedress and held it closed around her neck. "I have no idea," she said, and she closed the door.

25. Nora

JACK HAD NEVER BEEN a great sleeper. He tossed and turned some nights and sometimes he mumbled. In the beginning, I would try to decipher what he was saying, but it was always unintelligible and eventually I gave up. I asked him in the mornings what he had been dreaming about, but he never remembered.

In the three weeks following his letter to Ford, he actually sat bolt upright in his sleep on two occasions, in a state of terror. The first time he spoke clearly, saying, "I'm too hot. I'm dying!" He looked right at me, as if he expected me to be able to help. I was about to touch his face in case he was hot, but then he slumped down and soon enough he was snoring again. The second time he sat up panting, as if something had been chasing him. Again he looked right at me, his eyes wild and as big as saucers, and this time I took pity on him and pulled him down beside me and held him to my breast and whispered the sort of things I'd always imagined I'd whisper to our children when they had nightmares. I was still angry at him about the letter, but I was also still the woman I was, so when he became responsive—which is to say when he awoke and discovered himself in my arms—I proved myself to be as eager as he was to find pleasure in the situation.

All that time I held my tongue regarding Jack's letter, but as it happened, we were both standing in the foyer when the response arrived. I was getting ready to go out, to meet my fellow women's rights advocates. I'd just slipped my arms into the sleeves of my wrapper and pulled my cloche down tight over my head when the door opened and Jack walked in. "Good day today?" I asked as he got out of his jacket. I took it from him and hung it on the coat stand. "Good enough," he mumbled. "Stew's on the stove and still warm," I responded, and I leaned in for a hello/so long kiss, and just then the brass mail slot belched and in flew the letter.

It landed on the runner at our feet, front side up with the logo—the winged triangle with "Ford" in script in the middle and the words "the universal car" below it—in full view. Jack and I stared at it. Then he bent to retrieve it.

"Have a good evening, love," he said, and he went down the hall into the kitchen, all happy with himself, apparently, because he began humming. I watched from where I stood as he put the letter on the table and lifted the lid on the stew pot and inhaled, and then went to the cupboard for a spoon. And then I couldn't stand it any longer.

I marched in as loudly as I could, and I thought I saw him titter. "Why have you got a letter from the Ford company?" I demanded.

"I suppose because Mr. Henry Ford bothered to respond to a letter I wrote him," he said smugly. He turned to the bread tin and took his time pulling up the lid and fetching what was left of the loaf. Then he took the stew from the stove and sat down to eat it just like that, straight from the pot, with nothing between the pot and the table but an embroidered linen runner his mum had made us. I was too angry about the letter, and his behavior regarding it, to scold him about the runner.

"Yes, and so why did you write to Ford in the first place?"

He lifted an eyebrow. "Don't you know? I had the feeling you might have seen my letter lying about."

"You're a wicked piker, Jack Hopper. I asked you *why* you wrote to that lout, because the nonsense you invented in your letter, about trying to save that dearest man from a business blunder, can't have been your true purpose."

"If you know what the letter said, then why would you think I had any other motive? It meant what it said, nothing more, Nora."

"That's a whole lot of baloney! I want the truth." I realized how harsh I sounded and stopped to collect myself. "At the end you implied you had more to say about... About the jungle. That you would speak to him privately, and tell him things, clearly, that you never even bothered to tell me. That you would even travel to the jungle with him!"

He thought about that a minute. Then he smirked. "That was only to get his attention," he said. "I wanted him to take me seriously."

"Why? The man is a racist and an anti-Semite who hires thugs to beat his employees into submission when they don't do what he wants. Why would you possibly care what he does or doesn't do with his money?"

He put down his spoon. "I'll tell you why, Nora. I read in *Time* that he plans to increase rubber planting every year, until the whole jungle is fuckin industrialized."

"So? I read that too. He's bringing the *white man's magic* to the jungle. Very racist. Why should it matter to you?"

He opened his mouth and exhaled three times in rapid succession, as if he could hardly believe I would ask such a thing. "What happens in the jungle should matter to everyone! The magic *is* the jungle, the magic is the people who live there. Ford's business ventures and the money they generate are not the same kind of magic. Why does it matter to you what kind of housing Negroes have, or what kind of factories people work in?"

"That's me. That's what I do with my free time. But you're not one to—"

"Damn it, Nora," he shouted, and he slammed his fist down on the table. "I care about what happens in the jungle. The jungle is *my* cause."

"Your cause you never talk about? What kind of cause is that?"

"Don't judge me. You can't know what's in my heart."

"I'll agree with that, and I'd say that's a problem, wouldn't you?" I pulled out a chair and sat down hard and took a moment to compose myself. "It's not like he'll be successful anyway. He'll fail, as you explained so aptly in your letter. Let him get sick like you did and come back half dead and—"

"Nora."

I felt the heat of unexpected tears rushing to my eyes.

"Nora," he whispered.

He got up from his seat and came behind me and put his hands on my shoulders. I didn't want him comforting me just then, and I wiggled my shoulders to inform him. I snuffled loudly and took a handkerchief from my pocket and blew my nose. "Read the letter aloud, please," I said, nasally. "I want to know what that boob wrote to you."

He smiled. Remembering the letter, he was delighted with himself all over again, to think the famous man had taken the trouble to respond to him. "He's not a full-out boob," he said softly, walking back to his chair. "A lot of people get paid decent wages because of him. He just can't be allowed to destroy the jungle, that's all." He sat down. "And remember he showed himself to be a pacifist in the war. His peace ship and all that."

"Who could forget?" The ship had sailed from Hoboken in the early days of the war, supposedly so Ford could negotiate peace in Europe. But Ford got sick and when the ship arrived at its first destination in Norway, he abandoned his mission and sailed for home.

Jack pushed the stew pot aside and carefully opened the envelope. His jaw was quivering slightly; he was that excited. If Ford granted him an audience, and he went—or worse, if he invited Jack to travel to the jungle with him and Jack accepted—I would leave him, I promised myself. He cleared his throat and began.

Dear Mr. Hopper,

Forgive me for saying so, but Mr. Ford and I found your letter to be...

He hesitated, staring at the paper before him, his mouth dropped open.

"...*utterly audacious...*," he mumbled at last.

I stifled my impulse to laugh, which caused a strange squeak of a noise to escape my nose.

Jack continued to read, now slowly and apprehensively.

...and somewhat amusing. Do you think for a moment that Mr. Ford's decision to plant in Brazil was made over a cup of tea sitting in the parlor with a few good friends? Mr. Ford spent hour upon hour meeting with every sort of expert from every corner of the world so as to gather the best information available. And your conjectures aside, he has concluded that there is no place better to grow Hevea brasiliensis *than in its motherland.*

Further, let me say that I, as his personal secretary, was highly instrumental in this fact-gathering mission, and I agree with Mr. Ford's assessments one hundred percent. It is obvious, to me at least, that your attempt to dissuade him from going forward with his plan to establish the world's largest rubber plantation— which will not only ensure that we are no longer beholden to other countries for materials for our tires but will also help to bring civilization to what has henceforth been a country of savages— is based on your own bitterness regarding your personal jungle experience, to which, I remind you, you alluded in your letter.

Please accept my counsel and return to your tea packing and leave these matters to men who know what they are talking about.

Sincerely,

Mr. Ernest Liebold

Secretary to Mr. Henry Ford

P.S. In case you're wondering, Mr. Ford's amusement was derived from your assumption that he would be so ignorant as to need an explanation about how rain is generated in the jungle.

Jack put the letter down and looked off at nothing, his mouth still open. It was wicked of me to laugh, but I couldn't help myself. His letter to Ford *was* rather audacious. I hadn't thought of it that way before, because I was too busy being angry about its contents when I'd read it. But now I could see Ford's man Liebold was right. Jack's head swiveled in my direction. "What?" he barked. "You think it's funny, this bootlicker blowhard flunky talking to me like that?"

"Come on, Jack, it's amusing. The man is an arse, an odd bird, that's all."

"I'm not amused, Nora," he said, "and I'd be pleased if you'd restrain yourself, or if you can't manage, take it out in the other room where I don't have to see it."

It was my turn to find myself with my mouth dropped open. Jack never spoke to me like that. But I was taken aback only briefly. In that moment and in that context, it only seemed hilarious to me. I turned in my seat and covered my mouth with both hands to hold in my laughter, but it exploded anyway.

He watched me in silence and then he banged his fist on the table once again, harder than before, so that the stew sloshed over the edge of the pot and spilled onto Maggie's beautiful runner. When he saw he had my attention, he picked up the letter and ripped it in two, then ripped it again and again until it was no more than a handful of tiny squares swimming in the spilled liquid. "Go ahead and laugh," he said.

I laughed harder, folding in half until my head was near my knees. How could I help it? He was slaying me. I raised my hand to warn him to stop, but when I glanced his way and saw how he was watching me, with curiosity and maybe some concern, my effort only became more hopeless. For a long time I laughed—although I couldn't think what was so funny after a while—while Jack looked on, sober and bewildered.

My spell left me breathless. I looked away, for fear I'd start up again. I studied the sink, the cupboard, the clock, and concentrated on my breathing—until I saw with the corner of my eye that he was getting to his feet.

"I'm going, Nora," he said softly.

I shrugged. I assumed he meant he was going to bed, or going outside with his pipe.

He cleared his throat and said it again, louder. "I'm going. Back. To the jungle."

"What's this?"

"I'm going back to the jungle, Nora," he said once again, firmly. "As soon as I can make arrangements."

I stood too. My wrapper fell open and I saw his eyes slide down my body and up again. "Don't be ridiculous, Jack. All this time and now, a bolt out of the blue, you're going to the jungle? To the place where you almost died?"

"Yes."

"And what will you do there, Jack? Warn the Indians Ford is coming?"

"Maybe."

I laughed, but without humor this time. "Did you ever think maybe the Indians will be glad for the work? Who *are* you today? You're not yourself; that's for certain. And why are you so concerned about the jungle, now, after all these—"

"I told you, I've always been concerned. Every day of my life."

"My God, Jack! You never even speak of it."

"You never ask me."

I waved my hand dismissively. "I won't argue with you about this, because it's nothing short of ridiculous. I've tried our whole marriage to get you to talk about the jungle."

"'Course you did," he mumbled. "Years back, maybe."

"Don't put this on me, Jack." I half turned toward the hall but then I turned back again. "Anyway, you can't go to the jungle, because I won't let you."

Now it was his turn to laugh. "And how would you stop me?"

All of this was astonishing to me. Jack and I treated each other with respect and kindness, nearly always. I felt like an actor in a play, saying lines that had been written for me. Part of me was sick at the turn—a sudden turn indeed—our marriage seemed to have taken. Another part was glad to have forced the moment to its crisis. "I'm your wife. I simply won't let you go." I shrugged.

"If you're worried about Lipton, don't. He'll understand. He won't—"

"That's not what I'm concerned about and you know it."

"What then?"

I cleared my throat. I didn't know where to start. What if his health deteriorated again? What if he suffered more shell shock? What if, like Bax, he died and never came home? "Fine, Jack Hopper. You go if you want. I suppose I can't physically stop you." I narrowed my eyes. "But if you *do* go, which I'll only believe when I see it, I'll be at your side." And then I did turn, and I started down the hall.

"You can't come with me," he shouted at my back. "It's the part of my life that's private."

"Precisely. That's why I will," I said without turning. My meeting was probably almost over, but I intended to go out anyway, even if only to walk around the block. I heard him coming up behind me.

He hooked my arm and turned me toward him and held me by my shoulders. "You're not coming, Nora," he whispered. "This is something I have to do alone."

I looked deep into his eyes and asked him outright. "Jack, is this about returning to the place where Bax died?"

"No," he snapped. "I'd never find it. The jungle shifts and changes. But I'd want to get close, in that region, yes."

"Nevertheless," I said, and I pushed him away, but he came right back and leaned into me. "Nevertheless, if you're going, I'm going," I said. I slapped at his arms, though I couldn't get leverage pinned between him and the wall as I was. "You can't tell me what I can or can't do, Jack Hopper. I'll get my own passage if I have to and go on my own. I'll follow you there. The jungle, the jungle, the fuckin green jungle. The fuckin jungle swallowed Bax whole and puked you up and left you for dead. The jungle is a great green monster, isn't it, Jack? I want to meet him, face to face. I want to spit in his fuckin eye. I want to grab him by the bullocks and twist until... Why are you laughing, Jack?"

He took a step back, releasing me. Now he was chuckling uncontrollably, against the edge of a loose fist. It occurred to me that if Bax had been there, he'd be laughing too. We'd be spinning in circles laughing, the three of us, laughing at our bad behavior, bending ourselves in half, laughing like we were kids again.

But we weren't kids, and Bax was not with us.

I slapped him hard, across the face. He stopped laughing at once and slid his hand down his cheek. For a moment he was quiet. Then he whispered, "Not bad," still more amused than not. He pressed his body against mine again, leaving no doubt about what he was wanting from me now.

But he wasn't going to get it. "If you go, I go," I said firmly. "End of story." I pushed him away and went out the door.

Part 3

1928

26. Nora

A FEW MONTHS BEFORE my fourth birthday, an older slow-moving woman with a kind voice and hunched shoulders began to appear daily in our flat. My parents referred to her as the "nurse," though whether she was truly a nurse or simply a good-hearted neighbor I will never know. I never even knew her name. I only recall that she prepared simple meals for us and took our dirty laundry away and brought it back clean.

She was the one who packed my things and brought me to the O'Sullivans' when it was decided the time was right. I didn't realize I was leaving forever. When she took my hand and led me to my parents' room to say goodbye, my mother, who was sitting on the edge of the bed, brushing her red-gold hair, told me to be good and play nicely with the O'Sullivan boys, but not to let them push me around. I didn't question why her eyes were full of tears or why her voice was uneven. I blew her a kiss from the doorway, because I'd been told not to embrace my parents because they didn't feel well. My father was sleeping but I blew him a kiss too.

As we walked hand in hand to the building next door the nurse explained the word "contagious" to me, but she said nothing about the fact that she expected my parents to die from this contagious thing they had. It was Mrs. O'Sullivan who set me straight, sometime within my first half hour in her presence, saying my parents would soon be dead and did not wish me to witness their earthly departure.

I took her at her word. Somehow my four-year-old self assumed my parents passed just at that moment when Aunt Becky and I were waving our goodbyes to them from the front of their building a few days later. Then, perhaps a year after that, I overheard one of Aunt Becky's cronies mention "the beautiful sanitorium on the lake where people with consumption went to take the cure." When Aunt Becky turned away to speak to someone else, I asked the woman about it, and she said, yes, my parents had gone to that very sanitorium and they'd passed there months after I'd moved in with my aunt, in great peace and comfort, lying side by side on cots out on a lawn of emerald green under some shade trees where they could hear the birds and see the wildflowers surrounding the lake. But when I got older and began to ask more questions, Aunt Becky insisted her friend had deceived me, that sanitoriums were only for the wealthy and her friend should have known better. They'd died in their flat, she said. They were buried quickly, in unmarked graves in a place called Hart's Island, with monies collected by their neighbors. She didn't know herself they'd died until the death certificates arrived in the mail, some months later.

That they had died alone, needing more care than one old hunched woman could possibly have provided, and then been hauled off to an anonymous grave with no one to weep for them was too awful to contemplate. Yet the story I'd concocted about them wafting off to heaven on the gentle breeze of my whispered farewell was only childish, and my later belief that they had passed outdoors by the side of a lake was fantasy. My parents *were* poor; that I'd known. My father was a laborer, and my mother took in sewing. They would not have been taken to a sanatorium.

The death certificates, which Aunt Becky gave me just before she moved to Boston, stated that they'd died the same day. That was highly unlikely, my aunt said. Surely the "nurse" had stopped visiting when she saw they were close, and it was the smell of death permeating the building that eventually brought in the person or persons who arranged their passage to the potter's field. Who knew what days they actually died and how far apart?

Between shadowy truth and fantasy lay a pit of darkness. There were times I fell into it as a child, and there were times I knew it was there and was able to make my way around it. But always I was bewildered by it. In many ways my lack of certainty regarding my parents' last days defined me. I didn't believe in truth so much after that; truth was merely what you wanted it to be, what served you best. Perhaps my boldness in my younger days was a byproduct of that kind of thinking.

Jack never agreed it would be a good idea for me to accompany him back to the jungle, and I never backed down from my promise to do so anyway, whether he liked it or not. Over time it simply became a fact that we would proceed together, for better or worse. I didn't know exactly what was driving Jack's desire to return, but I knew what drove mine. If our trip could shed even a single ray of light on the darkness that shrouded Baxter's last days, I would be grateful. It would be something.

Four months passed between the night Jack received Ford's letter and the day in April when we finally boarded the ship to take us to Manáos. Jack wanted to arrive towards the end of the rainy season, before the river waters receded but after the worst of the storms. And we'd needed the time anyway to make our arrangements. Jack had to train someone to do his job while he was gone, and I had to find someone who had some knowledge of ledger-keeping to fill in at the bookstore. And most importantly, we had to find the right person for Maggie. She remained in good health, thankfully, but her legs bothered her and she did not like to go out alone for fear of falling. We hoped to find someone who could come by twice daily, once in the morning to do chores around the house, and once in the late afternoon to walk with Maggie to the market, or to go for her if the weather was bad. We wanted someone who was companionable.

We found the perfect candidate in Darlene Monaghan, a hearty young woman who lived with her parents on the block between our house and Maggie's. Darlene worked three or four hours a day cleaning for various neighbors, but she jumped at the chance to do more. She was getting married in mid-July—to Chester Duffy, who currently delivered our mail—and she wanted to save as much money as possible. Her only concern was that we return before then, because once she and Chester wed, they would be moving directly to Kentucky to work on his family's farm until they could afford a farm of their own.

As our departure time grew closer, Jack began to worry about my health. *Everyone* got sick in the jungle, he insisted. He still believed that his own range of jungle diseases had rendered him immune, but I was a city girl; the jungle would be a shock to my system. Each time he said so I laughed and reminded him that I'd never been sick a day in my life. Once we were on board and our ship was pulling away from the dock, I turned to him and said, "I don't want to hear another thing about my health." We were standing at the rail by then, waving frantically to Maggie and Darlene, who'd come to see us off. "You have my word," Jack agreed.

And sure enough, and probably because he'd forced me to crow about my good health for so long, I became seasick our first day out. Jack thought it might be because we had an interior cabin and there was no window. He said I would feel better if I could see the horizon. Accordingly, I allowed him to drag me up to the ship's deck on the morning of the second day, but the boat was bucking horribly at that moment, or so it seemed to me, and with Jack holding tight to my elbow, whispering, "Nora, lift your head and focus on the horizon line," I bent over the rail and vomited into the sea. The sea was less rough the next day, but still it was too rough for me, and so it went. I experienced various levels of nausea for the first several days of our twelve-day ocean passage.

I stayed in our small cabin almost the entire time, and I was miserable and did not try to hide it. Maggie had told me plenty of stories over the years of crowds of emigrating Irish packed into airless steerage corridors—in filth and surrounded by rats, sick night and day not only from the motion of the sea but also from diseases and starvation and the heartbreaking crises many were running from, some praying for Death to bring their wretchedness to an end. My suffering was nothing by comparison—I was a third-class touring passenger, in a private cabin—but still I felt alone with my misery.

I begged Jack to go up to the salon and talk to people and enjoy himself, but he refused to leave my side. The only time he left was to take his meals, and always he returned with crackers and ginger ale for me. By our sixth or seventh day out on the high seas, I was able to accompany him to the dining salon, but after each very light meal I was ready to return to the cabin. I just couldn't keep my stomach settled for long.

We were bored, Jack and I, especially the first handful of days when I was the sickest. We had books with us, but they were at the bottom of our trunk, which was beneath my cot. Jack dragged it out the first day on board, but the space between our cots was so narrow that he could not open the lid wide enough to reach anything that was not right at the top. Then, the fourth or fifth day, Jack went to the salon for supper and, amazingly enough, returned with a book. He held it up for me to see: Emily Post's *Etiquette!*

Had I been myself I would have laughed. "Where did you find that?" I asked.

"A lady Mum's age had it at the table. She saw me staring and asked did I want it. She'd just finished it. Someone had given it to her, and she was happy to give it to someone else.

"I couldn't see the title from where I sat so I said yeah, sure, I'd be happy for something to read, and she passed it to her companion, who looked at the cover and passed it to the man beside her, who also looked at the cover and passed it on to me. I suppose my face fell when I saw what it was because after a brief silence everyone at the table laughed, including the lady who'd given it to me. Someone quipped that I couldn't very well pass it back either, because that would be impolite."

Now I did laugh. "It'll be swell, Jack," I said.

"Yeah, swell. Who couldn't do with a wee bit more etiquette!"

And it did turn out to be swell, in ways I couldn't have imagined. Not only was the subject matter dreary enough to relax me, but Jack's reading voice was so even—so monotone, to be blunt—that it actually began to settle my stomach. Emily Post speaks of inflection in the pages, because of course how one says something can make all the difference between whether or not one appears to be gracious and polite. And yet Jack read with no inflection at all. The flatness in his voice became the horizon line I'd failed to see days earlier.

As I listened, I found myself imaging Jack sitting at the bedside of those with the Spanish influenza. He would have relaxed them too, with his soft, flat voice, even the ones who guessed they would be dead in a day or two. Suddenly I began to feel that I had failed to appreciate him sufficiently all these years—which is not to say I ever doubted my love for him. *To refuse to dance with one man and then immediately dance with another is an open affront to the first one—excusable only if he was intoxicated or otherwise actually offensive,* Jack read, whereupon I interrupted him to say, "They must have cherished you."

He looked at me, surprised. He didn't know what I was referring too.

"The people in the hospital annex, silly. When you read to them. With your lovely flat voice."

"Ha!" Jack exclaimed. He returned his gaze to the book page, searching with his finger for where he'd left off. But then instead he closed the book over his fingertip and looked aside, and I could see he was deciding something. He sat like that awhile. "There was a book in the jungle," he said softly.

"I remember. You brought several with you. And Bax brought an English-Portuguese dictionary." He wasn't listening.

"I might have mentioned once," he said, "that the books we'd brought with us, all of them, filled up with black mold when the rains came. Everything was wet all the time, our clothes, our hammocks, even the inside walls of our shack. But the books, they were the worst. The pages stuck together. They stunk. We threw them in one of our fires."

He was sitting across from me, on his cot. I was lying down on mine, with my head resting on two pillows and the blanket up to my neck. He took a deep breath and slipped his finger out of the Post book and placed it to the side.

"There was only one book that survived the mold and mildew. It belonged to Leon." He tipped his head and looked at his lap and then looked up again.

"Leon, and his friend, fellow by the name of Ted, were our campmates. They were from Pittsburgh. We were jazzed in the beginning, because we'd been paired with fellows our own age who were from the States and spoke English. We saw the potential there to have a bit of fun, you know? We made pacts, about how if one of us took sick the others would hold up his end, how we'd share our food, our whiskey, whatever we had. One for all and all for one, like the Musketeers."

He hesitated, one side of his mouth stretched into a smile. I nodded quickly, to show him I knew what he meant. In fact, I recalled that in one of his letters Bax had mentioned Leon and Ted. "Anyway," Jack continued, "point is, it went well at first—a lot of laughs we had ourselves in those early days—but by the time we reached our campsite, deep, deep in the jungle, we were all four of us sick as dogs with malaria and bordering on starvation. We were like four old men!" He laughed, joylessly. "We traveled first on a launch with some other fellows headed to another camp, and then, once the river narrowed, we traveled by canoe with C, fellow whose job it was to get us safely to our camp and teach us how to tap for rubber.

"This C fellow, he wasn't the pleasant type, if you get my meaning. But he did know what he knew, and he did teach us to build a shack up on stilts and a smoke house for smoking the rubber. And he did show us how to identify rubber trees and how to cut paths between them. And then the rainy

194

season began, and since you can't tap for rubber once the rains begin, our only job each day was to get out between storms and clean up the damage along the *estradas*—Portuguese word for the paths we made between rubber trees—and wait out the season so we could begin tapping once things dried out. And C, having no more to teach us at that point, and wanting to get back to Manáos while the river was high, left us on our own."

"Must have been frightening," I said.

"That and more. You have to understand. We had never recovered from being sick and starved or any of the other devilish things that plagued us daily. We were suffering all the time—from wounds and rashes and pains cutting through the empty parts of our stomachs—but also from boredom." Jack snapped his head to the side, almost as if he'd heard someone call his name. He stared at the wall for several seconds.

"But what I wanted to say," he began, turning back to me. "It was only the one book, Leon's, that survived the mold. And that was only because he took such care of it. Every night by dark we were all in the shack, you see. No one with half a brain would have been elsewhere. Not only was the threat of insects and animals worse at night, but when the rains came they brought branches and even whole trees crashing down, and fast-running creeks appeared where there hadn't been any before, looking to carry anything in their path straight down into the roaring river. So every night we sat in the dark, with only one candle burning because we had to conserve, the four of us, feeling like misery itself, and sick to death of the jungle by then, and sick of one another as well."

"Jack," I said. Anguish had crept into his voice.

"It was about Ted mostly. Bax couldn't abide him. He whined continuously, Ted did. Sometimes he mumbled to himself, nonsense stuff. He saw things that weren't there.

And he didn't try to pull his own weight. Sure he was sick, we all were. But he didn't make the effort. It was like having a child along, a disagreeable child.

"Leon coddled him, and Bax couldn't stomach that either. And I'd be lying if I didn't say it irked me some as well to see Leon so ready to defend Teddy's bizarre behavior."

Jack took in a deep breath and exhaled, producing a long, loud "ha."

"Anyway, the book, the book I'm trying to tell you about. Leon's book. I'm sorry I keep losing the thread. It was all so long ago, Nora."

I reached across the space between us and touched his knee. He was getting agitated.

"The book was an English translation of a German book about how to survive being a German immigrant in America. How to keep from being bamboozled by shysters waiting at the docks in case you survived the voyage over in your coffin ship, how to grow fruits and vegetables once you made your way to Pennsylvania, the destination of choice for German emigrants back then, according to the author. Leon's grandmum, German of course, had given it to Leon before he left Pittsburgh, for good luck. Even though he hadn't any interest in the subject matter, he stood it on its side near the candle flame each night, with the pages fluttered out so they would stay dry.

"And one night we're all sitting there," Jack said, speaking very quickly now, "—all of us on the damp floor, except Ted, who was, as he always was, in his hammock—thinking our dark thoughts and saying nothing, just listening for trees to start crashing down around us from the storm raging outside, when Ted starts with the mumbling again. Nonsense stuff. Doing it for no reason but to antagonize. And Bax makes a crack, and Leon comes back at him with something sarcastic, something defending Ted but you could tell it wasn't really about Ted. His issue was with Bax, and he was eager to get his goat on that particular night.

"There commenced a back and forth between them. It's hard to remember; I don't recall the exact words they said, but I can see their faces like it was yesterday. I knew everyone's range of expressions by then, and I could tell it was more serious than usual, that Bax and Leon were about to come to blows. And then I saw Bax's hand moving, flattening on the floor, like he was getting ready to hoist himself up. And Leon's hand started moving too, but his seemed to be heading for the candle. And I saw it all in my head then, how Bax would jump to his feet and Leon would grab the candle and throw it at him and...

"Our shack was no more than twice the size of this cabin, Nora. And our four crates, holding all we owned in the world, took up one wall, and there were the four hammocks hanging in the middle, the one at the far end containing the wee small body of Ted, who was still too busy mumbling to have realized what was about to happen. There was no space for a brawl. Everything being wet, a thrown candle wouldn't do much damage, but a full-out brawl...

"I grabbed the book, the arsewipe book containing everything you need to know to succeed in America. I didn't give it a single thought, I swear. I just grabbed the damn thing and I began to read, from the page that opened before me, randomly, and loud. And Bax and Leon were so stunned to hear me reading in the middle of the scene they were playing out that they forgot they wanted to kill each other in that moment and turned their wrath on me. But I only kept up reading, over their curses and yammers, in my lovely flat voice, as you called it, but loud, very loud, shouting the words to keep them off balance, and at some point they shut their mouths long enough to catch a word or two of the text, and as the words were about boarding houses, things that grew in the green fields of Pennsylvania, humming birds in the summer and snow in the winter, life as we had known it... You see, we were all so homesick by then, Nora. And heartsick too, for who we used to be before the jungle turned us into crude beasts. The words in the book not only sucked all the wind out of their wrangle, but it made us remember. It made me remember Mum and Da in particular, coming from the Emerald Isle to escape poverty. And when I finished the chapter and looked up, I found the others transformed too, Leon all guzz-eyed, probably with memories of his grandmum, and Bax asleep with his head against the wall and his mouth open. Even Ted was quiet. And after that, I read every night, until—"

"Until what, Jack?"

He looked aside. "Until the rainy season ended, until..." He laughed, again joylessly. "I'm sorry, Nora. I don't know what possessed me... I only wanted to point out..." He shook his head. "Well, I'm not sure what I wanted to point out."

I moved to the edge of my cot and grabbed his wrist. I had waited all these years to have the curtain drawn back, just enough so that I could have a peek. And now I'd had a peek all right, and it was more disturbing than I could have imagined. I had a hundred questions, but this was not the time for them, and I did not want to appear anxious for more than Jack was ready to give me.

I let go of Jack's wrist, and after a while he turned his head to look at the book lying beside him, *Etiquette*. He lifted it. "I'll read a bit more then, shall I?" he asked, and I nodded.

It was an enormous relief to feel like myself again, and I emerged from the experience with an abundance of gratitude—gratitude for everything in my life, particularly Jack, who had stood by my side throughout, placing cool compresses on my forehead during the worst of it, reading the Post book cover to cover twice, and keeping me company while I rested, stretched out on his cot and staring at the wall, his mind wandering to who knew where.

Although he didn't reveal any further details about his time with Bax and the others in the jungle, now that he had opened the door, I felt confident he would have more to say when the moment was right. In the meantime, I had plenty enough to ponder. I replayed the scene in my head, as Jack had painted it, over and over. I gave all four of them passes for their bad behavior, because—having just had an encounter with sickness myself, shallow and brief though mine was by comparison—I began to understand the vulnerability sickness carries, how it can wear a person down until he is truly not himself anymore. My heart went out to everyone who had ever suffered so.

We stopped briefly in Belém, the port city at the mouth of the Amazon, to pick up more passengers. Jack and I got up very early, hoping to view some of the sights, but it was still dark and there was little to see there at the docks. It rained that day, but not too hard, and the slight rocking of the boat didn't bother me as much as it had when we were still out to sea. And by the next morning the rain was gone, and we were able to view the sunrise on the river. It began as a solid gold line on the black river, with a blanket of rose above blending into a purple sky. Gradually the sun pushed itself up, dragging the rose hues along with it. Higher and higher it went, until the whole sky was aflame. While the river was wide, we were close enough to one bank that I was able to see the jungle for the first time: trees and trees and trees, pressed together, pressed forward, like congregants with a solitary purpose, their resolve mirrored in the water. It was glorious, all of it. I hadn't imagined it would be such a presence. It took my breath away. It seemed to say, *I am here and you are here and good things and bad things will happen, which is as it should be.* It filled me up, causing me to reflect on how empty I'd been.

I loved watching the mist dissipate to reveal the world more with every sunrise. I loved seeing the sky and the river shift from black to gold. I loved the sight of the assai palms, standing along the river bank like Narcissus, falling in love with their own reflections. I loved the squirrel monkeys chattering in the trees, the parrots screaming overhead, the pink river dolphins, the settlements here and there with boats tied to the trees and small houses up on stilts. Jack said to me, "So much for spitting in the jungle's fuckin eye, huh, sweetheart?"

Strangely enough, I felt beautiful in the presence of the jungle, perhaps for the first time in my life. It was hot and humid, and my body was damp all the time, and my hair became a muddle of unruly curls. Back in Hoboken the humidity would have annoyed me, but here it made me feel sensuous, as if I were another of the plants and trees, covered with dew. I felt intuitive, as if the energy from the jungle and the river flowed through me too. I felt compassionate, for no reason I can explain. I found the woman who had given Jack the book and thanked her with such a hearty embrace that she nearly choked with laughter. I talked to any of our fellow passengers who ventured into range. I asked them where they were from and why they were going to Manáos. The weather was still transitioning, from rainy season to dry, and while most days the river was as smooth as glass, there were plenty of days when the clouds gathered menacingly, and rain fell from the sky in quantities that were heretofore inconceivable to me. It poured from the sky, unlike any rain I'd ever experienced before. But even this I loved. I had crossed over into a state of pure wonderment.

27. Jack

THEIR MARRIAGE FELT AS transparent to Jack as the jellyfish he'd seen drifting at the side of the ship when they were still at sea. His journey to Amazonas years earlier had paved the way for their relationship, and now, he was certain, this trip back would end it—for he realized all their arguing about how she would fare in the jungle was really just a way to keep from talking about the more important issue of why she wanted to come along in the first place. Did some part of her believe she might find Bax, alive and well? No, it couldn't be that. But what then? And what about him? What were his reasons? He didn't know; or he did, but they were too complex to be organized into a single assessment.

The day before, in the early afternoon, they'd been steaming along very near to the bank of the river when a clear-winged butterfly came on board and landed on his sleeve. He'd almost cupped it, because it was that beautiful, and he wanted a closer look. It was Nora who stopped him, saying softly, "Don't. Let it fly off." The words were no sooner out of her mouth than the thing was gone. As he watched it flutter away, he thought to himself, *Nora would have gone too, all those years ago, if I'd been truthful.*

Maybe she sensed their time together was coming to an end as well, because ever since they'd boarded the ship, she'd been treating him with more affection than he'd known from her in some years. They'd always been lovers, and they'd always been friends, allies, but this was something more intimate, and simultaneously very provocative. He had felt it in the touch of her hand when he was caring for her when she was seasick. And since they'd left the ocean for the river and she was well again, she'd been standing with him out on the deck not only in the mornings when the sun came up—now her favorite time of day—but every night after supper while he smoked his pipe, close, leaning her back against his chest, so that he could pull her closer yet with his free arm. The last time he could remember her being so physically close so much of the time was during the war, when he'd been beaten outside one of her anti-war meetings, when she'd been worried he would be drafted, when people were dying from the influenza. It seemed she loved him best when she thought she might lose him.

They didn't speak much. Or if they did, it was quiet talk about the beauty of their surroundings, or quiet speculation about how Maggie was doing back home with Darlene, or how Nora's various committees were faring without her or how Lipton was managing without him. Nora often marveled about how different it felt to be chugging along on a ship with no need to pay attention to what time it was or even what day, whole days passing with nothing to do but look out on beautiful alien vistas, watching for butterflies, parrots, monkeys, river dolphins. Sometimes they talked about how reckless it made them feel, to have cashed in their stocks and gone deep into their savings, how youthful—though of course they weren't so young anymore.

How he cherished the long peaceful evenings with her at his side. He cherished the smell of her perfume, which he'd bought for her the year before, for Christmas. Since Nora was partial to *McClure's* and *The Mercury*, he'd borrowed a women's magazine from one of the girls at work and scoured it looking for the kind of gift that Bax might have chosen. The perfume was called Quelques Fleurs, which the ad said was "light, laughing, gay, sweet, for the girl who takes nothing seriously; something the rest of us need when we feel irresponsibly young—or would like to." Nora took most everything seriously of course, but the ad copy (which admittedly Nora would have hated because it was so overblown) made him think of Nora growing up, the smile she flashed whenever she wanted something—or wanted to hide something—the way she was around Bax, always laughing at his antics. She'd been puzzled when she opened the package. He could still see how her red-brown brow rose on her white forehead as she scrutinized it. And then she'd never worn it—until now. Now it had become part of the spell—her scent, the nearness of her body, the slow graceful movement of the ship on the river, the warm sultry embrace of jungle breezes, the lazy whispered conversations. The lull before the storm.

The last morning on the river they were up even earlier than usual, the only ones on deck who were not part of the crew. The steamer was scheduled to dock shortly, but passengers would not be allowed to disembark until the sun came up, for safety reasons. Most of them had gone to their cabins early the night before to get in a good night's sleep before their early departure. But Nora wanted to be on deck to see the lights of Manáos appear out of nowhere in the dark. They did not disappoint either; they were otherworldly after all their days on the Rio Amazonas.

The first thing Jack noticed once on land was that the city had declined significantly. The once grand hotels and stately residences were covered with black mold; roof tiles were missing; shutters hung unevenly on loose hinges. Webs and debris clung to what he knew to be imported French glass windows. Italian marble steps and patios were cracked and sprouting towering weeds. Gardens resembled small jungles. The only modern advancement was that there were cars in Manáos now, not many but those he saw were Model T's, of course.

They signed into their hotel, a modest three-story structure up the hill from the docks, and let the concierge know to expect someone shortly with their trunk. Then they went back out because Nora wanted to see the Teatro Amazonas, the opera house, which was only a few blocks away.

It was closed when they arrived. They stood in the great square opposite, the Plaza San Sebastian, turning in circles, admiring the architecture not only of the Teatro Amazonas but also of the Church of St. Sebastian and the other buildings surrounding the square, and of course the square itself with its grand monument dedicated to the opening of the "Ports of Amazonas to Friendly Nations" and its re-creation of the meeting of the waters of the Rio Solimões (the Amazon) and the Rio Negro in the design of the tiles beneath their feet. The buildings here were slightly better preserved than those they'd seen coming up the hill from the ship. Still, no amount of decrepitude could hide the fact that this had once been a great city that had attracted speculators from all over the world.

On the few occasions that Jack had been in Manáos years earlier, he'd had no reason to give any thought to the opera house—except its dome, which could be seen from out on the river—and this was the first time he was seeing it himself. It was spectacular, but even in its heyday the talent it was built to attract had stayed away after several famous visiting opera stars came down with malaria. An old woman happened by as they were standing there admiring it and told them in Portuguese, which Jack was happy to realize he still understood fairly well, that there hadn't been a single operatic performance in years. Since the end of the rubber boom, Jack surmised. "*Mas a cidade vai subir novamente,*" the old woman added. *The city will rise again.* She pumped her arm in triumph and laughed, revealing several black gaps between her teeth. In the meantime, she said, the lobby area was being used by the students from the music school. They weren't allowed into the theater proper, which was kept locked at all times, but the vestibule, which was large and had high ceilings that made for good sound, was opened each weekday morning and made available to them for a period of a few hours. If they were there to see the young musicians arrive, she reported, they'd have a long wait because today was Saturday and there would be no lessons. "*Muito triste,*" she added, referring to the situation generally, Jack guessed. *Very sad.* After she walked away, Jack and Nora went down to the harbor to look for a place to get breakfast. He'd noticed a dining area adjacent to the lobby back in the hotel, but he was rather elated to find himself back in this city and he wanted to explore. Nora did too. Along the way, Jack told Nora everything the woman had said about the opera house.

Mostly what was different were the people. Twenty years ago the streets were teaming with well-dressed folks—almost all Europeans—speaking a rake of colorful languages. You could tell by the way they carried themselves, by the way they spoke to one another, that they had more wealth than they knew what to do with. Their carriages were top-of-the-line; their horses were well-groomed and looked like thoroughbreds. And now they were gone. Even up near the hotel, just blocks away from the Teatro Amazonas, Jack had seen only dock hands and fishermen, and women wearing stained aprons over their dresses and scarves around their heads, their children running behind barefoot, in tattered clothes. The rubber money had pulled back from the city as surely as the river pulled back from its banks at the end of each rainy season. Nora had been in a state of bliss since they'd turned onto the river. Jack had worried that the decline of the city might impair her mood. But when he looked at her, he saw her angelic smile was still in place, her head turning left and right to take in everything.

They reached the docks. The ship they'd come in on was still there, being readied to bring passengers from Manáos back to Belém. It was the only ship of its size to be seen. Whereas once the harbor had been filled with grand ships from all over the world, now there were mostly fishing boats and timber rafts. From where they stood, they could see a bloated caiman floating by, belly up. Nora must have found the site grotesque, but she said nothing.

Jack had read in the newspapers that Abalo, the man who had hired Baxter and him—only to try to cheat them out of their wages—had moved from Brazil to New York and then back to Portugal. There was no chance he'd see him there in Manáos, and he didn't expect to see any of the other people he'd known twenty years ago either. Yet, as soon as they entered the Cachola Café, he realized there was something familiar about the proprietor, a middle-aged woman with skin the color of copper. "*Sente-se em qualquer lugar,*" she called out over her shoulder. *Sit anywhere.*

She was at the bar, washing wine glasses left from the night before. Even though it was early in the morning, she looked ready for a night on the town, with two strands of pearls around her neck and a low-cut flowered dress that clung to her large breasts. A young woman appeared at her side, and the woman in the flowered dress spoke to her in Portuguese, telling her to go and wait on the strangers from the boat and then get the rest of the tables set before the breakfast crowd came in. "*Estamos lutando contra o tempo esta manhã,*" she said. *We're fighting against time today.*

Jack was careful to give their orders in English; he did not want to call attention to himself as a stranger who happened to speak Portuguese. The middle-aged woman was Louisa, who had worked for Abalo as a young girl. Her face was recognizable, though she had been slight back then and now she was almost fat. Much as he would have liked to say hello to her, this woman who had befriended him and later helped to save his life, he did not wish her to recognize him, at least not while he was with Nora. He had no idea what he said to her the last time he'd seen her. He'd been delirious then, with fever. Maybe he hadn't said a thing. But maybe he'd told her about his brother staying behind.

In truth, he wasn't too worried about her recognizing him. The last time she'd seen him, he was half starved and nearly dead, his skin almost blue—and of course he'd been much younger. He would have loved to visit with Bruna to see how her life had turned out, but that would only hasten all the sorrow he knew was coming.

The young waitress appeared with a large tray containing their order. She was very pretty, tall and slender with long eyes and dark brows and a chin like a cat's. She smiled at Jack and Nora as she finished placing their plates and cups on the table. "What a lovely child," Nora said after she'd gone. Jack guessed she was Louisa's daughter.

In the end Louisa paid no attention to Jack, and he felt certain she hadn't the least idea who he was and cared less. Nevertheless, he promised himself that he would avoid the Cachola Café in the future. No point in taking chances.

28. Nora

Our first afternoon in Manáos Jack went down to the docks to meet with Fausto, the launch captain he had been corresponding with for weeks before we left Hoboken. Fausto, who spoke English, would be taking us into the jungle the following day. The plan was that we would carry a motorized canoe behind his launch, and when the river narrowed, Jack and I would take the canoe and venture into the depths of the jungle, along tributaries that Jack and Bax had navigated years earlier.

The enormity of what we were about to undertake left me at once breathless and elated—in a dither, Maggie would say. I could feel my blood pumping through my body at a quicker pace than normal. I unpacked our trunk, and to keep myself from overthinking what the next weeks might hold for us, I went downstairs to ask the concierge if she had a city map I could purchase. I didn't know how long Jack would be gone and I thought it might be fun to walk around a bit.

The concierge spoke almost no English, but I was able to get my point across by drawing zig zags on her desk with my fingertip, and eventually she reached into a drawer and handed me a folded map. It was free, apparently, because she pushed my hand away when I tried to give her a *real*. I brought the map back to my room and opened it on the bed. To my surprise I found it was not a city map at all; it was a map delineating the various countries that made up the continent, and the rivers that ran through them.

"What do we have here?" Jack asked when he returned. I opened my eyes. I'd fallen asleep on the bed with the map tented over me. "Are you planning on helping Fausto with the navigation?"

I had been sleeping heavily, dreaming the river, I realized. Jack and I were lost on it. In the dream we were terrified. I shook my head to free myself from the feeling of dread still clinging to me. I sat up and looked about, but it wasn't until I saw our trunk on the opposite wall, below the room's one window, that I remembered where I was. "Did it go well with Fausto?" I croaked as I tried to resurface.

"Ha!" Jack barked. He sat down on the edge of the bed and placed the two backpacks he'd been carrying on the floor at his feet. He removed the map from my lap and held it up to examine. "He's a hard one, Fausto is. Made me agree he could have our house if we lose his canoe."

"He didn't. You're razzing me."

"People disappear on the river all the time, Nora. He said if we don't make it back on time to whatever meeting place he designates when he drops us off, he wants the house."

"Screwy fellow, yeah. Our house, modest though it is, has to be worth a hundred canoes."

"That's what I said, but he made the point that if we don't make it back, we won't need a house." He twisted toward me and kissed me gently over my eye. "Don't worry. He was joking, mostly. His way of letting me know how dangerous it is to travel the rivers where we're going, and how much he values his canoe."

I considered telling him that I'd just dreamed we were lost on the river but decided against it. "Those are for us?" I asked instead, jutting my chin toward the backpacks.

"Yes, everything we need has to be made to fit in them." He turned back to the map and moved one finger along one of the tributaries of the Rio Negro. I watched over his shoulder. "You see here? This is the Rio Purus, where we'll be heading." His finger stopped. "Right about here is where Fausto will drop us with the canoe."

"Isn't this more or less where Percy Fawcett disappeared looking for his Eldorado?"

"Fawcett. I hope he turns up. More or less, yeah. But we'll be on a different river than the one he was supposed to have traveled, according to the stories in the papers."

I leaned in to have a better look. "There's nothing down there, Jack. Even the rivers dry up where your finger is."

He laughed. "They don't dry up, sweetheart. They're just not well charted. God knows how many there are yet to be explored. Anyway, Fausto will have a better map, I'll wager." He twisted around so he could look me in the eye. "It's not too late, you know, for you to change your mind. You could stay here at the hotel and—"

"Jack," I warned.

He shook his head. "All right then, Nora. I just need you to know that it's dangerous out there."

"Yes, I believe you've mentioned that once or twice before."

"Fawcett is only one example. And we only know about him because he's famous."

I raised an eyebrow, and eventually he stopped waiting for me to respond and turned back to the map. I said, to his back, "Jack, remember you said on the ship about the four of you, how bad things got during the rainy season, trapped in that tiny hut, all of you sick and angry? But then the rains stopped and you were able to work. It got easier then, didn't it?"

I saw the muscles tighten at the back of his neck. I had promised myself I wouldn't push. I blamed the dream, and the fact that I was still dazed from lack of sleep. And maybe I wanted to punish him for pushing me, even this far into our journey, about staying behind.

He took his time answering. "I was thinking about it this morning, when we were approaching Manáos... Seems like ages ago we were on the boat, doesn't it? Anyway, thinking about all that happened here years before is like looking at a photograph that's underexposed, where you can see the images, but you can't quite make them out. Do you know what I mean?"

"Sure," I whispered, though I couldn't think of a particular photograph I remembered to be that way.

He folded the map and placed it on the bedside table and kicked off his shoes. I moved over to make a space for him to lie down. He had to be exhausted too. We couldn't have slept more than three or four hours the night before on the ship.

"It's like that for me, Nora. When I try to remember the sequence of events, it's like the things that happened happened to other people, young fellas I was only told about. And it always makes me wonder, *If everything seems so long ago and far away, how is it I still* feel *it all?* In my heart, you know?" He yawned. Then he laughed. "I sound like the ninny I am," he said. "I'm tired, Nora. Very tired."

He put his hands behind his head and crossed his feet, his position of preference when he planned to sleep for just a short while, a holdover from his hammock days. The sun was going down already and the room had gone shadowy. We hadn't eaten since breakfast, and I assumed he would

213

doze for a bit and then we'd have a late supper, maybe here in the hotel.

I was getting into my own best resting position, with my pillow doubled over to elevate my head and my hands folded over my stomach, when Jack said, softly, "We thought things would improve too, but the work was too much for us, weak as we were by then. We got up each day in the dark and used torches to find our way tree to tree and cut the gashes in the bark and fasten the tin cans to catch the rubber, all just as C taught us. But it took an effort, Nora. By the time we got back to camp, it was late afternoon and we were worn out. We'd find ourselves with no more than an hour to eat our lousy *farinha* meals, the only thing we had in abundance, and rest a bit. Then we were back at it, trudging through the jungle to collect the rubber that had bled out earlier and then back to camp to smoke it. It was almost time to get up again when we finally got to bed. Every day, the same thing." He grunted. "Doesn't sound so bad, the saying of it now, but it *was* bad. We were miserable, all of us. And Ted…"

"Ted," I whispered. I turned my head to look at him.

He kept his eyes focused on the darkening ceiling. "Sort of lost his mind, he did, if you want the truth. Not that we weren't all on that same path. But Ted… For one thing, he believed we were being watched by monsters."

"Monsters, Jack?"

"Back when we were first on the launch, the other group of tappers we traveled with, four fellows from the northern part of Brazil, told us plenty of stories about local monsters, snakes that could mesmerize a man, creatures that had their feet on backwards to mislead people into following them… Wild stuff, folklore, you know, like the Fomorians of Ireland."

214

I thought I remembered the Fomorians as mythical sea raiders in Maggie's stories, but I wasn't about to interrupt to ask.

"Agggh," he moaned, "It's hard to talk about. But I promised—"

I held my breath. He'd promised who? Himself?

"Anyway, there was this day…" He drifted again. "Let me think for a minute, Nora."

"Maybe tomorrow, when we're—" My offering was a concession, because much as I wanted to know, I could see he was agonizing over it.

"No, not tomorrow. Fausto's launch is not that big. We won't be able to talk freely." He took a deep breath. "So, on this day, this day of all days, Ted stayed in his hammock when the time came and I went out with Leon to work their *estrada* in the morning and told Bax I'd work with him on our *estrada* in the afternoon, after our break. That seemed the best way to compensate for one man down. So we're going tree to tree, me and Leon, and we're talking, something we seldom got to do because Ted stuck so fuckin close to him all the time, and out of nowhere Leon reveals that Ted was the way he was in part because his mammy shot herself the year before."

"Oh, heavens!"

"Shot herself dead, right through the head, blew her brains out, like poor old Herta, and Ted was the one to find her. Leon said one of her eyeballs was dangling. That image stuck in my head. Anyway, Leon tells me all this and says I should tell Bax, his thinking being maybe Bax would let up on Ted a bit if he knew, because tensions were escalating between the two— among all of us, but the two of them especially. And then we go back to camp and have our little break and afterwards Ted, who was likely vexed all day knowing I was out with his friend—that's the kind of mad piker he was—gets his miserable self out of his hammock to do the second go-round with Leon. And I go out to collect with Bax, and…"

"And what, Jack?" I asked.

"We had our torch lit and were on our way back to camp, me and Bax, when I told him what happened to Ted's mammy. And we wound up arguing. I can't remember the nature of what was said, but I can see us standing there, shouting in each other's faces, when all at once we heard screaming, screaming coming from camp. We took off running, and when we got there, there's Leon, on the ground holding his leg—said he'd been bit by a spider—and there's Ted screaming his lungs out."

"A spider?"

"A wandering spider, Leon thought it was. Poisonous. Enormous thing. His leg was all chewed through, and we're trying to question him so we can be sure—because if it was really a wandering… And we can't hear a fuckin word he's saying because Ted is screaming for all he's worth and we tell him to shut the fuck up, but he keeps it up, and finally it's Leon who yells at him. And that shuts him down all right. But that's when he goes off the tracks completely too, and he looks at us and then he looks at Leon, and then off he goes, running faster than I'd ever seen him run before, into the jungle, screaming again, and next thing we know he's run beyond the entrances to both *estradas* and then we can't make out his torch light at all. We can't hear him either. He's gone, just gone. Swallowed by the dark."

"Oh, Jack."

He looked my way, but he didn't say anything. He was thinking, not really seeing me at all. I knew the look well.

He sat up suddenly and slid off the bed. The moon had come up by then, a delicate sliver with limited illumination, but enough for me to see where Jack was headed. On our way back from breakfast, we'd stopped in one of the outdoor markets to buy a bottle of Cachaça—a liquor made from sugarcane juice. The bottle sat beside two glasses the concierge had left for us, on a small table in the corner of the room. I sat up and fluffed his pillow and mine too so we could sit in comfort against the wooden headboard while he filled the glasses and brought them back to the bed. He handed me one. "That's not the worst of it, Nora."

He got back onto the bed with his glass. Clouds must have been moving across the sky because the room went dark just then. My stomach growled, but I didn't pay it any attention.

"Bax went off at once," Jack continued, "running after Ted, and I somehow got Leon into the shack meanwhile and cleaned his wound best I could. And time passed, and Leon is suffering something awful, half conscious and in a hell of a lot of pain, and his leg is swelling up worse and worse, and I'm wondering where in hell is Bax and why is he taking so long, and in he comes, finally. Alone."

I gasped.

"Alone, and bleeding like a goat from a wound he got on his own leg—up on his thigh—running through the jungle in the dark. Thorns, probably."

He stopped to drink. *Alone, and bleeding like a goat:* his words reverberated in my head. I could see Bax in that moment; I could see exactly what he looked like walking back into that shack, and I was terrified.

Jack must have drained his glass; I heard a clink when he placed it on the bedside table. "And I ask him where's Ted and he says he couldn't find him and then he got lost himself and never would have found his way back except he happened upon one of the *estradas*. And when I exclaimed, he tells me, and rightly so, I'll add, *Go out yourself if you think you can do a better job*, or to that effect. And out I go, but the jungle darkness... It's impenetrable. A solid wall of dark with all the shrill night sounds just reaching their apex.

"You see, we never left the *estradas*, even during the day. It was too easy to get lost. And Ted had gone out beyond them. And I didn't want to die, Nora. Not in that moment."

He must have turned his head toward me for his voice was closer to my ear. He must have heard me crying too. His fingers found my face, and he wiped my tears away on both sides. "I'm sorry to tell you all this, Nora," he whispered. "I'm so sorry." I could hear in his voice that he was crying too.

"And Leon?" I whispered.

When Jack's voice came again, it was no longer at my ear. "He passed that same night."

29. Jack

THE DAYS ON THE launch on the Rio Purus were harrowing, with *pium* diving into their faces just as Jack remembered from years before. The nights were filled with the yelps and screams of the jungle, with mosquitoes, bats, and the eyes of the caiman who watched hungrily from grasses along every bank. Yet Nora never beefed about any of it. She marveled at everything, which left Jack marveling at her. She was intrigued by the huge spiderweb configurations that stretched from branch to branch and shrub to shrub, glinting with silver dew each morning. She slapped at her skin when she was bitten by an insect and went right on studying the green walls that embraced them on either side. As for Fausto, she'd burst out laughing when he introduced himself as Lord of the River, and ever since they'd been teasing each other mercilessly, with him saying redheads brought bad luck on boats and her replying that if his self-proclaimed divine designation had any merit, he should be able to compensate adequately.

Nora wanted to know everything. Between the two of them, Jack and Fausto were able to tell her the names of several species of butterflies and trees and plants. Jack was the one to point out the Socratea trees, or Walking Palms, whose damaged stilt-like roots were always replaced by new ones, allowing the tree to actually "move" from its previous location. She'd seen them before, on the ship coming into Manáos, but now they were much closer, and she was thrilled. Jack told her that the stilts, which made the tree look like a birdcage, provided a hiding place for small animals being chased by larger ones. He and Bax had once seen a tapir in the clutch of a Walking Palm. Probably he'd gone in to hide from something and became stuck.

He hadn't shared any additional details about the events from days gone by since they'd boarded Fausto's launch. Nevertheless, it was a relief after so many years to be able to talk about his brother freely regarding the easy times they'd had on the river. He felt giddy with love for the both of them, himself and Bax, for the fellows they'd been before the jungle brought them to ruin. And even though he knew further disclosures about the bad times would not have a good result, for the moment he was happy, hopeful even. He was committed to giving her what she'd always wanted—the truth. He thought about Isabella, the fortuneteller, with her Ten of Wands card, the end of a burden-carrying cycle, she'd said. For better or worse, he would lay his burden down, at Nora's feet, before their journey's end, and maybe her reaction wouldn't be as terrible as he'd feared all these years. Maybe she would even forgive him.

But another thought was nagging him too: What if Bax was still alive? The notion that Bax had survived and simply never returned or bothered to contact him had come to seem more and more preposterous over the years, and Jack did not seriously believe it. But now that he was back in the jungle, Bax's presence had become so prominent in his mind that Jack could almost imagine his brother was very much alive, that he, Jack, had been dead wrong about that all this time. The feeling intensified when he realized they were navigating around the Teacup, so called because of the handle-shaped section of land that jutted out into the river. Jack had been eating a mango when he recognized it. He gasped, and to keep Nora and Fausto from asking what was wrong, he feigned choking. Nora jumped up from the crate she'd been sitting on and began to hammer his back. "You all right?" she cried. He continued to cough, right up until he felt reasonably sure they'd gone around the bend in the river and put the Teacup behind them.

The Teacup brought about an assault of memories. The launch he and Bax had traveled on years before had stopped at the Teacup first, to drop off the other men they were traveling with. Two days later, the launch had taken Jack and Bax and Leon and Ted and C as far as it was safe for a sizeable boat to navigate, and from there the five had canoed to what would become the second camp. Jack and Bax were back at the Teacup again at the end of the tapping season. They'd had to haul their rubber *pelas* to the Teacup via canoe to meet with the launch that would take them back to Manáos. The Teacup was the basecamp for all the tappers who worked for Abalo in the region.

It was at the Teacup that Jack and Bax first learned they would not be paid for the work they'd done that season. Two men down, and the two of them half dead, and here they were being told to go back to their camp and put in another season if they wanted to see a profit. They argued with C and his men, of course; they wanted their money. In fact, it would have come to blows if they had not been greatly outnumbered. Then Jack got to thinking C was only the middleman; there was no point in arguing with him about their wages. He changed his attitude from rage to reason and asked C to let him ride back to Manáos on the launch with the rubber, so he could speak to Abalo man to man. Bax was still howling, saying he would kill Abalo if he refused to pay them. He was a doodle in that way, a fool. He couldn't see he was hurting his own cause. C took Jack on board, but wisely left Bax behind. He had his men tie Bax's arms behind him with vines so he wouldn't try to swim to the boat. But as they pulled away from the bank, Bax got himself free and threw himself into the river anyway. Jack remembered the moment well, the boat moving out into the middle of the river, Bax splashing, screaming every curse he could think of, his voice getting smaller and smaller until there was only the hum of the boat's engine.

That was not the only thing Jack remembered about the basecamp. It was just to the north of the Teacup that he'd seen his brother for the last time.

When they reached the mouth of the Coragem the next day, Fausto untied his precious motorized canoe from the back of the launch and helped Jack and Nora to move their supplies into it. They would be on their own for the next several days. Fausto would meet them just where he'd dropped them and take them back to Manáos, where they would spend a few days relaxing before meeting the steamer that would carry them home.

The same company that had directed Jack to Fausto had also provided their supplies, and they were good ones—sturdy short-handled axes, machetes, tightly-woven hammocks, netting, a variety of canned foods, and so on—but that didn't make it any easier to set up camp each night once they were out in the canoe. Nora had her first encounter with a poisonous snake the first evening on the Coragem. She'd gone to tie one end of her hammock to a tree limb and there it was, lying along a branch, a slender tree snake, the same emerald hue as the waxy green leaves surrounding it. She noticed it just in time and withdrew her hand and stood motionless, with Jack whispering behind her, "Don't move, don't breathe," until the thing made a decision and slithered away.

Once it was gone she turned into his open arms and burst into tears, loud enough, Jack thought, to scare away anything else that might be lurking. But her moment of panic was just that, a flash, and, in typical Nora style, she pushed herself away from him and wiped her tears on her sleeve and went back about the business of tying her hammock. She had left all her pretty dresses and makeup behind at the hotel and dressed now in trousers and men's boots. She'd bought the boots back in Hoboken, the narrowest pair she could find, but she still had to wear two or three pairs of socks to keep them from falling off. On her head she wore a plain blue cotton cloche pulled down as far as it would go, with a wide-brimmed straw hat over it. Fausto had joked on the launch that she looked like a *dama elegante*. But she'd insisted it was the best way to keep the bats and insects out of her hair while also protecting her face from the sun. In spite of everything, she fell asleep almost immediately that night.

The second night out on their own they found a clearing on some higher ground and built a fire big enough to last until morning and tied up their hammocks and went right to sleep. But the third night they had to clear an area themselves to be able to build a fire big enough to boil water and heat a tin of stew. There were branches overhead and shrubs and tall grasses all around them. The fire was so close their feet burned. That night they returned to the canoe after they ate, removed the two boards that served as seats, and slept on the floor—head to head, between their supplies and the extra fuel tank—with mosquito netting over them. This was doable because they'd tied up in the current, and caiman and river snakes don't usually attack where there is flow. But Nora confessed in the morning she dreamed the line had come undone and they'd been carried far away.

The next night they found a clearing again and were able to tie up their hammocks side by side. But there were more noises than usual in the distance, and Jack knew Nora—who emitted sighs of exasperation every time there was an outcry from some animal—was having trouble falling asleep. Hoping not to trigger her outrage by letting on he knew she was afraid, he said, over the crackling of their fire, "Sleeping in the jungle is never easy. Each night you have to surrender to it. There's no other way to get there. There are so many things that can happen, but being exhausted takes precedence at some point, and then you just let go and hope you'll see the light in the morning."

Nora didn't answer at first. Then she said, "Jack, tell me a story of some sort, would you?"

He laughed. Nora did this now and then, especially if she was overtired or feeling low, asked for a story as if she were a little girl. Her Aunt Becky hadn't been much of a storyteller. His mum, on the other hand, was a superb teller of tales, making the best of her voice and her brow to convey drama. But by the time he and Bax had taken up with Nora, when they were nine and ten, the boys were "too big" for listening to fairy tales. But Nora wasn't, and she wasn't ashamed to say so. If Maggie offered, Nora's face would open with delight—while Jack and Bax feigned annoyance—and the three would sit and listen. Sometimes Nora would curl up so close to Maggie her head would wind up resting against Maggie's arm.

Then again, perhaps she was asking for another story about him and Bax. He'd been putting *that* off, waiting for the right moment to go on. He found himself thinking about how he and Bax used to talk in the dark, in their room, when they were boyos. And when they got older, how Bax would ask to hear the plot of a book Jack was reading, since he didn't care much for reading himself. So he told Nora about that, about Bax and him on the boat on their way to Manáos, clacking away about books. Nora listened, as she always did when Jack spoke of his brother, without comment, as if she was afraid she'd break the spell if she pried too deeply. But the fact was, the more he mentioned Bax, the more daring he felt and the more he was inclined to say. The narrator in Edgar Allan Poe's *The Telltale Heart* came to mind, the way the fellow gets louder and louder as he "chats" with the police inspectors, until he goes mad with the effort and finally declares his guilt.

30. Nora

SOMETIMES, WHEN WE FOUND ourselves in places where the river was as smooth as glass, we shut down the motor and used our oars. "Do you know what I love?" I asked Jack once when we were paddling through a large section of forest covered over by flood waters lingering from the wet season. It was so quiet that afternoon. Even the howler monkeys were taking time off. All around us treetops protruded from the water, some leafless and washed silver by the sun, epiphytes, ferns, bromeliads or orchids attached to them. "I love that the jungle looks like love, with everything you see embracing everything else. Vines embracing trees, epiphytes clinging to vines... Nothing standing alone. Even the sounds, the monkeys, the birds... It's as if it's all one."

Jack laughed. "You could say that, or you could say it looks like hatred, with everything competing with everything else—trees and vines and epiphytes—in a constant battle to get to sunlight."

Jack had said long ago that it was too far to travel to the place where Bax had died, that even if we could find it, which he doubted, it would cause us to be late getting back with Fausto's canoe. I was strangely all right with that, because the jungle *was* indeed one continuous thing, or many things but all of them connected in the most intimate way possible. As far as I was concerned, we'd been in the place where Bax had died ever since we'd gotten off the launch and into the canoe. Over the years I had come to think of Bax less and less, which wasn't to say I didn't think of him at all. It was more that my memories became faded, like patterned fabrics that have been laundered too many times. We'd been so young; in order to conjure up specific memories of Bax, I had to conjure up myself at that age too. And that was a girl—frivolous, outspoken, a bit of a daredevil—I didn't know anymore. I was a different person now, and if Bax were alive he would be a different person too. But here, in the jungle, on the river, I felt enveloped by a sense of timelessness. Here I recognized that young girl again, which made it easier to remember the young man who had always been at her side. Here in the jungle, on the river, I remembered how eager he always was for adventure, a by-product of his lust for life. Yes, he could be gruff and pushy at times, but no one could say he didn't love his life.

It passed through my mind that Bax had loved life as much as Jack had loved death... But no, that wasn't right. That hadn't been true in a very long time.

There were a few settlements along the shore. Jack said they probably belonged to tappers who still managed to eke out a modest living selling rubber for local applications. To date we hadn't seen any people since we'd been in the canoe, just a few boats tied up along the bank here and there and the roofs of a handful of shacks built back from the high-water line. Jack said we should keep an eye out anyway, because you never knew who was going to see you as a threat, who was going to shoot first and ask questions later.

Something bit me just below my left eye one evening when we'd gone ashore to make our fire, a smallish insect, if the size of the bite was any indication. But by morning the skin all around it was swollen and I couldn't open my eye at all. We had three different salves with us, and we applied each in turn, but the swelling refused to abate. And it was sore and itchy as Hades. Jack suggested a patch, which would at least keep me from scratching it. He made one, from a piece of what he thought was called *cordoncillo* leaf, which had some medicinal qualities, and thin strips of vine to hold it in place. It worked just swell.

Jack had stopped talking about events from the past before we boarded the launch, when Fausto's presence made it impossible to speak about anything personal. I thought he'd pick up again once we were in the canoe, but I didn't pester him about it. In order to rendezvous with Fausto, we would have to turn around soon. I still believed Jack would finish his story before then. The truth loomed ahead; I sensed it, and it felt irresistible.

And sure enough the following night, as we sat on our hammocks with our campfire burning between us, surrounded by darkness and the din of the jungle, wrapped in the knowledge that at any time a wild boar or unfriendly native or venomous snake or spider might appear, Jack picked up just where he'd left off the night in our hotel room.

"Once we'd buried Leon and given up our search for Ted, we went back to work—working not only our own *estrada* but theirs too. We were miserable, so, so miserable, Nora; we hated the jungle by then. I regret to say we argued constantly. The only thing we agreed on was that we would not stick around for another tapping season. As soon as the season ended we planned to hand in our rubber, collect our dough, and board the first ship out of Manáos and heading to the New York area. But then something amazing happened."

His eyes glowed larger in the firelight and I sat forward so as not to miss a word. "On that day of all days our misery got so bad it brought us to blows. Imagine us, half the size we'd been, near starving and dazed and confused from lack of sleep and ongoing sickness. And here we were rolling around on the ground in front of our shack whaling each other, or trying to; whaling's not the word for what we were doing. We were so weak we could barely make a fist let alone put it to good use. In no time we were overcome with exhaustion. And we roll off each other and just lie there, chuckling a little because it was comical really—really, it was the best moment we'd had in a long time—and I finally find the strength to sit myself up… And what do I see but four young Indians surrounding us, naked but for ornaments at their ankles and wrists and pieces of tree bark to cover their privates."

"Oh God, Jack, please tell me—"

"No, no, nothing like that," he broke in quickly, "though we didn't know that at first. And we wouldn't have cared anyway. Things had gone so arsewise by then; it seemed a better outcome to die at the hands of the Gha-ru, what these fellows called themselves, than to drag our miserable selves out on the *estradas* even one more day, wretched as we were.

"They took our guns, and one fellow—who had a small woven bag hanging from his shoulder—ran into our shack and right back out again. Didn't seem he'd had any time to take anything. They marched us through the forest, two days of marching. I had to all but carry Bax because his leg was so bad by then, oozing pus and smelling foul." He hesitated. "I'm sorry, Nora, I'm sorry to tell you all this, but—"

"Please continue," I whispered.

He took a breath. "We reached their village and it was… otherworldly. That's the only word I can think of for it. To think there were all these people, men and women and children, living only two days out from us all that time. And here we'd been starving to death, full of insect bites and wounds of every sort, constantly getting and recovering from malaria and who knows what other illnesses. And there they were, well fed and healthy and strong. It seemed impossible. They had everything, Nora, everything they needed. Nature had given it to them. Every kind of food, medicinal plants to cure every illness...

"There were three structures on their land, and our four captors led us into the largest of them and the chief was in there and came forward and took away our guns and the woven bag the one who'd run into our shack had been carrying. He peeked in, and when he saw me stretching my neck, for I hadn't realized the fellow had taken anything, he let me have a look too. It was the book, Nora! The damn book that I'd read so many times to keep us all half sane during the rainy season. The one about emigrating to Pennsylvania. How had they known about that? Anyway, the chief listened to our captors tell their version of capturing us and then he stuck some resin up his nose and put himself into a trance. And while he was there, getting advice from his ancestors or whoever was on the other end, he made the decision that we were not enemies. And that night there was a grand ceremony and first thing he did was heal Baxter's leg, with magic leaves and chants and these enormous ants he'd used as sutures."

I began to cry, quietly, tears of happiness mostly. It was as if I'd forgotten that Baxter would die anyway when the story came to an end.

"They made us part of the tribe after that. The wove us hammocks and set us up in the main structure, which was huge and home to many families. The four fellows who'd captured us became our guardians and took us everywhere.

Nora, they had this resin, from the bark of some tree, that they threw into the river to stun the fish long enough that they could pick them up and put them in baskets. Here we'd been starving, and they had this way of catching fish… Their gardens… They were living this wonderful life, right there, in the middle of nowhere. Their knowledge… That was what they had that we lacked. Knowledge of how to live in the world. They were a unit, one big peaceful system. Even the children were peaceful. In the mornings they got up and shared their dreams, the whole damn village. In the evenings they had these wild ceremonies… They sang to their plants. Everything they did was enchanting. Or nearly so."

He looked aside, remembering something. I stayed quiet and waited to see if he would tell me.

"Two weeks we were with them, and then one day our guns were returned to us and we knew it was over. We were to be cast out of paradise. I was worried. We'd gained back some weight and were healthier than we'd been in some time, but would we be able to make up for the work we'd missed before C returned to show us how to get our rubber to the basecamp?"

"What about Bax?" I interrupted.

He looked at me. "What do you mean?"

"You say *you* were worried. Wasn't it a worry for him too?"

He hesitated. "Yeah, sure, I guess. We didn't talk much in those days. Maybe we kind of thought the Gha-ru would take it wrong if we talked between ourselves in a language they didn't understand. They hardly talked at all, you see. They were a quiet people, like I said. We'd become like them in some ways. Anyway, we needn't have worried about not having enough rubber. The Gha-ru brought us back by canoe and then stayed on, for I don't know how many days. Ten, maybe? I can't remember anymore. Point is, they stayed on and they worked with us, to gather rubber, with one fellow always staying behind to hunt and prepare food. And then one day we got up and they were gone! Without a word! And then a few days later, C shows up. How did they know he was coming? My guess is this: They had these hollow logs they banged on to send signals when some of them were out in the jungle. We'd heard them from the beginning, but it only sounded like a rumble of thunder or more strange jungle noise before we saw them for ourselves."

Jack leaned forward, so that the firelight flickered over his face, making him look a bit grotesque. "They had to have been watching us, Nora, probably since the day we arrived at our camp. They knew exactly how to tap. And they'd known about Leon's book. They must have got the idea the book was some kind of magic thing—hokum was a way of life for them, you see. But there was something else too, though I don't know I should tell you. It's a detail you maybe don't need to hear and—"

"Go ahead," I snapped. "The more I know the easier it will be for me, in the end."

He sat back. "The day we realized we were going to be taken back to our camp, the four Gha-ru who'd befriended us escorted us to each of the three structures on their lands to receive some kind of blessing from each of the members of the tribe. Two of these structures we'd never been in before. One was just a smaller version of the main structure, with several families living within, and the other was where the older women lived. We visited that one last.

"All the doorways on all three structures were small, probably to deter enemies, but the doorway on this last one was smallest yet. We had to bend ourselves flat in half to get through, and as I was stumbling to the other side—Bax just behind me—I saw..." He broke off and tipped his face up to look at the treetops overhead. Then he turned his gaze back to me. His mouth was slightly open, and while I couldn't hear it over the crackle of our fire, I was sure his breath had quickened. "I'll just say it; heads. Human heads. Shrunken heads."

I gasped and covered my mouth.

"…and while I only allowed myself the quickest glance—because it seemed our four Gha-ru friends were watching for my reaction, I could swear Ted's was among them."

I looked at him. I wanted to put my hand on my heart, because I could feel the beating had gone jerky. But I didn't. Instead I told myself I was a tree, a giant kapok, two-hundred feet high and three-hundred-years old, a tree that had heard jungle stories all its life, and this was just another of them. Jack seemed to understand. Anyway, he gave me the time I needed. "Did Bax see him too?" I asked finally.

Jack shook his head. "He saw the heads. I don't know if he saw Ted's."

How can that be? I wanted to shout. How in hell could he and Bax have gone so far apart they didn't even discuss such things? I wanted to get to the point and ask him outright for once and for all how exactly Baxter had died. Everything else had come to feel irrelevant to me now. But I remembered the kapok and only nodded for him to go on.

C returned in his canoe, Jack said, and he helped Jack and Bax to build a second canoe, and they tied all the rubber balls, the *pelas*, to the two boats and floated them to the basecamp, which, Jack said, we'd passed when we were still on the launch with Fausto. Naturally C asked about Leon and Ted, and when Bax told the story of what had happened to them he made it sound like it had only happened recently, so as not to have to explain how the two of them had managed to collect as much rubber as they had. "Still," Jack added, "he couldn't have neglected to notice we were no longer the half-starved fellows he'd left behind months earlier. He must have had an inkling."

They'd expected to find Abalo at the basecamp waiting with their money when they arrived. The launch was there, to take their *pelas* back to Manáos, but Abalo was not. They were told he got tired of waiting and went back to Manáos on a different launch. His men had instructions to pay Jack and Bax.

"These men—their leader was a big Caribbean fellow who spoke some English—got the *pelas* on board and weighed them, and then the big fellow—his name has just come back to me: Magnânimo… Magnânimo says we did a fine job and our rubber has paid for our passage from New York and all the supplies we'd been given, but nothing more. We'd see no cash until the following season."

"Oh, Jack."

"Yes, no way out for us, is what he meant. We began to argue, loudly, which brought all the other men down from the launch. Along with C, they surrounded us, holding our arms behind our backs. Something had to be done, because we could not go back there and sit, the two of us, through the rest of the rainy season and begin all over again. Bax was still yelling, calling the men every bad name he could think of, saying he was going to kill Abalo, when I got an idea. Abalo was our only hope. I said to C that I wanted to ride back with them on the launch, to Manáos, to talk to Abalo. C laughed; he said Abalo would kill me. I said whether he killed me or not was not his affair; all I wanted from him was a ride back. Finally he agreed, and I went… Without Bax."

He looked at me, surely waiting for me to ask about him leaving Bax behind. When I didn't say anything, he defended himself anyway, saying, "I felt I had a sane idea, an idea worth trying at least, and there was Bax, screaming about killing Abalo. I had to go alone. You understand that, don't you? Two of us at his door, one of us screaming mad, was a threat.

"Anyway, we arrived one night at sunset and C told me to be back at the launch at dawn two days out if I wanted a ride back to the Teacup. I slept in some bushes behind a warehouse that night, and next day I made my way to Abalo's mansion. His maid, a girl named Louisa who we'd met our first time through, opened the door, and when she saw my face she told me to run, that Abalo wanted to kill me. I guess C had informed him the night before or earlier that morning that I'd come back to talk to him. Then Abalo appeared and Louisa edged back from the door to allow him access, and I told him, from out on the stoop because he didn't invite me in, that Bax and I wanted the money we'd been promised and he told me to go back and work another season, and I began to argue and next thing I knew he was holding a gun to my head. He said he'd kill me if he ever saw me again. Then he withdrew the gun and the door closed in my face. I was about to knock again when Louisa opened the door a crack and gave me an address, where Bruna, her friend, stayed, and told me to meet her there.

"I found the address, but I didn't knock until I'd walked off some of my ire, pacing up and down the dock there on the poor side of town where the fishermen lived. Bruna was another young lass we'd met our first time through Manáos. We'd become friends. I'd even sent her a letter, giving it over to the captain of the launch that had first carried us as far as the Coragem. The woman who answered the door looked me over suspiciously, for I was as filthy a sight to behold as you could ask for, but I said I was Bruna's friend and she asked me if I was the fellow who'd written the nice letter, and when I said I was, she let me in.

"She'd been drinking coffee with two other old women, and one young one—her name was Adriana—who had a small baby. They saw I was starving and they fed me, and later the door opened and Louisa and Bruna came in together. And when I told them all—the three old women and the three younger—that Bax and I had not been paid and would no sooner return to the jungle to tap another season than we would agree to throw ourselves into the river when the piranhas were running, they came up with a plan. You see, they hated Abalo too. He was a bad man who cheated everyone. They told me stories about him.

"The plan was this. Louisa would unlock Abalo's door in the wee hours of the morning, before dawn, when Abalo, who got drunk every night, would still be out cold, and I would enter and proceed to the tiny room at the front of the house where Bax and I had first met with Abalo and there I'd find the money Abalo had been receiving from the men he sold the rubber to. Louisa said I should take what was rightfully mine and get to the launch as quickly as possible, that with all the money her boss would be collecting he would never notice if some went missing."

"Bricky or stupid, I can't decide," I mumbled when he stopped.

He studied my face for a moment. Then he threw more wood on the fire. "You're tired. Why not sleep now and we'll talk again tomorrow."

I was thinking the same thing. I didn't want to hear his story anymore. I only wanted to know what happened to Bax. I put my feet up in my hammock and pulled down the netting I'd strung up over it. I heard him say goodnight, but I pretended not to.

31. Jack

JACK KNEW EXACTLY WHERE they were; they were closing in on the lands of the Gha-ru and he could hardly contain himself. He hadn't really believed they would get this far; the motorized canoe had made all the difference. They were also approaching the time where they would have to turn around if they wanted to meet up with Fausto—a necessity if they ever wanted to get back to Manáos.

Since he hadn't believed they could actually reach Gha-ru lands in the time they had been allotted, or that he would even recognize the area if they did, he hadn't thought out what might happen if they tied up and entered the village. And for that reason he hadn't mentioned their proximity to the village to Nora. Most likely, there would be nothing there; he had seen the destruction with his own eyes years before. But if by some chance—well, it would have to have been more than chance; it would have to be a miracle—Bax had been successful in rescuing the Gha-ru from their captors, and the Gha-ru had returned to their ancestral lands and rebuilt all they had lost, they would be there today. And Bax would be with them. *If, if, if.* He tried to imagine what it would be like to push through the thick brush into the clearing and see his brother standing on the other side. He'd be speaking the language by now. He'd be the chief, knowing Bax, with a crown of macaw feathers on his head and a wife and a slew of naked children at his side. The shock would be too much for Nora. He couldn't risk it. But then he remembered that Bax had never come home, had never sent a message. That alone was proof positive that he was dead. Why did his mind persist on playing this ruthless trick on him?

A half hour later he cleared his throat and exclaimed from the back of the canoe, "I know where we are! I recognize it."

Nora turned to look at him. He was moving his head from side to side, pretending to be studying both banks. He didn't want to make eye contact with her. "If I'm right—and by golly I believe I am—we're approaching the lands of the Gha-ru!"

"The Indians?" she squealed. "Should we stop?"

"They may no longer be there."

"Why? Why would they not be there?"

"It happens like that," he said inanely. It was too much to explain in that moment.

"But we can go and see for ourselves, yes? We'll be able to travel there and still get back for Fausto, won't we?"

"I can't believe this, Nora!" he said, hoping to change the subject. "The river changes its shape constantly. When it's swollen and moving fast like now, it spreads out and creates lakes and streams where there weren't any. When it pulls back at the end of the wet season, it takes chunks of terrain with it, creating banks where there weren't any. And immediately trees and shrubs and grasses sprout up, making the new banks look like they've been there forever. The waterways and the jungle around them are in a state of flux all the time. And yet I know where I am like it was only yesterday."

Nora had said hardly a word to him that morning when they were packing up their hammocks and settling into the canoe. He couldn't decide if she was just in a mood or if he had said too much the night before. He worried he might have somehow painted Bax as the bad brother. He'd lied to her when he'd said back in their hotel room that he couldn't remember what he and Bax were arguing about the night they heard Ted screaming from the camp, the night everything went arsewise. He remembered very well. He'd told Bax what Leon had told him, about how Ted's mom had taken her own life and how Ted had been the one to find her, and Bax had agreed that it was bad business but he still didn't see the point in mollycoddling Ted; that part was all true. But then Jack went on to say Bax had never given Ted a fair shake to begin with, and that's when Bax got loud, shouting that Jack despised the little piker as much as he did, maybe more, but that Jack was a fake whose intention was always to make out he was the good brother, the tolerant one, and Bax was the bad egg. It seemed to him that he'd gone out of his way not to tell Nora how cruel Bax had become in those last weeks. He'd never said a word to her about how relieved he'd been when he saw Ted's shrunken head in the Gha-ru shack, because a part of him had feared Bax was responsible for Ted's disappearance. But maybe unknowingly he *had* painted Bax as the bad one, regarding lesser conflicts at least. Was that possible? Ever since this Freud fellow had begun spouting his half-baked views, everyone was talking about "unconscious behaviors." Jack had always thought it was a lot of hokum, but maybe he'd been wrong.

Nora turned to look at him again. "You didn't answer me, Jack? Are we stopping, or are we not? If there's time, I want to stop."

In spite of her adamant tone, her eyes were dancing, or at least the visible one was. She looked damned elated, Nora did, even with one side of her mouth pulled up at a peculiar angle due to the swelling. He opened his mouth to answer her but in the end he couldn't coax out a single word, so he simply nodded. The problem was that his heart was in the process of breaking, because in that moment he realized that after all these years and all his lies—or was it only the one lie that he'd stood behind for so long that it had come to feel like many?—Nora too held some hope that Baxter was still alive. The full force of what he had done to her came at him like a sudden blow to the gut. He deserved whatever he got.

An hour later they motored into the hidden cove where Jack and Bax had once bathed with the Gha-ru, with suds that came from rubbing two pieces of bark together. For every modern convenience they had in Hoboken, nature had provided the Gha-ru with a counterpart. How had they known which tree made suds and which made poison and which produced the sap that would put you into a trance? He tied a line to an overhead branch and turned the canoe around so he could get out first. Holding the canoe steady with one foot, he stretched his arm toward Nora. She took his hand but held it only long enough to get her footing. "Wait," Jack said. He felt like he was suffocating. He needed to tell her something, right now, before they went any further—to prepare her, in case. But she was already moving toward the thick wall of green.

Jack led the way inland. The process was arduous, in part because the foliage was thick and in part because his machete was dull. He cursed himself for not having bothered to sharpen it for some days. The smell of decay was everywhere. Nora asked why they hadn't experienced it before, and he said it was because they'd never been far enough inland. "It's the odor of rotting leaves and fallen, decaying trunks, Nora. It fills your nose and mouth and lungs with its putridness.

This is the other part of the jungle, the part that doesn't feel so much like love."

She didn't answer.

Every few yards he stopped, either to clear the sweat from his eyes or to check his compass. If they got turned around, they would never find their way out. She was mostly silent behind him, but she yelped once and when Jack turned, he saw a snake slithering away along the thick mat of leaves beneath her feet. It was a yellowish thing, with black markings. He remembered encountering one years back. "Non-venomous," he mumbled.

Eventually they broke through some brush and they were there, in the Gha-ru clearing. Nora gasped. "Is this it?" she cried. "Where are the people? There's nothing here!"

Jack didn't answer. As he said in his letter to Ford, once a tract of jungle is thoroughly cleared and there are no trees or plants to absorb the rainwater, the rains continually wash away the soil nutrients, making reforestation a slow process. Accordingly, the gardens surrounding the clearing had reverted back to jungle, but the clearing itself was the way Jack remembered it. The three structures had been burned to the ground years before, of course. But he'd been afraid there might be bones or skulls lying about. Fortunately they'd washed away too. Nor was his brother standing there with his family waiting for him because he'd had word from his scouts that a white man who looked just like him was approaching by canoe. Still, he cupped his hands around his mouth and yelled, "Gha-ru!"

"What are you doing?" Nora cried, shrill.

"If there are Indians anywhere in the region, this will bring them."

"And what if there are and they don't know you anymore? What if they think we're enemies?"

"They wouldn't," he mumbled. He turned to look at her. Her lips were pressed tight, but with the patch over her eye and her blue cloche pulled all the way down to help hold it in place, the effect of her anger was neutralized.

They waited in silence. No one came. He was hot and itchy and deflated. He had come all this way for this moment, he realized.

He walked to the middle of the *maloca*, to the place where he and Bax had once slept side by side on banana leaves. Nora followed. They stood for a long time turning in circles, shielding their eyes from the glare of the late afternoon sunlight.

"We'll stay here tonight," he said, "and leave tomorrow early to meet up with Fausto."

He was thinking they would have to motor the entire way, but barring a serious problem, they would make it on time.

He had Nora detach her hammock from its place at the bottom of her gear pack. Then he used some rope to tie both their hammocks side by side between trees at the edge of what was once the garden. He went in search of dead wood for the fire they would soon need. The jungle was quiet. As he dragged limbs into the clearing, he was aware of Nora's silence particularly. She stood in one place, her hands at her sides, following his every movement with her good eye. He could almost feel her questions building behind it, like water behind a dam. Her unease was palatable. It was as if she already knew what he was going to say, as if she hated him already. He got the fire ready, but it was still too early to light it. He sat on the ground to wait.

Nora wandered around the clearing for a while and then came back and sat too. The sun was nearly below the tree line by then and the light was fading. Jack lit the fire and Nora opened a tin of meat for them to share. It wasn't until it was dark that he finally found the courage to speak.

"I took the money. There was no time to count it. I took what felt about right in my hand. Then I ran out of the mansion and down to where the launch was being readied for its trip back to the Teacup. C was there, moving crates of supplies around on the boat. But he jumped off right before we left the dock.

"This concerned me. I'd assumed he'd be traveling back with us. If Abalo realized some of his money was gone, C would know right away who the culprit was.

"Days later we arrived at the Teacup, but before I could get Bax alone and tell him I had the money, another launch, a smaller, faster-moving one, appeared, and C was on it. I was there on the bank to see it coming in. First thing I noticed was C's brow was sliced and crudely stitched, the whole affair black and swollen; Abalo must have clobbered him with his pistol when he realized some of his money was gone. After all, C was the one responsible for me and Bax, and he was the one who allowed me to ride back to Manáos in the first place.

"C was burning with rage and so was I. He'd come all that way to take back what was rightly mine. He accused me and I denied it. He made me strip. He was greatly disappointed to find nothing on my person. When he got in my face, shouting, his machete up in the air like he planned to split me in two, I lost my mind and punched him. Someone shot at me from the boat just then, from C's boat—both launches were there, both with a few men aboard and more on the ground. The bullet missed me, probably was meant to. They'd get no information from a dead man.

"C's men had my arms behind me in no time. C lifted his machete and was in the process of drawing a fine line beneath my jaw when Bax appeared—he must have heard the shot up at the camp—and got into a fray with some of the other men. They had him strip too, and seeing nothing, C's men went up to check the fellows at the camp. They came back empty-handed of course. It began to storm, hard. There was thunder and lightning. We were well into the wet season by then. I had untied and dropped the pouch holding the money back when I'd first seen the launch coming around the bend. The ground on the bank was mud; all I'd had to do was press it into the sludge with my foot. When C and his men knocked me to the ground and began to beat and kick me, I made sure to fall on the place where the pouch had fallen. Eventually C and his men came to believe I wasn't guilty after all and they got back in their launch and motored away.

"Once we were alone, I produced the pouch and showed Bax. He took it and hid it. We agreed we had to leave the Teacup first thing in the morning, before C concluded he'd been had and came back. I had a few broken ribs and a swollen face and neck, and our first night on the river I came down with a fever like none I'd ever had before. I began spitting up blood too. I was sure I was dying. Bax brought me here, to the Gha-ru. They'd saved his leg; he thought they would heal me too. He also thought they would hide us until we could find our way back to Manáos and get out. Get home."

Jack put his hand over his eyes and waited for his emotions to wear themselves thin. He took a deep breath. He dared to glance at Nora. She was still, staring into the fire, her visible eye as hard as a marble. "What we found was... When we got here... Was that the Gha-ru had been attacked. Their huts were burned to the ground, still smoldering. There were bodies, mostly older women and young children. They'd been shot mostly, but some..." His voice cracked. He couldn't go on.

So many nights in his dreams he had seen those bodies, their precise placement, the angles at which they lay. But now that he was here, in the very spot, he couldn't remember just how it had been anymore.

"Three Gha-ru women," he said finally, "hiding in the forest. Two of them, they took Bax to see where the others, the ones who'd been taken prisoner, were being held. The other—she had a baby—stayed behind, to care for the babe. And me, I guess."

Jack wiped his eyes and let the moment revert back into silence. The stillness of the jungle was absolute, as if every animal, every leaf on every tree, had waited all this time for him to tell the truth.

"I don't know how long they were gone, Bax and the two..." He glanced at her and then back at his feet. "Maybe a long time. I slept. I didn't know anything. When they got back Bax tried to tell me everything, but I could only take in so much. My head wasn't on straight. The sickness. Bax and the women had gone somewhere on the river, in the canoe, to the place where the Gha-ru had been imprisoned; that much I got. The Gha-ru were being made to cut brush to clear paths for rubber tapping. Men with whips and guns behind them all the time. If they faltered, they were beaten and thrown onto a pile of bodies, some dead and some almost."

He looked up at the stars and then again at Nora's face, which hadn't changed at all. His own face was wet again, but he didn't bother to wipe it. "Magnânimo, the one who captained one of Abalo's launches, the one whose launch had taken me to Manáos and back again... His boat was there, at the new camp, where the Gha-ru were being forced to work. He must have gone to drop off supplies after he left the Teacup. I'd wondered why he'd gone in the wrong direction. His presence left no doubt that Abalo was behind the... enslavement. Not that that was ever much in question. How would anyone even know there were natives deep in the forest if not for the fact that C had found Bax and me in good health—with lots more rubber then we should have had, the two of us working alone—when he came back for us at the end of the tapping season? Bax had the women hide, and when he saw Magnânimo back on the river, he canoed out to him. He didn't let on he knew anything about the Gha-ru. He told Magnânimo I was sick and useless to him and offered Magnânimo money in return for my safe passage to Manáos. Magnânimo had to know where the money was from. He didn't care. He said he'd do it."

Nora's head moved slowly, until she was looking directly at Jack. She stared at him for a long time with her marble-hard eye before turning back to the fire. He leaned back on his elbows and spoke to the stars. "So that's where it ended, Nora. We—me and Bax and the women—canoed to the rendezvous spot Magnânimo and Bax agreed on, a place just beyond the Teacup, and..."

A bird called out in the distance and Jack recognized its deep, throaty whistle. It was a *potoo*, a night bird. All his time in the jungle he'd never seen one, but he'd heard one one night on the river traveling with the other men. Paulo, one of the men who'd gone to tap at the Teacup, said no one ever saw the *potoo*, because when he slept, during the day, he blended in with the bark of the branches he slept in. But it was good luck to hear one, because they brought messages from the dead. Jack wondered if this *potoo* could be carrying a message from Bax. He nearly smiled through his tears. He wanted to tell Nora about the *potoo*, the way he'd told her about the Walking Palms and other mysteries of the jungle. But she'd begun to cry now too, so softly he hardly heard her at first.

"And what of Baxter?" she whispered hoarsely. "You said he was dead."

"*Dia Uas*. Last time I saw him, he was alive."

He waited, but nothing changed. The stars kept their vigil in the sky. The moon, half hidden behind a cluster of cloud, held its murky beam. "So you're saying you lied," she said. Her voice was low and flat, but he could hear the danger in it.

"Yes, I lied."

"And him? What was his plan? To become one of them? A Gha-ru? A white native?"

"He had his rifle and mine, and the women indicated they knew where there were more. The Gha-ru had saved his life; he felt obligated to do what he could to save them."

"I can't believe this," Nora hissed. "Couldn't you have—"

"No, I could not have," he said. He was calm now, relieved; the worst was over. "I loved him too, Nora. If there was anything I could have said or done, I would have. He'd made up his mind. I was half dead at the time. I could hardly think."

"But you didn't *try*."

"You don't know that. I did try. He'd come under their spell, when we were with them. He wanted to be one of them. And then, when he saw what had been done to them..."

"So why are we here, Jack? Was it necessary to come all this way so that you could tell me this?"

He shrugged. "Maybe. Maybe it was." He found a stick near his feet and began to draw circles in the dirt. "I don't know why we're here. I only know I knew one day I'd come. Maybe some part of me thought he might have been successful after all, Baxter and his three women." The thought made him laugh. "It sounds like bunk, I know, but there were nights when I lay awake imagining he'd rescued the Gha-ru, and they all came back, to this place, their land—where their ancestors are buried and where their gardens once flourished and where they knew how to find the plants they needed to heal one another, where the spirits spoke to them—and started over."

He dared to look at her. Her face was wet, glistening in the firelight. He took a deep shuddering breath. "There were nights I imagined he'd lived long enough to have a child, with one of them. I daydreamed I'd come here and run into a young man who looked like him, and when I asked the boy, he'd say his mother was Gha-ru and his father was the man who saved the tribe, years before." He laughed without the least bit of pleasure. "What a doodle I am." A log shifted and he watched the light from the flare dance over Nora's face before looking away. "I couldn't control the fantasies. Half the time I didn't even realize I was making them up. It was like being awake and dreaming at the same time. I knew none of it was true. I knew he was dead. But I'd still find myself making up stories with better outcomes than…"

"You should have told us, me and your mum. We could have come back and looked for him, right away, before it was too late."

"It was a time of madness, Nora. Abalo wasn't the only one enslaving Indians. The greed for white gold had reached a peak. What Abalo did was small scale compared to other stories I heard. People didn't seem to think there was anything wrong with making Indians work for rubber. They were savages as far as most were concerned. Baxter made his decision, Nora. He wanted to stay."

"And you? If you were so sick, how did you manage to get on a steamer in Manáos?"

"The same women who'd helped me when I'd come to talk to Abalo hid me. They wanted me to stay until I got better, or until I died, I suppose, whatever came first, and maybe I should have. Maybe if I'd remained in Manáos I could have found a way to go back, to look for Bax, or to join him. But every day I was with them, Bruna and Louisa and the other, the one with the baby, Adriana, put them in jeopardy too. So when they told me there was a steamer leaving for Belém and then New York Harbor not four days after I'd arrived in Manáos, and a captain they thought would take the rest of the money—it was in the pouch, tied to my person—in exchange for my passage, I left." He threw the stick he'd been drawing with into the fire. "Well, I went, I should say. The three of them had to carry me to the ship in the night, because I couldn't walk a single step on my own."

Nora said nothing. When he turned to look at her again, he realized she was no longer at his side. "Nora?" He looked over his shoulder. She was in her hammock staring up at the sky.

32. Nora

I WAS NUMB, A rock, more a feature of the earth than
something living on it. There were too many thoughts
colliding in my head: *Bax was alive when Jack last saw him.
Jack lied to me. He tricked me.* I longed for home, but I had no
home. I could never return to Hoboken. Maggie would be
lost to me, because I would not make her choose between us.
I had nowhere to go, and I wanted to die.

In the morning I forced myself to leave the relative
security of my hammock and follow Jack through the forest
and back down to the canoe. I didn't look down; I didn't
care if there were snakes or spiders wandering near my feet. I
didn't look side to side. I was indifferent to my surroundings.
I let my good eye stare ahead, unfocused so that Jack was
no more than the vague shape leading the way. When he
stopped to hold a branch back for me, I stopped too. I stood
still and stared at nothing until he got the message and went
forward himself. At one point he turned to me, his mouth
opened to say something. I shook my head fast and mouthed
no.

It was torture to be in the canoe with him. Mostly I
maintained my numbness, but there were moments when
I became aware of a red-hot lava coursing through my veins.

In those times I felt less a rock than a mountain, with rocks shooting up with full force from the center of the earth and striking out at my heart. I wanted to explode. I wanted to erupt. I wanted to scream and hit him. I wanted to choke him. But it would only impede our progress on the river. And what I wanted most was to be off the river, away from him. I focused on my breathing, one breath at a time, until I fell back into a numb state.

He tried to touch me a hundred times. He tried to help me out of the canoe whenever we tied up, but each time I flicked my hand at him in warning. I'd have sooner let myself fall into the river and be eaten by piranhas than have him lay a finger on me. I'd have sooner crawled over the edge of the canoe on my hands and knees. He tried to help me tie up my hammock, but I repeated the gesture, preferring to struggle with the apparatus. I wouldn't eat the food he prepared over the fire in the evenings. I ate my meals, what little I could stomach, out of the can, unheated. I wouldn't drink the water he boiled. Each night when he was done at the fire, I boiled my own supply. Several times in the evenings when our hammocks were tied up—side by side out of necessity— he turned to me and said my name, but I never responded. "Please," he added every time. Once I heard him crying. It made me sick. And it broke my heart as well. I had loved this man. I could not seem to bear the rage and grief together.

We arrived at our rendezvous point on the morning of the day we were to meet Fausto, but he wasn't there yet and we had to wait. That was the only day in all the time since Fausto had dropped us off that we saw other people. A long dugout canoe carrying several Indian boys, most older but a few as young as four or five, passed by on the opposite bank. The children stared at us with wide eyes. When they were almost past, Jack suddenly shot to his feet, as if to let the children have a good look at him. I hated him more than ever in that moment. Was he still holding out hope that Bax was alive? Was he hoping the children would recognize him as someone who looked like someone they knew?

The first thing Fausto said when he arrived was, "What happened to your eye, Missus?" but I only shook my head to let him know I didn't want to discuss it. He didn't say much at all after that, to me or to Jack, for which I was grateful.

Once we tied the canoe to the launch and got underway, I said my first words to Jack since the night on the lands of the Gha-ru: "Show me where you saw him last."

"It will be sometime tomorrow," he mumbled.

The next morning he came into the cabin and I followed him back out. Then we stood together at the rail for several minutes. Eventually his hand shot out. He pointed. "There."

He kept his finger extended, and I kept my eyes directed on the spot he pointed to, a small beach surrounded by jungle. I imagined Bax, standing there on the bank with his hands on his hips, watching the boat as it carried his brother away. "What he did was noble," I whispered, so Fausto wouldn't hear. "Unless he miraculously survived, which doesn't seem likely, he spent what he had left of his young life trying to save those people. He should be famous for that. If you had only told someone… Maybe someone would have written about him. Maybe his story would be known by now. Maybe he'd be in history books where he'd inspire acts of courage in others. We all live such meaningless lives, looking out for ourselves, unconcerned with anyone else. Get ahead, save money, accumulate… And here he broke out of the cycle… And *you*, you were the only one who knew, and you kept it to yourself. You should be ashamed."

I marched back to the cabin before he could respond. Later I heard Fausto say, "The missus, ain't she feeling good?"

"No," Jack said.

We had to return our backpacks to Fausto along with the hammocks and other supplies. I found a burlap bag and stuffed my clothes into it when we were still a full day out, and then when I saw Manáos coming up in the distance the following day, I stood near the gangplank with my stuff ready to disembark the second we docked. As I flew past him, I whispered a thank you to Fausto and hurried away while Jack was still searching for something to carry his things in.

Breathless from walking uphill carrying the bag, I went directly to the hotel's front desk and asked the concierge for a second room. She looked alarmed when she saw me, and no wonder. I was wearing a black eyepatch now, which Fausto had given me to replace the leafy one. She must have thought Jack had walloped me—and in a sense he had. I pointed to the wooden board behind her, where she kept the room keys dangling from nails, and eventually she gave me a key. I was in the process of trying to explain that I had no money on me and would be back later to pay when the door opened behind me. "I'll take care of it, Nora," Jack said.

"Good," I replied without turning, "and since I have more clothes than you, please remove your stuff from our trunk and have someone bring it to my room."

"I'll do that too," he said.

"Thank you," I responded curtly, and I hurried up the stairs to find my new room.

Oh, but it was a relief to be alone. I opened the window and stretched out across the bed diagonally. Jack and I were scheduled to board the ship that would take us back to New York in a week. When we'd come in with Fausto, I hadn't seen any ships at all at the docks, but I planned to walk down early the next day and see if there might be one coming in sooner, if I could somehow change my ticket.

In all this time I hadn't been able to concentrate on a plan of action. My rage—or the lethargy I experienced in those moments when it was absent—had taken up all the space in my head. But now that I was alone, on the bed staring at the ceiling fan revolving slowly above me, I could see that it would be a bad idea *not* to return to Hoboken. I had friends there. I had my job. I'd lived there almost all my life. I didn't know how to live anywhere else. And while I never wanted to see Jack again as long as I lived, I had to be able to see Maggie. I would have to rent a small flat in a boarding house like the one I'd lived in with my aunt. People would talk—a divorced woman, living alone—but then they'd talked years before, when my aunt first left, and I suddenly found myself an unmarried woman living alone. Hoboken it was. *Heaven, hell, or Hoboken*, as the dough boys used to chant heading off to war and already dreaming of their return.

Two porters came with the trunk in the afternoon, and in the evening someone knocked again at my door. I opened it a crack and angled my head so I could see the intruder with my good eye. "Please have supper with me," Jack whispered.

His face was full of petition. If he had been a stranger, I might have opened the door and embraced him; he looked that sad. "No," I whispered back, "but I need money," and I closed the door as quietly as possible.

A minute later several *reals* began to appear under the door, one after another. As I watched them pile up, I realized there couldn't be much left. We'd calculated back when we'd first arrived in Manáos and concluded that once Fausto was paid, money would be very tight.

The bills stopped coming. All was silent for a short time, and then I heard his footsteps retreating down the hall.

Later I went downstairs thinking to have supper in the hotel. But as I entered the lobby I saw Jack sitting at one of the tables in the adjoining dining salon, just off to the right. He was sitting near the entrance, facing the lobby; apparently he had positioned himself so that he would see me as soon as I came down. I kept moving, through the lobby and out the door onto the street.

The streets were narrow and dark and all of them looked the same to me. I knew my way down to the docks and I thought I would know how to get up to the opera house, but the docks were too far for a woman walking alone at night, and I didn't recall any eateries near the Teatro Amazonas. I kept to the same road I was on and entered the first eatery it led me to. Unlike the café we'd eaten in down on the docks our first morning in Manáos, this place was small and rather dirty, and as all the tables were full of locals jabbering in Portuguese, I had to sit at a counter between two burly men who smelled of dead fish. But having eaten almost nothing for several days, I was ready to devour whatever was put in front of me. When the waitress appeared, I pointed to the string of words at the top of the chalkboard menu that hung on the wall behind her. She turned to look and then turned back and asked me a question, to which I nodded affirmatively.

I had no idea what I'd ordered. I sat tall on my stool with my arms pinned to my sides and stared at the wall in front of me and listened to the voices and the laughter coming from behind me. Every now and then the two fishermen on either side of me spoke to each other, but they were kind enough to lean back and talk behind me rather than in front. When the waitress appeared again, she was carrying a huge bowl of fish stew and a platter of cheese and sliced bread. As soon as she withdrew I tasted the stew. It was wonderful, with three or four different kinds of fish, judging by the floating colors, and some vegetables I didn't recognize. I ripped a slice of bread in half and commenced in earnest. For the next twenty minutes I didn't give a thought to Jack or my situation. I ate like I'd never eaten before. When I finished the stew I lifted the bowl to my mouth to drink down the last bit of liquid. That made the fellow on my right laugh, and I turned to him and smiled. He said something to me in Portuguese and I shrugged, and we both laughed.

When I was returning to the hotel I happened to glance up at the second floor in time to see Jack withdrawing from behind the curtain of the window in the room that had been ours. That softened me towards him just a little. For the first time in several days I was able to say to myself, *Jack Hopper is not a bad man. What Jack Hopper did was wrong, but he himself is not evil.*

The next morning I got up with the sun and hurried down to the dock to see about exchanging my ticket. I found the ticketing office just near the Customs building and in it a clerk who spoke perfect English. Sadly, he informed me that the first and only ship leaving for New York Harbor in the near future was the one I was already booked on, now six days out.

I wasn't surprised but I was greatly disappointed. I asked him if there was at least a way to change out our two-bunk cabin for two smaller cabins without altering the ticket price. If he said no I planned to ask if I could work on the ship for the cost of the purchase of a second room; I could clean cabins on the first-class deck or serve food in the salon. Anything would be better than sharing a tight space with Jack Hopper. I was still angry with him, of course, but the feeling of uncontrollable rage had abated. I no longer felt like a mad woman capable of dangerous behavior. I was simply a woman scorned, a woman who had been deceived, like so many others throughout time. I couldn't risk putting myself in a position where I would become explosive again. The ticket clerk said all the available single rooms were reserved for folks getting on in Belém, but if Jack was willing to bunk with other men and I was willing to bunk with another woman or two, it could be done. I told him that would do, perfectly, and he said he would go ahead and make the arrangements and have our new tickets ready for us the morning of our departure.

Afterwards I walked a bit and then sat down on a bench with a clear view of the river. I was so preoccupied with my thoughts that I didn't realize someone had sat down beside me until I heard him clear his throat. I looked up. "Fausto? What are you doing here?"

"I be the River Lord, remember? I be always here. See, there's my boat." He pointed. Indeed, there was his boat, between two others, tied to the dock. "I saw you come from ticket office when I was at breakfast," he added.

I sighed. "You probably realize Jack and I—"

"Yes, yes, you don't have to say it. My Ana Maria leave me four times." He held up four fingers. Then he winked and laughed. "She always come back. But you...you two, I know the signs, Missus." He clicked his tongue and shook his head. "Sad, so sad. The ride out I think, now this *um casal feliz*, a happy couple. But coming back..." He shook his head again, sorrowfully.

I looked down at my lap. I didn't know what to say.

"Missus Nora, I go in one minute," he said, staring at his boat. "Today I take four men for *arapaima*. You know *arapaima*?"

"No, Fausto. What's *arapaima*?"

He laughed with pleasure. "*Arapaima* special, Missus Nora, like you with your *chapéu elegante* and eyepatch. They big as a man, big as me, and weigh more. Monsters. Ugly, ugly, but good to eat, very good. We travel to spot on the Rio Negro and untie canoe and paddle to lagoon where water is receding fast now at end of rains. The *arapaima*, they so big they get stranded when river recede. We sit long and quiet." He lowered his voice to a whisper to set the scene. "And when *arapaima* come up for air... It has a lung, you know? It breathes water and air. Then..." He made his voice loud once again. "Then we jump off canoe all at once with nets and knives and... *Aqui é*! We got him!" He shouted the last bit and snapped his fingers in front of our faces. Then he looked across the way toward his boat. "See that *companheiro* standing by my boat? He waiting for me. He on time, other three late." He looked at me. "The women, you know how they make their nails?"

"You mean polish, to make them shiny?"

"No, no. To make shape." He shook one hand over the nails of the other to gesture buffing.

"Oh, you mean to file."

He laughed again. "Yes, file. File, file, file. The scales on *arapaima* are good files. For nails. For women. All women in Manáos have them. If we catch *arapaima*, I bring one back for you. *If.*"

"That would be lovely, Fausto. I'd love a nail file made from a fish scale." Having been such miserable company on the boat I was glad to have the opportunity to converse with Fausto about something as unoffending as fish scales. "I'll walk down to your boat tomorrow at this time and see if the fishing went well. *If.*"

Three more men arrived together on the dock and joined the one already standing near Fausto's boat. Watching them,

Fausto got up slowly from the bench. "Now I go," he said. For a moment he seemed distracted. Then he turned toward me. "But tomorrow, tomorrow, tomorrow. Tomorrow I leave very early, at dawn. I take many people very far to meet another boat to take them all the way to Fordlândia."

"Fordlândia?" I exclaimed. "Fordlândia! You mean where Henry Ford is building his rubber plantation?"

"You know Henry Ford, Missus?"

"I do. I mean, I don't know him, but I know about Fordlândia!"

"Yes! Everyone want to go to Fordlândia now, to work for the American. He building a great city, like Manáos, all around his rubber trees." He laughed a deep belly laugh. "Go look at the map, at Biblioteca Publica. They happy to show everyone. But *arapaima* scale. Come not tomorrow but day after for *arapaima* scale. That day I take men fishing again. I be here at this time, just like today."

He began to walk off, but I called out to him, "Fausto, where is the library?"

He stopped. "Library?" He rubbed his forehead. "You mean biblioteca! Yes, yes, Biblioteca Publica. Very beautiful." He gestured with his hand. "Near Teatro Amazonas, opera house. You find it easy." He pointed to his eye. "You tell them you are *um pirata,* a pirate lady, and friend to great River Lord, Fausto. They treat you nice." He laughed heartily and went on his way.

33. Jack

JACK HEARD A RUSTLING sound, but after so many nights of drifting along on the surface of sleep without ever actually arriving there, he was finally sleeping deeply, and he accepted the noise as a component of his dream. He would not have chosen to retreat from this dream even if he could, because Bax was in it. He was sitting at a desk that looked very much like Jack's desk at Lipton's—a somewhat incongruous sight. Jack didn't remember ever seeing his brother at a desk before. Bax hadn't even liked sitting at the kitchen table to do his homework when they were boyos. He'd always preferred the rocker near the window, with his books piled precariously on his lap. He liked to rock, and he liked to be the first to know when one of their friends appeared out in the street. *That* was Bax.

But if *that* was Bax, the one in the rocker chewing on his pencil while his eyes drifted from the open book at the top of his book tower to the great outdoors on the other side of the window, who was this fellow who looked just like Bax sitting at Jack's work desk?

While Jack watched, Bax's impersonator folded a piece of paper and slid it into an envelope. As he licked the envelope he looked up and beamed at Jack. That's when Jack realized it was not Bax *or* his double. It was him, Jack! He was looking at himself, and his image was smirking back at him!

He awoke. Immediately the dream began to fade. But he sensed it was important and he lay still and tried to find some vestige of it to cling to. Despite his effort, all he could see was the expression he'd seen on his own face, that smirk. He wasn't a smirker; no one would ever say he was, would they?

When there was nothing left at all of the dream he allowed himself to remember that Nora, the love of his life, hated him now, and that it was his fault. In his attempt to do everything right, he had done everything wrong. He hated himself as much as she did. Maybe more. If she ever spoke to him again, he would ask her if she wanted to hold a competition, to see who hated him more. They could each make a list of things they despised about him and see whose was longer. He didn't feel like getting out of bed. He didn't feel like dressing. He was hungry but he didn't feel like eating either. He only wanted to go back to sleep.

He turned his head to the right, away from the window, because the sun was just coming up and the light hurt his eyes. That's when he noticed the sliver of white under the door. It took a moment, but he came to realize it was a piece of paper. Someone had tried to slip him a note but hadn't given it enough of a thrust to make it fully into his room. A jolt of current shot through him, and in the next instant he was out of bed and on his feet and reaching for it. Nora's handwriting. He could hardly breathe.

He didn't bother to brush his teeth or wash his face or even lock the door. He simply put on the clothes he'd left on the floor the night before and ran down to the dock as quickly as he could. Fausto was just untying the lines.

"Wait," he cried. "Wait."

Fausto turned and looked behind him. Jack looked too. There had to be thirty or forty people on board the small launch, along with their possessions in crates and burlap bags. Fausto turned back to him. "She don't want to see you, man."

"Come on, Fausto. Let me on board. I have to talk to her."

Fausto wagged his head from side to side. Then he sighed. "*Mulheres, mulheres, mulheres,*" he mumbled. *Women, women, women.* He'd already pulled the gangplank up. He stretched out an arm and Jack grasped his hand, and bracing one foot against the side of the boat, he swung the other over the rail and Fausto pulled him on deck. As Fausto released him he said, "No trouble on my boat, you hear?"

Jack waited until Fausto was in the tiny wheelhouse at the front of the cabin, and then until the boat was turned around and heading toward the middle of the river. Then he broke away from the rail and began squeezing through the crowd—men and women and children—until he espied Nora standing outside the cabin on portside, leaning against it. He saw her shudder when she saw him. Her mouth fell open. He approached her quickly, before she could scream for Fausto. "Fordlândia, Nora? Is that what you want?"

She stared him down with her good eye. "You must either get Fausto to turn this boat around right now or jump off and swim. We cannot both be on this boat."

"What did you expect me to do when I saw your letter?"

"I didn't expect you to see my letter until we were well underway."

"Please talk to me, Nora. At least tell me *why* you're going to Fordlândia. I'd say you owe me that much, but that wouldn't be true. You owe me nothing. Still… Where did this come from? What are you doing to yourself? You're upset with me so you're going to Fordlândia, a place in the middle of the jungle that you know nothing about?"

"I'm feeling impulsive these days. Leave it at that." She looked away. "I really don't want to talk to you."

"What will I tell Mum? If I'm to go back without you, I need to know what to say. And what will I tell the girls if they come around asking for you? That you went off to live in Fordlândia? I can't say that. They won't believe me. They'll think something awful happened to you and I don't want to say."

"Do you see how easy your mind jumps to lying as a solution? I'll write to your mum. You needn't worry."

"Nora, please. All our years together, all we've been through. I can't have lost you so completely that you would just disappear."

She didn't answer for a long time. He saw her gaze sweep over the crowds of people, the river beyond them. Finally it fell on him. "I'll talk to you under one condition, and only because I don't know how long it'll be before I can get a letter to Maggie, or to Mr. Fitzgerald or any of the girls."

"Anything you say."

"And then you must leave me be."

He nodded eagerly.

"This boat is going some seven or eight hours down the river. Then it will meet with another boat, the *Liliana*, which is coming up from Fordlândia. The *Liliana* is bigger, with hammocks, because the second leg of the journey will be longer. There will be a passenger exchange with the *Liliana*, and then Fausto will take the people coming from Fordlândia to Manáos and the *Liliana* will take the rest of us to Fordlândia. When I get on that other boat, you will ride back to Manáos with Fausto. You must promise me that."

"Nora, you can't—"

"That's the deal, Jack Hopper. You cannot travel to Fordlândia with me."

Jack's eyes filled with tears. Nora's one eye did too, and he wondered if it was because there was some small part of her that still cared a little or if hers were tears of anger, of rage.

"All right," he said. He shrugged. "So, why? Why Fordlândia?"

"I'm hoping to teach. Once the building of the city is complete, many families will come, from Dearborn but from other places too. There will be many Indians and mixed-race people. There will be children, and they will need teachers."

"What if you don't get hired?" he said, stupidly, because who in their right mind would turn down a chance to hire Nora.

"I went to the library yesterday to see a map of the area where Ford is making his plantation. The head librarian turned out to be bilingual. We had lunch together. She told me everything she knew about Fordlândia. She wrote me a letter of recommendation."

Jack was speechless. "But you hate Ford," he said finally. It was the only thing he could think to say.

She almost laughed. "This has nothing to do with Ford, Jack. This is about me, about an opportunity to do something, well, noble, before it's said and done."

"Noble," he whispered under his breath. "I can't think what you're talking about. You've lost me. You've always lived a life of…" He drifted off.

She leaned in toward him and spoke in whisper too, but hers was bitter and through her teeth. "Listen to me, Jack Hopper. I'm changed, and not just because of… The river changed me. Being here changed me. I'm no Aunt Becky, but I always thought I'd do something important with my life. And I always thought I'd have children who could learn from me, and who would teach me too."

"You did important things. What about the war? Your parlor meetings…"

"Don't be ridiculous. We attended a few meetings a long time ago. Now we're complacent, the lifestyle we live. Our radio. Our refrigerator—"

He pictured their electric refrigerator. It had two compartments, one over the other in an oak cabinet. Nora had opened and closed the doors so many times on delivery day that he'd feared she'd break them. But he knew better than to mention that now. "Let me come with you, to Fordlândia," he begged. "Maybe I can make things up to you. Maybe we can be noble together."

This time she did laugh, without any mirth. "No," she said simply.

"But…" But *what*? he asked himself. He couldn't think of a single argument to make on his own behalf. Then something came to him. "But I've told you how the Indians were exploited. This will be that all over again."

"Most of those Indians have been acculturated now—which of course is terrible, but that's apparently what's happened. That's what the librarian said. Besides, for all that Ford is a despicable racist, he's always been known to pay a fair wage. *You're* the one who always reminded me of *that*. Think how this will help the economy here. It will bring so much much-needed money to the region. And I can do my small part to make sure the children are educated to understand they must never become oppressors, to make sure what happened to the Gha-ru never happens to anyone else…"

"You can't make them all little socialists. That's not the way it works."

"Who says I can't?"

"Nora, I don't see how I can allow you do this."

She stared at him, her exposed eye glaring. "I intended not to put the blame on you regarding what happened to Bax, but you must admit at the very least you stole my heart under false pretenses. You lied to me. You tricked me. That all but negates our marriage, on moral grounds if not legal. So please, don't tell me what I can and can't do."

He thought of the bed, back at the hotel. Suddenly he was exhausted. "I wanted to tell you the truth, Nora, every day. But the more time passed, the more... And the truth wouldn't have brought him back anyway."

She waved her hand in front of her face, as if to cast away his words. "This is a conversation I don't feel like having. What's done is done. I don't want to talk about it." She pushed herself off from the cabin wall. "If you'll excuse me, I'd like to stretch my legs."

He turned to look at the crowd. Stretching her legs would be impossible, but he was too befuddled to mention that. He moved out of her way.

34. Nora

I MADE MY WAY around to the opposite side of the boat and squeezed into a small space beside one of the bins Fausto used to contain the fish he caught. It stunk, but at least it left me something to lean on. Not only were there too many people on the boat, but almost all the women had cloth bags with them, full of food, no doubt. They'd been carrying them when we left the dock, but now many balanced them between their feet, taking up even more space.

The bags reminded me that I'd forgotten to tell Jack that I'd taken our trunk; it was on board, currently hidden under a pile of smaller crates and sacks near the bow. I'd meant to mention it in my note, so he'd be sure to buy himself a valise for his trip back to Hoboken. In the rush to get to the docks I'd forgotten. Alas, there were hours and hours to go before the passenger exchange with the *Liliana*; undoubtedly, and unfortunately, I'd get a second chance to tell him.

All around me people were chatting in Portuguese, a language I would have to learn myself if I wanted to make the most of my time in Fordlândia. I'd never tried to learn another language before, but I thought I might be good at it. Already I felt an affinity for it; I'd grown accustomed to its particular music.

I realized I was smiling. I'd never thought of myself as an adventurer, but now I saw it was possible that an adventurer was exactly what I was. Surely my time in Fordlândia would result in additional opportunities to discover hidden abilities I possessed but had never tapped into. I couldn't wait to get there.

I was still wearing my eyepatch. I'd checked my eye in my hand mirror the night before, and while the swelling had gone down some, it was still puffy and red, and my eye remained more closed than opened. I had thought to be done with it by this time, but now I was glad to be wearing the patch, because if nothing else, it was attention getting. Frequently people, especially the women, turned in my direction and stared at me with curiosity. I smiled at them when I caught them looking, and most of them quickly looked away. But now and then one made an effort to smile back. I would have to win them over one at a time because they would be part of my community and I would be part of theirs. We would see one another daily. We would work side by side. Some of their children would be in my classroom.

Jack appeared again, turning left and right to tack through small spaces and make his way to me, and this time I didn't mind so much. In fact, I found myself feeling sorry for him. I'd be making a new life in the beautiful jungle and he'd be returning to work at Lipton's, managing a room full of tea-packers. It wasn't that he hated his job, but he did hate being indoors so many hours each day. I couldn't help but think that Bax never would have stood for it. Even if he'd been the one to come back sick and too weak to work the docks, as soon as he was strong again he would have quit Lipton and gone right back to the shipyards. He wouldn't have let a sizeable paycheck and a cozy relationship with the boss keep him office bound.

"So, will you go back to Lipton's?" I said when Jack reached me.

He snorted. "What else would I do?"

"Maybe you should think about finding work you'd enjoy more."

He studied my face. He was trying to make sense of the change that had come over me since we'd spoken on the port side of the boat. *Good luck*, I thought. I couldn't make sense of it myself. "Something noble? I assume that's what you're getting at," he said.

"Why not, Jack? What about that book you always said you'd write one day? The novelette for *Adventure*? Why not actually do it? Life is short."

"You're damn right about that," he said. "I may very well do that, quit my job and write that story…"

He was doing his best to play along, but his heart wasn't in it. He had to be thinking we'd spent most of our savings, that he'd lose the house before he ever finished a book. But he'd never quit his job and take the chance anyway. That wasn't Jack. Jack was steady. Jack was loyal—except regarding me. As for his writing, I'd seen bits and pieces of it over the years. His story was about two men, pirates traveling the high seas. But for all that he had the skills—clean, well-structured sentences—his characters never got very far along on their way to their destination. I couldn't count the times I'd come across the pages of one of his efforts crumpled in the trash and, knowing he was really writing about himself and Bax, had myself a peek to see if I could learn something new. I never did.

Jack turned slightly, as if he had suddenly become interested in the line of trees along the riverbank. I knew the stance; he didn't want to talk to me. The sun was nearly overhead now, and every minute it seemed to get hotter and more humid. Couples had begun to argue, and older children were whining while smaller children begged to be picked up and held. I was having trouble staying upright myself. I leaned back further against the fish hold and accidentally tipped a bucket that had been stashed on a wooden shelf above it. I turned just quickly enough to save the bucket from falling into the hold, but not in time to keep it from dumping a long streak of green slime all along the back of my trousers. I found a rag on the same shelf and began to wipe furiously at my bum, much to the amusement of some of the other women standing nearby. "Can I help?" Jack asked, turning back to me.

"No," I snapped. The women laughed again. In that instant I forgot my good intentions toward my new community members and glared at them.

Some men chatting nearby began to laugh too. Jack took a step in their direction and a moment later he joined the conversation, which was unfolding in Portuguese, naturally. He asked a question and one of the fellows answered and everyone laughed harder. When he was back at my side, he said, "I asked them what they'd be doing in Fordlândia, and one answered, *Taking revenge on Henry the First.*"

"I don't get it," I groused.

"Henry the First is Henry Wickham, the English fink who stole all those rubber seeds so long ago. They hate him around here. If not for him, the rubber boom would never have come to an end. Now they think Henry Ford will bring the industry back to Amazonas. They call him Henry the Second."

Suddenly it seemed easier to make casual conversation than to stand side by side saying nothing. Anyway, it made the time pass. "And you still don't think it can happen? That Ford with all his money can't make this work?"

"No, Nora. I told you before. Rubber trees might grow swell on plantations in places where there's no blight, but here it can't be done. Ford will fail, and the sooner the better."

I jutted my chin and looked away.

The adults were drooping now, and many of the women and just about all of the children had slumped to the deck floor. They had to hold their knees to their chests, the women and girls with their skirts tented over them, to keep their feet from being stepped on—not that anyone was in a position to move more than an inch or two. We were all wet with sweat. In my little corner, body odor from the group at large had begun to mix with the fish smell. The only good thing was that we were far enough away from the shoreline that the mosquitoes and other insects weren't bothering with us.

Later in the afternoon, I managed to tip yet another pail and this time a small fishing knife tumbled out and hit my arm before falling to the ground at my feet. Jack turned at once and reached for my arm, but I pulled it back from him. I was bleeding. I could tell it wasn't deep, but it was going good. Jack picked up the knife and threw it into the hold where it wouldn't do more damage. In the meantime, one of the women who had laughed at me earlier, when the slime had spilled on me, pulled a clean piece of fabric out of the cloth bag she'd been holding between her feet. It looked like diaper fabric. She handed her bag to a girl about seven or eight and more or less pushed Jack out of the way and used the fabric to tie around my arm to stop the bleeding. She said something to the girl, who in response pulled a colorful shawl out of the bag. The woman, the girl's grandmother most likely, then made me a sling. She spoke to me soothingly in Portuguese all the while she was adjusting it on me, and by the time she was done I was nearly in tears and missing Maggie very much.

Eventually we saw the *Liliana*, tied to a dock protruding from a small sandy beach. The boat had two decks and looked plenty large enough to satisfy us one and all. As we approached, we saw that the people who had been on the *Liliana* were all on the beach, sitting alongside their possessions. One by one they got to their feet and began to pump their arms in the air and cheer. "They must have been waiting a long time," I whispered to no one. I was cradling my wounded arm. Between the sling and my eyepatch, I imagined I looked fierce, if somewhat clumsy. I imagined the hirers at Fordlândia would ask me what happened and I would tell them the details with good cheer, so they would know I wasn't a griper. Then I'd produce the recommendation letter from the librarian.

I looked up from my woolgathering and found Jack staring at me. "What?" I whispered.

"Nora love," he whispered. "I love you. Don't do this."

I could only stare at him. His whispered words connected me to a thousand pleasures of the past. I shuddered and looked away.

The people on the beach became even more animated as our launch pulled up to the dock. By the time Fausto had tied up, some of them were already making their way towards us. Fausto shouted in English and then in Portuguese that they would have to wait until his passengers disembarked, but they continued to come, yelling and pushing their way forward, and finally he darted into his little cabin and returned with his gun and fired into the air. Everyone quieted. Again he told the people from the *Liliana* they would have to wait their turn. He nodded to those of us on his boat that we should proceed.

I hung back. When I'd first come on board, Fausto identified two young men who would carry my trunk to the

272

Liliana for me, but they would do it last, he'd said, after the smaller crates were gone. There was a lot of shuffling about, people clamoring to get to their possessions and line up to depart down the gangplank. In the confusion, one of the men who had been on the beach, a white man in his fifties, managed to climb on board. He approached us straight away, Jack and me, perhaps because we were the only whites on Fausto's boat. "Not headed for Fordlândia, are you?" he asked in English.

"I am," I said before Jack could answer.

The stranger, who was clearly American, turned to Jack. "And you?"

"She's on her own."

"To teach," I added quickly.

By then the American's wife had managed to push her way on board as well, appearing just in time to hear the end of the conversation. She looked me up and down, taking in my eyepatch and makeshift sling and green-slimed trousers. "Don't go," she said. She slapped her hand on her heart and took a second to catch her breath. "It's the end of the world there."

I was immediately indignant. "I've spent time in the deep jungle, thank you very much. I know what to expect."

"Oh no you don't, sweetheart," she countered. She was short and pudgy, older than me though not as old as her husband. "The whole forest is burning."

I barked a laugh. "Of course it is. They're clearing it to—"

"No. Listen to me. The idiots couldn't get the trees to burn, because everything's still wet from the rains. So they poured kerosene on everything. The flames that went up after that! We couldn't sleep, Hank and me, because all night long you could hear the animals screaming, monkeys and jaguars and God knows what else, all being burnt to death and not so far from us! It was horrible. It was a nightmare. You could actually see the birds bursting into screaming balls of flame as they tried to fly away. Five days the forest burned. The sky was red, then black, then ash fell everywhere, like we were under a volcano! You know what that's like, when the whole world as far as you can see is covered by ash? When there's no color anywhere? When you can't take a breath without feeling something twist in your lungs? And everything dead silent for the simple reason everything *is* dead! And the smell! The end of the world. I couldn't wait to leave. I'll never go back. And when I get home I'm going to pray every day that I never live through anything like that again. It's changed me, by God, and not for the better."

The man put his hand on his wife's arm to calm her, but she shook him off. Her own hand remained on her heart, and her face remained an angry red. She caught her breath and was about to start up again when someone else appeared, a young man, perhaps eighteen or so. He took off his cap and wiped the sweat from his forehead with his handkerchief. "You telling them about the attacks?" he asked the pudgy woman. He was American too, maybe the couple's son.

"No," the woman said sarcastically. "The fires!"

"What attacks?" I managed.

"The people," he lowered his voice, "the *caboclos*, some of 'em went crazy. They weren't satisfied with conditions—"

"You wouldn't be satisfied either if you was them," the pudgy woman interrupted. She turned back to me. "We got houses, because we're all Dearborn and our job is operations. The workers, they got lean-tos with hammocks. No screens or nothing to keep mosquitoes out. Or if they were foremen, they got a sweltering hot bunkhouse with no ventilation. Half of them have malaria. Everything is filthy. There's no sanitation set up yet. They say it's coming, but it ain't there

274

now. They're throwing their waste in the creeks. You can't imagine the mosquitoes, the flies… I told Hank, I'm going home. If you don't want to come, good enough. That's your choice, but… Do you know some of them got families there living like that? One young woman had her baby snatched up by some bird of prey! The baby's all right now, but—"

"Enough," Hank interrupted.

I saw with the corner of my eye that Jack was watching me carefully. He looked sober enough, but I knew he was smirking on the inside. He let his gaze slide to the couple. "So you're both leaving for good?" he asked them. There was complicity in his tone. This was what he'd wanted all along: confirmation that the great Henry Ford—who would never understand the spirit of the jungle or the people it belonged to—would fail.

"Damn right we are. And all these people coming on board," the woman continued, turning to sweep her arm to indicate those still on the beach waiting for the departing passengers to finish moving their crates, "they're leaving too."

"The heavy equipment we were promised never arrived," Hank said dryly. "I'm supposed to oversee running it, but it never showed up. We had men half dead with fever clearing logs by hand. A few were bitten by Bushmasters, vipers six feet long with huge fangs." He spread his arms out to show us.

"Why is it all right for you to talk about Bushmasters and I can't say about the baby?" the woman interrupted. She was close to tears. "At least it didn't die."

Her husband ignored her. "Half of them bitten died before we could get them medical attention, because the Bushmaster will strike again and again, injecting more venom each time. Awful song to go out on."

"All that's a lot of bellyaching," the young man interrupted. He turned to address himself directly to Jack. "You got to expect snakes in the jungle, right? And vultures too. Ain't that so? The real problem is humans. Crazy humans, you don't expect. The people went off their nuts and attacked us. They decided they didn't like the meals they were being fed—"

"Everything covered in flies," chirped the pudgy woman, talking to me. "I wouldn't like it either."

"And so they rioted, with their machetes."

"They wouldn't have hurt anyone," the woman said. "I've told you that."

"They chased us into the forest, threatening to kill us. One of the bosses promised them good meat and better pay and got them to back off, but the tension didn't go nowhere, and who knows what will set them off next. I for one won't be there to find out."

"The place is cursed," the woman agreed. "If Ford has his way, he'll turn the whole jungle into one giant plantation. And his boy Edsel, saying Fordlândia is a sanitary campaign against the jungle? The cheek!" She shuddered.

Chaos had broken out on the deck, and we all turned to look. People were boarding with crates and trunks while others were still trying to disembark. Two men shouting in Portuguese looked very close to exchanging blows. Someone got in the middle and tried to calm them but then someone else came up from behind and started shouting at the do-gooder.

I was watching all this when Jack startled me by laying his hands on my shoulders and turning me towards him and speaking an inch away from my face so he would be heard above the fray. "You said in your note if I tried to interfere with your plans you'd never speak to me again. That's fine.

Don't fuckin speak to me. I can live with that. But I'm not letting you go to Fordlândia. I will pick you up and drape you over my shoulder and keep you there until this boat turns back. That's the way men do it here, you know. And you can stay angry with me for the rest of both our miserable lives, I don't give a bullocks." He jerked his head toward the American woman, who was now managing the placement of her trunk, which a couple of the *caboclos* had carried up for her. "She's right," he said. "Fordlândia is cursed."

I pushed him away from me. I was breathing so fast I was almost hyperventilating. Fausto approached just then, his finger extended in the direction of my trunk, his brows raised as if to ask whether I still wanted it moved to the *Liliana*. I answered his unspoken question, sharply, my eyes on Jack Hopper. "Take it!" I said. "My plans have not changed."

Fausto gave the signal and the two young men he'd appointed earlier lifted my trunk and began to move off with it. When Jack turned to look at them I said to his back, "You'll need a valise to get home. I meant to mention it before now."

He whipped back toward me. "If you insist on going, I'm coming with you," he said.

"You can't. You made a promise!"

I got behind the men who were carrying my trunk. Jack jerked forward, to get behind me, but just then Fausto appeared and pushed himself in front of Jack. He still had his gun. He didn't aim it at Jack, but he made sure Jack saw it, and next I knew two other young men, more of Fausto's helpers presumably, appeared on either side of Jack and grabbed his arms and jerked them up behind his back.

Everything quieted. Everyone had stopped shouting to watch the unfolding drama.

Everyone but me. I was crying, hard, but I forced myself to keep moving, down the gangplank. When I reached the beach I dared to look back. Jack was still struggling against the two men, twisting himself side to side to keep a watch on me. His face was red with anguish. Fausto was still standing there too, his gun at his side. Jack leaned far to the right, to catch my eye. "That's what's done me in all me miserable life," he cried. "Promises, Nora. All the fuckin promises I made."

35. Nora

LATER I ASKED THE captain of the *Liliana* if I could visit my trunk for clean clothes, but he said all the trunks and crates were locked away for security reasons; no one was allowed into the baggage area. And thus I spent the night in a hammock that smelled of all the bodies of all the people who had used it before me—and I came to believe the number was great, beyond comprehension—in clothing stained with blood and fish guts and my own body odors.

It began to rain in the middle of the night, hard. The boat rocked and my stomach twisted, but I didn't vomit, because I'd had nothing to eat or drink. I hadn't known to bring food, and no one invited me to share theirs. Moreover, my arm, which had not bothered me so much during the day, began to throb as the gray light of dawn pushed through the absolute darkness. I touched it. It felt twice its normal size.

It rained all day, dissolving the sight of even the banks we traveled between. No one spoke to me, but they spoke plenty amongst themselves, and the furrowed brows and somber expressions assured me that word about Fordlândia had spread and I was not the only one concerned.

By midday I was starving. Had my disposition been the same as when I'd first boarded Fausto's boat, I might have tried to charm one of the families nearest me into sharing just a bit of their bread, which they seemed to have in abundance. But a dark cloud had formed over me, as dark as the one that traveled along with our boat, and I found I preferred wallowing in my own misery to the prospect of filling my stomach. Anyway, the boat was still rocking some and the chance was great I would only be sick.

Bax had told Jack to tell me and Maggie he was dead and buried; I knew that now. That's what Jack had meant when he'd raged about his "fuckin promises." It hadn't occurred to me before, but now that he had spelled it out—or spit it out, as was the case—I realized it was precisely the sort of thing that Bax would do.

There was an incident years before, one I would never forget. Baxter Sr. had jammed his finger between two pieces of steel down at the docks, and when he removed his glove and saw how deep the laceration was, he asked permission to go to First Aid and get it wrapped so he could get back to work. But the nurse on duty—a German woman, the niece of one of the foremen—said he needed stitches and would have to go to St. Mary's. He fussed; he didn't want to leave work. But the nurse insisted, and he went. She had him come back the day after so she could ensure the swelling was going down, and then a week later he returned again so she could remove the stitches.

The First Aid station was located in a small room at the front of the Small Parts warehouse, and one day—a good month after the accident—Bax was sent to Small Parts to find a bucket of resin to waterproof something in the cargo hold of the ship he was loading. He had to go right past First Aid, and as the door was open, he looked in. He saw them in there, the nurse sitting at her desk and Baxter Sr. beside her, leaning over her, both of them looking into the other's eyes, with love and yearning, Bax said.

I was furious with Bax at first. How could he be sure what was going on in their heads? Baxter Sr. loved Maggie, heart and soul. He was as happy a married man as one could be. My own future happiness seemed to rest on the truth of that. But Bax insisted it was the look of love he'd seen on their faces. *How do you know the look of love?* I asked him, and he answered, *I know it well, for it's there on your own lovely face at times.* Besides, he added, what was his father doing in the nurse's office otherwise? His finger was healed. He had no business there.

Bax never confronted his father. And he made me promise to keep the matter to myself too. If word got back to Maggie, he said, it would crush her. And for what? Surely it was no more than a passing thing. We agreed Jack should not be told, that he could not be trusted with the information. But he found out anyway, because he was there with Bax some months later when Baxter Sr. came out of a burning apartment building all but carrying the German nurse.

Baxter Sr. had told Maggie he was working late that night, at the docks. But he'd been with her, the German lady, and they both died, her almost immediately and him later in the hospital, both from smoke inhalation. Bax made sure no one put it together that they'd been in the nurse's flat when the fire broke out. He told Maggie his father had told him— when he'd come out of the burning building, in the moments before he'd passed out—that he was on his way home from the docks when he saw the flames and ran in to save as many as possible. Bax painted him as a hero. And the next day he sent me to the house to make Jack promise he would never tell his mother otherwise. It took some doing, because Jack was upright in those days. But in the end I convinced him that truth had to bow to deception when deception had the power to comfort.

Knowing Bax had prompted the lie that Jack had told me did not make me any less angry. If anything, I was angrier than ever, at the both of them now. I was dizzy with all the anger swirling through me.

I was standing at the leeside rail, in the rain, which was light by then, cradling my arm and thinking what it would be like to climb overboard and drop into the river when I heard these words in my head: *And here you made this trip to find Bax.* The words came at me as if from someone else, though I didn't believe them for a minute. Jack had said Baxter was dead, and I'd never had reason to doubt him. But this much was also true: Since the night I'd learned what really happened, I'd been thinking to myself, *What if Bax is still alive? What would it be like to encounter him after all these years, here in the jungle?*

The speed of the boat changed; we were slowing down. Gradually the bank came into view, and with it a terrible sulfurous smell mixed with a pungent kerosene odor that stung my exposed eye. Eventually the people on the dock came into view too, a long line of them, all facing us as they waited for us to tie up so they could begin their journey back to Manáos.

Out of nowhere it came to me: I had been betrayed, by the boy I loved when I was a girl, and the man I loved when I became a woman, by my parents, who hadn't let me know I'd never see them again, and by my aunt, who couldn't wait to get on with her life, even if it meant leaving me behind in a drab boarding house. And how had I survived? By becoming an opportunist, perhaps at the cost of betraying myself.

What a wretched woman I was! Had I not married Jack to save myself from a life of bitterness and loneliness? I'd wanted a family, and so I took myself one.

I was no better than he was.

We were still too far away for me to see the faces of the people who had lined up to leave Fordlândia, but their resolve was evident in their collective posture. Their possessions were in piles at their feet, half sunk in mud. Beyond them I could see the vague outline of some structures, and beyond that some trees, spread apart, black and leafless, the dark gaps a betrayal to everything I had come to love about the jungle.

We have all been betrayed, I thought, *and we have all become betrayers.*

36. Jack

Jack was sitting in the hotel dining salon, working through his third glass of Cachaça, when the lobby door opened and Nora flew in. He'd been drunk, more or less, for three days running now, and at first he thought it was his mind playing tricks on him. What would Nora be doing here? Hadn't she gone to Fordlândia to live a life of nobility? This woman—she had to be an imposter—was filthy, wearing stained trousers and with her arm wrapped in a blood-stained scarf. Her hair was matted and there were streaks of dirt on her face. But no one else in Manáos had red hair, so it had to be her! He watched as she struggled to negotiate a room with the concierge. He wanted to call out to her—*Hey sweetheart, come and sit down and have a drink with me! You look like you could use one!*—but even in his inebriated state, he knew better.

Once she was given a key, Nora turned to the staircase and disappeared. A moment later, Isabella, the fortuneteller, pushed her way into the disorder of Jack's thoughts. *She'll be angry, but she'll get over it*, she said. Jack moved his glass aside. He sensed it was time for his binge to end.

Jack was busy packing his clothes in his room the next day when there came a knock on the door. "Come in," he said. He had his back to the door and his new cheap secondhand suitcase opened on the bed before him. He glanced over his shoulder to see Nora's head protruding from the doorway. "Since I'm the one wanting this breakup," she announced in a voice devoid of emotion, "I should be the one to leave the house. That's only fair."

Jack put down the shirt he'd been folding and turned to face her fully. Her hair was wet; she'd washed it. He'd been awake all night, willing her to come to his room and tell him she'd had a change of heart. It took all the restraint he could muster not to go to hers. And now she *had* come, finally, but only to confirm that nothing between them had changed. He found himself wondering if she would be able to procure a divorce. He wasn't a bigamist. He hadn't committed adultery, and she wasn't the type to lie and say he had. As far as he knew, there were no other circumstances under which a divorce could be obtained. "Nora, don't be foolish. I'll leave the house. I can get a room—"

"No," she snapped, "I'll be the one to leave. I insist. I can stay with Quinn," she said, referring to a friend who was a war widow.

"All right, that's swell," he said. And he might have said more, because her flare of anger had infected him and now he was angry too, but her head disappeared and the door closed, and he went back to packing. Not ten minutes later she knocked again.

This time she didn't wait for him to answer. She pushed the door open and said, "Actually, if you don't have any grievances about it, I may stay with your mum. Once she gets over the fact that we've gone our separate ways, she'll be pleased as Punch to have me around. I hope that won't present a conflict for you. I can be out when I know you're planning a visit."

"Whatever suits you, Nora."

She nodded. "Good," she said, and she closed the door.

The cheap valise he'd bought was not going to be big enough after all. He removed all the garments he'd already packed and laid them out on the bed and started over again, this time rolling each article of clothing into a tight sausage. He'd be dashed if he was going to go down the hall and ask her if he could share the fuckin trunk. He'd leave a few things behind first. He was glad to see he still had a lick of pride. He would find someone else to love him for whatever little time he might have left. Or go without. People did it all the time. Look at all the women who'd lost lovers to the war. They'd reconciled. Half of them found other women to love. Everyone found what they needed—or otherwise they just stopped looking. And there were always the brothels across the river. The reform laws had chased them underground along with the saloons, but that didn't mean they'd ceased to exist.

Not five minutes later there came yet another knock. "Come in," he said, and he hoped she heard the annoyance in his tone. He could only imagine what kind of beef she was planning to hit him with now. He continued to roll up his clothes, but after a few seconds of silence he straightened, and sighing more loudly than was polite in any circumstance, he turned, ready to take it on the chin, so to speak. But it wasn't Nora's head protruding from the doorway. "Louisa!" he gasped.

She marched in, and two other women followed behind her. Jack was so amazed that it took him a full minute to realize the last of the three was Bruna—his Bruna, with whom he'd spent a beautiful night once so long ago, all grown up, with a well-padded middle and a bum to match, but still a beauty in her way.

"Jack," Bruna said, tearing up, gripping the handle of her purse with both hands. "It really is you!" She spoke in Portuguese. "I was certain you were dead. But you made it home somehow. And you got better! And now you're back!" She stepped forward and hugged him awkwardly with one arm, and since he only stood there stiffly, unable to make sense of the moment, she quickly stepped away again. He glanced beyond her. He wanted to ask her to please shut the door but it seemed an inappropriate request at that moment, and it would have seemed even more inappropriate for him to sidle between her and Louisa and the other woman and close it himself.

All three women were dressed up, wearing the fuller skirts and longer hemlines that Nora had packed away years ago. All wore their hair pulled back tightly, mostly hidden under their hats. Louisa's and Bruna's hats featured feathers that stuck straight up into the air, and the other woman—he realized now it was the same young woman who'd waited on them in the café where he'd recognized Louisa that first day in Manáos—wore a bonnet with a lot of stiff netting sitting on top like a bird's nest too jumbled to be useful.

Louisa broke the spell with her trademark laughter. "You must be wondering how we found you, Jack, dear," she said in English.

He smiled stupidly. She hadn't known English twenty years ago. He wanted to ask her about it, but three days of hard drinking followed by a night of sleeplessness had rendered him speechless.

"A man and his lady came in at the restaurant where I work some weeks back," Louisa said, reverting back to Portuguese. "Estela here..." (she indicated the young

287

woman) "...waited on them. He resembled you, but I thought, No, can't be Jack Hopper. Poor old Jack is dead and gone. And even if he's not dead, why would he come back here? And if he did come back, wouldn't he want to say hello to me? Of course he would! So I gave up the idea as quickly as I'd taken it on. But then we heard there was a woman down at the docks, asking one of the captains about passages to Fordlândia, that place on the Tapajós where the American with too much money and not enough brains is making the rubber farm, and someone said she'd called herself Mrs. Jack Hopper."

"What's this?"

Everyone turned to see Nora standing in the hall with one hand on her hip and the other holding one of Jack's shirts. She dangled it from her finger, as if it were a dirty thing. It had gotten mixed in with her things in the trunk apparently. There was a rustling of skirts as Louisa and Estela moved to the left and Bruna moved to the right and Nora stepped into the space they'd created and closed the door behind her. Jack closed his eyes. This could not end well.

"I heard them say my name. Tell me what's going on."

He found his tongue. "Remember I told you about the friends who hid me when I came to meet with Abalo? And then again, when I came through the last... They put me on the ship that brought me home."

"This is them? Why are they talking about me?"

"They only said they heard there was a Mrs. Jack Hopper down at the docks, that that was how they found me. They're here to say hello."

"Why didn't they keep you longer and nurse you back to health before they put you on that ship?" she snapped. "Ask them that, would you? Why did they put you on the first ship that came along when you were practically..."

He didn't know how to tell Nora that at least one of the women spoke English and knew what she was saying. "I insisted, Nora. I explained this to you. Abalo would have killed them, or hurt them somehow, if he learned they were hiding me." He looked at Louisa, then at Bruna, then at Nora again. "But this is not the time for such a discussion."

Nora clamped her lips and jutted her chin with indignation, but she took a conciliatory step back and leaned against the door. Her arms were crossed; her wound was only bandaged now, her arm no longer in a sling—though she was still wearing her eyepatch.

Louisa and Bruna looked at her and then at each other. They seemed baffled now that she'd made her grand entrance. Finally Louisa spoke, louder and more formally than before, and in perfect English. "Well, of course we had to see you, Jack Hopper. I hope you don't mind. We had to see for ourselves that you were alive and well."

Jack moved to Louisa and embraced her fully. "I'm not myself," he said by way of apology for his poor manners. "My wife and I have had some…" He looked at Nora, with her patch and bandaged arm. It dawned on him that they'd think he'd beaten her. He almost laughed. He moved to Bruna, and this time he embraced her properly. "It's lovely to see you again after all these years. You're as beautiful as ever." He turned to the young woman, Estela, and took her gloved hand in both of his. "Very good to meet you, my dear." Estela curtsied.

Louisa placed her palm on the side of Jack's face. "Ah, Jack, you came back here looking for your brother, didn't you?" she said, switching back to Portuguese. "I knew you would one day."

He nodded.

"What's she saying?" Nora asked softly. "Why doesn't she speak English?"

Louisa ignored her. "You learned what happened then?"

"I know he's dead," Jack lamented in Portuguese. "I don't guess I told you much last time I saw you because of how sick I was, but we'd become friendly with a tribe of Indians. They were captured... And my stubborn brother got it in his thick skull he could somehow rescue them. Him and a few women, against a great number of butchers working for..." He hesitated. He wondered if she knew her former employer had been involved in the massacre.

Louisa sighed. "You don't know then," she said. She turned to look at Bruna. They stared at each other with their eyebrows lifted. Louisa turned back to Jack. "Ah, Jack, I never imagined I should be the one to tell you. That tribe, yes. And others. Horrible what happened. Those who survived, you will see them working as boat paddlers, or if they're women, whoring. You can tell them by their scars, whiplashes, and missing fingers. And worse. Much worse, if we had the time. But your brother didn't die with them, thank God at least for that."

"You don't mean to say he's alive?" Jack whispered, his heart crashing up against his ribs.

"What's going on, Jack?" Nora asked.

"Oh, Jack, how I wish I could say so." Louisa looked at Bruna, hard, and Bruna shook her head fiercely, as if to say, *No, not me.*

Louisa took a deep breath. She turned to the side and looked at the bed. Jack quickly gathered the loose clothing and threw it in the suitcase and made a place for her to sit. She sat heavily and took another breath. "There's no easy way to speak of such matters." She sighed again. "He showed up here."

"Here? What do you mean?"

"He showed up at the house, at Abalo's. A few weeks after we put you on the steamer and sent you on your way.

I answered the door but I never got to say a word to him. Abalo was expecting a lady friend that evening, a married one who didn't want her activities made public, so he got to the door same time as me. When he saw it was your brother, he shouted, *How dare you show yourself here?* Your brother, he started raving, saying Abalo and his men were murderers, and Abalo backed up to the cabinet where he keeps his gun and pulled it out and shot him dead, straight to the heart. Just like that. It was over in seconds. He had me run for a blanket, and he covered him up, and when his lady friend arrived not a moment later, he had her step over him."

Nothing she had said made sense to Jack. They were words with no significance. He wanted to ask her to say it all again, but he couldn't formulate the request. Louisa stood up and took his arm. "Jack, it was fast. He felt no pain. I was there. I can promise you that. Jack? Jack, are you all right?"

"Jack?" screeched Nora. She was trembling and close to tears. She moved forward, and Jack wondered if she would come to him too, but she didn't. "Jack, what's happened? What did she tell you?"

"He came back for me," he whispered in Portuguese, to no one in particular. "And I was gone."

"Maybe he did and maybe he didn't," Louisa said. "No one will ever know."

Bruna stepped to his side and took his other arm.

"Please tell me what's going on," Nora begged.

Jack glanced at her, but he couldn't explain.

The moment froze, as if it were a photograph, Louisa and Bruna holding on to him, their faces full of petition, Nora crying softly by the door, and Estela, her eyes downcast, as still as a statue in the middle of it all. Finally he managed to lift his head and glance at Nora. "She loved him too," he said to the others.

Louisa and Bruna scrunched their faces sympathetically in Nora's direction, but neither moved.

"Was he properly buried?"

Louisa squeezed her eyes tight, then opened them again. "Abalo's men took him to the river."

"What did she say?" Nora asked. "I know it's about Bax. Why are you not telling me?"

"I'll tell you once they're gone," he mumbled. He shook his head hard and added, speaking to Louisa and Bruna, "I knew he was gone. I've known it for years. Yet hearing how... Learning that he'd come back for me..."

"You don't know that, Jack," Louisa said again. "More likely he came back to challenge Abalo, and Abalo got him first."

A minute passed. Then Louisa let go of his arm and looked at Bruna. "I think we should go now, dear. I think we should leave him alone with his wife." Bruna quickly nodded in agreement and stepped away.

"We had more to say," Louisa began, turning back to Jack, "but we'll come back tomorrow or the day after, when you've had time to think about all this." She patted his arm. "We've upset you enough for now."

"There is no tomorrow," Jack managed. "Tomorrow we leave for New York, first thing in the morning."

Louisa sighed. "Well, you've answered our question then. You're still in New York."

"Across the river, yes."

"I remember. Hoboken. That's what we thought. When we realized you were here, we thought we should bring Estela."

The young lady bent one knee and curtsied once again.

Louisa placed her hand on Estela's shoulder. "This is surely not the right time to mention, but maybe, as we won't get a chance to see you again..."

Jack nodded encouragingly, though he didn't know what she was talking about.

Louisa hesitated and began again. "Estela, as you know, works at the restaurant with me, but her dream, since she was a little girl, is to be a singer at the opera. She attends music school daily, in a special program that takes place in the vestibule of the opera house. She's very talented, everyone says so, and very brave too. And so, like many who are talented and brave, and maybe a little crazy in the head, she wants to go to New York and be part of your big opera there." She looked at Estela with pride and love. "You wouldn't think such a snip of a thing could have such a powerful voice. Anyway, when we heard you were here, we considered you were probably still living in New York, and we thought you might give her your address, in case she has any trouble. We know no one in New York. We don't even know anyone else in your country. Estela is saving her money and hoping to leave in a few months. She won't be a bother to you. She's not like that. I'm sorry to be telling you all this when you've had such a shock. But we're worried about her of course, living in a strange country, and—"

"What are they saying, Jack?" Nora asked. She had stopped crying and was using his shirt to dab at her good eye.

Jack had only taken in the essentials, but he got the gist of it. He moved to the bureau and found a scrap of paper and a pencil. His hands were shaking and he could hardly write. To Louisa he said, "Tell her to contact me when she arrives. I can help her find safe lodging. No, second thought, tell her to write as soon as she has an arrival date. I'll find a room, a boarding house with other young women, before she even arrives. That way..." He saw his brother floating in the river, bloated, like the caiman he and Nora had seen when they'd first come to Manáos. He stopped speaking and waited for the image to dissipate. He looked at Nora, who seemed to be mumbling to herself. "The young woman sings opera," he said in English. "She's coming to New York and may need our... My help."

"She's familiar," Nora whispered.

"The first day. She waited on us in the café down at the docks." He folded the scrap of paper and handed it to Estela. She curtsied again.

"They didn't have trouble arranging for her to travel?" Nora asked. It was no secret that the darker one's skin the less chance one had of being permitted to emigrate. That was one of the causes that Nora had been championing back home. She'd even written a letter to C.C. Brigham, the professor of psychology at Princeton who was determined to get everyone on board with his belief that dark-skinned people were stupid and shouldn't be allowed into the country. He'd never answered her, but the local newspaper had reprinted her letter, stirring up a controversy in town.

Louisa took a breath, and addressing herself to Jack in Portuguese, she said, "Her birth record shows her father is American. That helped." She cleared her throat and turned to face Bruna. "Tell him," she said, lifting her chin. Bruna's face darkened and she looked down at the floor. Louisa stepped beside her and put her hand on her friend's back. "Go ahead," she coaxed. "This is the only chance you'll ever get."

When Bruna looked up her eyes were wet. She bit her lip. "Estela," she said, as if that explained everything. "My husband was good to her while he was alive. He was a father to her. Still. When we heard..."

Jack could hear Nora insisting on a translation in the background. She spoke softly, as if something essential to her spirit had abandoned her. He reached out a hand and found the edge of the bureau and used it to balance himself.

"You mean to say...?"

Bruna and Louisa nodded solemnly. Estela kept her head tipped, her eyes on the floor.

Jack's throat went dry and his legs began to grow rubbery, and when they could no longer support his weight, he dropped to his knees. For a moment no one moved. Then Estela stepped in front of him and put her hand lightly on his head. Her touch overwhelmed him, and he lifted his hand to cover his eyes and began to sob.

"What?" Nora was screaming now. "What is happening?"

All at once Jack was surrounded by taffeta, the rustling skirts of the three women, Louisa and Bruna and Estela, tightening in around him, their hands on his head and shoulders. "I've botched everything," he wailed. He wrapped his arms around his daughter's knees and sobbed into her skirts, soaking the front of her dress with his grief.

37. Jack

JACK GOT UP AT dawn and hurried up the hill to the opera house, the once great Teatro Amazonas. The concierge had known about the students who practiced there and had advised him of the time she thought they began when he'd inquired the night before. Now he stood at a distance, near the monument in the square across the way, and watched as the students started to arrive. He didn't see Estela, and he began to worry she might be part of a second group that came later. But then there she was—if he was not mistaken; it was hard to be certain from where he stood—running up the grand staircase to the lobby.

He sat down on a bench and closed his burning eyes. He hadn't slept at all, for two nights in a row now, and the fatigue he felt was crushing. His head spun in circles all through the night, and it was spinning now. Among his many thoughts was the realization that his ship would be leaving soon, was probably fully boarded already. The concierge had promised to have someone carry his valise down for him ahead, when they came for Nora's trunk. Still, if he wanted, he told himself for the hundredth time, he could stay behind. But where would he stay? He was very nearly out of money. And how would he get home?

These questions had answers, surely, but he couldn't work his way through the logistics of them.

Eventually he began to hear music, and only then did he get up from the bench and cross the square and climb the staircase. He inched open not the main door in front but, as there were several to choose from, a door all the way to the right, and the sounds grew louder. When he'd been there before, on the day he and Nora arrived in Manáos, the doors had been locked. Now his instincts had served him well. The door he found himself peering through opened into a small cubicle, which opened into the great lobby by way of an archway. He could easily listen without being seen.

He peeked out. The student musicians, maybe thirty of them, were tuning their instruments: oboes, English horns, clarinets, flutes, violins, a viola, a cello, a bass. The instructor, a small man with thick white hair, nodded as he watched them. Jack didn't see his daughter anywhere, and he began to worry again that this was not her group after all. In addition to the musicians, a number of students sat on the floor in front of them. He looked them over carefully. Estela was not among them either. *How were children in this poor community able to afford such instruments?* he wondered, and he concluded the music school had a sponsor, someone not from Manáos.

"*Todos prontos?*" the instructor asked when it was finally quiet. His students nodded. He picked up his baton. The students playing clarinets and oboes and flutes and horns lifted their instruments to their mouths. They began quietly, evoking a setting that filled the grand lobby of the Teatro Amazonas as softly as a dream. Then came the strings.

The lobby was immense, with marble floors and columns and frescoes and statues and elaborate woodwork on the ceiling and huge chandeliers. Everything needed painting, refreshing, or in the case of the marble, cleaning, but Jack could well imagine what the place had been like in its heyday. He thought of the great hopes the city had had back then for its lovely opera house, for the people who would come to see performances as the rubber industry flourished. That hadn't worked out, but at least the lobby was being put to good use.

He closed his eyes—so sore from too much Cachaça and too little sleep—for just a moment, to better enjoy the music, to think about what it would be like to hear it in the actual theater. The students were good. It was easy to imagine he was listening to seasoned adults. He was drifting into a dream when heard a female voice and opened his eyes and peeked around the archway. And there was his daughter, Estela, standing between the musicians and her classmates, off to the side so as not to block the musicians' view of the instructor. She began softly, singing in Italian. She was wearing a sleeveless, shapeless white shift that fell to just below her knees, so unlike the long taffeta skirts and stiff bonnet from the day before. She was almost too beautiful to look at, painfully beautiful, with her dainty chin and her wide dark eyes, her wavy black hair tumbling down her back, her small delicate hands clasped in front of her as she sang something sad, very sad. *Saudade*—it was a word he had learned from the *cabaclos* he'd traveled with twenty years earlier—a sadness so extreme, so exquisite, it defied a precise translation.

Her lament changed pace, growing sadder yet, and louder too, her voice filling the lobby, her expression so doleful it took up all the space in his heart. Every note was perfection. He'd never heard anything like it, not from someone so young, not from anyone. Although she was singing in Italian, it was close enough to Portuguese that he could pick up a few words. He thought she was singing about a tree, a willow. He was all but ignorant when it came to opera. He'd gone to the Metropolitan Opera across the river with Nora once, to celebrate her birthday. But he didn't remember anything about the performance. The truth was he'd slept through part of it. What he remembered was that it had been a glorious night. Nora had been so happy. She'd pressed herself close to him on the ferry on the way home and he couldn't stop thinking about how much he loved her.

Jack felt tears welling up, and he didn't know how much was his daughter's sad song and how much was the memory of what Nora's love felt like when it was at its peak and how much was simply his eyes, sizzling with white-hot pain.

Estela's soprano was strong, full of range. She let her body sway with the music, his little girl, herself a willow. She pressed her hands together tighter and lifted them to her throat and lifted her eyes to the ceiling, praying with her body and her face and her voice for things to be different than they were. He felt her every movement in his heart, her every emotion, her defeat in the face of tragedy. Then she lifted her voice to reach an even higher note, one overflowing with lament, and in that second there was another sound, a short, sharp wail. It had come from behind one of the cubicles on the opposite end of the lobby, across from him. Everyone in the audience glanced in that direction and then quickly turned back to Estela.

It was Nora, fleeing. She must have passed right by him, when he'd been sitting on the bench, resting his eyes in the plaza. She'd turned so fast he wouldn't have known it was her if he hadn't caught a glimpse of her carrot-colored hair. The only redhead in Manáos, he thought, chuckling to himself.

The evening before, after the women left, she sat on the edge of his bed and listened while he told her what Louisa had told him, about Bax, and what he had just learned about Estela. She stared ahead with her visible eye wide and unfocused the entire time. When he was done, she got up and drifted to the door and left the room, as quiet as a ghost.

He turned his attention back to his daughter. He could think later about what it meant that Nora had been there too. What he wanted now was to fill himself with Estela, to breathe in enough Estela to last until she came to New York. She would be brilliant in New York. All the city would fall to its knees before her, as he had the day before. And he would be there to savor her success, going to her every performance, her every rehearsal. Their lives would overlap. They had to; she was his daughter.

Estela lowered her hands over her heart, one on top of the other, then she turned just slightly, and all at once she was looking right at him, singing to him. Had she known all along he was there? He stepped out where he could be seen and stared back at her boldly. She was the best thing that had ever happened to him, and he knew he would treasure this moment for the rest of his life.

No one else noticed him standing there. All eyes were on Estela, or in the case of the musicians, on their music. The song was ending. She shifted once again, to face her audience of fellow students more directly. She dropped her hands to her side, a gesture of utter helplessness. As the last notes played, she tipped her head and looked at the floor. Her posture was the essence of *saudade*. He wondered if her life had been one of great sorrow, because no one could mirror such complicated and heavyhearted emotions so perfectly, no one could act them so well. But then when the last notes of music were dying away, when the last violin string had almost ceased vibrating and the lobby was just about dead silent, and the students were just in the process of lifting their hands to applaud, in that one solemn fragment of a second, his daughter, his Estela, broke into a Charleston—a step forward, a kick, a step back, a back kick—and everyone, including the white-haired teacher, laughed.

It was a relief to laugh after so much *saudade*. Even Jack, who'd lost everything—his wife, his brother, all the years he could have been loving Estela if only he'd known she existed— laughed. He bit his lip and wiped his burning, tearing eyes with the back of his hand and glanced once more at her, hoping to catch her eye one last time. But she was engaged now, talking to other students, her hand on the shoulder of a young man who had risen to his feet with sheet music in his hand. He looked at his watch.

He had exactly eight minutes to get to the docks.

38. Jack

THERE WERE TWO VERY small cabins aft on the lower deck set up for single women to share, and Nora stayed in one of them with an elderly woman who needed a cane to get around, while Jack stayed in a triple on the lower bow with two other men. When he approached Nora in the dining salon the first night, hoping she would sit with him, she introduced him to her cabin mate—whose name he didn't catch—and then got away from him as quickly as possible. He dined with a group of businessmen who had all bought land on the Tapajós, thinking that the values would soar as Fordlândia got underway. Now they were even more jazzed than they had been when they'd first invested because there was a rumor afloat that Ford, whose deal with the government of Amazonas required that he plant only one thousand rubber trees on the more than two million acres granted to him, was really not interested in rubber at all. Rubber was a coverup, people were saying, because Ford knew the land concealed oil and gold, and he intended to extract both. The businessmen were so animated they could hardly contain themselves. Jack ate as quickly as possible and excused himself and went up on the promenade deck to smoke his pipe and nurse his immense *saudade*.

On the second night out, as the ship was passing the lights of Santarém, Jack was startled from his reverie by a hand that came out of the dark and clasped his wrist. He turned to see Nora standing beside him, in tears. "What is it?" he asked.

"I was thinking," she said, "about what Bax would have made of the world we live in, so different from the way things were back then. You think he would have liked it? Vacuums that plug into the wall? Spin dryers? Toasters?"

"He would have liked Charlie Chaplin," Jack said flatly.

"You're probably right about that, but what of the rest of it? I'm talking about the bigger picture." Nora was agitated. Jack had to step back to keep her spittle from hitting his face. "Look at Lindbergh, Jack. How long until anyone with money can get on an airplane and fly across the country? You think he would have liked that, or you think he would have hated it?" She stepped closer and took hold of his lapels and shook him lightly. "Why, Jack? Why didn't he think of me? Why didn't he leave with you?" She barked an unhappy laugh. "I guess I didn't mean that much to him after all."

He couldn't think how to answer. He seemed to be stuck on Charlie Chaplin, on picturing Bax laughing out loud during a showing of one of his films. It wasn't that long ago that he and Nora had gone to see *The Gold Rush* in a theater across the river. Bax would have loved that. His laughter would have boomed out over the sound of everyone else. He would have been slapping his knee, bending forward in tears laughing. He would have talked about it for days. He would have told all the boys down on the docks. Nora was still staring at him, waiting for a response, apparently. "He was only a boy," Jack said.

She held onto him a moment longer, her one visible eye wild in its socket, then she turned and began walking toward the passageway that led to her cabin. "Nora," he called after her, but that only made her walk faster.

That night Jack lay in his berth listening to the snores of his two companions and thinking how he might have answered differently. He should have talked about how thoroughly Bax had lost himself after Leon's death and Ted's disappearance. He'd lost his mind; that was the truth of it. And the Gha-ru gave it back to him again, though it wasn't the same as it had been. Still, they gave him purpose. They were an irresistible force, and Jack might have fallen under their spell himself if he hadn't been so sick.

He wondered what had brought Bax back to Manáos in the end. Maybe he thought he could get Abalo to understand the evil he was doing and give it up. Or maybe he *had* come to kill Abalo and see if that would bring the atrocities to an end. The last time Jack had seen Abalo, when he'd gone to argue for their wages, Abalo had said if he showed his face again, he'd kill him. In Abalo's mind, one brother was the same as the other; he didn't see a difference between them. Jack had been over the possibilities a hundred times, a thousand times, in the last few days—and nights. He still couldn't sleep more than an hour or two at a time. Instead he drifted through questions that had no answers, often with Estela singing in the background. He didn't want to live that way anymore, sleepless, hopeless. He wanted to pinch some joy from life.

When he finally fell asleep that night, he dreamed he was explaining to Nora everything, the whole story all over again. But in the dream he was brilliant. He described every event precisely, and he could see by her expression that she finally understood how it had been, how Bax could not have done other than stay behind and how he could not have changed Baxter's decision. But when he awoke in the morning, he couldn't remember a single word of his skillful narrative.

The following evening Nora wasn't at supper. He thought of knocking on her cabin door to make sure she was all right. But he'd seen her companion dining with a few other women, and as they had been engaged in a cheerful conversation, he concluded that Nora was fine and would not want to be bothered.

The next day, though, he saw her in the morning, standing out on the promenade deck looking out at the jungle. When she saw him staring, from some twenty feet away, she lifted her hand, but then she went back to eyeing the view and he decided again to leave her alone. They'd been like that, standing in their places, for several minutes, when their ship turned a bend in the river and a large steamer came into view, being pulled by a tugboat. It was heading toward them, which was not a problem as there was more than enough room for the vessels to pass on the wide river.

As the steamer got closer, Jack saw that it carried a steam shovel, tractors, stone crushers, concrete mixers, prefabricated building materials, even a railroad car. A whole city could be built from what was there. It could only be the shipment that Hank, the American from the *Liliana*, had been talking about, the one expected months earlier. When Jack looked away from the spectacle, eager to catch Nora's eye, he realized that lots of people had come out on deck to watch the barge go by. Some of them were cheering and pumping their fists. More investors, no doubt. Who else would want Fordlândia to succeed? He continued to look for Nora but he couldn't find her in the crowd.

On the sixth night out on the river she appeared at his side again after supper and leaned back against the rail. "I'm not sleeping," she said flatly.

"I'm not either."

"I keep going over it again and again. If only you'd waited. A few more weeks. You would have left together. I know you couldn't have known, and I know you were sick, but I wish you hadn't left him behind."

She was relentless, and Jack had had enough. "Did I leave him, or did he leave me, Nora?" He looked her straight in the eye. He'd never felt so disregarded, so scorned. "And why is this always about you anyway? Why is it always *your* loss?"

A few people who had been chatting nearby glanced at him and moved off. He'd spoken loudly, but he couldn't stop himself. "He was my brother." He drummed his chest with his knuckles. "We slept all our lives in the same room. We caught each other's colds. We listened to each other snore and fart. He heard me when I cried. I heard him when he got pissed and couldn't calm himself, when he punched the mattress and a few times the wall. We were like one in that way. We were different but we understood how the other ticked as well as we understood ourselves. We shared secrets now and then; and now and then we couldn't stand the bloody sight of each other. But it was all swell, because we knew our blood was thick as mud. Right up until the jungle, it was swell and we both knew it, whether we were fighting or not, we both knew if it came to it, we would die for each other. That's what we had. That's what I lost, in case you're interested."

Nora took a step back. He'd frightened her, and he was glad. "You can say I left without him, or you can say he abandoned me, put me on a boat more dead than alive with a man he knew to be evil—on the slim chance he wouldn't throw my sopping, miserable self overboard for the piranhas to pick apart—and assumed I would somehow find my way back to New York on my own. Maybe he came back because he regretted leaving me that way. Or maybe he saw the hopelessness of trying to save the Gha-ru and decided to come home after all. Or maybe he came to kill Abalo. We'll never know what was in his mind, will we?"

He turned toward the rail, but then he had another thought and turned back.

"And how do you think I felt returning without him, Nora? I was guilty out of my mind for carrying a torch for you all my miserable fuckin bullocks of a life. Since we were kids I hoped and prayed you and Bax would break it off and somehow you'd see I was the one… Then when he didn't come back with me, it felt like I'd made it happen somehow, like it was my fault, like I caused it by wanting you so bad. But I didn't ever want this, Nora. I never wanted to lose him. I would rather have done without you a million times over than see anything bad happen to him. He was first; he was my brother. I need you to hear for once and all what I'm saying to you. I am sick of hearing about your loss in a way that disregards mine. So leave me alone. Gnawing at me about how God-awful it's been for you is not going to change a thing. It's not going to bring him back."

Nora opened her mouth to respond but before she could he caught another wind. "I don't want you to talk to me anymore about this. I've got things to work out in my head, not about the past either. I'm done with the past. I've been living with the past ever since Bax put me over his shoulder and carried me to Magnânimo's boat. I have to go forward now. I have a daughter. I have to think about how to be a father. I don't want you to distract me." He turned his back to her, to relight his pipe and to give her the moment she needed to stomp off, which is what she did.

And it was true; he couldn't stop thinking about Estela, about how it would be when she arrived. He was already concerned he would somehow alienate her, the way he had alienated his wife. He hadn't thought to ask for her address, but he was sure he could find her easily enough. He would write to her in care of the café where she and Louisa worked. He planned to write the moment he got home. He would tell her not to wait, to come at once, that she had a grandmum who'd be giddy with joy when she learned about her. No need to look for lodging. She would have her own room in his house. She could take the ferry into Manhattan when she needed to be there. Surely that would put Bruna's mind at ease too.

He'd been thinking as well about a dog. He'd always wanted a dog himself, a big one, one that looked like a wolf. But whenever he imagined one, he wondered if Estela might prefer something small that would curl up in her lap like a cat. Or maybe she'd simply prefer a cat! Whatever pleased her. *How do you know she likes animals?* he'd asked himself several times already. The answer was there in the little dance with which she'd ended her aria. She liked everything. She loved life.

He felt like an old woman, unable to stop blubbering with emotion. Sometimes it was all he could do to keep from interrupting his investor cabin mates—who spoke endlessly of the riches that would soon befall them—to tell them about his own riches. *Ha!* he wanted to shout, *You fellars think you got lucky? You don't know the half of it!* But then he would remember that his wife had left him. Nora, whom he had loved nearly all his life.

He went to supper early the next night, because he didn't want to see Nora. Now that his anger had finally come to the surface, he realized it felt better than any of the other emotions he'd experienced regarding her recently. It was precise; it had a target. He ate at a corner table with four strangers, none of whom said a single word. When he was done, he hurried up on deck. It had stormed violently hours earlier, but now it was clear, and the setting sun filled the sky and the water with a thick golden light. He lit his pipe and watched the honey-gold fade to silver and then vanish into the darkness, and he found to his immense surprise that he was at peace.

39. Nora

IT WAS THE LAST night on the great river. In the morning we would be stopping in Belém to pick up more passengers and then heading out into open seas. To celebrate, the captain announced during supper that music would be played on the phonograph in his cabin and several loudspeakers along the promenade deck would broadcast it out to the river, the jungle and beyond. We were leaving our mark, he said, making sure the jungle remembered us as much as we would remember her. He wanted everyone to drink, dance, and be merry. "After all," he reminded us, "Prohibition awaits." We laughed uneasily and raised our glasses.

The night was spectacular; the moon was nearly full, and it cast a soft silver glow on the water and the banks of the jungle in the distance. The temperature was perfect, and there were neither clouds in the sky nor thunder grumbling in the distance. Leaning over the rail, I could see the silhouettes of the dolphins swimming at the side of the ship, and it reminded me of the stories Jack had told me about how jazzed he and Bax had been seeing them for the first time all those years ago. I could picture the two of them, hanging off the side of the boat, shouting and laughing, having not the faintest idea of the misfortunes that lay ahead.

It took me a moment to find Jack, because he was standing at some distance from the crowds who'd already come outside to wait for the music to begin so they could dance. He was smoking his pipe and looking out over the river when several seconds of harsh static erupted from the ship's loudspeakers. Then, as promised, the speakers began to blast music, the first tune of which was Gene Austin's "Bye Bye Blackbird."

I wanted to dance. I'd been miserable for days, but somehow my misery abated some once I knew there was to be music. Part of it might have been the eyepatch, which I removed before supper when I realized the bite had finally healed. The skin was lighter in the area where it had been, but it had to be an improvement over the black pirate patch on my pale white face. I'd changed my outfit too. I'd worn a plain green shift to supper, but I'd returned to the cabin and changed into a white sleeveless dress with a pale blue sash at the hips. A string of pearls—Jack had bought them for me years ago—was knotted and hung down to my waistline.

The song ended and then the static came again, and then the "Baltimore Buzz." Ragtime. Even though the tune had nothing in common with opera, I thought of Estela, her lovely voice, her casual embodiment of grace and beauty. I wondered if she had a radio in her home, or a phonograph. It was possible she and her mother didn't even have electricity. The past could not be changed, Jack had said; he was looking forward now, to the future. He had his daughter to think of. He didn't want me to distract him.

Someone tapped my arm lightly, a fingertip, and I turned to see a man about my age. He was my height too, and a bit overweight. He wore a handlebar mustache, and a wool cap, which, on a night like this, could only mean he was bald and intent on hiding it. His light-colored eyes were cheerful, and he seemed like a swell enough fellow. "I've seen you in the dining hall," he said, smiling. He tapped the skin above his eye. "I almost didn't recognize you now, without the patch. You're traveling alone, yeah?"

I faltered. I was alone but I wasn't alone, because Jack was on the same boat and I was never not aware of him. Jack, who had his daughter to think of now. He'd been there that morning just before we boarded, at the opera house, too. I'd seen him peeking out to look at her from the opposite end of the lobby. "Yes, alone, mostly," I said vaguely.

He ignored the fact that mine was a non-answer. "And what brought you to Manáos? It seems a long way for a lady traveling on her own."

"My daughter," I answered. I almost laughed; I had no idea why I'd said that. "She's staying with friends in Manáos," I continued, "but she'll be coming home soon."

The song ended and there was more static, and then Mamie Smith singing "Crazy Blues." People were still pouring out of the dining hall and dancers were everywhere now. I looked in the direction where Jack had been but I couldn't see him. He had probably returned to his cabin, miserable recluse that he was.

"Lovely night," the stranger said.

"It is," I agreed, and I turned instinctively toward the rail to look at the moonlight on the river. The stranger turned too, and we stood like that for a moment, side by side, leaning forward with our elbows on the rail, smiling indecisively and saying nothing. I remembered how enticing the river looked to me that rainy day on the *Liliana*. For a few short moments I'd wanted oblivion, and the river seemed to offer it.

"What's your name, if you don't mind me asking?"

"Nora."

"Nora, that's lovely. I'm Scott." He cleared his throat. "Nora, would you care to dance?"

"Why, all right," I managed. "Why not?"

I offered him my hand and he led me away from the rail. But just at that moment a couple dancing nearby moved off and I glimpsed Jack, all the way down at the end of the deck, almost to the stern, as far away from the commotion as he could possibly get. If I was not mistaken, he was looking back at me.

My companion lifted my hand to his shoulder and I turned toward him, but not to dance. "I'm very sorry," I said. I waved a finger in Jack's direction. "I see someone I know. I must speak to him."

Confusion registered on his face. "Thank you, though, Scott," I added, already moving away. "Thank you very much."

I watched Jack watch me approach. I had always loved the way he looked at me, unequivocally and with a kind of solemn admiration, as if I was something special, something exotic stepping out from the shadows and into his view and not the too tall, too thin, flour-faced old bird I actually was. Part of me wanted to pick up our argument where we'd left it, with him saying I was a distraction, because he had a daughter. The other part of me wanted to tell him I thought I had come to understand the meaning of closure these last days, though I wasn't certain.

I took a final step and landed right in front of him, face to face. I was feeling bold but nervous too, and I found myself playing with my beads, gently pulling them from side to side at the back of my neck. I made myself stop.

"What?" he said.

"Baxter told you to say he'd died, didn't he? Because he thought it would be better for me and your mum. That's what you meant by promises—"

"That slipped. I didn't mean it to come flying out of my mouth. I'm sorry for that. I've made my apologies to him too, wherever the hell he is." He chuckled unhappily.

"It was wrong of him to put that burden on you, to force you to lie."

He looked surprised. "He was a boy. I was a boy." He tilted his head. "Nora, do you love him yet, after all this time?"

I took a moment before I answered. I wanted to be sure what I said was true. "No. The girl I was loved him well enough. But I haven't been that girl in a long time now. I can't say I haven't wondered over the years what it would have been like if he'd come back and we'd been together. It might have been good, and it might not have been. It's something we'll never know."

"You said he was noble, what he did..."

"Yeah, noble. Foolish too. He didn't have a chance to succeed. He chose to throw his young life away, stupid boy. And he abandoned me. There's that."

He stared at me awhile. "It's my fault you feel that way. I'm truly sorry."

I shrugged.

"Nora," he went on hesitantly, "I know you hate me now, and I don't blame you, but... You did love me once, didn't you?"

"I want you to understand this, Jack. If you had done something terrible, say you'd met some other woman and spent a night with her, then it would be hard but I could forgive it, because it was one moment of recklessness. But lying about Bax, that was ongoing, not a moment's recklessness but something that presided over every moment of every hour we spent together. It was the thing that grew between us, though I didn't know what it was at the time and you did. He shouldn't have told you to lie. And *you* shouldn't have done what he said. But the lie itself was a solitary incident, like a night with another woman would have been. Like you said, he was a boy and you were a boy. But the deception that followed... You brought that into manhood with you. You brought it into our marriage."

He hung his head. "You're right. I can't say you're not. Right as rain."

I touched his collar with a fingertip, then dropped my hand to my side. He seemed not to realize I hadn't answered his question. He took a deep breath. "It all feels so complicated, Nora. I give myself a headache every time I think it through from start to finish." He shook his head. "I can only say I'm sorry. If I could say it a thousand times without wearing you out, I would. If I could do it over again, I would do things differently."

He turned back to the rail and I fell into place beside him. We didn't speak for a long time. The riverbank oozed moonlight. I would miss the beauty of the jungle.

"And now there's Mum," Jack whispered. "I can't imagine telling her that I lied all this time, that Bax was alive when I left him. *Why put her through it all again?* I ask myself, but now, after what's happened to us..."

"She's getting old, your mum. It seems a bad idea to give her more grief than she's already endured. But it's worth thinking about."

He nodded. "Yes, I'm thinking about it. Thinking and thinking. It seems it's all I ever do anymore. I'd like to take a vacation from thinking even for a short while. I think all day and then I climb into my bunk and think all night. I never sleep. I just think."

I watched him watch the tree line. I hadn't slept much either. "Jack Hopper, would you like to dance with me? You can't be thinking and dancing at the same time, can you?"

He barked a laugh and sobered immediately after. Then he bent towards me and I saw him take in that my eyepatch was gone and my eye was healed. How he hadn't noticed before I cannot say.

A minute went by, and still he searched my eyes, as if looking for the meaning behind my simple question. Finally he mumbled, so close to my face that I could feel his breath, "I'm thinking of getting a dog, Nora."

A dog. Is *that* what he was thinking about? I myself was thinking we would have to turn the attic into a second bedroom, for Estela. And we would have to convert the nursery—the junk room—into a lavatory. It was about time too. We'd need to take out a loan. "The more the merrier," I said.

"A cat too."

"Is there a message here I'm not getting, Jack?"

He looked over his shoulder. I turned to look too. I'd almost forgotten the deck was full of dancers. It was breathtaking to find them there now, their silhouettes shimmering in the moonlight as they moved about, everyone smiling, looking into the eyes of their partners. Their presence seemed vital in that moment. I turned back to Jack. "So do you want to dance with me or not?"

He laughed again, but this time with real pleasure. "Of course I do."

Now it was Irving Kaufman's "Tonight You Belong to Me" playing. We had the recording at home. It was one of our favorites. We'd danced to it many times, pushing the furniture out of the way so we could move comfortably in our little parlor.

He took me in his arms and we began to dance slowly. I'd forgotten his scent: pipe tobacco, mixed with a sweep of sweat. When he started to hum, I tipped my head back, to see his face. He smiled at me and I smiled at him. I found myself thinking, *Any dance might be one's last; and that's precisely why we must always say yes to the chance.* He pulled me closer. "Love me, Nora," he whispered in my ear.

And in that moment I knew I did and always would, and I told him so.

Acknowledgments

THANKS TO EVERYONE AT Five Directions Press. In particular, thanks to C. P. Lesley for creating a beautiful interior book design for this series, and for all the other many things she does on a daily basis to support Five Directions titles. Thanks to Courtney J. Hall for creating lovely, intriguing cover designs for Books 1 and 2. Very special thanks to Ariadne Apostolou, who read not one but two drafts of *Gifts*, with as much care and consideration as she would have her own work, and then offered the kind of suggestions that can only come from someone who is a constant reader and a brilliant writer. It is a great joy to work with all of you.

Thanks and much gratitude to Paula Coomer, another brilliant reader and writer whose recommendations are always golden. And thanks as well to Paula—who, unlike me, gets out in the world—for carrying around and handing out postcards about my work.

Thanks to Michael Dooley, always my first reader, for supporting my work in every way possible.

Thanks, once again, to Carlos Damasceno of Manaus, Brazil, for sharing his incredible knowledge of all things Amazonas, and to Julián Larrea, Ecuadorian guide, for a blissful experience on the Pastaza River and in the deep jungle beyond.

Many books informed and inspired *Gifts for the Dead*. I am grateful to have come across the following titles:

- Scott Addington, *World War One: A Layman's Guide*
- Mark Black, *World War One*
- Patricia Florio Colrick, *Images of America: Hoboken*
- Michael D'Antonio, *A Full Cup: Sir Thomas Lipton's Extraordinary Life and His Quest for America's Cup*
- Doug Gelbert, *A Walking Tour of Hoboken!*
- Susan Goodier, *No Votes for Women: The New York State Anti-Suffrage Movement*
- Greg Grandin, *Fordlandia: The Rise and Fall of Henry Ford's Forgotten Jungle City*
- David Grann, *The Lost City of Z*
- Theodore Roosevelt and Roger B. Wood, *The German Spy in America*
- Howard Zinn, *The Twentieth Century: A People's History*

The Author

J<small>OAN</small> S<small>CHWEIGHARDT</small> <small>IS</small> <small>THE</small> author of seven novels, a memoir, two children's books, and various magazine articles. She lives in Albuquerque, New Mexico.

ALSO FROM FIVE DIRECTIONS PRESS

River Aria

RIVERS, BOOK 3

1928

WHEN TIA ADRIANA'S OUTBURSTS first began, JoJo thought it was because she would miss him so much. And surely that was part of it. But the bigger part was that she had lied to him, long ago when he was a little boy. And as there didn't seem to be any harm in her deception, as it made JoJo happy in fact to hear her build on it, Tia Adriana had done just that. She'd embellished it; like clay, she kneaded and stretched it; she worked it until it was as high and as stalwart as the tallest ships that come out of the night to rest in our harbor, until it was as vast and mysterious as the river itself. She even made it official, hauling it to City Hall to be recorded and made public for anyone who cared to see.

Many times in the weeks before JoJo and I left for New York, Tia Adriana tried to tell JoJo the truth. But every time she opened her mouth, her effort turned to sobbing. She would drop her head into her hands and cry with abandon. And when JoJo crossed the room to lay his callused palm upon her heaving back, she would only cry harder.

She wept so much that at one point JoJo said he wouldn't be coming to New York with me after all, that he would rather stay in Manáos and live the life he had than leave his *mamãe* in such a state. He made a joke of it; he said if his mother kept crying that way, the wet season flooding would be twice as bad, and everyone in the city would drown and it would all be on him. He wasn't joking; he was playing with the idea of changing his mind.

It was then that the other two got involved, my mother (Bruna) and Tia Louisa, who were sisters—in heart if not in blood—to Tia Adriana, and to each other as well. "Is that what you want for your son?" Tia Louisa scolded when JoJo was not around. "You want that your only child should grow up here, fishing for a living in a ghost town? Dwelling in a shack up on stilts and likely to flood anyway? Every day a sunrise and a sunset and barely anything worth remembering in between?" My mother would chirp in then, adding in her quiet way, her coarse fingers extending to cover Tia Adriana's trembling wet hands, "Adriana, wasn't it because you wanted more for him that you lied in the first place?"

The three of them became philosophers once my mother and Tia Louisa had calmed Tia Adriana sufficiently that she could think past her misery. They weighed JoJo's future, how it *would* unfold if he stayed, and how it *might* unfold if he left. Would and might: it was like weighing mud and air. Could he be happy, they asked themselves, eking out a living on the docks for the rest of his life? Blood and fish guts up to his elbows? Endless squabbles up on the hill trying to get the best price for his labors? Drawing his pictures on driftwood—because between us all we couldn't keep him in good paper—or on the shells of eggs, or even on our shabby furniture?

Was that what was best for our beloved JoJo? Or was it the alternative that promised more? America! *America! O my America! My new-found-land!* In America he would be attending an art school—the grandest art school in the grandest city in the whole country—not because he, our JoJo, who had grown up ragged and shoeless, had ever even considered that he might travel to New York, but because a man named Felix Black, the protégé of a famous American artist and a former teacher of art himself, had come to Manáos to study our decaying architecture some months ago. And as fate would have it, he wandered into Tia Louisa's restaurant and saw JoJo sitting in the back booth with some paints he had probably stolen, painting the young woman sitting across from him (me, as it happens) on a canvas so scruffy it could only have come from someone's rubbish pile. And this man, Felix Black, watched for a while and then bent over JoJo and whispered in his ear—startling our dearest JoJo because, except for his eye and his breath and the fingers holding his brush, he was barely there in his own body when he painted—to say that he was a benefactor at an art school far away in New York, and if JoJo were to come, he would help him to *realize his full potential.*

Mud or air? Foot-sucking muck from the bottom of the river or the breath of the heavens, sweet and suffused with bird song? Stinking dead fish or *full potential?*

We knew what was best for JoJo; there was no doubt in any of our minds. And we knew that JoJo, who was fearless—though he could barely read or write—wanted this chance more than anything he'd ever wanted in all his twenty-one years. But the fact remained that Tia Adriana could not bring herself to tell him about her lie, and he could not be permitted to arrive in New York without knowing about it.

I didn't know the lie was a lie myself until one week before our scheduled departure. Being more than a year younger than JoJo (and loose-lipped, if my mother and *as tias* could be believed), no one had been foolish enough to trust me to keep a secret of such consequence. Innocent as I was, I had even participated in the lie, which was nearly as exciting to me as it was to JoJo.

Accordingly, when my aunts and *Mamãe* first began to look for ways to throw light on the truth, they didn't include me in their conversations. But when they failed to find even a single solution, they called me into Tia Adriana's shack and sat me down at the table and told me the whole long story from beginning to end.

While they spoke, interrupting one another with details as always, I slouched in my seat and leaned my head back, until I was looking directly up at the ceiling. Our images were up there: Me and Tia Adriana and my dearest *mamãe*, and Tia Louisa and Tia-Avó Nilza, who was Tia Adriana's mother (and JoJo's grandmother, of course). Three years earlier, JoJo had painted all of us on a large rectangular *cumaru* table top that Tia Louisa was throwing out from the restaurant because two of the table's legs had broken. When JoJo claimed the piece of wood for himself, Tia Louisa reminded him that his mother's house was far too small to hang a thing that size. But then an out-of-towner who'd been listening to their conversation over his fish stew told JoJo about The Sistine Chapel, which JoJo had never heard of before. And so impressed was JoJo with the stranger's story of the how the famous artist (Michelangelo, whom JoJo had heard of) had come to paint on the ceiling of the Pope's chapel, that JoJo decided then and there that he would nail his painting—which he dubbed the Sistine Chapel of Rua Estrata—on his mother's ceiling, where it would be out of the way. And that is where it remained. Instead of scenes from the Bible depicting man's fall from grace, however, JoJo had painted us floating through our labors as if we were saints—me and Tia Louisa at the restaurant, serving rowdy wage earners, and my mother and *as tias* sitting in a row on the bench outside Tia Adriana's shack repairing fishing nets while they gossiped the day away.

Usually when I looked at the painting it was to marvel at how young I was back then, how much I'd changed. But now I was thinking that with the exception of myself, JoJo had unwittingly painted the very women who knew about the lie from the beginning, who had probably helped to shape it, knowing how they were when they were all together. I felt my face grow hot, with anger first and then with embarrassment and then with despair. And then Tia Louisa, who was just hoisting the story into the present moment, suddenly changed her tone and snapped, "Estela, are you listening?"

I sat up straight at once.

"This is important, so you must pay attention. Once you're safely on the ship on your way to America, you need to tell JoJo about the lie—"

"And the truth it was meant to conceal," Tia Adriana broke in, nodding excitedly.

"And the truth it was meant to conceal, yes." Tia Louisa closed her eyes and sat in silence for a moment. Then she went on. "You'll be almost four weeks traveling, the two of you sharing a cabin. He'll have nowhere to escape to. When you arrive in New York, we'll want your full report, your letter saying he knows and has accepted…"

"And that he loves me…us…in spite of everything," Tia Adriana cried, her eyes filling with tears.

I looked at their faces. Only my mother was leaning forward, waiting anxiously for my response. The other two trusted me better, especially Tia Louisa, who sat back and folded her arms under her ample breasts, as if to declare that her work here was done.

I let them wait. I looked beyond them, at the cast-iron pots and pans hanging from hooks over the wood stove, the dishes out on shelves, the cot in the corner where Tia Adriana slept, the old tin washtub in the opposite corner, the curtain, worn to gauze by years of handling, that separated the kitchen from the back room, where Tia-Avó Nilza and Avô Davi and JoJo slept.

"Yes, of course," I said at last.

It occurred to me that *I* would have to lie to *them*, in the event that JoJo was unforgiving. What other option was there?

ALSO FROM FIVE DIRECTIONS PRESS

Before We Died

Rivers, Book 1

1910

It was Clementine, the old Italian hag who passed herself off as a fortuneteller, who started it all. Mum began seeing her regular after Da died, as she purported to know exactly what Da was thinking over there on the other side. How many times me and Bax gave over all our energy trying to make Mum see the hag was only after her dough, what little she had of it. But she would hear none of it. Then one day, after one of their "sessions," Mum tells us Da told the hag—and the hag told her—that we, meaning Bax and me, needed to get away from the docks and have ourselves an adventure, because we were for fair spending too much time being miserable since Da's passing. We knew Da didn't say no such thing, but we also knew he would have said *just that* if he could look down from above and see the sorry state we were in. We *were* miserable. Me more so than Bax because he at least had the lovely Nora to console him. Mum was all for it back then, this adventure idea, when it was fresh from the hag's lips to her ears. Fuck, she was all for it as recently as the day before.

But now here was our ship—all twenty thousand tons of her, double-masted with one great funnel, booming her kisser like the wild sea lass she was—preparing to cast off, and here was Mum, clinging to our shirt sleeves, bawling and keening like it was Da's funeral all over again.

Nora was there too, of course, with her arm wrapped around Mum's shoulders, trying to persuade her to let us go before it was too late. "Just pull away," she snapped at Bax, her ire on the rise. We looked at each other, me and Bax, but we only continued to try to reason our way out of Mum's grip. She was our mammy after all.

Finally her shrieking became a whimper and she let go of us and we kissed her quick and ran like hell. And sure enough, we were the last two to board. By the time we got up on deck and pushed our way to the rail, we were already pulling away from the dock. "There," Bax hollered. He'd found her in the crowd—her yellow dress, her hat that looked like a rose garden planted on a steep slope—hunched over and sobbing into her handkerchief like an old woman as Nora led her away. I thought my heart might break, it was such a sorry sight. But just then Nora—ever the rip—who'd been bent over Mum, consoling her, straightened and looked back over her shoulder, right at us, and flashed her most winning smile, all gums and bright white teeth. I laughed, because at first it seemed she was beaming at me. Then I felt my cheeks go hot. She was beaming at Bax, of course. He was wearing the new black derby she'd bought him to remember her by. He took it off and bowed and she blew him a kiss. Then she turned back to Mum and resumed her caretaking.

Our sea journey took fourteen days. I brought along a satchel of books, and while Baxter was off becoming intimate with the captain, the crew and all of our fellow travelers, I finished off Jack London's *The Call of the Wild*, which I deemed appropriate given our destination. In the evenings, when Bax had knackered himself sick making new friends and it was too dark for me to read (we'd been told not to light lanterns unless it was an emergency), Bax would ask me how my book was going, which was his way of saying he wanted the story in as much detail as I could remember.

We'd established the pattern back when we were kids, because Da didn't give much credence to a boy who spent too much time behind a book, and while I had nothing to lose going against Da's whims—as I was never going to be the favorite anyway—Bax had the nut hand there and he could not afford to lose it. So Bax got the benefit of my hard work; I read and then I summed things up and related them to my brother, enabling him to learn almost as much as me about books without having to actually crack one. It could have been our little secret too, but Bax was too spirited to try to get away with something like that. "My brother's the bookworm," he'd tell anyone who cared to listen. "I get all my learning secondhand from him." Sometimes he'd add, because it made people laugh and also because it was mostly true, "And he gets all his living secondhand from me." The only book Baxter had brought along was an English-Portuguese dictionary, because he was determined to be able to speak to our fellow *seringueiros* (rubber tappers) in their native tongue.

Nora had been in the same room with Jack London just the month before, when she'd gone across the river to Manhattan with her auntie to attend a lecture given by Mary Ovington, one of the leaders in the women's rights movement and a member of the Socialist Party. Nora had come back jazzed, saying she planned to work with the socialists while

Bax and me were away, to advocate for affordable housing for the Negroes. My first thought at the time was, *Now, ain't that ironic? Here she don't really even have decent housing herself, her and her auntie.*

Nora's parents, native-born in New York but from Irish Catholic stock like our own, died of consumption when she was a toddler. All she remembered of them was their coughing, their spitting up of blood. She'd been raised by her Aunt Becky, her father's sister, a short round woman who never married, a socialist and anti-imperialist who gave speeches and rallied workers to fight for their rights, and who often dragged her niece along with her to secret meetings—*so as to indoctrinate her,* Mum and Da always said with a good ounce of scorn. They lived in two tiny rooms in a dilapidated boarding house for women on Jefferson Street. Aunt Becky worked in a garment factory when she was younger—which was where she first took note of workers' rights, or lack thereof—but now she had enough dough (Mum and Da had always speculated the socialists were paying her a stipend to keep her gob running) so that she didn't need to work at all and could spend all her time rousing others to higher states of social awareness. It couldn't have been all that much though, that stipend, judging by their living conditions.

We'd been sitting in the parlor that day, listening to Nora go on and on about how handsome he was, London, how smart, and how she planned to read all his books, which she could do easily enough as she worked in a bookstore now that she was out of school, and she got her books for cost. He was my man too, London was. Here was a fellow could clean a clock when he had to but could also write what was in his head and even what was not. I hoped to do as much myself one day, maybe writing stories for the papers or for a magazine, so long as I was never chained to a desk in an airless office where the risks and thrills of a life well-lived could be denied me. I wanted to ask Nora if he'd talked about his adventures in the Klondike, but just as I was about to open me useless gob, in jumps Bax, saying, "This London fellow… Would you say he's handsomer than me?" Nora stared at him a moment, her mouth open and her eyes wide, feigning to be aghast he would ask so impertinent a question. But then all at once she'd squealed with delight and leaped off her chair and planted a loud smacker on Bax's cheek and told him no, never; no one was as handsome as he was, except maybe me (and her gaze came sliding my way, leaving me, as always, with my cheeks ablaze) as I had the same genetic coding, if Gregor Mendel with his pea plants could be believed.

While he didn't care for reading, it was Bax who put our plan together, him and Nora. They combed the newspapers and made a list of New York agents and exporters working rubber in South America and wrote letters to a few of them. Or, to be more accurate, Bax dictated and Nora did the writing; neither of us had good penmanship. One agent-exporter, a Portuguese by the name of Manuel Abalo, wrote back, and when he was in New York on business, Bax took the ferry across the river to meet with him. Abalo wanted to meet me too of course, but our boss on the docks, German fellow who Da had had great respect for, said he'd fire both our skinny arses if one didn't stay behind and get the work done.

Nora and Bax were standing at the door when I got in from the docks that night. I had to plow my way through to get inside and out of my jacket. Even Mum was standing nearby, wringing her hands and looking jazzed. Bax had been back from his meeting for a while by then, but he'd made the ladies wait till I got home, not because he didn't like to repeat himself—old Bax never had a problem there—but because he wanted to feed the drama, as was also his way.

"So he says to me," Bax said to us soon as I sat down, referring to this Abalo chap. "How do I know you can do the work? Why would I want to be pouring money into men I have no proof can keep up? I heard longshoremen were a shiftless lot."

Bax took a step back, so that he was dead center in the room, to demonstrate how he answered. With his chin raised, his legs apart, and his arms folded over his chest, he could have been Hercules himself standing there. "Shiftless, you say? Listen here, I says to the old kinker, I could well name some shiftless bods out there on the docks, but me and Jack would not be among them. I says to him, Me and Jack, we've carried sugar, flour, beef and coal, and much more, in crates weighing twice as much as our own woebegone selves on our young backs, and no one ever saw us as much as flinch. Me and Jack have labored in the piercing cold of winter morns, before there was even a glim in the sky, and under the hottest midsummer sun, working sometimes twenty hours straight, doing what must be done to get our ships loaded and out to sea. We have worked with sponges tied over our ugly gobs to keep the fumes from some of them hauls from choking us down. We have worked bruised and cut and oozing pus from the bottoms of our feet. We have worked sick as dogs. We have worked bleeding like goats, me and Jack have. We have forced our big bodies into wee narrow spaces to take on cargo, and we have lifted above our heads barrels that would kill us fast if one of the other macs was to lose his footing. So say what you will about longshoremen, my good man, but don't dare say it about Jack and me, and never say it again in my presence."

Baxter nodded once, to let us know the drama was over for now—though he maintained his heroic stance in the middle of the room. Nora turned to Mum at once, her jaw dropped open with delight. Mum stretched her lips out flat in response, closest she could get to a smile these days. "And what did he say to that?" I asked. My brother could be a doozer when he wanted. I was the serious one, the thinker. Sometimes I found me miserable self with thoughts behind my thoughts. But I could never have come back at Abalo the way old Bax did. And I will not deny it grieved me some to be lacking Baxter's fire.

Bax waited to be sure he had our full attention. "He said, You and your brother, you've got yourself a job."

We all laughed then, even Mum. I got up to shake my brother's hand, and Mum and Nora stood up behind me, just to be nearer.

Abalo would become our *patrão*, Bax explained, meaning he would arrange our passage to Amazonas and provide us with the tools we'd need to get started as *seringueiros*. We would have to pay him back at the end of the first tapping season, but if we did a good job and brought in enough rubber, we'd have more than needed to cover our expenses. Abalo said we might even want to become agent-exporters ourselves after a few seasons of hard work. There was *that* much money to be made in the industry.

We whooped and hollered when Bax was done with his blather, and the three of us—Mum was watching from the entrance to the kitchen by then—began to dance in a circle, our hands on one another's shoulders just as we did when we was wee wild brats. "We're going to be rich!" Bax cried, and he leaned over to plant a smacker on Nora's bobbing cheek. "We'll have ourselves our own business," he went on. "We'll take turns going to South America to oversee, but eventually we'll hire an overseer, and then we'll conduct our business from here. I'll take you to Paris…" (this to Nora, naturally) "…and we'll have tea with your precious Picasso. We'll live here, of course—because if you can't live safe and full on the Emerald Isle, where better is there than here in Hoboken in the grand state of New Jersey—but we'll have ourselves a swank office on the top floor of a grand building across the river just like Manuel Abalo. Just like him, we'll look out the window and see the Flatiron reaching for the sun each day, making us feel like anything is possible. It'll be a fine life after all."

His "after all" hit me like a bolt of lightning. "I only wish Da was here to share it," I said. I dropped my hands from Baxter's and Nora's shoulders and our little jig fizzled to an end.

Mum sighed loudly and excused herself, and we watched as she disappeared into the depths of the kitchen. Then Baxter laughed. "If the hag is right," he whispered, "Da knows all about it already!"

"The hag's nothing but a hocus, and you know it as well as I do," I snapped at him. "She wants us to have an adventure for fair, but not because Da's spirit said so. More likely it's a plot to get us out of the way so she can glom even more of Mum's money."

"Whatever your mum pays her," Nora broke in in a rapid-fire whisper, "it's a small sum for the hope and happiness she receives in return. Besides, your mum told me Clementine refers to things she can't possibly know, things that were intimate between them two. So there may be some truth to it after all. Consider that. Or at least respect it."

Her eyes flashed from me to Bax and back again. They went a deeper blue when she got beefed. We took the argument no further.

http://www.fivedirectionspress.com/before-we-died

One large, fascinating tapestry.
—Literary Fiction Book Review

THE
LAST WIFE
OF
ATTILA THE
HUN

A NOVEL

JOAN
SCHWEIGHARDT

Winner of the ForeWord Book of the Year
and Independent Publisher Book Awards

Two threads are flawlessly woven together in this sweeping historical novel. In one, Gudrun, a Burgundian noblewoman, dares to enter the City of Attila to give its ruler what she hopes is a cursed sword; the second reveals the unimaginable events that have driven her to this mission.

Based in part on the true history of the times and in part on the same Nordic legends that inspired Wagner's Ring Cycle and other great works of art, *The Last Wife of Attila the Hun* offers readers a thrilling story of love, betrayal, passion, and revenge, all set against an ancient backdrop itself gushing with intrigue. Lovers of history and fantasy alike will find realism and legend at work in Joan Schweighardt's latest offering.

"The hero-tales of the Germanic peoples form a glowing tread in the tapestry of European literature. [This story] presents one of the greatest of those legends from a woman's perspective, with emotion as well as action, bringing new meaning to an ancient tale."—Diana L. Paxson, author of the Wodan's Children trilogy

http://www.fivedirectionspress.com/the-last-wife-of-attila-the-hun

FIVE DIRECTIONS PRESS

Literary Journeys along Paths Less Traveled

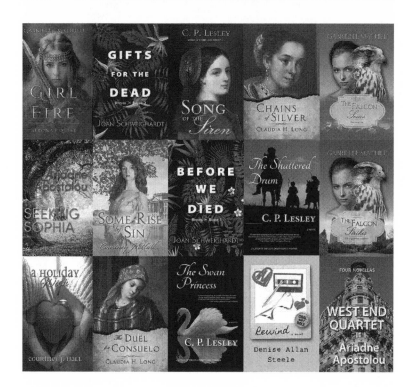

http://www.fivedirectionspress.com/books